Skinny Lizzie

ELIZABETH WAITE

sphere

For Doris, whom I still miss every day of my life

SPHERE

First published in Great Britain in 1993 by Warner Books
Reprinted 1993, 1994 (twice), 1995, 1997, 1998, 2000
Reprinted by Sphere in 2010

Copyright © 1993 by Elizabeth Waite

The moral right of the author has been asserted.

a ret... ...out
the pri... ...lated
in an... ...ned

ISBN 978-0-7515-0045-5

Phototypeset by Intype, London
Printed and bound in Great Britain by
Clays Ltd, St Ives plc

Papers used by Sphere are natural, renewable and
recyclable products sourced from well-managed forests and certified
in accordance with the rules of the Forest Stewardship Council.

Mixed Sources
Product group from well-managed
forests and other controlled sources
www.fsc.org Cert no. SGS-COC-004081
© 1996 Forest Stewardship Council
FSC

Sphere
An imprint of
Little, Brown Book Group
100 Victoria Embankment
London EC4Y 0DY

An Hachette UK Company
www.hachette.co.uk

www.littlebrown.co.uk

– into the kitchen, which was always a scene of great activity, women coming and going in all directions, calling Christmas greetings to their mother, not pausing long enough for an answer. Hanging her own and their coats on the hook behind the door and donning her flowered, wrap-around overall, their mother would hand tea cloths to Lizzie and Syd and then start work. Plates piled high, vegetable dishes and soup tureens, gravy boats and stands, platters so large that they needed two hands to lift them, glasses, cups and saucers.

She would fill the deep sink with hot water, adding soap flakes and a handful of common soda from the large brown earthenware jar which stood on the window sill, and then the washing-up would begin. With her arms in soapy water up to her elbows, her back and shoulders stooped low, she barely stopped to take a breath, let alone have a rest. She worked away until the stacks grew smaller, Lizzie and her brother hardly able to keep up with the drying.

The last stage was the worst. Every glass had to sparkle. Taking three dry glass cloths from a line strung beneath the shelf which was high above the kitchen range, Nellie Collins would help her two children. Each glass had to be held up to the light, checked that there were no smears or finger marks.

There was one thing in the Dawson's favour though. Mr Dawson always drove them home in his car, probably because he knew they were all too tired to walk.

Chapter One

1932, London

'Aw, COME ON, Mum, if we don't get a move on we'll be late for the concert.'

'Oh, do shut up and stop fidgeting. It's no good us going out this early.'

Ten-year-old Lizzie Collins, thin as a whippet and just as quick, shook her long fair hair and accepted her mother's scolding with goodwill and cheerfulness. All the week she was able to take life as it came, but this was Saturday and Saturday evenings were different. They were the highlight of her life.

The Collins family lived in a typical back street in south-west London. Aunt Daisy took on the role of head of the family because each day her mother would be up early and off to her job at the Dawsons. Lizzie hated the Dawsons. They always seemed to come first with her mother. Half a crown a morning they paid her mum, and for that she did every menial task asked of her, even down to scrubbing the doorsteps.

Even Christmas morning was the same. Ever since Lizzie could remember, she and her younger brother Syd had walked to Balham with their mother. Down the back area steps they would troop

Once home, Lizzie stopped envying the Dawson children their huge Christmas tree and toys and got ready to enjoy herself. All preparations for the Collinses' Christmas meal had been done days in advance and Aunt Daisy always had the cooking well under way. Lizzie loved Aunt Daisy, who was like a second mother to her. Daisy was her father's unmarried sister, and since he died Mum always said that if it hadn't been for Daisy they would have fared a lot worse.

Lizzie didn't miss her dad. He had hardly ever been at home anyway. Besides, there was always Leslie and Connie to turn to.

There were eleven years between her mother's first two children and Lizzie and only eighteen months between Lizzie and young Syd. Having Leslie for an older brother made up for the loss of her father. He adored Lizzie and she knew it, and Connie was the best of sisters. In fact, Lizzie felt so secure within the love of her mother, Aunt Daisy and her brothers and sister that it never entered her head that she should feel deprived.

Nellie Collins had been born within the sound of Bow Bells, making her a true cockney. Her actual place of birth had been The Cut or, to the uninformed, The Lambeth Walk, and she passionately loved London and its people. She had come to live in Tooting when she married Albert Collins, for better or worse as she had vowed – over the years it had turned out to be a bit of each. She was in her early forties now, with a tiny face to match her stature. She was still a good-looking, slim woman after having had four children and not exactly an easy life. Early on in her days in service to the upper classes, Nellie had formed a set of high principles. But, as time passed and circumstances worsened, she had tempered them with down-to-earth common sense. She loved her children and lived for them, though Lizzie worried her more than the other three put together. Lizzie was skinny, far too skinny.

Not that she was undernourished, far from it. Maybe they didn't always have the best of everything, but Daisy, who did all the cooking, was a marvellous cook and no one in the house ever went hungry. Daisy would say, 'Our Lizzie has hollow legs.'

'Wiry, that's what our Lizzie is,' Nellie would proudly tell folk. The truth was, she was never still for two minutes at a time. She had reckless energy and was brainy with it. Her teachers at school wrote glowing reports of her work at the end of each term, but still Nellie worried about her. She was far too strong-willed for her own good. She wanted the moon and the stars to go with it and God alone knows what else.

An atmosphere of excitement always hung over the house on Saturdays. The nearby Fairlight Hall, which was run by the Shaftesbury Association, was known far and wide. Church services, Sunday school, prayer meetings, mothers' meetings, Girls'

Brigade, Boys' Brigade, magic lantern shows, all were weekly events at Fairlight Hall, but the Saturday concerts were the favourites. These were mixed entertainments with singers, dancers, comics and magicians. Short sketches always seemed to include a rich old gentleman with a heavily bandaged, gouty foot which the maid would accidentally trip over, and although this sketch in various forms would be performed each week, the feigned extreme pain on the face of the old man and his blasphemous curses never failed to bring roars of laughter and loud hooting from the audience. An entrance charge was made for these shows; sixpence for seats at the front of the hall and threepence for seats at the back. The Collins family couldn't always afford to go – until, that is, Mother got her job when Toc H decided to sell refreshments during the intervals.

Although Toc H was started as a club for soldiers during the 1914–18 war, it continued to do good works after the war, particularly in poor city areas. So, when a local member had approached Nellie Collins with the offer of an evening's work each week for the princely wage of three half-crowns, Nellie gasped in surprise and pleasure and accepted at once.

By this time Leslie had joined the Army, and Connie was 'walking out' with her boyfriend. So at about eight o'clock, Aunt Daisy, Mum, Syd and Lizzie would set off for Fairlight Hall. Their first job was to set out rows and rows of cups and saucers, for it was a very large hall, packed every week with eager audiences. Then, as the lights were dimmed and the opening musical number began, an official of Toc H would find them empty seats in the house. Often Syd and Lizzie ended up sitting on the floor between the gangways, but they didn't care; they got to see the concert for nothing. During the interval, it would be Aunt Daisy with her arms deep in soapy water at the sink doing the washing-up, while Syd and Lizzie dried. Nellie thought she had the easiest job, collecting the dirty crocks on large tin trays, making numerous trips from hall to kitchen and back again. All four of them were given a free drink, with iced or Chelsea buns for the two children. As a bonus, any refreshments which remained unsold were given to Nellie free of charge, plus those precious three silver half-crowns. Imagine! It took her three whole mornings to earn that amount at the Dawsons!

When saying her prayers on a Saturday night, Lizzie never forgot to say, 'God bless the Toc H.'

Between having their midday meal and getting ready to go to the concert, the shopping had to be done. It was always Lizzie who accompanied her mother on these expeditions to Tooting market. There were times when Lizzie found the bargaining that went on a great source of amusement, but on Saturdays she felt irritable and hoped her mother wouldn't take too long deciding just what she was going to buy.

It was a busy scene that confronted Nellie and her daughter on this particular evening, much as it was every Saturday evening. The open-fronted shops, the street traders and barrow boys, all plying their different trades, shouting their wares, each a keen competitor for customers. Shopping for food amongst the working class was undertaken on a daily basis, mainly because their income was earned and paid daily. The prosperity promised in 1918 at the signing of the Armistice had never come about. It was 1932 now and still men walked long distances in search of employment. One-day odd-jobs found eager takers; even one good day's work and pay made life look a little rosier.

'Are we going to the market first, Mum?' Lizzie wanted to know.

Her mother shook her head, 'We'll try the Mitcham Road first. Meat's the most important, we can get our vegetables on the way back.'

Late-night shopping at the butchers, of which there were at least four in the Mitcham Road, had become a battle of wits. Those well enough off to be choosy about their weekend joints would have shopped earlier in the day, but at this time of night it was a different matter. It was essential that the butcher sold off all his perishable items by the time he pulled down the shutters that night. Anything left would definitely not be in an edible state come Monday morning. Better to sell it off cheaply; a blessing in disguise for the poor.

Nellie had stopped at two butchers, hesitating while Lizzie impatiently scuffed her feet. She put a loving arm about her daughter as they walked on.

'Don't worry, love, they'll start auctioning the joints off soon, then we won't be long. We shan't be late for the concert, I promise.'

True enough, further along the road, a crowd of women had assembled on the pavement in front of the next butcher's shop. The proprietor was deliberately keeping them waiting, allowing the tension to build. The laid-out enamel trays were still full of meat, although the fresh parsley, arranged so neatly between the rows at the start of trading early that morning, was now visibly wilting. The men working at the blocks still wore their blue and white striped aprons, so clean and fresh at the day's start, now stained and bloody. The master butcher had donned a straw boater before coming out, setting it at a jaunty angle on his head. To his upper lip he had attached a false waxed moustache. This always made Lizzie laugh as it did all the other children in the crowd.

The November evening had turned bitterly cold, having rained heavily earlier on in the day. The pavement on which the women now stood was not only wet but had begun to harden into ice. Hardly any one amongst them was wearing boots or shoes that were weather-proof; their toes and fingers were stiff with cold; their winter coats far too thin to keep out the biting wind. Cold, tired, with hardly more than a few shillings in their purse each would be hoping for – no, praying for – the chance to pick up a bargain. In her mind's eye each woman was already seeing a joint roasting in the oven for tomorrow's dinner, big enough to feed the whole family and, with any luck, enough left over to be served up with bubble and squeak for Monday's meal.

That's the dream they had. It was often not the reality. Many a woman went home with her shopping-bag holding little more than odds and ends: a scrag of mutton, a piece of leg of beef (fit only for stewing), or a bit of belly of pork. Still, these working-class women were marvellous cooks, producing meals of great nourishment, roughened toil-worn hands making the lightest of pastry for a pie.

Finally, the master butcher came to the forefront, placed a large wooden crate dead centre to the waiting women, climbed up on to it and raised his megaphone to his mouth. The megaphone made his voice audible even at the back of the crowd where Lizzie stood with her mother. His patter started; a few bawdy jokes which were lost on those cold women, who were after food, not comedy: 'Git your money ready, ladies, I'm gonna give you all a treat tonight. Move in closer, there will be bargains for everyone.' Two assistants now took up their places on either side of the crate on which the butcher was perched, armed and ready with a stack of brown paper bags. When a price had been agreed and a buyer found, the meat would be tipped into a carrier bag, held up by one of the assistants. No effort was made to wrap each item separately, this being deemed an unnecessary luxury for the poor.

'Look 'ere me darlings, Sunday joint, sausages for the ol' man's breakfast and dripping to put hairs on yer chest.' Loud and rough, his voice droned on. Most in the crowd had heard it all before; it was the meat on offer that they were interested in, not his commentary. Still he kept trying to gain their good-will, working hard to induce amusement, even hoping for a laugh, but only provoking the odd half-suppressed giggle. He gave up. With an exaggerated sigh he shouted, 'Right, now to the serious business . . .'

He picked up an empty enamel dish. Silently he turned to the display of meat in front of which he was perched. Taking down a rib of beef, he held it aloft for a moment before placing it into the dish; two breasts of lamb were added with great cere-mony, a thin end of belly of pork, two long strings of sausages, and to top the lot a wax packet contain-ing beef dripping. Lowering the dish to the eye level of the women at the front of the crowd, brandishing the contents in front of them, he quietly said, 'Eight bob.' No response. Straightening himself upright, he yelled, 'First hand up gets the lot for seven and six.' Again no response. Everyone knew it didn't pay to rush. 'Six shillings,' his voice boomed out even without the use of his megaphone. No one in the crowd uttered a word. Leaning forward, the butcher focused his stare on a fat woman. 'Look luv, didn't you hear what I said?' Raising his voice even higher, 'Six bob the lot.' The woman shifted uncomfortably, saying nothing, averting her eyes away from his stare. 'Well, I'll to go hell and back. You lot can walk up and down this street till midnight, you won't find a better bargain.' He spoke quickly, 'Tell yer what I'll do. Do yer like offal? Yer should do, it's bloody good for yer.' Lowering the dish he scooped up a large handful of liver from a tin pail which stood on a bench to the left of him. Into the dish it went, slithering and slipping over the strings of sausages, now entwined amongst the red meat. 'Wait for it. I'm not finished yet.' A whole shoulder of lamb was quickly placed on top of the now overful dish. 'That's the lot.' This decided, there was a long pause before the butcher, his endurance now pushed to the limit, shouted, 'Now it's got to be worth three half-crowns of anybody's money.' Setting his feet more widely apart, he drew a deep breath. Again he threw out the challenge. 'Seven and sixpence.' Self-consciously, the women looked at each other. There wasn't one amongst them who wouldn't have dearly loved to call out, 'I'll have it,' but three to four shillings at most was their mark. Frustrated to the point of anger, the butcher lost his temper; as yet he had not made one sale since starting his auctioneering. 'Right, who'll take the bloody lot for nothing!'

'My Mum will. My Mum will.'

Lizzie's voice rang out sharp and clear. Nellie put her arm out to restrain this impetuous daughter of hers but Lizzie had gone through the crowd like lightning, not slowing down until she cleared the ring of pushing women. Then the audacity of what she had done dawned on her. Lizzie's heart was racing. 'Dear Jesus, let the ground open and swallow me up,' she prayed.

Nervously, she looked up at the great hulk of the butcher towering above her, still holding that dratted dish of meat between his hands. Hastily she dropped her eyes and hung her head. The silence which followed seemed to last forever.

Then the mumbling from the crowd began. 'Gawd bless the poor little mite,' one woman called out. Then the fat woman, who had been made to feel a fool earlier on, decided to put her twopenny worth in.

'Gawd bless her my arse. Cheeky little cow. Bloody good 'iding is what she needs.'

Normally Lizzie would have rounded on the woman, quick to repay in kind. Not now, though. She felt sick. Bending his knees but keeping his back perfectly straight, the butcher brought his face down almost level with Lizzie's. Her nostrils filled with the smell of dried blood coming from his stained apron and she felt even more sick.

Speaking gently, with a soft, quiet voice, the big man said, 'For your cheek, love, it's all yours.'

Straightening himself up, he turned to an assistant. 'Hold open a carrier,' he ordered. Slowly, deliberately, he tipped the whole contents of that enamel dish into the paper carrier-bag; liver clung to the sides of the dish, he removed it pushing with the flat of his hand. Now, for the first time, he stepped down from the crate, folding over the top of the brown paper bag. Not trusting the handles, he held it out towards Lizzie. Using both of her arms, she clutched it to her chest but found she couldn't move. She remained rooted to the spot, staring at the man.

'Off you go missy, you ain't as daft as you look,' and with that he laughed out loud.

This comical remark suddenly made Lizzie relax. She turned and walked back towards her mother. The women parted to make a path for her, and she stared insolently at the lot of them.

'You little bugger showing me up like that!' One of her mother's hands grabbed her, the other raised in anger to strike. Instinctively, Lizzie ducked. Still the blow caught the side of her head, leaving the ear stinging and the tears burning at the back of her eyes.

Rebellion seethed in her as her mother pushed and shoved her along the pavement. Hiccuping, trying to stifle her sobs, Lizzie asked herself angrily what had she done wrong? The butcher had offered the meat free and surely you had to be out of your mind not to accept an offer like that. Why was her mum so mad at her? She forced the tears back. She was not going to cry; she would not let her mother see how much she had hurt her. 'I'm never gonna come with her again to get the rotten shopping,' she vowed. Still holding the carrier-bag tightly to her chest but trying to think how she could get rid of it, they turned the corner of the street into the darkness of a side road.

'Lizzie, I'm sorry. I'm sorry,' Lizzie heard the sob

in her mother's voice and realized that she, too, was crying.

This sudden change of attitude not only baffled Lizzie but also set her off crying again.

'Can we go 'ome now,' she snivelled.

'Don't cry, don't cry,' her mother implored her. 'I didn't mean to hit you, truly I didn't.'

She relieved Lizzie of the dreaded carrier bag, totally ignoring the wet stain on the front of her coat caused by Lizzie having clutched it too closely, allowing the blood to soak through from its unwrapped contents, and dropped it whole into her large patchwork shopping-bag. Before moving, Nellie drew her young daughter into her arms and hugged her so tightly Lizzie rocked on her feet. Lizzie decided she would never understand adults, they seemed to have their emotions well and truly mixed up.

Walking quickly now, Lizzie's hand was clutching tightly to her mother's free one. Back in the brightly lit Mitcham Road, the gutter was packed with barrows. Barrows piled high with fruit; barrows offering vegetables, salad, flowers, even shell fish; the barrow boys had it all.

Nellie ignored them all, making a beeline for the cooked-meat shop. Pungent, delicious smells filled the air yards before they actually reached the shop. What a layout! Pigs' trotters, faggots in hot gravy, rissoles, shiny fat sausages, pease pudding, meat pies in all shapes and sizes, even pigs' heads split in half and roasted – the choice was endless. Lizzie's mouth was watering; suddenly she felt very, very hungry.

'What would you like, love?'

Lizzie couldn't believe her ears. Sometimes on a Saturday evening while shopping, her mum would buy a tuppenny pie and they'd have half each, eating it walking along. But it didn't often happen. Usually they passed this shop; her mother's finances didn't stretch to shop-bought cooked meats. Now she was being offered a choice. What a decision! Inside the shop nothing mattered at that moment but the fact that they were going to have something hot and tasty to eat.

Behind the counter an imposing lady with a fat red face smiled broadly at them as she asked, 'What's it to be, missus?'

Nellie had only a moment of indecision. 'Four meat pies, please.'

'Mince or steak and kidney?'

'Oh, steak and kidney, please.'

'Blimey,' the word came quietly from Lizzie's lips, they were the dearest and Mum was buying four!

Wrapping the hot pies in two large sheets of white paper the woman beamed as she handed the parcel to Nellie.

'They're nice. You'll enjoy them,' she said.

Nellie smiled and nodded as she bent to place the pies most carefully on the top of her shopping-bag. Then, opening her purse, she paused and impulsively said, 'And one hot saveloy for us to eat now, please. Oh, and would you mind cutting it in half?'

' 'Course, I will, luv.'

Taking a long, black-handled knife from the bench behind her, the woman easily sliced the large, red, spicy sausage into two equal parts, then, tearing off a strip of white paper, she wrapped each uncut end of the saveloy, leaving the hot, steaming end protruding.

Handing one half to Nellie and the other half to Lizzie, she asked, 'What 'ave you done my darling to deserve this treat?'

Lizzie smiled but didn't answer; she was impatient to get her teeth into the fleshy sausage.

'Well now, that'll be one and a penny, four pies at threepence each and one saveloy a penny.'

Nellie counted out the money and said, 'Thanks a lot.'

'You're welcome,' said the woman. 'Tat-ta lovey, 'ope to see you again.'

Lizzie, her mouth filled with hot sausage, grinned. Then, as chirpy as any sparrow, she called back over her shoulder, 'I hope so too. 'Bye for now.'

Nellie, having finished eating her half saveloy, hoisted her heavy shopping bag up into her arms and mother and daughter quickened their pace as they rounded the Broadway and made for the covered-in market.

Lizzie knew the routine off by heart. Passing Emanuel's and their beautiful layout of imported fruit and vegetables, 'Far too expensive,' her mother muttered.

'Hello, Jack,' she called as she propped her shopping-bag against the front of Smith's stall, where the sheet of imitation green grass hung down. 'Got an empty box for me?'

'Sure, Nellie, help yourself,' swarthy looking Jack Smith called in answer as he came towards them.

Nellie went behind the stall into the depths of the area at the back used for storing empty crates and unpacking them at the start of each day. She appeared a moment later, holding a light-weight wooden box; the bottom was firm but the sides were only slates of wood. Jack Smith bent low and lined the bottom with a thick wad of newspapers.

'Potatoes, Nellie?'

'Yes please, Jack, five pounds, and a pound of carrots and onions mixed.'

These items having been weighed and tipped into the box, Nellie added, 'One swede, two parsnips and a cabbage. That's the lot, thanks,' she said, opening her purse to pay.

'No fruit this week, Nellie?'

'I dunno,' she was slow to decide.

Reaching for a large orange as a specimen, Jack told her, 'These are as sweet as a nut. Penny each, but ter you, seven for a tanner.' Before Nellie even had time to agree, he crouched down and from beneath the stall produced a cardboard box. 'There's some specky apples here and a few loose bananas. Want the lot for tuppence?'

'Go on then, I'll have the oranges as well.' There was a wide grin on Lizzie's face as the fruit was added to the rapidly filling box.

'Right, that's one and ninepence the lot.'

Nellie took a florin from her purse and, as she passed it over to Jack, she exclaimed, 'Oh God, I've forgotten the celery.' Aunt Daisy would have been upset. Sunday tea was not complete without a stick of celery.

'Penny more to pay then, Nell. Fourpence a head it is,' he said as he totted it up.

Wrapped in newspaper, the great bunch of celery topped the vegetables and fruit, its green leaves, looking bright and fresh, sticking out from the rolled newspaper.

'Can we go home now, Mum?' Lizzie pleaded.

Opening her purse again, Nellie said, 'Just run up to Eggee's for me, there's a good girl. Get two pennyworth of pieces a bacon and that will be our lot.' Seeing the desperation in Lizzie's eyes, her mother added gently, 'It won't take you two minutes. We'll be home with plenty of time to eat our pies before we set off for the concert. Go on, love, I'll wait here with all the shopping.'

Lizzie took the threepenny piece from her mother's outstretched hand and ran off. She didn't mind going to Eggee's stall because it fascinated her. As the name implied, Eggee sold eggs. It was an extra large stall, divided into two halves. On the egg side was a grading machine, its many lights giving off warmth as brown, white and speckled eggs gently came down in a continuous line, to be sent off in different directions according to their weight and size. Mid-week her mother often sent her here with a basin to buy cracked eggs. She always came willingly, knowing that there would then be scrambled eggs for their tea. Besides she and Syd had great fun making the toast; kneeling in front of the bars of the grate, red hot from the range fire, they would use the long-handled, three-pronged toasting forks, daring each other to get closer all the time until the slices of bread ended up with burnt stripes. Making the toast was always a good laugh. No – it wasn't that she minded running the errand; she just didn't want to be late for the concert.

It was to the opposite side of the stall that Lizzie needed to go now. Every variety of cheese you could think of was sold here, plus bacon. Lizzie liked Mr Eggee. She was repeatedly scolded by her mother for not calling him by his proper name which was Mr Goldberg, but to her he was Mr Eggee and there was no disrespect in calling him that. He was a heavy-set Jewish man with black hair and bright dark eyes which now had a gleam of amusement in them behind his rimless spectacles as he watched Lizzie approach.

His voice was friendly as he called, 'Hallo, Skinny Lizzie.'

'Hallo, Mr Eggee,' she returned.

'Is it bacon you were wanting?'

'Yes, please. Mummy said, may she have twopennyworth of pieces?'

'Your mamma certainly may. Pieces, we have plenty. 'Tis a good time you choose to come.' Turning, he tore down a large greaseproof paper bag from a string of them hanging on a steel rail. Walking to the slicing machine, he began to fill the bag from a white enamel tray which lay beneath the cutters. Too small to be sold as rashers, he regularly sold these pieces quite cheaply.

'There you are then, young Lizzie. Now be sure my regards you give to your mother.'

Reaching up, she was given the bag of bacon pieces plus one penny change from the threepenny bit. 'I will, Mr Eggee. 'Bye, thank you.'

Her mother was right, Mr Goldberg was a kindly, generous man, and Lizzie liked him because he was always so friendly. There were not many she would allow to call her Skinny Lizzie, not without giving tit for tat. But with Mr Eggee Lizzie knew that it was said affectionately.

Aunt Daisy always maintained that these pieces of bacon were the best value to be found this side of heaven. Firstly, she would sort out all the lean pieces which provided a good breakfast for them all. Next, the thick ends would have onions and sage added, rolled in a suet crust and boiled in a pudding cloth to create a good dinner. Lastly, the real fat lumps were rendered down in the slow oven at the side of the kitchen range to supply dripping for their toast.

Still waiting by Smith's greengrocery stall, Nellie looked rather woebegone. 'What's the matter, Mum?' asked Lizzie.

'Nothing, love, a bit weary, that's all.'

Making a space amongst the vegetables, Lizzie placed the bacon in the box. Now, how were they going to get this lot home?

'Come this side of me Lizzie.' Balancing the shopping-bag in the crook of her right arm, Nellie placed four fingers of her free hand underneath the first row of slats on the side of the wooden box, leaving her thumb on top. With a nod of her head she made a gesture for Lizzie to do likewise. 'Lift,' she instructed. Walking with the box between them required bodily effort. Nellie, although only five feet four inches tall, was a good deal taller than Lizzie. Unevenly balanced and looking peculiar to say the least, they made their way out of the market.

Outside, the weather had turned decidedly worse; the harsh wind was bitter, threatening a severe storm. They had to wait for their chance to cross the main road which was still busy with traffic. Trams rumbling, clanging and swaying, travelled in both directions. Lorries, cars, push-bikes, everyone seemed hell-bent on greater speed. At last there came a break in the traffic and they stepped forward, walking awkwardly, and, more by luck than judgment, they reached the far pavement in safety. They stopped a moment and drew a deep breath.

In Selkirk Road, the jellied eel shop was now open. Nellie called a halt.

'Put the box down, love.'

'We're not gonna have eels as well, are we?' Lizzie
wanted to know.

'No, we're not.' Taking two pennies from the
pocket of her coat, Nellie held them out to her
daughter. 'Just go in and ask Beccy to put twopennyworth of mash in a bag.'

Of all the shops, the eel shop was Lizzie's favourite. Fish and chips was all right, even good sometimes, but pie and mash was better, and eels and
mash with its green liquor was the best treat of all.
The liquor (or gravy) was supposedly parsley sauce,
but, as Aunt Daisy said, no parsley ever made her
sauce as green. It was a well-guarded secret of the
Harrington family who owned the business. On the
rare occasions that Syd and Lizzie were given a
penny each at suppertime, Syd would opt for a
pennyworth of chips, while Lizzie would go for a
penny basin every time. All the basin contained was
mashed potato and the green liquor for a penny.
Eels were three pence a portion. At the rear of the
shop, there were many marble-topped tables with
high-backed benches for seating; each table had its
own huge tin pepper and salt pots and, best of all,
chilli vinegar. Chilli vinegar was not like the vinegar
they had at home; small red strips of cayenne pepper
floated, clearly visible through the glass bottle.
Seated at one such table, in the noisy, steamy atmosphere, greedily spooning the liquor, lavished with
pepper and the hot, spicy vinegar, into her mouth,
always hoping that an odd piece of eel had slipped
in, was a treat indeed to Lizzie.

'Lizzie, come down here,' Beccy Harrington, the daughter of the shop owner, had spotted her in the crowded shop. Blousy, very fat, common even, but with a heart of gold was a good description of Rebecca. She and her parents lived directly opposite the Collins family. 'What-cha want, ducks?' Beccy asked as she bent low towards Lizzie.

'Would yer put twopennyworth of mash in a bag for me mum, please?'

'No bother, luv, wait there.'

Within two minutes, Beccy was back, handing Lizzie a parcel that was not only heavy, but very, very hot. Taking the two pennies, she bent and planted a smacking kiss on Lizzie's cheek.

'Off to the concert, are you?' Without waiting for a reply, Beccy pushed Lizzie in the direction of the shop doorway. 'Night, night Lizzie. See yer in the morning. God bless,' Beccy called affectionately.

'Night, Beccy. Thanks ever so much.'

Turning at last into Graveney Road where they lived, they found it deserted. Not teeming with children as was normal. No clanging of meat hooks against steel hoops, no girls skipping, chanting their timeless rhymes, no tops being slashed down the centre of the road by means of home-made whips. The cold weather brought a change of character to the street, giving it a desolate air. For once, the youngsters had obeyed their parents, staying indoors in the warmth of the family kitchen. Lizzie and her mother stooped and placed the wooden box on the pavement. Lizzie unlatched the front garden gate, took the shopping-bag from her mother's arm, and went ahead up the path to the front door. Using her knee to lever the box waist high, Nellie held it in front of her stomach, one hand on each side. Pushing with her hip and bottom, she got the front door open and called out, 'Daisy, come an' give us a hand, will you?'

The kitchen door opened, the lights from the gas mantles in the room beyond streamed out, lighting up the passage. Daisy's bulky frame filled the doorway. A few steps forward and Daisy stopped dead in her tracks.

'God above,' she exclaimed, 'whatcha do, rob a bank?' Nellie leaned against the wall, suddenly helpless with laughter, while tears streamed down her face. It took her a couple of minutes to collect herself and to be able to speak, during which time Daisy stood watching her dumbfoundedly.

'Help us get it all in,' Nellie managed to say, and then, speaking as if to herself, she added, 'you're never gonna believe it.'

Young Syd, hearing all the commotion, put down the comic he had been reading and came into the hallway. He was feeling irritable, his mum seemed to have been out for ages, and he was sure that Lizzie would goad him. 'I've had half a hot meat pie,' she would tease, 'it was ever so good.' Well, if she had, he hoped it choked her.

'I'm starving, Mum,' he whined.

'All right, son, give me a minute and we'll all eat.'

Grudgingly, he helped his auntie drag the box

down the passage and into the kitchen. Nellie worked as she talked. Four plates were placed in the oven at the side of the kitchen range. Daisy and she began to take the meat, piece by piece, from the sodden, bloody carrier-bag as Nellie told her tale, right down to the last detail. Lizzie, sitting on the fire box at the end of the fender warming her feet and holding her hands out to the red glowing coals, was tired of listening to them. Endless questions and answers.

'She never did,' said Aunt Daisy for the umpteenth time.

'She did, brazen as you like.'

'Mum. You've bin all through it a dozen times. Can we 'ave our pies?'

'Yeah, pie and mash,' Syd added, glinting at his sister as he sat up to the table. At last. No one was talking. The pies were good, much better than the twopenny minced meat ones, Lizzie decided. The pastry was fluffy, flaky, the inside piping hot, with a generous amount of meat and thick rich gravy. Definitely worth the extra penny if you could afford it.

Her plate now empty, Lizzie sat back and smiled to herself. It was because of her that her mum was able to buy those pies; it couldn't have been such a bad thing she'd done. No. 'I'd do it again an' all,' she promised herself, but she was level-headed enough to fathom that chances like that don't come twice in a lifetime.

*

Eventually they were ready. Aunt Daisy, as ever looking as neat as a pin, used her long hat-pin to secure her navy blue felt hat securely to her head. Mum had her best coat on, a hand-me-down from the Dawsons which secretly Lizzie admitted looked very nice, the fur collar framing her mother's lovely face and keeping her ears warm. Syd and Lizzie brought up the rear, each warmly clothed, long scarves wound around their necks. They all set off for Fairlight Hall and their Saturday concert.

Chapter Two

THE NEXT DAY was Sunday. Grandma's day. Grandma Collins was a small, weather-beaten woman only just turned sixty, but years in the open air selling flowers from her stall at the Broadway had dried up her skin so that she looked older than she was. Her shiny silver hair swept up on top of her head and her firm mouth reminded Lizzie of Queen Mary.

Harriet Collins had rarely, if ever, shown either of her two children the affection they deserved. Widowed while still young, she had become hard and bitter. Yet somehow Daisy had grown into a cheerful loving woman, despite the fact she had never married, and Albert had grown into a jolly, outgoing man, charming all the women with whom he came into contact. Half the time his affairs were no more than infatuation, but for Nellie, his wife, each new affair was disastrous. Disastrous because she truly loved him and suffered terrible rejection and humiliation.

Seeing Nellie's distress had brought anguish to her mother-in-law and she had often prayed that Nellie would come to terms with the inescapable facts of life about her son. When, however, Albert Collins was involved in a fatal accident, Harriet had reflected bitterly that maybe she could be held somewhat responsible for her son's attitude to life. Yet, even at the funeral, she had not felt able to voice her feelings. Warmth and sentiment were lost to her. Much as she admired her daughter-in-law, even loved her, and longed to relieve her own pent-up emotion, she could not get the words out. 'Perhaps,' she told herself wearily, 'I've left it too late.'

Only Lizzie was the exception. 'Mischievous little monkey,' her gran was often heard to mutter, but those cold eyes would soften at she gazed at her youngest granddaughter. Only Lizzie, with her exasperating ways, was able to penetrate the invisible barrier and somehow manage to get her gran to show her feelings.

Harriet Collins came in from the scullery, carrying a scuttle of coal, as Lizzie opened the front door of her grandma's cottage.

'Hallo, Gran. Mum says dinner will be on the table for one o'clock and we've not ter be late.'

'She did, did she?' Harriet dumped three big lumps of coal on to the glowing fire and then upended the colander into the centre. The fire hissed and steam rose as the wet vegetable peelings and stale tealeaves banked down the heat. 'An' what 'ave you been up to this week, Lizzie?' Gran asked as she twisted round from the hearth and got to her feet.

Lizzie raised her eyebrows and put her hand over her mouth. 'Eh, I don't think I better tell you. Wait till you see what we've got for dinner today. Aunt Daisy said we can 'ave a choice.'

'A choice? What of – a stew or a pie, I suppose.'

'No, Gran, real roast. Honest. You'll see. Me, Mum and Aunt Daisy will tell you all about it. So come on, get yer hat and coat on.'

You bet they'll tell Gran the whole story and it'll take them for ever, Lizzie told herself. She was getting a bit sick and tired of her aunt's probing of every little detail and Syd's quizzing of the affair.

While Gran was getting herself ready, Lizzie had a good old poke around. To her, Gran's cottage appeared like something out of a story book. Silverdore Terrace has just five cottages, set beside Blunt's market and almost opposite the central hall in Mitcham Road. It was just a few minutes' walk from Tooting Broadway, and yet to anyone discovering these dwellings for the first time, it was as if time had passed by this tiny corner of South London. Outmoded, ignored, but loved by their elderly occupants, each cottage boasted a hundred-foot-long front garden. There was nothing at the back except a small yard, an outside lavatory and a cold-water tap. The front of the dwellings made up for this. A joy to behold at any season of the year, flower beds, flowering shrubs, and tall hollyhocks were tended with love and efficiency. In spring, flowers in abundance would nod their heads in the pale sunshine, while in summer, rose bushes bore blooms of every conceivable colour – pale pink, dark pink, white, yellow, peach, orange and every shade of red, all seemed to bloom for ever. There were lavender bushes and hydrangeas with flowers as big as dinner plates. Gran even had a holly bush in her garden and as Lizzie looked this cold Sunday morning at the bright red berries with which it was covered, she mulled over in her mind once again the difference between Silverdore Terrace and the street of back-to-back houses where she lived. It was only a two-up-and-two-down dwelling and the front door opened directly into the living room, but to Lizzie the garden alone made it a special place.

When they got to Graveney Road it was half-past twelve and Gran followed her usual procedure. She went upstairs and locked herself in the bathroom where she used the toilet and washed her hands, then went on up the extra five stairs into Nellie's big front bedroom and laid her hat and coat on the bed. This ritual took about ten minutes. Afterwards, she came downstairs and went straight through into the kitchen. Outside in the scullery, Daisy would grin at Nellie and under their breath, in unison, they would murmur, 'Inspection over.'

Connie had already laid the table for seven; Bill, her young man, having been invited to Sunday dinner this week.

'Sit up, all of you,' Nellie inclined her head towards Grandma and at the same time opened the kitchen door and called up the passage, 'Come on, Syd, and you, Lizzie, sit up at the table.'

As they took their places, Daisy brought the vegetable dishes in from the scullery, and set them down in the centre of the table. Nellie, her face red and wisps of hair escaping from her usually immaculate coiled plaits pinned each side of her face, entered, carrying a huge willow-patterned meat dish on which lay the now roasted rib of beef and the shoulder of lamb which she set down in front of Bill.

'Would you do the honours please, Bill?' Nellie quietly asked. 'I always feel a man carves meat much better than us women do.'

Bill Baldwin was grateful to Nellie; he had felt a bit out of place amongst all these ladies but she had set him at ease. 'I'd be honoured,' he told her as he picked up the carving knife and bone-handled steel which Nellie had set down beside the dish. With an exaggerated flourish he criss-crossed the blade of the knife back and forth against the hardened rolled steel, winking at young Syd as he did so. Satisfied that the knife was sharp enough, he asked, 'Now, Mrs Collins senior, what is it to be, beef or lamb?'

Nothing had been missed out today. Nellie had chopped the dried mint which hung in bags above the copper, adding a liberal amount of sugar before pouring on the hot vinegar; Daisy had dug up a root of horseradish from the backyard and had persevered with the grater, even though the strong herb had brought tears to her eyes. Daisy handed the plates around and soon there was a heaped plate set before each of them and they all began to eat.

The conversation was noisy until Aunt Daisy

pleaded, 'Let's eat up while it's all hot. You can all ask questions and get your answers,' she said, looking directly at her mother, 'when we get to pudding.'

The kitchen was warm, the fire burnt brightly as they continued to sit around the table. Apple pie and custard had been consumed by each of them, despite the huge first course, and now the tea tray with its large brown earthenware teapot stood centre of the table and a Sunday-best cup and saucer stood in front of each person. Daisy removed the woollen tea-cosy and began to fill the cups, having first poured in the milk. Explanations were over. Gran had gasped as Nellie had, for the hundredth time according to Lizzie, gone through the whole story. Connie and Bill thought it was hilarious.

Lizzie had had enough of being made to feel a fool. 'Well, Gran, what would you 'ave done?' she asked in a loud voice. 'There was this bloke propped up on a wooden box looking right comical an' all I can tell yer, what with his false moustache an' daft straw hat, doing his best to sell a load of meat. What 'appened? He got carried away. Nobody could afford all what he put in that dish and he ended up losing his temper. T'was his own daft fault. Showing off he were. "Who'll 'ave the bloody lot for nothing",' Lizzie mimicked. 'What yer supposed ter do? Stand there all posh an' quiet like, pretend you 'aven't heard him. Only a half-wit would do that. Anyway, I noticed you all enjoyed your dinner. Free or not, it never worried any of you.' Lizzie's tirade

came to an end. It had to; she had run out of breath.
Everyone glanced at each other.

Nellie finally broke the silence, 'Oh Lizzie love,
we didn't mean to upset you.'

Then Daisy's voice held a note of pleading as she
said, 'Of course we didn't, come on now, give us a
smile.'

Lizzie's temper had burned itself out; slowly a
smile came to her lips and quickly became a great
grin as she felt Syd kick her leg beneath the table.

'Oh Lizzie! Lizzie!' Gran moved her face until it
was touching Lizzie's and then pressed her lips
against her granddaughter's cheek.

Dumbly Lizzie raised her hand and felt the place
where her Gran had planted a kiss. Suddenly, everything was wonderful. Great. She began to laugh.
The laughter was infectious, and soon everyone was
laughing fit to bust. As Harriet Collins wiped her
face, she cast her glance ceilingwards. It didn't do
to have a favourite but how could she help it? One
in a million was this harum-scarum granddaughter
of hers. If she could hold on to that temper of hers
she'd go far. Got a sensible head on her shoulders,
our Lizzie has, if only life would give her a few
breaks. One thing was for sure, no one could ever
say that Lizzie was backward in coming forward.
Harriet was surprised to find herself admitting that
she loved her youngest granddaughter with all of
her heart.

It was nearly dark when Lizzie got home from

school on Friday afternoon to find Syd sitting on the doorstep.

'What are you doing out here?' she asked.

He didn't answer and she tutted as she pushed by him. Opening the letterbox she slipped her hand in and pulled on the length of string which hung down with the key inside the door.

She unlocked the door and pushed it open with her knee. 'Come on Syd, you go first and light the gas mantle and as soon as I've got me coat off I'll make us a drink.'

Syd was on his feet now, but he hung back and hesitated. It dawned on Lizzie that Syd was afraid of the dark. Mum and Aunt Daisy were away at their mothers' meeting. They went every Friday afternoon to the Central Hall and didn't get home until about five-thirty. It was still only half-past four. If Lizzie hadn't come straight home, what would Syd have done? Stayed sitting on the cold flagstones? He knew the front door key was on the string. She wanted to hug him, but Syd wouldn't stand for being mollycoddled.

'I'll go first,' she said softly. 'What would you like, a cup of tea or Oxo?'

'I'd rather have Oxo, an' Lizzie, I'm starving. 'Ave we got to wait till Mum comes home before we get our tea?'

Lizzie laughed out loud. 'We'll find something,' she assured him.

Ten minutes later, after Lizzie had put the poker into the banked-down fire, the two of them sat on the hearth rug, each with a thick slice of bread and dripping, smothered with pepper and salt and a mug of scalding-hot Oxo.

'Wonder what we got for tea,' Syd said as he sniffed hungrily at the appetizing smell that was coming from the side oven.

'Smells like hot-pot,' Lizzie told him. They both liked that, plenty of vegetables, dumplings and gravy.

'Hope we've finished our tea before Tim and Joey come round,' Syd muttered to himself, while staring into the fire.

'Oh no!' Lizzie exclaimed, very annoyed. 'It's not bath night for the Hurleys tonight, is it?'

'So Tim said when I left him. "See you later for our bath", that's what he said.'

'I wonder why Polly never mentioned it,' Lizzie mulled this over in her mind.

The Hurleys lived in Selkirk Road, and their house stood back to back with number thirty Graveney Road which was where the Collins lived. John and Kate Hurley were warm, friendly people. John Hurley was a fortunate man in as much as he had a regular job; storeman up at the Co-op. Kate, his wife, was everyone's friend, a hard-working woman, whose hair had once been a lovely blonde colour, now turned grey. A lovely smile was always on her face, showing exceptionally good white teeth, and it lit up her merry blue eyes. There was a saying Kate Hurley was fond of: 'Never bother trouble till trouble bothers you', and by that she seemed to set great store. The Hurleys had three children, two boys, Tim aged eleven, Joey just nine, and Polly, who was older than Lizzie by just four days. Lizzie couldn't remember, or even imagine, life without Polly. They were best friends, always had been.

The bath routine was a palaver Lizzie could have done without tonight. She had wanted to go round to Polly's house and discuss what Miss Roberts had been talking about so earnestly before she dismissed class – the dreaded scholarship exams. Still, never mind, these bath occasions often turned out to be quite jolly gatherings and she'd still get to see Polly.

There weren't many houses in the district that could boast a bathroom. Indeed, Nellie would tell it that when Albert Collins brought her from Lambeth to Tooting as his bride, there were three things that immediately made her take to the house. One, bay windows upstairs and down. Two, Venetian blinds. Three, a bathroom with an indoor lavatory. Once, the great cast-iron bath had stood gleaming white against the wall, now its under-belly and huge claw feet had turned rusty. Dust had collected beneath it in far unreachable corners. There was no running hot water – there never had been. Just the solitary brass tap which gave out only cold water. Two years ago, the landlord had made life somewhat easier. His workmen had removed the big old copper from the scullery and filled the space with a gas cooker and a gas copper. No longer did a fire have to be lit beneath the grey hearthstoned beast in order to heat the water. All that was needed now was a supply of pennies to feed the slot-meter and just one match with which to light the jets, which were set underneath the bottom of the copper.

Having this new-fangled copper did not eliminate all problems. A water supply was not connected to it. Cold water still had to be drawn from the tap above the scullery sink which stood at least six feet away on the opposite wall. Bucket after bucket needed to be filled and carried across to the copper. When boiling, there was a tap placed low down from which the water could be drawn out. Then the fun would begin. From the scullery, through the kitchen, along the passageway, and up the stairs into the bathroom, buckets had to be lifted almost chest high in order to tip the boiling water into the bath.

At seven o'clock, Nellie was trying hard to get cleared up. The copper was nigh on boiling and condensation was running down the scullery walls. 'Move your books,' she said to Lizzie, as she threw the dark red chenille cloth over the scrubbed table top; she didn't want Kate to see the place in a mess.

Daisy was laying sheets of newspaper over the linoleum up the passage, which would soak up some of the water that would inevitably get slopped in the process of reaching the bathroom.

John Hurley preceded his family, taking off his coat as he came into the kitchen. He was a short, stocky man, with strong brawny arms. Kate followed, wearing her Sunday coat and hat. Tim, the eldest boy, had a sly look about him, in Aunt Daisy's opinion, while young Joey, with huge brown eyes and a mop of dark curly hair was everyone's favourite.

'Right, out the way kids,' John Hurley ordered, 'we'll soon have the bath filled.'

Lizzie looked at Polly and a nod of her head suggested that they made themselves scarce in the front room.

An hour later, John Hurley had taken himself off to Wimbledon dog track. Using the long, hooked poker, Daisy had removed the top plate of the hob, leaving the fire open. The flames, now exposed to all the draughts, were leaping and flickering, giving out extra warmth. Tim and Joey, wrapped now in towels, glowing and clean, their well-scrubbed faces a shiny red, sat giggling and laughing, playing marbles with Syd. Polly, who had bathed first, was dressed; her hair now straggled round her face in damp tendrils. Nellie came in from the scullery carrying a wooden tray; three cups and saucers holding strong, sweet tea were set down for the women and five tin mugs of cocoa were handed out to the children.

All eyes were turned to Daisy and dribble came from young Joey's lips as she asked, 'Who wants a lump of bread pudding?' Rich and dark, full of fruit and peel, the top heavily dredged with sugar, its spicy smell filled the kitchen.

'I do,' five voices called while heads nodded in eager agreement.

Time for bed. Lizzie and Polly clung together. 'See you in the morning,' Lizzie called after her friend.

'Yeah, night. God bless you,' Polly answered.

'Thanks, Nellie, you too, Daisy. It's bin a real treat,' Kate hugged them both.

'You're more than welcome any time,' they told her.

Closing the front door behind the Hurleys, Daisy grinned at Nellie as she gathered up the sodden newspaper. 'Only don't make it too often,' she muttered.

Pouring another cup of tea for themselves, Nellie and Daisy marvelled at the rigmarole they went through every time they or their neighbours wanted to use the bathroom.

'I'd just as soon sit in the old tin bath in front of the fire,' Daisy exclaimed.

Nellie gave her sister-in-law a lopsided grin and then both of them burst out laughing. Each was fully aware that that was exactly what Daisy did whenever she had the house to herself.

Christmas that year was marred for Lizzie by two things. Leslie was now stationed in Malta. Without Les, things couldn't be the same. Lizzie adored him, he was a father to her as well as a brother. The second thing really narked Lizzie. Her mother insisted she still had to go to work for the Dawsons on Christmas morning.

But there were some compensations. Snow was forecast and that meant great fun out in the street with all the other kids or even up on the common if Mum felt up to the walk, and Connie was getting engaged to Bill. Bill Baldwin was like one of the family already. He was a big husky lad with light brown hair, not a bit shy now he had got to know them all. Bill was devoted to Connie; he loved her with all his heart, and had known she was the one for him from the moment he'd set eyes on her. Since there was only him and his widowed mother, Nellie had invited them to join the family for Christmas dinner.

A week before Christmas, Bill came upon Syd arguing with Lizzie in the backyard. 'What's up, kids?' he wanted to know.

Syd confided in him, 'We've only got four bob in our money box and the present we want ter buy for Mum and Aunt Daisy costs five bob.'

Bill looked at them thoughtfully. 'That's a lot of money to spend on one present.'

'We know that,' said Lizzie, 'but it's what they want. We heard them talking.'

Bill worked in Billingsgate Fish Market. The hours were long and the work hard but he made good money working on commission. It was a problem how he could give these two nice children a shilling without hurting their pride. A penny from him every Saturday had become quite acceptable but a shilling was a lot of money. He was too wise to offer it outright.

'Tell yer what. I haven't got round to cleaning my bike for more than two weeks now. The front lamp is so dirty it's a wonder a policeman hasn't stopped me, and the rear light is not much better. Just 'aven't had the time.' He drew in a deep breath and pretended to be considering the matter. 'If I give you two sixpences each, you wouldn't clean me bike for me, would you?'

A great grin spread on Syd's face while a flash of hope lit up Lizzie's blue eyes. ' 'Course we will,' they chorused. Rags and a tin of Bluebell metal polish were produced and they set to with a will.

Once inside the china shop, Lizzie gazed fondly at the twenty-one-piece tea services set out on a stand behind the counter.

'Which one do you like best, Syd?' she said.

He pointed to a blue willow-patterned set. 'What d'you think of that one?'

'Oh, no. Gran's got that pattern, so has Mrs Hurley; let's buy Mum and Aunt Daisy something different.'

Twice the blonde assistant with the red-painted fingernails asked if she could help them.

'No, we won't be a minute,' they told her – but they were. At least twenty minutes had passed before they settled on a cream-coloured set with a honeysuckle design.

Handing over their shillings, sixpences and pennies, Syd nudged his sister, 'Go on Lizzie, ask her.'

The assistant smiled, 'Ask me what?'

'Please . . .' still Lizzie hesitated.

'. . . Deliver it to our house.' Syd got it out in a rush. 'It says goods costing five shillings or more will be delivered free of charge.'

'That's quite right, young man,' the assistant told him, as she reached for a pink form.

And so, on Christmas Eve, a puzzled Aunt Daisy signed for and accepted a large wooden box.

Lizzie and Syd clutched at each other's hands, squeezing every now and again as they watched their mother and their aunt discard the straw on to the kitchen floor and extract six cups, six saucers, six tea plates, a milk jug and sugar basin, and, lastly, the large bread and butter plates. Nellie's face was wet with tears, and Daisy, her eyes brimming, stared in amazement at the china and the straw now scattered widely.

'Come here, ducks, and give your old aunt a kiss,' Daisy said as she drew Lizzie to her.

Even Syd was smiling as he brushed at his cheek with his fist to remove the dampness where his mother has planted several kisses.

Christmas was good. Mrs Baldwin had proved to be a jolly sort, joining in games and giving a solo of 'Silent Night' whilst Nellie played for her on their upright piano. And on Boxing Day it did snow. Waking to a stillness that only comes with snow, Lizzie ran to look out of the window. A pure white, unblemished blanket covered everything except the tips of the chimney pots. The only sound was from a few sparrows visible in the yard, twittering away near the back door asking to be fed.

'Come on, Syd, wake up!' Lizzie shouted as she ran to the small box-room which Syd had as a bedroom all to himself. 'It's bin snowing.'

As she pulled the covers from his bed, Lizzie looked around the small space. Syd had a bookcase, which Leslie had made for him; it was full of comics and paperback books. He also had a small table and one chair, ideal for doing his homework, except that Syd never bothered to do any.

A thought came to Lizzie, as she tickled her brother's toes and he gave her a brutal kick. If, in the new year, Connie was to marry her Bill, she would then have a bedroom of her own. In her mind's eye, Lizzie was already seeing the room she now shared with her sister set out as she would like it, if only she could wheedle her mother round to her way of thinking. That should be easy, she told herself, and if her mum wasn't forthcoming, there was always Gran. Gran had some lovely pieces of furniture, much more than she needed. Yes, Lizzie was confident the new year would see her settled very nicely into a room of her own.

Chapter Three

AS ALWAYS, JANUARY was bleak, with short hours of daylight, and dark, bitter-cold evenings. One day, as Lizzie came through the school gates, she heard her younger brother yelling coarsely, 'Wait for me, Liz. You'll never guess what,' he panted as he drew near. 'Our teacher says we can 'ave all the tar blocks we want so long as we've got something to carry them 'ome in.'

'You're barmy,' Lizzie retorted. 'What would we want with a load of messy old tar blocks?'

'Bet Mum would be glad to 'ave some. Save her coal, wouldn't it?'

Lizzie pondered on this. Syd was a likeable little dare-devil with his friendly and carefree approach to life, and at times he could be very thoughtful, even loving.

'If I mend the wheel on me barrow, will you come up the High Street and 'elp me get some on Saturday? Will yer?' he pleaded. 'All the other boys are gonna get some.'

Lizzie nodded; her eyes were merry and her lips smiling as she took hold of his hand.

During the short walk home, Syd chatted away very excitedly, telling her what his teacher had told the class. The Ministry of Transport had commanded that all the tram tracks in the centre of main roads had to be renewed. Removal of the old tracks meant the discarding of wooden blocks embedded on either side.

As it turned out, the whole district was on to a good thing once work started. Men were taken on as labourers, digging out the existing rails, thrilled at the prospect of a few weeks' steady employment. There wasn't a kid who didn't enjoy the excitement of it all as they lined the gutter and stared in amazement. Pick-axes were vigorously swung, by tough, weather-beaten young men, in a repeated rhythm. The piles of old tar-sodden blocks grew larger as heap after heap was tossed aside. Great cauldrons of hot tar stood on the edge of the pavement, each with a fire glowing brightly beneath, and filled with thick jet-black steaming liquid with a pungent smell so strong it took one's breath away.

'Breathe deep,' mothers were admonishing their children. 'It'll do yer chest a power of good.'

If it didn't burst your lungs first, Lizzie thought, as she and Syd joined the scrambling, pushing, shoving mob to fill their barrow once more.

The whole show moved with great speed. All too soon the length of High Street from Trinity Road at Tooting Bec, right through to Tooting Broadway was completed. Four lanes of shiny steel rails were set centre to the road and the gangers moved on towards Colliers Wood and south Wimbledon.

Nellie went back and forth from the pavement, where Syd and Lizzie had tipped their load, to the backyard, transporting six to eight blocks at a time in her shopping bag. Daisy toiled away, stacking the rough, dirty blocks of wood as high as they would go in the garden shed.

'Don't sit on them chairs,' Nellie called out as Syd and Lizzie came in through the back door, 'and both of you get them dirty boots off.' She glanced across at Daisy, 'Look at them, right filthy the pair of them!'

In no time Nellie had stripped them of their outdoor clothes, made sure that they had washed their faces and that their hands were thoroughly clean. By now, Daisy had the table laid with a sumptuous feast of sausage and mash, with jam roly poly and custard to follow.

The tar blocks proved to be a godsend. The next few weeks were bitter. Snow lingered and turned into dirty, mushy heaps, ice formed in the gutters and no water came from the scullery tap. All the outside pipes were frozen.

Inside, the kitchen was warm and cosy. The fire roared away all day and was well banked down at night, never allowed to go out. It spurted and crackled dangerously as the children sat doing their homework while Nellie knitted and Aunt Daisy sewed. The tar blocks were pitted with gravel and as the tar melted the tiny stones were shot out, making sounds like pellets being shot through the air as they hit the hearth. Lizzie and Syd would laugh aloud and protest as their mother placed the fireguard in position.

'The only person not showing a profit from all of this is the local coalman,' commented Nellie.

'You can say that again,' Daisy retorted. 'Thanks to our two kids, those blocks will help eke out the coal for many a long day.'

Nellie nodded her agreement. 'And you know what, Daisy, there shouldn't be half the children bad with chest ailments this winter. You've only ter open the front door to realize that.' For there was hardly a family who hadn't amassed a store of tar blocks and everywhere the air was acrid with the fumes of burning tar.

As winter at last gave way, the pale early spring sunshine brought out the women to gossip over the back fences once more. Then there was another upheaval in the district – hard to believe, but true. Electricity was coming to Tooting. Arguments ranged back and forth as to the merits of this wonder. The municipality was undertaking to provide this service free of charge for a limited number of points in each house. Any additional sockets would have to be paid for.

Upheaval came to the back streets this time. Pathways and roadways were dug up and wide open trenches were laid bare during the laying of the cables. Boisterous kids harassed the workmen. Floorboards were taken up in downstairs passages and women fought a losing battle against the dust and dirt. When completion was almost reached, the inevitable official in his bowler hat appeared. Hold-

ing his clipboard firmly, pencil poised, he raised his
eyes to the top of the front door.

'Ah, yes. Number thirty, Mrs Collins, right?
How many extra points will you be wanting?' he
enquired in his posh accent.

Daisy and Nellie answered in unison, 'None,
thank you.'

'You do realize our free instalment offer only
covers the ground floor?'

Nellie wrinkled her brow but said quietly, 'Never
mind, we'll just have ter make do.'

'My dear lady,' he replied, 'you will have no light
or power points in the upper regions of this house.'

Daisy scowled at the man, 'We've got by with gas
all these years and it won't kill us now not to have
electricity in the bedrooms.'

He smiled sardonically, turned away, then hesitantly said over his shoulder, 'If you change your
mind over the next three days, the same offer will
stand.'

They didn't change their minds, no more than
many other occupants of the road did. In fact, it was
a long time before the electric light which had been
installed in the downstairs rooms was put to full use.

'Switch it off, switch it off,' Nellie screamed at
Syd, who had demanded the honour of being the
first to flick the brass switch.

Nellie was in a state of panic, 'It makes the place
look so dirty,' she sadly remarked.

'Indeed, it does,' agreed Daisy.

The ceilings were smoke-blackened from the constantly burning kitchen range, and the gas jet fixed above the mantle shelf which gave out heat as well as providing light had left a filthy stain on the wall. The new light with just a bare bulb illuminated the room so brightly that it clearly showed the grime which had previously been ignored.

Lizzie was glad her bedroom still only boasted a gas bracket. At times, to save money, even this was not lit. She and Syd would be given a candle, placed in a saucer of water, to light up their rooms while they got into bed. Lizzie even liked to lie and watch the weird patterns on the walls and ceiling made by the flickering flame, but she hated the smell which lingered when her mother snuffed out the light between licked finger and thumb.

Tomorrow would be Good Friday and school had broken up at midday. There would be two whole weeks' holiday. Lizzie was spreading dripping on a slice of toast but her thoughts were elsewhere – on the fact that she had sat her scholarship exams.

After tea that evening, Lizzie walked round to Polly's house. She was longing to ask Polly what she had thought of the exam questions. The light was on in the kitchen and the fire glow showed clearly through the back window, so she knocked on the door and opened it, as she always did, and called out, 'It's all right, it's only me, Lizzie.'

The kitchen was deserted, but someone was moving about upstairs. Surprised to see neither Mr nor Mrs Hurley, she went to the bottom of the stairs and called up.

Polly answered, 'I'll be down in a minute.' She clattered down the linoleum-covered stairs, and came into the kitchen, grinning at Lizzie and pointing to a chair. 'Pull it up to the fire,' she ordered, and threw herself into another chair opposite.

Lizzie sat down and Tibbles, the Hurley's tabby cat, hugged against her legs. 'Where's your mum?'

'Gone to the pub with dad. Won't see them before closing time.'

Lizzie laughed, 'I'm glad they've gone out, I was going to ask you about the exam. How d'you think you got on?'

Polly frowned, 'Wouldn't like to say, really. How about you?'

Lizzie shook her head. 'Dunno. Glad it's over, though. Don't suppose I got many questions right.'

Polly protested, 'Oh, come on, Lizzie, they weren't that difficult, were they?'

Lizzie forced herself to agree. Now that she had found out what she wanted to know, she wished that they could just forget the whole matter. It would be weeks before they got the results. 'I hope we both pass,' she said listlessly.

'Well, worrying won't make it so. Will it?' Polly laughingly answered, as she suddenly stood up. 'Come on, let's go round to the Selkirk Pub. If we call through the door, me dad's sure to buy us a ginger beer and a Darby biscuit.'

Together they ran down the road, quickening

their steps as they neared the pub, taking the front steps two at a time. Polly saw her dad as soon as they opened the door, slumped in a chair near the dart board, a frothy pint in his hand.

'You've got a cheek, the pair of yer,' he told them, but his cheerful face was creased with laughter as he turned towards the bar.

Side by side, the two friends sat on the steps, glass in one hand, large round biscuit in the other. Easter would begin tomorrow. On Holiday Monday they would probably all go to Mitcham Fair. The scholarship suddenly didn't matter so much.

'Glad we came out, aren't you?' Polly asked.

'Yeah. Your dad's great,' said Lizzie. All the worry and agony of sitting the exam seemed remote and dim now. 'Want to come with me ter see me gran tomorrow?' she asked.

'Love to,' said Polly.

The lovely month of June came again. For the past weeks, there had been great excitement in the Collinses' house. Nellie had baked rich dark cakes which the local baker had promised to ice. Aunt Daisy had sewed a white silk dress for the bride and a pink dress for the only bridesmaid. Connie was to marry her Bill and Lizzie was to be her only attendant. Disregarding the cost, tradition was adhered to. Nearly all the neighbours were inside the church and everyone held their breath as Connie came down the aisle on John Hurley's arm.

Lizzie had always thought of her sister as plain,

even straitlaced, but nothing was further from the truth today. A crown of orange blossom with a froth of white veiling framed her face. She carried a small posy of pink roses and the colour matched her rosy cheeks. Lizzie stood shyly behind her sister and offered up a silent prayer that when the time came for her, too, to be married, she might look as beautiful as Connie did today.

Once outside, the crowd began throwing confetti and yelling good wishes. Syd was wearing his first pair of long trousers and Lizzie could scarcely believe that this clean, tidy, blond, curly-haired boy was her young brother.

The reception was a cold salad meal laid out in the function room of the Selkirk Pub. At six o'clock, when the public bars opened, spontaneous gaiety broke out and a good time was had by all.

Connie's departure from the house was not such a wrench. She and Bill had rented the top half of Dolly Whitlock's house, which stood at the far end of Graveney Road and meant that Connie would still be a daily visitor.

The wedding was over but excitement was still in the air. The summer horse-race meeting at Epsom was due and on the second day the most famous race of all would take place – the Derby. The Fountain Public House in Garratt Lane was running an outing, with four bus loads of people. The whole Collins family, with the exception of Gran, was going to Epsom for the day. Six-thirty in the morning and the pub was packed as folk filed through and out of the back door to board the buses.

'Can we go upstairs?' Polly yelled at her parents.

Mr Hurley set down the crate of booze he was helping his mates to load on board, wiped his sweaty forehead with his forearm and grinned at his only daughter, 'Yes, all right, but sit still. See the boys don't run about till yer mum and me get there.'

Five children made a dash for the stairs. Polly and Lizzie grabbed a seat together, while Syd, Tim and Joey squashed up on a double bench. Finally, to loud cheers, they were off! As they left London behind and entered the green Surrey countryside, they joined the already jam-packed main road to Epsom: open-top buses, hackney carriages, motor cycles with side cars, charabancs, all their seats filled to capacity.

Pearly kings and queens, regally seated in their horse-drawn carts, rubbed shoulders for the day with true royalty. Bumper-to-bumper with cars and commercial vans were Daimlers and Rolls Royce limousines, their occupants smiling and waving just as enthusiastically as everyone else.

They finally arrived at the course and were directed by policemen into a special parking area reserved for buses. Shopping bags and boxes were unpacked and food in plenty was set out on the grass. Serious drinking began for the adults. And the kids had all the pop they wanted. Spread out wide, away from the course, was the fairground. Coffee stalls, beer tents, tipsters, gypsies, fortune tellers and racketeers, all contrived and schemed to earn a few quid from the day's racing.

It was a brilliant day and the sun shone with a vengeance on the thousands who had turned up to chance their luck on the horses.

'They're off,' the cry went up as the first horses left the stalls.

'Quick,' Lizzie grabbed Polly's arm, causing her to drop the long iced bun she was munching. 'Let's get to the rails.'

They elbowed their way through the crowd, the shouting and cheering so loud it was enough to burst the eardrums. The two friends held on to each other tightly as the horses came into sight, their hooves pounding the track as they thundered past between the rails.

Later that afternoon the mums gathered the children together and took them over to the fair. Toffee apples, candy floss, humbugs and bags of hot chips combined with rides on the roundabouts and the big dipper.

All too soon it was time to go home, but the fun wasn't over by any means. Crowds lined the pavements, dozens of children to the forefront.

'Chuck out yer mouldies,' they bawled. By now ninety per cent of the racegoers were tipsy and they responded willingly. Handfuls of farthings, half-pennies and pennies were chucked over the sides of carts, out of the windows of cars, buses and the charabancs into the road. Dodging the traffic, evading the horses hooves, pushing, shoving, struggling with each other to reach the coins first, the children swarmed, unaware of the dangers, enjoying the rough and tumble and laughing gleefully as the toffs in the big cars raised their top hats to them.

Dirty and bedraggled they alighted from the buses in Garratt Lane. 'You go on 'ome with the kids,' John Hurley slurred as he and his mates tried to rouse one man who was paralytic with drink, unable to move from the pavement where he sat.

Wearily, the four women and five children set off for home. At the gate of number thirty, all good-nights having been said, Daisy almost as an after-thought asked, 'How much did you win, Kate?'

With a humorous grin on her face, Kate answered, 'Five pounds one shilling – not bad, eh? You and Nellie aren't out of pocket on the day, are you?'

Daisy looked at her sister-in-law and they both laughed. 'No,' they both answered, and Nellie added, 'We made a bob or two.'

Chapter Four

THE LETTER ARRIVED on a Saturday morning. Lizzie picked it up from the mat and stared at the envelope for a long time. Franked London County Council, she knew exactly what it contained and dallied with the idea of throwing it into the fire unopened. 'Oh, Jesus!' she whispered in an agony of frustration. 'What am I going to do?'

Lizzie lay in bed that evening and thought confusedly about her day and in particular about the examination for the scholarship. She had passed and that was something she had not really imagined would happen, although she had allowed herself to dream that it might.

Her delight was tinged with guilt. Why should she be privileged when her brothers and her sister hadn't been? To go to the High School would cost money. Maybe she would be entitled to a grant, but it certainly would not cover the cost of uniforms, books, travel to and from school and many more untold items.

Her mother's delight as she read the letter had been a joy to see. Tenderly she had hugged Lizzie to her, murmuring, 'Well done. Good girl.' Aunt Daisy's congratulations had been more hearty. She had grabbed Lizzie, sweeping her off her feet, and was triumphantly swinging her round and round when the kitchen door opened and Gran stood there.

'Our Lizzie's passed her scholarship,' Daisy quickly told her mother.

'I'm not a bit surprised; ever since she could toddle, she's had her nose stuck in a book,' the old lady retorted dryly.

'Oh, say you're pleased, Gran,' Lizzie pleaded.

'Of course I'm pleased,' she said quietly. And she was.

To Harriet, this little girl was everything. She wanted to pet and cuddle her but she was not used to showing affection. Silently, she vowed that nothing, if she had her way, would stand in the way of her favourite grandchild being granted the chance of a good education.

In the scullery, Lizzie was putting on the kettle when she heard her elders in the kitchen discussing finances. She wanted to put her hands over her ears as she heard her mother sadly say, 'I only hope we can afford it.' Whichever way she looked at it, Lizzie knew the cost would be far more than her mother could manage.

Double delight: Polly had also passed.

'How did your dad take the news?' Lizzie asked, as she cut two lumps from the cold bread pudding.

'He was very pleased,' Polly assured her, smiling at the memory. 'Mum said afterwards, it knocked him all of a heap. He wouldn't believe it at first, kept saying brains didn't run in the family. He said he is coming round to talk to yer mum about money, and how they are going to manage.'

During the whole of the summer, endless opinions were exchanged and ideas debated. Leslie wrote from Malta that his blonde whippet of a sister was a genius and for his mother to buy Lizzie a bicycle on the never-never and he would give her an extra sixpence a day to pay for the instalments.

John Hurley voted this a good idea for the pair of them. 'I'll see what Nick Shephard can do,' he told Nellie.

She grimaced. Nick was their insurance man whom Nellie never quite trusted. Black hair smarmed down with grease, blue eyes and a pencil-slim moustache and always smartly dressed in the up-to-date fashion, he was a hit with most women, though not with Nellie.

Every Saturday morning he called for the weekly payments on their Britannia insurance policies. 'Royal Britannia, two tanners make a bob, three make eighteen pence and four make two bob,' the kids in the street would chant as he did his rounds.

Nick Shephard had a sideline. He sold things on the weekly. Towels, sheets, boots, shoes, you name it, he would do his best to get it. Where from was a closely guarded secret.

'Two bicycles?' His brow puckered then suddenly he was grinning. 'Leave it ter me. I'll have them for you by next Saturday.'

He shook hands with John Hurley but Daisy

blocked his way as he made to leave their kitchen. 'These are for two young girls. We don't want no rubbish nor yer stolen bikes. Do you understand me?' She looked sternly into his eyes.

'Trust me, Miss Collins,' he entreated. 'As if I would do anything to jeopardize the good relationship I've had with this family for years now.'

But her next words were menacing. 'Just remember what I've said.'

The evening before school started found Polly and Lizzie in the big warm kitchen of the Collinses' house. Nellie and Aunt Daisy had taken themselves off to the Selkirk for a glass of stout and a singsong, and Syd had gone to his Boys' Brigade meeting. The two girls sat one each side of the kitchen table, labelling their books and sportswear.

'All finished,' Lizzie said as she put her plimsoles on top of her books and shut the lid of the small case.

John Hurley had bought Polly's uniform from Morley's, the official school outfitters, but Lizzie's had been lovingly and expertly made at home by Aunt Daisy. The regulation cloth and colours had been available from Smith's in the Mitcham Road. Both girls had been taken by their mothers to the Royal Co-operative Society. There, by means of mutuality cheques, navy-blue knickers, black stockings, shoes and plimsoles plus vests and blouses had been bought.

Mutuality cheques were a godsend and repayments were strictly weekly. If you had a Co-op representative call, one shilling in every pound had to be paid extra as interest. However, if you took your weekly payments to the Co-op bank (and this entailed climbing a flight of forty steps) for twenty consecutive weeks without fail, no interest was charged. Come rain or hail, Nellie went to the bank religiously each week. Using mutuality cheques, she and Daisy could buy while prices were at their lowest.

'So,' Polly concluded, 'tomorrow is the big day.'

Lizzie grinned, 'And about time too. Wonder how we'll get on, it still seems too good to be true. You and me going to the Elliott High School in Southfields.' She nudged Polly and they both giggled. 'Hope the other girls in our class are not stuck up.'

'Who cares if they are,' Polly looked lovingly at her friend as she squeezed past the new Raleigh bicycle which stood propped against the wall of the passage. 'We'll have each other. We'll get by,' she declared.

' 'Course we will,' agreed Lizzie.

Chapter Five

IT WAS NEARLY Christmas once more, the third since Lizzie had been at the Elliott School. Alone in the house, Lizzie, not yet dressed, sat in the old armchair by the fire. There was only one person outside her family who she had bought a present for, and that was Polly.

Lizzie disliked her classmates more than she dared to admit, and the very thought of Miss Dawlish, her headmistress, filled her with a forlorn air of defeat. Without the company of the happy-go-lucky Polly, she would really have hated school.

Miss Dawlish was a snob. There were no two ways about it. 'It is a privilege that should never be taken lightly,' she would intone from her high dais each morning as she gazed over her pupils at assembly. 'You are members of my school at the expense of the ratepayers,' she would insist. 'You owe it to them to prove that you are the cream of the cream.' Lizzie had never worked out the meaning of that statement.

Miss Dawlish failed to accept the fact that she had pupils from an impoverished background. A great charity worker, she would regularly urge her girls to bring donations for the relief of the poor.

Lizzie's contributions were small; more often than

not only what Gran gave her. She knew only too well how her mother struggled to provide the elementary necessities for her to attend the Elliott, and so she rarely made a difficult situation worse by asking.

'Old bitch,' Lizzie would mutter to herself when Miss Dawlish smiled sweetly as better-off classmates ingratiated themselves.

'Boot-lickers,' Polly would mumble. She agreed whole-heartedly with Lizzie about Miss Dawlish, and certainly there was no love lost between her and her condescending classmates.

However, she didn't fare as badly as Lizzie. She had a father in full-time employment and was able to acquire such things as her own sports equipment. Although she willingly shared with Lizzie, it still left Lizzie vulnerable to their sick jokes.

The highlight of the past year had been their street party. Polly had let the cat out of the bag at school. 'A street party! How disgusting,' the tall, freckled-faced teacher's pet Marion had mimicked.

All south London had street parties in 1935. King George V and Queen Mary had been on the throne for twenty-five years and their Silver Jubilee was a grand excuse for a celebration. For weeks ahead, men had collected pennies up and down both sides of the street every Sunday morning. 'It's to give the kids a good time. God bless yer,' they would say at each house, as coppers were pushed into their collecting tins.

The men were as good as their word. The great day had been declared a public holiday. From the pub, stacks of trestles were brought forth and set up in the centre of the road from one end to the other. Large planks of wood formed table tops, red, white and blue paper cloths were laid, and endless rows of benches provided the seating.

High above, lines stretched from upstairs windows were joined to their neighbours on the other side of the street. Banners and flags made out of old cloths dyed in tin baths to all shades of red, white and blue, showed how patriotic the Londoners could be.

Children were seated near to their own front doors and were waited on by the adults. There were jam, fish-paste and cheese sandwiches, lemonade and ginger beer, fancy cakes and chocolate biscuits, with jelly, blancmange and ice-cream to round it all off. 'Smashing,' was the unanimous verdict.

When darkness came, children sat along the kerb stones, watching the antics of the adults. Tunes were pounded out on old upright pianos, and accordions took over when the piano players had a rest for a few pints. 'Knees Up Mother Brown', 'The Lambeth Walk', 'Knock 'em in the Old Kent Road', 'My Old Man Said Follow the Van', 'My Young Man is Up in the Gallery' – these and many more well-loved songs were sung lustily, if not tunefully, as neighbours weaved their way back and forth across the street. In the morning, there were empty bottles by the dozen, beer bottles, pints and quarts, cider bottles, lemonade bottles all stacked up along the pavement.

'Wonder if we could nick a few, get the money back on the empties,' Syd considered as he went to call for the Hurley boys.

'Tell you what. It wasn't only the kids that had a good time,' Daisy declared as she swept the front path and Nellie retrieved more empty bottles from the front garden.

Lizzie found herself laughing at the memory as she told herself to get cracking and get dressed. Blow the Elliott, Miss Dawlish, and all those posh girls, who thought they were much better than anyone else.

The bells sang the arrival of 1936. Neighbours came out into the roadway to sing 'Auld Lang Syne' and to kiss and hug each other. Only one person was missing; that was Leslie. Lizzie missed her big brother. She wrote him a regular weekly letter, telling of her progress at school, which was surprisingly good, and skilfully she outlined her grievances. His replies never failed to make her laugh. 'Don't stand for no argy bargy from them. Give as good as you get, Lizzie,' was his advice.

The year had scarcely begun and the whole country was in mourning. King George V was dead. Connie said she didn't want to go to see the King's lying-in-state.

'I do,' Lizzie said. 'Please, Bill,' she implored her brother-in-law, 'will you take me?'

' 'Course I will, love, if your mum says it's all right.'

They came out of the underground tube station to find everyone else in London had decided to pay their respects; mounted police were controlling the crowds. They queued for well over an hour on a bleak January day made worse by a keen wind that was blowing off the River Thames. At last they entered Westminster Hall. It was difficult to see anything at first as they slowly shuffled forward in step with everyone else. Gradually their eyes became accustomed to the dusk interior.

A solitary wreath lay on the coffin and tall, beautiful floral tributes nearby made the air sweet and heavy with perfume. Women and children wept. Men looked solemn. Lizzie was afraid to look, attracted far more by the soldiers and their uniforms as they stood guarding the body – heads down, perfectly still like statues. As they passed out at the other end of the hall, Bill squeezed Lizzie's hand; she had never let go of his since entering the hall.

'There, Lizzie,' he said, 'you'll never forget the death of King George V, will you?'

'No, I won't,' Lizzie solemnly agreed.

Plans for the coronation of Edward VIII were going ahead, but all the time Mrs Simpson was on the scene. She became the main topic of conversation everywhere, discussed in shops, on buses, in the streets and pubs – not always discreetly. Boys and girls alike sang saucy songs about her, ridiculing her for having designs on England's future King. Opinion was divided. Many thought he would be a good King because he had shown a keen interest in social problems. Others were opposed to a marriage because she was a divorced woman and an American. Preparation for the ceremony of crowning the sovereign continued. Edward would be crowned King in Westminster Abbey, but would Mrs Simpson be his Queen Consort?

At last, in the following December, Edward VIII finally announced that he would abdicate. 'Good riddance to bad rubbish,' declared Harriet Collins. But the repercussions of his action were colossal. Souvenirs that had been made in their thousands for the coronation were now utterly worthless. There would be no coronation, and traders sustained great losses. No one escaped. From the largest stores down to fairground traders and barrow boys, all were left with coronation mugs, cups and saucers, wall plaques, bowls and teaspoons on their hands. Now they couldn't give them away, let alone sell them. Edward VIII's renunciation of the throne had been disastrous in more ways than one. Folk looked back over the past twelve months as 1936 drew to a close and shook their heads.

Lizzie wrote an essay as part of her English exam and for once won congratulations from Miss Dawlish. 'The past year has to be one of the most important years in the history of the Royal Family,' she wrote. 'Three different Kings had each sat on the throne of England in such a short space of time.'

The following year, 1937, was relatively uneventful in England, although there were disturbing rumblings from Germany, where Adolf Hitler was initiating a large re-armament programme.

'He won't stop till he dominates the world,' declared Fred Johnson, the milkman for the whole street.

'Rubbish,' declared Jackie Jordon, Nellie's next-door neighbour. 'We've sat on them once, you don't think we're daft enough to let 'im drag the Germans into another war?'

'We'll have to see, won't we?' Gran put her two pennyworth in, as she opened the front gate.

Actually, she wanted to get Nellie and her daughter inside, off the doorstep. She had more personal worries to discuss. She had lived through enough wars and wasn't about to get upset over something that might never happen. She'd bigger problems to worry about just now. Compulsory purchase of her house and the ground it stood on, that's what the letter had said. Well, she'd see about that!

''Allo, Gran, who's upset you?' Lizzie cheekily asked as her grandmother pushed past the knot of people on the doorstep and made her way down the passage and into the kitchen.

'Never you mind, just put the kettle on,' she snapped. Her eyes were blazing and her cheeks flamed as she savagely removed her hat-pin and hung her hat behind the door. It was not a bit like Gran to be so short-tempered, least of all with her beloved Lizzie.

By suppertime, the whole street knew that Silverdore Terrace was to be pulled down. The very thought of Gran's lovely home disappearing made Lizzie feel sick and she burst into tears and threw her arms about her Gran's neck.

'Stop it! Crying won't help. I'm going to the solicitors first thing tomorrow; I'm also going to make sure the newspapers hear about this.' Gran, pale and very angry, snatched her letter up from the table and shoved it into her bag. 'They'll 'ave ter do more than just send a letter if they want my house. Lived in Silverdore since I were married at seventeen – that's coming up for fifty-four years. Try chucking me out! Just let them try!' Gran yelled threateningly.

The young lady in the solicitor's office was brisk and efficient as she ushered Daisy and Harriet into the main office. Mr Martin came from behind his desk to shake their hands. Tall and neatly dressed in a navy-blue suit, striped shirt with a stiff white collar, he epitomized his profession.

Having read through the letter, he cleared his throat and with one finger eased the stiff collar about his Adam's apple. 'I'm afraid this is watertight,' he said. He was all sympathy. 'It's an odd business, I don't like it one bit,' he told them. 'Legally, though, there is not much I can do about it.'

With a melancholy nod of her head, Harriet Collins made to rise.

'Wait,' Mr Martin himself rose. 'Perhaps it would be better if you let me explain the situation fully,' he suggested. Harriet sat down again and nodded dumbly.

Mr Martin carefully weighed his words. 'Your ownership of the cottage is not in dispute. It is the land on which it was built. The freeholder, as he is known, owns the land for ever and he has fairly wide powers to do with the land as he wishes. These cottages were built in 1816 when a lease on the ground was granted for a fixed period only. Over the years, all owner-occupants, including yourself, Mrs Collins, have paid ground rent to the freeholder and observed the terms of the lease granted by the original freeholder. That fixed period came to an end twenty years ago. Clearly, then, the freeholder has been lenient and is now well within his rights to ask that the land be given back. There is nothing we can legally do to restrict the freeholder from having use of his land.'

Daisy felt utterly inadequate. Her mother sat still, eyes cast down, her body slumped; a sad sight indeed. Until two days ago, Harriet Collins had thought of herself as a house owner. Apparently she had been deluding herself. Ownership had been meaningless.

'No one will be harassed,' Mr Martin assured them as he saw them to the door. 'Indeed the company involved are being quite generous. They are offering compensation to all owners although the amounts will be relatively small.'

Harriet had a determined air about her in the days
that followed and everyone was careful not to ask
what her plans were come the day when she would
have to leave Silverdore.

'She'll tell us when she's ready,' Aunt Daisy told
Lizzie, but Lizzie still regarded her Gran with cau-
tion.

Then one day Lizzie called in unexpectedly and
found her Gran crying. It almost broke her heart.
'You must come and live with us, Gran. We'll take
care of you,' she said.

Gran nodded and held her arms out wide. Hugging Lizzie close, she pressed her lips to the top of
her granddaughter's head. 'Oh, I'm just a silly old
woman clinging to the past. I'm fine now that you
have come to see me.'

They had tea together and Harriet sat watching
Lizzie as she ate, with the light from the fire dancing
on her long, silky hair and her young, unlined face.

'I'll never see her grown into a woman,' Harriet
sadly told herself.

Sunday was a lovely spring day, really warm and
with just enough breeze to stir the leaves on the
trees. The sky was cloudless and the birds were singing as Lizzie set off to bring Gran back to spend the
day. Turning the Broadway, she broke into a trot.
Gran always had a treat ready for her every Sunday
morning: a brandy snap, a fairy cake hot from the
oven, or even treacle toffee.

'Your Gran's sleeping late, not like 'er,' old Mr

Thompson told Lizzie, his gnarled fingers clutching his walking stick as he leant heavily against his front gate.

'No. She'll be out the back,' Lizzie reassured him.

'I'm here, Gran,' she called as she opened the front door.

There was no answer. Lizzie didn't move for a long time, but stood looking at the cold ashes in the grate. No matter what time of the year, Gran always had a fire. A lump rose in her throat and tears stung the back of her eyes and she couldn't move.

She wanted the comfort and happiness of seeing her Gran. She wanted to be hugged and kissed. Intuition told her to be afraid. Her Gran had said no developer would get her out of this house alive. Lizzie's glance took in the orderly state of the room. The furniture shone, antimacassars on the chair backs were set dead straight and the brass firearms and fender gleamed. The room was perfect except for the dead ashes in the grate, and the total silence.

Slowly, Lizzie climbed the stairs.

Her grandmother lay still in her bed. She must be dead, Lizzie thought, trying to stay calm as she watched the sunlight playing on her grey hair. Around her Gran's lips, a slight sweet smile lingered such as there had never been in life. Such sadness swelled up inside Lizzie that she didn't know what to do, so she just stood there for an endless time beside the bed, her eyes never leaving the face of this grandmother she had loved so much. Then the tears came and she raged, 'You can't be dead, Gran. It's Sunday. I've come to take you to our house. I can't bear this. What will I do without you, Gran? Please, don't be dead.'

Lizzie only vaguely remembered walking home. First her mother, then Aunt Daisy held her and stroked her hair and wept with her.

The funeral was on Friday and Lizzie was surprised at the number of people who crowded into their front room. She was pleased, though, at the numerous funeral tributes which lay on the pavement outside their house. Going to the lavatory was the only excuse she could think of to escape when the black hearse, drawn by sleek grey horses, turned into the road.

She couldn't stay and watch the flowers being placed around the coffin which held her Gran's body. Relief was all that Lizzie felt when finally it was all over. Aunt Daisy was grey-looking and tired, and Nellie had cried so much she was unable to speak.

Lizzie did her best to console them and later it was she who coaxed her mother and her aunt to eat. When night came, Lizzie went wearily to bed, wondering if the terrible aching and longing for her Gran would ever ease. Saying her prayers, she still said, 'And please, God, bless Gran.'

Weeks had gone by when the letter from the solicitors arrived. No one, except Lizzie herself, was surprised to learn that Harriet Collins had left her house and all her worldly goods to her granddaughter, Elizabeth Louise Collins.

The special pieces of Gran's furniture John Hurley offered to store in his large shed. Wrapping the legs of chairs, tables and bureaux with sacking, he carefully stacked and covered it all. The rest was sold.

Once all the legal transactions of Lizzie's legacy were settled, there had been two hundred and forty-one pounds left to her, plus the settlement the developers had promised to pay when demolition of Silverdore took place. Her mother and her aunt persuaded Lizzie to put the whole amount into a Royal Arsenal Savings Account and forget about it until she was older.

By September, several things had happened in Tooting, all tied up together, changing the Broadway for ever.

A new market opened and Silverdore Terrace was destroyed completely. Once the clearance scheme started, it made great progress. The developers' intention was to build a cinema on the site. The surrounding ground would be a car park.

Lizzie went back only once more to see her little bit of countryside set back from the busy Mitcham Road. It'll be gone soon, she thought, and she felt angry at God for letting it happen and even more angry that He had seen fit to take her Gran. It was just a peaceful row of five white cottages, each with its own extremely long front garden full of flowers, but there simply wasn't anywhere else like this peaceful haven. Not in Tooting there wasn't.

Chapter Six

IT WAS BITTERLY cold out of doors and not much better within. The wind roared and found every nook and cranny. Windows rattled and curtains moved and the draught beneath the doors was enough to cut your feet off. Ice formed on the inside of the bedroom windows and still the snow didn't fall.

'Would be a damn sight warmer if it did snow,' Aunt Daisy said as if she were a weather expert.

The year of 1938 was only two weeks old and it had brought nothing but misery. Lizzie and Polly couldn't ride their bikes to school, not in this weather. The tram fare was a penny return but wherever they got off the tram, they still had a long walk. Southfields was such an awkward place to get to.

Polly stood with her hands spread to the kitchen range which, despite all Nellie's efforts this morning, was refusing to burn properly. A sudden gust of wind brought smoke swirling out into the kitchen. Usually, Lizzie was ready and waiting when Polly called for her, now she came into the room, flinging her woollen scarf twice around her neck.

'Oh, it's perishing upstairs,' she said, blowing on her fingers, putting on her gloves. ''Bye Mum, 'bye Aunt Daisy,' she called as the two of them went up

the passage. It was a quarter to eight and it was still
dark as they let themselves out into the street. It
would be dark again by the time they reached home
tonight.

Daisy wondered just how long her loving niece
with the soft blue eyes and long fair hair would be
able to stand the pace. She worked so hard, persever-
ing at her homework every night, determined to be
at least within the top ten girls in her class. As she
had remarked to Nellie over the Christmas holidays,
their Lizzie was far too thin. Her arms were so frail
and her legs were like sticks, and just lately she had
developed a dry cough.

Lizzie wasn't looking forward to going back to
school. She had earned the respect of her teachers
with her academic achievements and admiration
from her classmates for the way in which she
excelled on the sports field. Only Miss Dawlish
remained a thorn in her flesh.

At first her mother had been reluctant to attend
the school nativity play, in which Lizzie had been
cast as an angel. On numerous previous such
occasions, Nellie had been only too aware of the
headmistress's condescending attitude and had been
hurt by it. The audience had loved the show, jumping to their feet and applauding loudly as the whole
cast took the last curtain call. It should have been
such an enjoyable evening and Lizzie knew how
proud her mother was feeling. She had, however,
watched with dismay as Miss Dawlish approached
her mother, manoeuvring her into a corner of the

hall with great skill – expert that she was! Lizzie was fuming, knowing there was nothing she could do. By now, she was used to her headmistress's ruthlessness – but her mother was not.

Kind and compassionate herself, Nellie was nonplussed, not understanding this educated woman's self-assurance and worldly attitude.

'The old bitch,' Lizzie muttered aloud, 'she certainly picks her time.' But it was typical of the woman – the bigger the occasion, the more important Miss Dawlish felt. Lizzie was trembling as her headmistress turned away and her mother came towards her.

There was an uneasy look on Nellie's face, but she forced herself to smile and took hold of Lizzie's hand. No reference was made as to what had taken place, yet Lizzie could see that her mum was confused and had been thoroughly embarrassed by whatever Miss Dawlish had chosen to say. Unforgivable. That was Lizzie's reaction.

One day, she vowed. That woman will get her come-uppance – arrogant old cow!

All went smoothly that first day back at school. Lizzie hadn't been singled out at assembly by one of Miss Dawlish's barbs although she had fully expected to be. And her form mistress showed great kindness and concern about her.

At break time, Polly and Lizzie had decided to stay in the classroom. Lizzie shivered as she held her handkerchief over her mouth, trying to quell a fit of coughing. Miss Lemkuler looked into her pupil's face and felt pity and admiration. It was a shame that this girl came from such a poor home, but in spite of this she worked hard and was determined to make something of her life. To some extent she understood Miss Dawlish's attitude; so many girls from working-class families had been forced to leave the school without completing their education. Places in good schools should only be allocated to pupils whose parents could afford to keep them there until they were at least sixteen years old. Education, according to Miss Dawlish, was wasted on the poor of this world, and it was not in her nature to make an exception.

'You shouldn't have come to school this morning, Lizzie, if you are unwell,' said Miss Lemkuler, as she placed her hand on Lizzie's forehead.

'I'm all right,' said Lizzie abruptly. Then, involuntarily, she let out a cry as a pain shot through her side.

Miss Lemkuler calmed Lizzie down and sent Polly to the cloakroom to fetch her outdoor clothes. 'You are to go home and go straight to bed,' she said.

It was more than an hour later that Lizzie, dragging her feet, came down the front garden path. Aunt Daisy met her at the door, asking no questions. She flung her arms around Lizzie and led her into the kitchen. Within minutes, Lizzie had her face bent over a steaming bowl of boiling water to which Daisy had added Friar's Balsam, with a Turkish towel covering her head, and soon Lizzie was sweating profusely.

By the time Nellie arrived home from work, Lizzie was seated in a chair in front of a roaring fire. She was pale and silent, all her pains eased for the moment. A wad of thermogene wool had been placed on her chest by Aunt Daisy, kept in place by two strips of red flannel.

Two bricks, heated in the oven, and a stone hot-water bottle were carried upstairs and placed in Lizzie's bed. Nellie made her a cup of Oxo and told her to stay by the fire and give the bed a chance to get warm.

Three days later, and still Lizzie did not feel well.

'I think you should take her to see the doctor,' Daisy said as she and Nellie stood gazing at the sleeping Lizzie.

Nellie tucked the bedclothes tightly about Lizzie and sat beside her. 'If only she'd eat,' she whispered.

'Come on now, let's go to bed and make up your mind to get her to that doctor tomorrow. She'll be fine, you'll see,' but Daisy spoke without conviction.

The waiting-room was depressing. The lower half of the windows were crudely painted with dark green paint, keeping out almost all available daylight. A single gas bracket set on the wall to the left of the black iron fireplace struggled to burn brightly but only succeeded in casting gloomy shadows.

The buzzer sounded for the third time. 'Come on, dear, it's our turn,' said Nellie. Two old men moved their feet and one woman sneezed and shook her head as they walked by.

'Do we have to go in?' whispered Lizzie furtively. She was scared of doctors.

The surgery was more brightly lit and infinitely warmer. Doctor Pike did not bother to stand up, just raised his head from the book in which he was writing, and silently motioned Nellie to sit in the only available chair. It took only minutes for him to examine Lizzie. Blushing, feeling awkward, she stood before him in her vest, knickers and black woolly stockings.

'Deep breath . . . breathe out . . . say ninety-nine. All right, get dressed.' Turning to Nellie, he almost recited, 'Not enough sleep. Not the right diet. You might try her on cod-liver oil and malt; she needs building up.'

Washing his hands at the small sink in the corner of the room, Doctor Pike half turned and added, almost as an after-thought, 'Perhaps you should take her to St James's. I'll write a letter; it won't take me a minute.' Licking the flap, he sealed the envelope and passed it over to Nellie, saying, 'Outpatients, tomorrow morning, eleven o'clock.'

The consultation and advice cost two shillings.

Coal and food were expensive and money was short, so it fell to Daisy to take Lizzie to the hospital, whilst

Nellie was away doing her morning stint at the Dawsons.

That awful smell of carbolic! The long draughty corridors, loud footsteps ringing out on the stone-tiled floors, people in white coats hurrying in all directions. Shunted from one cubicle to another, Lizzie was weary. She had coughed so much, her chest was sore and her very bones ached. Lying now on a high metal couch, covered by a red blanket, she just wanted to sleep. Aunt Daisy pulled aside the curtain that divided one cubicle from the next, bent over and smiled lovingly at her niece. Lizzie stared at her with penetrating blue eyes, 'What's happening? Are we going home now?'

Daisy hesitated, her own eyes glistening with tears. 'They want to keep you in, Lizzie.'

'What?'

'Sh!' said Daisy. 'You mustn't get excited.'

Lizzie was shaking visibly and her big eyes looked at her aunt full of pleading, wanting to be taken home.

A sister-in-charge came. 'Now then,' she said, 'we'll put you into a chair and get you up to the ward.' Her voice was soft, but unwavering.

The kitchen was crowded. People seldom popped in and out of Nellie Collins's house. She didn't encourage them. Now Jackie Jordon and his wife Doreen stood by the fireplace, Mrs Beasley from number nineteen with her youngest baby cradled in her arms, Alfie Brown, the street bookmaker and his runner, Tommo, all were there. All had come to commiserate because young Lizzie had tuberculosis.

'Christ, that's infectious, that is,' wailed Nora Beasley, ''as it affected both her lungs?'

Neighbours and friends were all very well, but Nellie wished they'd go home. She appreciated their kindness but – but what? She hadn't really taken in what Daisy had so patiently explained.

All she knew, her Lizzie had been kept in hospital. Dare-devil, tomboy Lizzie had consumption. She'd seen it coming and shut her eyes to it.

'It's all my fault,' she reproached herself. 'I could see her getting thinner every day, and what did I do about it? Nothing! Oh, it's not fair, it's awful.' She backed away as Doreen Jordon tried to console her, took refuge in the scullery and gave way to a flood of tears.

Lizzie remained in St James's for six weeks. Her mother visited daily, and Aunt Daisy came with Kate Hurley when visiting times were allowed. John Hurley came up some evenings bringing Polly and young Syd with him, but they were only allowed to see Lizzie and wave to her through the window. No children were allowed in wards where patients had infectious diseases. Even adults had to don white masks which covered the lower half of their faces.

One day, two doctors endeavoured to explain to Lizzie why she couldn't go home. Instead, she was being transferred to a sanatorium.

Pinewood Sanatorium was at Wokingham in

Surrey, but as far as Lizzie was concerned it might just as well have been hundreds of miles from London. She had never seen anywhere remotely like it. She was settled into a room with just four beds, white walls and ceiling and white-and-black tiled floor. The curtains and bedspread and draw-around screens, all matching, were made from a flowery material so pretty as to delight the patients, and seeming to bring the garden into the room.

It was not a bit like the many-bedded ward she had just left. Through the wide-open windows, Lizzie could see a view that was unbelievable. As far as the eye could see there were trees; tall, stately, dark green pine trees. She had hidden her head beneath the bedclothes last night and cried herself to sleep. She didn't want to go to no rotten sanatorium, miles away from London, with no visitors – not even her mum.

A fresh-faced, smiling young lady gently placed a tray on the table which straddled Lizzie's legs and propped her up against a great mound of pillows. The smell of the cooked lunch was good and suddenly Lizzie realized she felt hungry.

It wasn't going to be so bad here after all, she told herself as she picked up her knife and fork.

Chapter Seven

AFTER WHAT, TO Lizzie, seemed endless examinations and tests, she was back in her bed. 'I feel sick,' she moaned. A nurse ran forward, grabbing a dish from the shelf; she held Lizzie's head whilst she vomited into the bowl. Then she wiped her mouth and laid her back on to the pillows.

Lizzie began to cry. She felt frightened and lonely. Had she been abandoned by her family, sent to this place out of the way? It wasn't fair. It wasn't her fault she'd got tuberculosis. Why, if she had to be ill, did it have to be something that was catching. In despair, she began to thrash about. The nurse came back over to her; gently she sat on the bed and drew Lizzie's head to her breast.

'There, there now, darling,' she said. 'Susan's here. I'll stay with you.' She rocked Lizzie to and fro and stayed with her until she sank into a natural sleep.

The next morning, after breakfast, the nurse Lizzie now knew as Susan draped Lizzie's dressing-gown around her shoulders. 'You look beautiful,' she told her, adding, 'and that's good, because Doctor Bennett is coming to see you.'

Lizzie looked startled. 'I haven't got to have more things done to me today, have I?' she asked.

Before Nurse Susan had time to reply, a jovial-looking young man approached the bed. He towered above Lizzie, smiling broadly, his hands in the pockets of his white coat, a blue striped shirt open at the neck.

Lizzie snuggled deep into her pillows, fear showing in her eyes. 'What are you going to do with me now?' she demanded to know.

'Tell you my name first,' he said, drawing a chair up close and taking hold of Lizzie's hand. 'You had a rotten day yesterday, didn't you?' Lizzie made no reply.

'Well, never mind. My name is Stephen Bennett. I know yours is Lizzie Collins and I am going to be looking after you.' Still Lizzie made no comment. She wasn't in a chatty mood this morning.

After a moment of tension, he nudged her with his elbow, leant forward and winked. 'Tell you a secret. I've only been here three days longer than you have. I don't know anyone and Nurse Susan doesn't cuddle me to sleep like she did with you.' Susan blushed scarlet and Lizzie stared at him in astonishment, dumbfounded as to how he knew about that.

'Come on, Lizzie,' he said casually, 'be my friend.'

'Well,' Lizzie appeared to be considering it, 'not till you tell me what else you're going to do ter me.'

The doctor stared at her and she stared back. Then he grinned. 'It's a deal,' he said, holding out his hand which Lizzie solemnly shook. 'Usually, when people are ill with tuberculosis, we have to give one of their lungs a rest. So, we do an operation which cuts the cord holding the lung up and it collapses. To keep the lung rested and to enable the patient to breathe, we pump air into it. Artificially we do the work the poor old lung would be doing if it wasn't so poorly.'

Lizzie's eyes had never left his face while he had been relating these details. Now she moved away warily. 'Well, you ain't gonna do that ter me,' she said.

'Let me finish, Lizzie,' he pleaded. 'All that business we put you through yesterday told us you don't need an operation.'

'Thank God for that,' Lizzie exclaimed defiantly. 'So can I go home now?'

Across her head, the nurse looked at the young doctor and they smiled at each other and he said, 'We've got ourselves a real bright spark here.' To Lizzie he begged, 'Be patient, there's a good girl.' Then, with a gentle expression on his face, he told her, 'You have fluid on your right lung and you need to stay with us for quite a while. Still, we shall get you into a healthy routine and you'll find out that those of us who work here are not such a bad lot. You might even come to like us.'

His lips were smiling as he finished and his eyes had a mischievous glint in them.

After several days had passed, Lizzie was well aware of the routine, though she was astounded to learn that she would still have to spend at least six more weeks lying in bed. At eleven o'clock each morning either Susan or Linda (Linda being the other nurse assigned to Lizzie's room) would stand over her as she swallowed a raw egg. Even beaten up in a glass with milk added, Lizzie found it revolting.

To follow was a section of a fresh orange on to which halibut liver oil had been dripped. Lunch was at one o'clock. By two o'clock, complete silence. 'Break it if you dare,' the red-headed freckled-faced Linda had warned Lizzie, though a smile had lingered about her lips as she spoke. Not a soul moved anywhere until four o'clock.

At bedtime, one of the nurses would command, 'Open wide', and two spoonfuls of Gee's Linctus would be poured into her mouth. Never did she have to settle down to sleep without a good-night kiss.

The two nurses liked her and Lizzie liked them. They giggled with her and made fun of Sister Cartwright, who bustled in and out of the ward, her eyes taking in everything, but who really was a nice old softie. They told her humorous stories about the doctors and they showed her affection. It didn't stop Lizzie missing her mum and Aunt Daisy or Polly, and as for her brother Syd, who was more often than not a little devil, she missed him like hell; but when Susan and Linda were around, she didn't feel quite so lonely.

Visitors were allowed once a fortnight on Sundays. When Nellie Collins had received the visitor's pass she had sighed deeply and sought advice from Daisy.

'I could just about scrape the coach fare together but that would mean going empty 'anded,' she dolefully told her sister-in-law.

' 'Lotter good that would do our Lizzie,' said Daisy, ever the practical one. 'No. Get together the things we know she likes, some embroidery or knitting to keep her occupied and fer Christ's sake don't forget her books. Toc H will let yer 'ave as many books as yer want.'

'Then what will we do with them? Cost a fortune to post a parcel like that,' Nellie's voice almost broke. She was very upset.

'We'll take 'em up to the Elephant and Castle on the tram. Stop worrying. It'll be all right. You'll see.'

Come Sunday morning they were up and ready early. Syd was sent to spend the day with Connie and Bill.

'Wind's still cold,' Daisy warned, 'we'd both better put a scarf on.' Then they were off to catch the tram from the Broadway, each carrying a heavy parcel.

An inspector at the bus station pointed out the coach. 'Runs right into Pinewood grounds it does, missus,' he told them. 'Fare's four and six each.'

Nellie couldn't bring herself to make the request, but Daisy was not to be put off. 'That's what we come 'ere for,' she muttered to herself as she approached a group of drivers. 'Excuse me,' she called, 'which one of you drives the coach going to Wokingham?'

'I does, as it 'appens,' said one of them, separating himself from his mates. 'What can I do fer yer, luv?'

Daisy hesitated. He was a big, red-faced man, smartly dressed in his uniform overcoat, a white silk scarf knotted at his throat.

'You wouldn't oblige me, would yer?' she got out at last. 'Take a parcel for me niece? She's down there in the Sanatorium.'

'Don't yer want ter make the trip, lady?' He could have bitten off his tongue as soon as the question left his lips. Nellie had come to stand alongside Daisy.

Two more forlorn-looking long faces, Ted Baker told himself, he hadn't seen in many a long day. Yer silly sod, he chastized himself, they ain't got the money for the fare. God, he wished it was up to him. He'd have them on that coach all right, and bugger whether or not they could pay. 'I'll take it fer yer with pleasure,' he said.

'There's two parcels,' Nellie spoke quietly.

'All the better, luv. What's the young lady's name?'

'Lizzie Collins,' they answered in unison.

'Well, if yer Lizzie comes ter meet me coach, I'll tell 'er you both send yer luv, shall I?'

'She's confined to bed,' Nellie said with a sob in her voice.

'Well, never mind. This is me regular run. Nurses are used ter me 'anging around fer two hours every other Sunday, give me a cup of tea, regular as clockwork they do. They'll see your Lizzie gets her parcels all right.'

'Mister, you're a good sport,' Daisy said.

'No trouble at all, darlings, and if yer want ter make it a regular thing, yer know every other Sunday I'd be more than happy ter oblige.'

'Please, have this for your trouble,' Nellie said, holding out a sixpence.

Ted Baker told his mates afterwards that a lump the size of a billiard ball filled his throat then. His big hand gently closed round Nellie's, curling her fingers inward over the coin. Kindly he whispered, 'Put it away, missus. I might need someone ter do me a good turn some day.'

They lingered long enough to watch the coach pull out from the bus station, a sad-looking pair. Daisy, a healthy buxom woman at least four inches taller than her sister-in-law, looked neat and tidy in a well-fitting brown costume with a lace-collared cream blouse. She worried about Nellie and wished that she had been able to afford to pay her coach fare.

'I miss Lizzie so much,' Nellie said, as she groped in her bag for a handkerchief for she was blinded by tears.

'I know yer do, luv, but she's in the best place. We'll have her home soon, you'll see.' And as she uttered the words, Daisy silently prayed that they were the truth.

Lizzie was thrilled. Fruit, boiled sweets, a new face flannel and lovely scented soap were in one parcel, and in the other were wool, knitting needles and a nice slip-over pattern, which had been cut out from *Woman's Own*, and there were lots of books as well!

'Look at all the letters you got,' cried Nurse Susan, as she tidied Lizzie's bed. 'Well, I'm off for my tea now, I won't be long. Don't go getting too excited.'

When she had gone, Lizzie began reading. One letter was from Mr and Mrs Hurley, who now signed themselves, Aunt Kate and Uncle John. That was nice. One was signed by several of the neighbours, and enclosed were four stamps. One was from Connie and Bill with a postal order for two shillings.

Tears trickled down her cheeks as she read the next one. 'Be good now, whippet. Eat all your food and take your medicine because I want to see you fat with rosy cheeks when I come home.' Oh Leslie, so far away in Malta.

She was slightly put out as she read one her mother had received from Miss Dawlish. 'We do wish Lizzie well, her classmates miss her, as does the entire staff. Such a bright pupil of whom I have great hopes.' Had she misjudged her headmistress all these years? Lizzie doubted it!

The longest letter was from Polly. 'Soppy old thing you, Lizzie, getting ill like that,' was how she started it. 'You'll never guess; I've got a boyfriend.

Fred Holt is his name.' Lizzie brightened up a bit as she scanned the pages. A good laugh was Polly, and a good friend. She read on, 'The Granada is open, you'll have to come when you get home. Expensive, though. Costs ninepence downstairs. Fred took me upstairs. You have to walk through a hall of mirrors. Costs one and threepence. Reginald Dixon was playing the organ in the interval. You know, we've heard him on the wireless. He plays in Blackpool Tower. Oh yeah, and everyone going into the pictures that week got a free stick of Blackpool rock. Want a lick? – HA, HA! Seemed funny though, Lizzie, going to the cinema built on the place where your Gran's house used to be.' Not funny, thought Lizzie, as she folded up the letter, real sad.

Lizzie had had a bad week. It started on Monday. Nurse Susan and Sister Cartwright had pulled the curtains around her bed, sat her up and removed her nightdress.

'Knees up my lovely,' said Sister Cartwright, 'lean forward, head down.' Her voice was kindly, but the determination was there.

Two older doctors talked *about* her, but not *to* her and Lizzie didn't like that. Doctor Bennett appeared, smiling broadly, his fair hair tousled, in need of combing; he winked at Lizzie as she raised her head. Tap, tap, the doctor's fingers beat along her ribs.

'Ah, there it is. Just a little prick, Lizzie,' he said casually. It wasn't. It hurt like hell and Lizzie cried out. Both Nurse and Sister held her hands.

'Be brave,' Susan whispered, 'it won't be long.'

It seemed to take hours and Lizzie got hot and flustered. One tall doctor loomed over her. 'All over, child,' he said. 'Look, we struck gold.' He held aloft a large syringe, the tube of which was filled with a murky yellow fluid. He patted her head and moved away with his colleague.

'Please, Nurse, may I have a drink?' Lizzie pleaded.

'Of course you may, pet,' said the motherly Sister Cartwright, pulling Lizzie's head towards her ample bosom. 'You've been a good, brave girl. You will get better now that the doctors have got that nasty fluid off your lung.'

Sister was right. Two weeks later and Lizzie was up and about. She was weak as a kitten at first, and the nurses laughed at her first attempt to stand. Her legs buckled beneath her. Dressed in a navy-blue skirt and neat white blouse, with shoes on her feet for the first time in weeks, Lizzie was ready to leave the main building. She was going to the camp.

Long rows of wooden huts, partitioned off to give each patient a single room, set in the heart of sweet-smelling green pine trees. All through the woods tracks had been cut and laid over with cinders. Each room had a large window in the outside wall, but no pane of glass. Whatever the weather, there were no shutters. If it rained too heavily, beds were covered by a tarpaulin.

Exercise, rest, and good food was now the order

of the day. Walking the cinder tracks between the tall pine trees was a morning routine. Each week the distance was extended. The afternoon two-hour bed rest was still obligatory. Twice a week, patients listened through headphones to a recorded message. 'Your illness probably started with a common cold,' the voice droned on, 'built up to bronchitis, developed into pleurisy, thus causing tuberculosis. The remedy is to eat fat. FAT builds up bodily resistance. It is good for you; you must eat it.' Lizzie vowed that she would.

The rooms on either side of Lizzie were occupied by young girls, for which Lizzie was grateful. In the main building, her room had held, besides herself, three older, very sick ladies. Nice enough, but not very companionable. Twenty-five-year-old Mary Gibson had a fresh, healthy face and didn't look at all ill. 'Blimey, she's young,' had been her first words when introduced to Lizzie. A proper cockney lass, was Mary. Do I speak like she does? Lizzie wondered after a day or two, and promised herself she'd try to do better.

Anne Caxton was almost twenty. Just the opposite from Mary, slightly frosty at first. Her eyes were deep brown and framed by long, stiff black lashes. Her expression was discouraging, as she eyed Lizzie up and down. Happily, she thawed as the days passed and Lizzie was pleased to have two friends.

Lizzie, arriving at the gate to pick up her weekly parcel from the coach driver, stopped to listen to what the older patients were saying.

'There is going to be a war,' said a tall, educated-sounding lady.

'Yes, you can bet on it now,' said another.

'We shall all be sent home,' a third patient told the group, as if she were privileged to prior information. Lizzie liked the sound of that. The thought of the country going to war didn't particulary worry her.

The coach turned in at the gates and came to a halt with a squeak of brakes. Ted Baker and Lizzie had become friends and, as the door of the coach opened, he grinned down at her and gave her the thumbs-up sign, nodding his head backwards. She looked in the direction he indicated and was flabbergasted. Her brother Syd was kneeling up on a seat, his nose pressed flat against the window. His eyes were wide and he was grinning like a Cheshire cat. In the gangway, crushed with passengers, was her mum. Further down was Aunt Daisy. Lizzie was overjoyed. She jigged up and down on the spot. She couldn't believe it, she had visitors.

Nothing could spoil that day. They had a picnic in the woods, Lizzie showed them her room and took them to the main building to meet Nurse Susan and Nurse Linda. The time went all too quickly. Suddenly the bell went, summoning them back to the coach.

'Don't forget to say thank you to Ted Baker, will you Lizzie,' her mother said. 'Heart of gold that man's got, his mates too. It was them that helped us out with the fare.'

Ted Baker brushed aside Lizzie's thanks. 'See you in two weeks,' he called, as the coach door closed. Lizzie ran alongside waving until her arm ached.

'Crikey,' Mary said, 'you've got real nice folk, ain't yer?'

'Yes I have,' Lizzie agreed.

The patients didn't get sent home and England didn't go to war. Prime Minister Neville Chamberlain went to Germany to talk to Adolf Hitler. He was sincere in his efforts, and came back waving a piece of paper, saying, 'Peace in our time'.

At first Lizzie was disappointed not to be going home, but not for long. November came and Lizzie was much better. Now she could go home!

The ambulance came to a halt in Graveney Road, and when the doors had been opened it seemed to Lizzie that the whole street had turned out to welcome her home. Tears choked her. What a homecoming, what a surprise! The strong, tanned arms that lifted her down belonged to her eldest brother Leslie. His service of seven years in the Army was over. He had been given his discharge. Lizzie was happy, so happy! What a wonderful Christmas this will be, she told herself.

And it was.

Chapter Eight

ANOTHER NEW YEAR. 1939.

The papers were full of dire predictions and most people hoped they were exaggerating. Many others knew war was only a matter of time.

Leslie Collins was amongst those who were not lulled into a false sense of security by the words of Neville Chamberlain. Council offices were offering Anderson Air Raid Shelters free of charge and Leslie collected one. The erecting of this caused so much interest amongst the neighbours that the local paper sent a reporter to investigate. Come Friday, Leslie's picture was in the local paper. With Syd beside him, their shirt-sleeves rolled high above their elbows, they stood beside this ugly, weird monstrosity which now stood deep in the backyard. Both brothers had blond, almost white hair, masses of tight curls which hugged their heads and which they both hated. Their teeth were also alike. The top rows were white and even, the lower ones showing gaps.

'Lucky that is;' said Nellie, 'if you can put a six-pence between your teeth' (and both of her sons could) 'you were born lucky,' she insisted. They differed only in height. Syd, at fifteen years old, was already almost as tall as Leslie.

'Like his father,' Daisy remarked, 'gonna top six foot, you see if I'm not right.'

'Hope so,' said Syd. He badly wanted to get into the Army. If war did come and he was really tall, he could put his age up and get away with it, he told his mother. Nellie shuddered at the thought.

Lizzie didn't go back to school; she got a job.

Spring came and the trees on the Common were loaded with blossoms. On Whit Monday Leslie took them all to Hampstead Heath. Folk loved the Heath on a bank holiday because of the fair. Lizzie was breathless as she enthusiastically threw her last wooden ball at the elevated coconuts.

'Hopeless you are,' Syd told her, pushing her aside. Syd threw each ball with grim determination. He struck with his third attempt and Lizzie shrieked with delight as the coconut fell to the ground. Syd ran to retrieve his prize.

The stallholder put in a replacement. 'You're good you are, sonny,' he said, as he patted Syd's head.

'Yeah, bowl for England he might one day,' yelled an admiring onlooker.

Leslie and Bill treated them to rides and Lizzie found the swing-boats exciting. 'Pull harder,' Syd ordered, as the swing began to soar. Boys were hooting with laughter as they watched from the ground. Girls' dresses were billowing high, giving glimpses of petticoats and legs in silk stockings.

Mum and Aunt Daisy found them and said it was

time to eat. Families were flocking to the grass areas for picnics. Hard-boiled eggs, ripe tomatoes, cheese sandwiches, Swiss jam roll and fruit cake – everyone tucked in; Daisy poured tea from two vacuum flasks and there was lemonade for those who wanted it.

As they left the Heath, music still blared out from the merry-go-rounds. Shrieks and squeals still mingled with loud shouts of laughter. London families were still enjoying their bank holiday.

No gloom and doom talk of war. It had been a smashing day.

The sun had shone for weeks on end as if to defy the bad news. 'We definitely will have a war,' said John Hurley as he passed the official letter back to Leslie.

It was the beginning of August, only eight months since Leslie had been demobbed. He was to report to Aldershot. He was on the first-reserve register.

Seven days later, and again the local paper carried a photograph of Sergeant Collins who was receiving new recruits, known as militiamen, into Aldershot Barracks. Two weeks after that he was home again, this time on a forty-eight-hour pass.

'Remember, sleep in that shelter,' he repeatedly told Nellie, 'don't take chances.'

'Oh, they won't bomb London,' cried Aunt Daisy, wanting to evade the subject altogether.

When Leslie went back to barracks the goodbyes and hugs were emotional. Daisy had lost a fiancé in the last war and memories flooded back. Nellie's heart was full of fear as she held her first born. Syd made a joke, 'Have a uniform ready for me,' but Connie wiped away a tear and Lizzie locked herself in the bathroom. She didn't want Leslie to go away again and couldn't help herself. She had to cry.

Sunday morning, 3rd of September.

Folk were out on their doorsteps and all front doors were flung wide open. Those fortunate enough to own a wireless set had the volume turned full up, blaring out for all to hear. Big Ben chimed, then struck eleven o'clock. There was a silent air of expectancy throughout the whole street.

'It is with regret that I have to inform you a state of war now exists between ourselves and Germany.' Neville Chamberlain's voice came over the air with a feeling of finality.

The silence remained in the air for a full minute. Maurice Smith from the other side of the road broke it. 'What the 'ell did we go through the last bleeding lot for?' he stormed aloud. Everyone glanced at the pinned-up left sleeve of his jacket. It was twenty-two years ago that he had lost his arm in the First World War. His next-door neighbour let out a stran-gled yell of rage and then everyone began talking at once.

'Oh, the poor kids,' wailed Doreen Jordon, 'they'll all have to be evacuated.'

'I'll join up, soon as I can,' vowed Syd.

'Oh Christ, my Bill will 'ave to go,' Connie said, brushing away tears.

'What the 'ell is that?' The question came from several mouths as the air was rent by the wailing of the sirens.

'Bloody eerie, ain't it?' said one old woman.

Nellie gathered her family together and took them back inside the house. 'Let's hope it's only practice,' she said as she filled the kettle and got down the flask in readiness for the air-raid shelter.

But it was a false alarm, and soon the moaning, long drawn-out, all-clear sounded.

'We're all right now,' Daisy said calmly.

Nellie offered up a silent prayer and made the tea.

Children up and down the street were saying their goodbyes. Labels hung round their necks stating their names and addresses. Carrier bags held their sandwiches and gas masks in cardboard boxes hung over their shoulders. Women threw their aprons over their heads so that their tears wouldn't be noticed as teachers marshalled groups down the road. The street seemed different after that. Abandoned, clean and tidy, and far too quiet.

To top the lot, council workmen came with lorries to take down the iron railings which had adorned low garden walls, and dismantle the chains which had hung for years between posts. Wrought-iron ornamental gates were wrenched from their hinges and all were carted away.

'What the 'ell is going on?' residents wanted to know.

'It's to help the war effort,' was the only explanation the elderly council men could give.

Weeks turned into months and all the young men were getting called up. Connie's Bill went into the Navy and Leslie was back with his regiment in Malta. The new year came and wartime in London became a reality. Food was rationed, coal was short, fresh meat and fish were hard to get and corned beef was a handy substitute. Every single thing was rationed. The Ministry of Food dealt with the issuing of ration books. Fawn coloured books for adults, green coloured for children under five years of age.

Rationing made life hard for wives and mothers and rows brewed up in shops.

'Whatcha mean, I've had me tea ration?' they would shout.

'I dunno what the world's a coming to,' grumbled another. 'Not a bit of sugar in the 'ouse an' she says I can't 'ave any for another four weeks. A bloody month, mind you!'

Life was tedious. Stockings were hard to come by. Sally Silverman's stall in the market looked dull, dusty and empty.

'Only got lisle ones ter offer you gals,' Sally miserably told them.

'Not even fully fashioned, are they?' Polly asked.

'No, love, fully fashioned they ain't. Turn them inside out, cut the edges from round the heel why don't cher? That way they don't look so bad.'

'They don't look so good either,' grumbled Polly.

Silk stockings from Sally had cost one shilling a pair since God knows when, and they'd been fully fashioned. Now she wanted one and ninepence for lisle ones. They hated this boring old war; they hated the blackout and were already sick to death with shortages.

The last few days of May 1940 were like a nightmare. Rumours were unbelievable. France had fallen to Germany. British troops were stranded on the beaches of Dunkirk. German planes bombarded the helpless men. The sea lay in front of them, German troops behind them.

Old men stood in the Selkirk Pub and cried openly in frustration as they listened to the news on the wireless. The obscenities they yelled did little to relieve their anger.

Boats of all shapes and sizes were put to sea. Men who hadn't navigated a vessel for years volunteered. The Navy did their bit, under horrific conditions thousands of men, not only British soldiers, but French and Belgian also, were plucked from those beaches. Trip after trip was made and men still cried. Some were speechless with shock. A mass of dead bodies covered the beaches, with more floating gently in the sea. Yet it had been a miracle, the evacuation of Dunkirk.

Britain now stood alone.

Not long afterwards the bombing of London began. Night after night the sirens wailed the warning. Deep shelters in parks and on commons were filled with families. Hundreds more made for the Underground stations, sleeping on the platforms. Young and old alike endured the hardship, too nervous to be above ground where bombs were falling and the noise of anti-aircraft guns was deafening.

Lizzie got home later each evening. She had landed a good job as a ledger clerk with A. T. Hart, the quality butchers. With the outbreak of war, she, along with all the clerical staff, had had to leave the comfort of her office and come out into the shop, serving customers, wrapping meat, marking ration books and taking money. Because of a shortage of staff she sometimes had to work in different shops. For three weeks now she'd been in the Chapel Street shop. It was near the London docks, an area that was a prime target for the German bombers.

Sure enough, they came over early one evening. It was the roughest raid so far. Incendiary bombs rained down and flames shot high into the air; clouds of dust rose up and the acrid smell was choking. Lizzie walked over London Bridge, coughing and spluttering, her eyes were red and sore. Air-raid wardens and policemen were everywhere.

'Where yer making for?' someone asked her.

'Tooting,' Lizzie managed to mutter.

'Come along, this way,' a hand guided her.

'Buses are few and far between, but you might be lucky. Tube stations are all closed,' volunteered the warden.

'Thank you,' Lizzie blubbered, just wanting to get home.

The next morning, Lizzie awoke with a headache and sore throat. She staggered downstairs into the kitchen and gratefully sipped the tea that her mother had made for her.

'You'd better stay home today,' Nellie insisted.

'All right,' Lizzie croaked.

She pushed aside the plate of toast Aunt Daisy offered, but held out her hand as her aunt said, 'There's a letter for you.'

At that moment Polly pushed open the door and burst into the room, waving a buff-coloured envelope. 'Snap!' said Lizzie, waving her identical one. She tore open the envelope and a long whistle escaped from her lips.

'You too?' Polly asked. Their letters were the same. Call-up interview, Thursday, two p.m., in the Central Hall.

In just two weeks' time, they would both be eighteen.

Smiling slightly, the woman on the other side of the table agreed to interview them together. 'Stay calm,' Lizzie told herself. There was no way she was going to go into the Forces.

'How about munitions?' the posh voice asked.

'Oh no!' Polly looked at Lizzie and they both shuddered at the thought.

'Work in a factory?' was the next suggestion.

'Never!' they both agreed.

'How about the ATS? At a later date, of course,' the genteel lady offered.

'Me dad says it will be all over come Christmas,' said Polly defiantly. 'We ain't gonna go in no army.'

'We shall see,' the woman sighed. 'Meanwhile, these forms have to be completed.'

The interview wasn't going at all well. The lady took off her spectacles and rubbed the bridge of her nose. 'Land Army?'

They both gagged at the thought.

'The trams or the buses?' she put forward in desperation.

The two girls giggled. 'Don't fancy the trams,' said Lizzie, 'buses might be all right.'

'Yeah. Nice uniform they have on the buses,' said Polly.

Relief flooded through the interviewer. She was anxious to be on her way. London in the blackout was no place to be.

'So, I'll state your preference for war work with London Passenger Transport,' she said, writing on the forms, not waiting for an answer.

They contained themselves until they were at the bottom of the stairs, then the pair of them fell about laughing. Boisterously, they punched each other, 'We're gonna be clippies.' The very thought brought forth more laughter which echoed loudly against the tiled walls. Swiftly they ran out into the Mitcham Road. Who'd have believed it? They were going to help the war effort, they were going to work on the buses.

Chapter Nine

THREE WEEKS' TRAINING at Chiswick, on full pay, had gone remarkably well – except for one incident.

Alan Cooke, a retired driver, having served twenty-four years at Shepherd's Bush Garage, was in charge of the class. Twelve girls in all, Lizzie and Polly going to Merton Garage, the others to various depots.

What Alan Cooke didn't know about schedules wasn't worth knowing. Tall, good-looking in a rakish kind of way, he fancied he was God's gift to all women – even at his age. At break-time, Lizzie was unusually quiet.

'What's the matter?' Polly asked, as she set two large mugs of tea down.

'I can't stand that man. He's 'orrible,' said Lizzie.

'Why? What's he done now?'

'He pinched me nipple.'

'You're joking!' Polly couldn't help it, she laughed out loud.

'So you think it's funny, do yer? Well I 'ope he does it to you.'

'I'll bloody kill 'im if he tries,' said Polly, her temper rising.

During the afternoon session, Polly kept her eyes on Mr Cooke. He approached Lizzie, coming up from behind. Leaning forward, he placed his two arms over her shoulders, supposedly to check what she was writing. Quick as a flash, Polly was out of her seat. Between thumb and fingernail, she pinched a lump of his backside, giving it a good, hard nip.

He sprang backwards and let out a cry of pain. His instinct told him it was Lizzie's mate who had attacked him, but he couldn't prove it.

'He won't try his tricks on you again in a hurry,' Polly said with a satisfied smirk on her face as they walked to the bus stop.

'You're a bitch, Polly,' Lizzie laughed as she spoke. 'Did you notice he didn't sit down all the afternoon?'

They ran up the road, giggling as they went.

They left Chiswick the proud owners of a full uniform. A leather shoulder bag with two compartments, and a wooden ticket rack completed their issue. How neat they looked – Lizzie, small-boned, fair complexion, her long hair tucked into a snood; Polly, tall and slim, her dark hair cut to shoulder-length and worn with a fringe. Their only complaint was that the serge trousers were itchy.

Six weeks later, and they had taken to their wartime job like ducks to water. Both girls were on the same shift, but not the same route. Lizzie loved the job, she liked meeting people, but she did get tired.

The grimness of each day seemed to get worse. The air raids were becoming a habit, a fact of life accepted as an inconvenient annoyance but no more than that. Even the stories of bombed factories, direct hits on shelters and folk losing their homes didn't shock people as it had at the beginning of the war.

Lizzie, and many like her, began to think that it was safer to be in the open during a raid, rather than huddled up below ground. It was bad enough coming home by tube late at night. At Tooting Broadway, the whole platform seemed to be a tangled mass of humanity, huddled together, no room to turn, let alone move about. The stench of bodies was awful. Once clear of the arms and legs, Lizzie would run like a wild hare. At midnight, steel floodgates would slam shut and folk sheltering below were then entombed until the next morning. Lizzie couldn't bear the thought.

Finally, she decided she had had enough of their Anderson shelter. If she had to spend one more night sleeping against the damp wall, listening to Aunt Daisy snore, her mother sucking boiled sweets and old Mrs Ticehurst, whom Nellie had taken under her wing, cluck away at her loose false teeth, not to mention the lapping of water under the floorboarding and that horrid musty earthy smell, she'd go mad.

When she got home, she went straight upstairs to bed. Nellie objected, then pleaded. 'You'll be killed,' she wailed.

At least I'll die in comfort, thought Lizzie as she snuggled down in her clean, comfortable bed. She ignored the gunfire, the searchlights, which criss-crossed the sky and lit up her room, even the bombs, and had her first good night's sleep for months.

'About time we saw a bit of life. Never go anywhere now do we?' Polly sounded right fed up.

'Two toast and cheese,' Elsie called from behind the canteen counter. Lizzie rose and went to fetch her snack.

'You were a long time. What were yer talking to Elsie about?' Polly wanted to know.

'A night out for us, actually,' Lizzie said, wrapping up the large piece of cheese and putting it in the pocket of her overcoat. Her mum and Aunt Daisy looked forward to the bits and pieces she smuggled out from the canteen.

'A night out where? The last one didn't turn out so well,' grumbled Polly.

They had been on early shift, so one evening they had gone up to Rainbow Corner at Piccadilly. Talk about the League of Nations! Yanks, Canadians, Australians, Poles. The dancing was all right, they certainly didn't lack partners; it was the close clinches that bothered them.

'Elsie said troops are moving on to Garratt Green.'

'So?'

'Whatcha mean, so?'

'Well, what difference will it make ter us?' Polly grunted through a mouthful of rissole.

'Fairlight Hall is putting on a dance Saturday night, you know, to welcome them.'

'Only be a gramophone. Bet yer life they won't have a band.'

'Oh, for Christ's sake, what's the matter with yer, Polly?' Lizzie asked in desperation.

'Sorry, Lizzie,' Polly said apologetically. 'Don't mind me, I'm just having one of those days.'

On Saturday night, they fished out their high-heeled shoes and long skirts, made up their faces and curled the ends of their hair with hot tongs and went off to this sevenpenny hop at Fairlight Hall.

Lizzie looked across the hall at a dark-skinned, blue-eyed, wavy-haired lance corporal and fell head over heels in love. She felt good in her long black skirt and pretty pink chiffon blouse as she danced close to her new-found friend, whose name was Charlie Wilson.

Polly was getting on well with his tall, lanky friend, who was called Frank. So well, in fact, that when 'In The Mood' came blaring from the gramophone the two of them gave an exhibition.

Their bodies were as one as they matched their steps to everyone's favourite quick-step. Partners fell back, leaving Polly and Frank a clear floor. The record came to an end and they hugged each other, hot and sweaty as they were. A burst of clapping showed admiration and Polly blushed.

'Who's Taking You Home Tonight', was the last record to be played and couples dreamily danced the waltz with the lights dimmed. Charlie sang, his lips close to Lizzie's hair, "I'm pleading, please let it be me."

The four of them left the hall together Polly and Frank lingered in Garratt Lane, and Lizzie yelled back, 'We're going on, Polly. I'm on at a quarter-past five in the morning.'

'All right,' came Polly's reply, 'see you tomorrow'.

Charlie left her at the gate. He hadn't attempted to kiss her and Lizzie was disappointed.

'We'll be here for a while. I shall see you soon,' he promised, and Lizzie hoped it was a promise that he would keep.

On Wednesday when Lizzie finished her shift at one-forty-five at Tooting Bec, Charlie was there waiting for her. He bent down and gave her a swift kiss.

'Okay, Lizzie?' he asked as natural as you like, as if they had known each other for years.

His uniform was well pressed and you could see your face in the toe-caps of his boots. Lizzie gave him a lovely smile and he smiled back.

Catching her in his arms, he swung her in the air. 'Oh, I haven't been able to get you out of my mind, Lizzie. I want to spend every spare minute I get with you.'

Lizzie laughed; she liked his authoritative tone. He went back to the garage with her, waiting while she paid in her day's takings, then they walked all the way home to Tooting, talking non-stop.

Her mother and her aunt warned her to be careful. 'Take things slowly, please,' Nellie pleaded. 'Couples rush to get married in wartime and live to regret it,' she wisely told Lizzie. Their words were wasted.

Eight wonderful weeks and she had been with him wherever possible. Now, as the leaves on the trees began to turn beautiful shades of red and brown and the evenings drew in, Charlie came to say goodbye. His battalion of the Royal Artillery Corps was moving on. On the doorstep Lizzie snuggled close and Charlie covered her lips in a long kiss. It was wonderful. It was different from all the others kisses, long and passionate.

'You will write to me, won't you?' Charlie begged.

'Of course I will, darling,' Lizzie promised.

'If I get a long leave, will you marry me?' he asked.

'Yes, oh yes,' she answered, her eyes wet with tears.

''Allo, Lizzie. Long time no see.'

Lizzie's face broke into a smile as she punched the threea'penny ticket and handed it to Sadie Braffman. 'How's yer mum?' she asked.

'She's better. Misses me dad a lot though.'

'Yeah,' Lizzie muttered thoughtfully. 'A lot of people do.'

Bernie Braffman had been a great character and had had two stalls in the market for years. Lizzie had stood at the corner of Blackshaw Road and watched his funeral procession pass.

One bystander had uttered a statement that had struck in Lizzie's mind. 'In this life, you're as rich as the number of friends you got. Well, Bernie Braffman was a rich man.' What better epitaph could a man have?

'You finishing now?' Sadie asked as she watched Lizzie pick up her ticket box from underneath the stairs.

'Yep. Thank God. Not a bad duty, this one though. Six-three out of the garage in the morning, finished now at Tooting Bec twelve-forty-five. Two journeys to Shepherd's Bush, only one up to Crystal Palace.'

'Come and 'ave a cuppa coffee with me?' Sadie suggested hopefully.

' 'Course I will, can't stay long, though. Gotta pay in at the garage.'

They sat facing each other across the oil-cloth covered table in the steamy cafe, while Lizzie sipped her coffee and Sadie poured out her troubles.

'It's no joke 'aving to cope with two stalls,' she complained, staring fixedly at Lizzie, her stout body pushed tight into a grey costume which emphasized her ample bosom. Her jet black hair and olive skin were lovely, her best features really, thought Lizzie, who found herself feeling sorry for Sadie without really knowing why.

Lizzie listened attentively and made noises of encouragement. 'What's ter do, I don't know,' Sadie went on. 'Since my brother David got called up and me dad's gone, I 'aven't opened the bedding stall.

It's not worth it. Coupons for this, dockets for that, queues at the warehouses and what for? Nothing. You wouldn't believe it.'

Sadie paused for breath, 'I have to keep the grocery stall going, don't I? 'Asn't been too bad so far, but now, staff I can't get. Not a soul. I tell 'yer, Lizzie, a man I wish I was. Off ter the war I'd be.' Then she shot a question at Lizzie out of the blue, 'Have you finished for the day?'

'Yes, I told you already.'

'Same time all the week?' asked Sadie.

'Till Friday,' Lizzie told her. 'Saturday and Sunday rosters are different.'

'Oh, Lizzie,' Sadie practically shrieked, 'you could help me out no end.'

'Me? How?' But already Lizzie suspected what was coming.

'Do a few afternoons on the stall with me, and what about when you're on late turns, a few mornings, eh? You'll do a few mornings maybe, then?' The worried look on Sadie's face tore at Lizzie's heart.

'Well, I'll give it a try. Nothing definite, you know. See how it goes.'

'Oh, d'yer mean it?' Sadie said and, to Lizzie's embarrassment, she flung her arms round Lizzie's neck and kissed her noisily.

So now Lizzie had two jobs.

It was pouring with rain when Lizzie came out of the garage. Wearing a long mac, with her hair covered by a scarf, she looked tired and dejected. All she really wanted to do was to go home and get into bed. Instead, she was doing a stint up at the market this afternoon.

She shouldn't grumble, she told herself. In the couple of months that she had worked for Sadie, she had done pretty well. Sadie was grateful, kind and generous, and what's more, they had a good laugh most of the time, especially when Polly was able to do a turn on the stall as well.

Lizzie was pleased to see her sister Connie in the scullery when she pushed open the back door. Short and sturdy, bursting with energy, she wore a smart, long dress. Being pregnant suited Connie.

'Hallo, love,' she smiled and greeted Lizzie warmly. 'Mum told me what time you'd be home. I've boiled some potatoes and I've got a tin of pilchards. You 'aven't eaten in the garage, 'ave you?'

'No,' Lizzie answered, 'I wasn't gonna bother.'

'I really wanted ter tell you about our Syd,' Connie said as she vigorously beat at the potatoes in the saucepan with a fork.

'Why? What's up with Syd?' Lizzie sounded angry.

'All right, all right,' said Connie, trying to calm her.

A few weeks before, the police had been round. Syd and his mates had stolen a bike. Since Bill had been called up, Syd had lived with Connie. It was better than being on her own, Nellie had decided.

''As he been a nuisance or 'as he been pinching again?'

'Nothing like that, 'onest Lizzie. Give me a chance. The fact is,' Connie hesitated, 'he's run off. Gone to join up.'

'What?' roared Lizzie. 'He's too bloody young.'

Connie plopped a spoonful of mash on to the plates, which each held two pilchards, then spooned the tomato sauce from the tin over the fish. Lizzie felt afraid; Syd could be a right little sod, but he was their young brother, the baby of the family. Trouble was, he looked so angelic. He could lie through his teeth, smiling all the time and folk believed him.

She ate her lunch without really enjoying it and was grateful when Connie cleared away their plates.

'Well now, what's Sadie got to sell that's special today?' Connie asked, as Lizzie pulled her trousers off and stepped into a brown tweed skirt.

'Dunno till I get there. Might be Camp coffee,' she suggested.

'Well, whatever, don't you go overdoing it, love,' Connie said kindly, 'and don't start worrying about Syd. What's done is done, and there is nothing we can do about it now.'

'Does mum know?' asked Lizzie.

'Yes, she does, and she didn't take it too bad.'

Lizzie wrinkled up her face. 'Poor old Syd,' she said. 'He's not so bad, you know; I hope he's got a guardian angel.'

There was a lively atmosphere in the market that

afternoon. Most of the stalls were open and each seemed to have something to offer because queues had formed everywhere.

'Marvellous, ain't it?' one woman remarked to Lizzie as she counted out her change. 'Now there's plenty of work about and we've gotta bit of money, the things ain't around to buy any more.'

Tommy Clarke's stall had oranges today and young women with babes in their arms, toddlers in push-chairs and prams waited patiently. Old Tommy served them from an open wooden crate only if they had green ration books. Oranges were only for the under fives. Probably the first time some kiddies had ever seen one.

Mrs Scott, seventy if she was a day, resolutely kept her son's hardware stall going. Today she had a few Axminster rugs but the supply would run out long before the queue had dwindled.

Sadie's voice was persuasive as she walked the length of the line of women who clutched their canvas and paper bags. 'Custard powder, matches, some bottled coffee, Daddie's Sauce, even a few Chivers' Jellies we've got today. So, spend some ration points with us, please.' It was only by taking coupons and bundles of points to the Ministry of Food that traders were able to obtain dockets which enabled them to replenish their stock from the warehouse.

Lizzie had just finished serving old Maggie Watson. She was a good customer, with a houseful of daughters and children, and she had at least a dozen ration books. Women gazed in envy as she packed jars of jam, packets of sugar and tea into her bag.

Sadie smiled sweetly and, turning to Lizzie, said, 'Let Mrs Watson 'ave another coupla jellies. A lot of children she's got to feed.'

'Fanks, Sadie, yer a sport,' said Maggie Watson, handing over the extra coppers to Lizzie.

'Next, please,' Lizzie called, after having paused to blow her nose. Her mum stood in front of her.

Nellie passed a dog-eared fawn-coloured ration book over to her daughter, saying, 'I'll 'ave all that's going and a tin of spam, please, don't think there's enough points left for anything else.'

Lizzie placed a packet of Foster Clarke's custard powder, a large bottle of Camp coffee, Scott's porridge oats, one jelly and one box of matches on the counter. 'Sorry, mum,' she said, 'all the Daddie's Sauce has gone. I want twelve points for the spam, please.'

With scissors in hand, Lizzie bent her knees and cut the strip of points marked C from the ration book and let them fall into the already overflowing tin, which was on a shelf beneath the counter. Flicking through the pages, Lizzie found what she already knew, no tea coupons, no sugar allowance, no soap docket. She hesitated. Then, with grim determination, she straightened her back and got up on to her feet. Boldly, she took two quarter-pound packets of tea down from the shelf, a two-pound bag of sugar, two tins of spam and a tablet of Lux toilet soap. Setting the lot down, Lizzie quickly totalled up the amount. 'Five and tenpence ha'penny, please, Mum,' she said, handing back the ration book, and reaching for her mum's shopping-bag in which to pack the goods.

'See yer later,' she said cheerfully to her mother, getting in return only a nod and a frosty stare. The queue moved up and Lizzie worked on.

Lizzie felt done in as she opened the front door. Hardly had she got inside the house when Nellie started.

'What d'yer think yer up to? Eh? You knew we didn't 'ave coupons for those things,' stormed Nellie.

'So I gave you a few extras, that's all.'

'That's all!' her mother yelled. 'Yer could go ter prison, so could I, so could Sadie!'

'She never meant no harm,' cried Aunt Daisy.

'Don't you side with 'er,' Nellie turned on her sister-in-law. 'You weren't there. Bloody awkward I felt.'

'You took it all though, didn't you?' Lizzie retaliated.

She regretted this remark immediately. Her mother went berserk.

Lizzie had had enough. 'Right,' she screamed, as she let her fist come down so hard on the table that the cups jumped. 'Put it all in a box and I'll take it back to Sadie in the morning. I'll tell 'er what I did. All right. That satisfy you?'

Silence. Silence so great you could cut it with a knife.

'Well?' Lizzie yelled so loudly that her mother and her aunt backed away. 'Well?' Lizzie repeated as she watched her mother shake her head and wring her hands.

'She can't,' Aunt Daisy said quietly.

'She can't what?' demanded Lizzie.

'Give it all back. Yer mum's given some of it away.'

Nellie put out a hand. 'Don't be cross, Lizzie,' she implored.

'Jesus Christ,' Lizzie muttered, gazing at her mother with perplexity. 'One minute you're gonna kill me, next yer tell me not to be cross. I don't believe this. So go on, tell me.'

'Well we didn't need the coffee. Not now we've got the tea. So I let Mrs Gregory have it.'

'And?' Lizzie asked loudly.

'Well, old Mrs Durrel's only got one ration book, living on 'er own. I gave her a tin of the spam.'

Lizzie looked across at her aunt. Daisy was having a helluva job controlling her amusement. She winked at Lizzie. That did it.

Lizzie suddenly saw how comical it all was. It was like a slapstick scene from the Saturday concert. Her hands flew to her mouth, but it was no good, laughter bubbled out and Aunt Daisy joined in.

The relief was apparent in Nellie's voice as she said, 'How about a nice hot cup of tea?' It was too much. The last straw. There hadn't been any tea in the house for the last three days, and wouldn't be now if it wasn't for this afternoon's do!

Chapter Ten

THE JUNGLE OF London's back streets now showed signs of being war-torn. Where once panes of glass had let the daylight into houses, now there was darkness. Windows shattered by bomb blasts weren't replaced, merely boarded over.

The raids tended to be lighter now and mostly on the coastal towns. People became complacent and none more so than Lizzie – until one night the droning of the incoming bombers throbbed menacingly once again. Bombs streamed down from the sky, one landing with a thud which shook the houses but did not explode.

Lizzie didn't realize just how near it had fallen until she left the house just after four o'clock the next morning. She found a scene of activity. In the darkness, torches flashed, voices came from all directions.

'Hoi! Don't go down there,' shouted an air-raid warden but his voice only panicked Lizzie into hurrying faster. Reaching the corner of the road, she came to an abrupt halt, trembling and unable to move she stood rooted to the spot.

The unexploded bomb had torn into the end wall of the first house. Its nose was embedded, its fin tail protruding at least two feet. Voices yelled at her from the darkness.

'Move. Come on, yer silly cow, move yerself,' a cockney voice boomed out.

'Cross over to the other pavement and walk towards me, slowly,' instructed a voice firm with authority.

Lizzie did move slowly, praying as she went, 'Please don't let it go off.'

Safely round the corner she wanted to be sick. Nothing had prepared her for this. Half of Selkirk Road had gone. Just a pile of rubble remained. Lizzie stared, speechless with shock, terrified for Polly and the Hurley family.

By some miracle, their side of the road had only caught the blast. 'Thank God,' she murmured; and again, 'thank you, God,' as Aunt Kate and Uncle John came towards her, dusty and battered, but otherwise unhurt. Now Lizzie began to cry, her legs were trembling. 'Where's Polly?' she whispered.

'It's all right,' Aunt Kate told her, 'she's been taken to hospital. She was cut a bit by the flying glass.'

Hardly had the mobile canteens moved off and the firemen rolled up their hoses, having hosed down the blackened framework and steaming bricks, than the sirens were wailing again.

At ten minutes to eight, the Bendon Valley Laundry suffered a direct bit. Only those who were late for work that morning escaped. Over seventy women, including Mrs Baldwin, Connie's mother-in-law, were killed in that raid.

Later the same day, the Bomb Disposal team safely defused the unexploded monster and carted it away on an army lorry. The gaping hole in the side wall of the house was crudely repaired.

A sad silence settled over the district for several days but life went on.

London became fairly quiet after that, as the air raids became far less frequent.

Connie gave birth to a seven pound boy, whom she named William after his father, and everyone was sad that Bill's mother had not lived to see her grandson.

Lizzie was doing very nicely financially. She drew her wages from Sadie and put them into her Post Office Savings Account. There were weeks when she was also able to save a substantial amount from her bus wages. This was because of spreadovers.

Crews took the buses out from the garage very early in the morning, carrying office cleaners and factory shift workers. The next couple of trips would be for the office workers. Then, to save petrol, the buses would be parked in the City, and the driver and conductors travelled home by tube train. They had four to five hours' free time before going back to collect their bus and doing the homeward runs. For these split duties, wages were paid from signing on to signing off – as much as thirteen hours for some duties. Lizzie was surprised at just how much she had managed to put away.

She was also surprised at the speed with which Polly decided to get married.

Polly had been badly shaken when Selkirk Road had been hit by bombs and had been allowed to leave her job on medical grounds. She had become good friends with Arthur Scott, who had lived in the same road all his life, and whom she knew quite well. It wasn't until Arthur was invalided out of the Army that Polly and he became interested in each other. He was a strongly built young man, aged about twenty-two, with broad shoulders and thick forearms. His reputation had always been tough and there was a rawness about him that made Lizzie feel apprehensive, but he and Polly seemed to suit each other well enough.

They had found a house to rent in Wilton Road, Colliers Wood, and had set the wedding date. The fact that Polly was pregnant probably brought the date forward.

The preparations for Polly's wedding made Lizzie feel quite envious. Charlie wrote regularly, but it wasn't the same.

There were sandbags piled up each side of the doorway at Wandsworth Town Hall, which slightly put the dampers on the wedding guests, but Polly looked lovely, her dark hair gleaming beneath the pale blue wisp of a hat she wore, and her bright eyes sparkling with happiness. The coupons for her cream-coloured two-piece had been begged and borrowed, but the outcome was worth it.

Arthur Scott looked quite presentable dressed in a suit, with white shirt and dark tie. He stood grinning as the registrar pronounced them man and wife. Suddenly Polly Hurley was Mrs Scott.

Wilton Road was only ten minutes' walk from Merton Bus Garage and Lizzie became a frequent visitor there. The house Arthur had found to rent was large and comfortably furnished. Lizzie loved it from the moment she walked through the door, even though most of its windows were boarded up. In the front room there was an open-ended sofa and two big armchairs, drawn up beside a blazing coal fire.

'Crikey,' said Lizzie, 'ain't you lucky? How long have you got it for?'

'Till the war ends, I suppose,' said Polly, shrugging her shoulders, 'but come on upstairs, I want to show you something.'

Polly flung a door open on the first landing, 'What about that then?' she cried.

Lizzie stared in amazement. 'A modern bathroom with a geyser an' all, oh, ain't you lucky!' she said again.

Seven months later, Polly gave birth to a tiny scrap of a girl. Strange how big, strapping Arthur was so gentle with the baby, and so proud of Polly. They named the baby Lucy, after his mother.

*

Lizzie picked her way carefully through the garage. She'd been on middle shift, having just paid in her takings. It was a quarter-past eight, no one was about and the great depot was eerie. Pitch dark. Because of the blackout, what few lights there were were covered by black tin shades with small slits to let through just a faint glimmer. Buses were shunted into position, ready for the morning, the concrete floor was smeared with petrol and diesel and the air smelt foul.

A man stepped forward, blocking her way, and for a moment Lizzie was petrified. The smell of the uniform told her it was a soldier. An arm stretched out and a familiar voice said, 'Hallo, Lizzie, my darling.'

'Charlie?' she asked with some apprehension.

'Who else meets yer from work and calls yer darling?' he answered and she knew he was smiling down at her.

'Oh Charlie,' she whispered, before his lips covered hers.

Holding her close, he said, 'I've got four days' leave before we take off again. I've been ter your 'ouse, yer mum said I can stay there.'

Four whole days, it seemed too good to be true. They clung to each other in silence until Lizzie said, 'Polly's is nearest, let's go and 'ave a cuppa with 'er and Arthur.'

Lizzie couldn't take her eyes off him as Polly busied herself making the tea. His mop of dark hair grew thick and curly at the nape of his neck and she longed to run her fingers through it.

Lizzie telephoned the garage and was granted leave. The next few days were bliss, every minute they spent together. At night, with Charlie lying so near in what was Syd's room, her longing for him grew. If only there had been enough time, they might have been married. If only . . .

Lizzie tried to take everything in her stride, but when Charlie left again, she felt very low. It seemed this war was lasting for ever.

They only got occasional letters from Leslie. The wireless told how the island of Malta was being bombed day and night. And young Syd was in Germany; they received a few airmail letters from him with many words crossed out by the censor.

Connie had left London, she and baby William were down in Plymouth. That way, whenever Bill got shore leave, he and Connie could be together. Like many other families, theirs was totally split up.

Lizzie's heart missed a beat when one lunchtime she got home and found not one letter from Charlie, but two. Aunt Daisy was away, doing her bit for the war effort (every afternoon she manned the mobile canteen on Balham Station), and her mum was busy ironing. Nellie took up another flat iron from the range, held it to her cheek, then spat on it, finally wiping it with a clean white cloth. 'Don't sit there musing over yer letters, Lizzie, open them, for Christ's sake!'

'I'll make us a cup of tea first,' Lizzie answered, playing for time.

Setting a cup down on the dresser, Lizzie said, 'Drink it while it's hot, Mum. I'm gonna take mine upstairs.'

Nellie sighed. Lizzie was such a good-hearted girl, a worker an' all. She proved that, but she didn't seem to have much luck. Life hadn't been that good to her so far, and Nellie hoped against hope that this Charlie was the right one.

Upstairs it was dark, chilly and drab in her bedroom. With the window boarded over for so long, she'd forgotten what it was like to be able to look out of the window, and with the wallpaper peeling from the walls it wasn't exactly the most pleasant of places to be. Lizzie lit the gas, lay on the bed and tucked the eiderdown tightly round herself.

The first letter was ordinary, saying how much he had enjoyed seeing her, thanking her mother and her aunt for putting him up. Only the last paragraph made Lizzie shiver with fear. 'God only knows when I'll see you again, Lizzie,' he wrote, 'we have been issued with tropical kit.'

The second letter was oh, so different. 'I love you, Lizzie,' was how it began. She could feel her heart thumping. The words were so sincere. A glorious feeling came over her; she closed her eyes and hugged her pillow.

They seemed to have had such a short while together and it was only from previous letters that Lizzie had heard about Charlie's earlier life. His

mother had come to London from Scotland to be in
service. She had died only days after he was born.
No one had ever told him of his father and he had
been brought up in a Shaftesbury Home for orphans
near Blackfriars Bridge.

Now Charlie had opened up his heart to her and
poured out his true feelings. He had been so moved
by the sight of Polly and Arthur in their nice, clean,
warm house and baby Lucy had been the icing on
the cake for him. 'I've never had a family. Come to
that, I've never had a home, not even a room of my
own.' The words of his letter blurred as Lizzie's eyes
filled with tears. 'Will it ever be our luck, Lizzie?'
he asked. Sadness gushed through her. This rotten
war, the loneliness, the longing, it seemed as if it
was lasting a lifetime. 'Oh Charlie,' she cried, turning face down in her bed to muffle her sobs.

Later, she rinsed her face and hands under the cold
tap in the bathroom and went downstairs to have
her evening meal with her mother and Aunt Daisy.
But her thoughts were miles away with Charlie.
Come the end of the war, she'd have a home ready
for him. A place that would be theirs, and they
would have a family. She'd make it up to him for
all those long lonely years.

By the time the day was over, she had made a
firm decision.

She was going to buy a house.

Chapter Eleven

1943 CAME IN bitterly cold. Every single thing seemed to get worse, except for the fact that they no longer had to endure the Blitz.

All the STL registration buses disappeared from Merton Garage and were replaced by Daimlers. No longer were the passenger seats padded and upholstered. Rows of plain wooden benches had to suffice.

Lizzie, used to digging her knees into the sides of the seats in order to keep her balance when collecting fares, now found it much harder in more ways than one. After only one week, her shins were black and blue with bruises. 'Look on 'em as yer war wounds,' Polly laughingly told her.

Lizzie's bus route had also been changed as had her driver. She was now on the 118 which ran through Streatham Vale to Clapham Common. The route was mostly through nice suburban districts but in the Vale there were quite a few factories. Now her passengers were mostly young factory girls and women, her kind of folk and she liked the change a lot.

The Smith meters factory was on war work and the girls told Lizzie it was all very hush hush. And Payne's firework factory now made rockets and varicoloured lights for the Merchant and Royal Navy.

Pascall's sweet factory gave Lizzie the greatest laugh. 'God knows what their wartime turn out is,' she remarked to her mother one evening as she told of her day's work.

'But 'ow about this, Mum. One girl told me, if you go there on a Friday morning and take two pounds of sugar, yer can get a pound of boiled sweets or toffees in exchange.'

'Really!' Aunt Daisy butted in. 'But where does the sugar come from?'

'That's exactly what I asked her, Aunt Daisy. Who the hell's got two pound of sugar to spare? Seems some folk have, this girl told me. Big families mostly, I suppose. Still, she's promised ter bring me some off-cuts. Broken bits of sweets they are. They don't get many, but she said she'll try.'

'Cor, that would be nice,' said Nellie. The sweet ration was eight ounces every four weeks which didn't go far.

Also in Streatham Vale was the big cemetery and at its gates was a new double-fronted florist shop. Lizzie's new driver, Bill, jumped down from his cab and came round the bus to talk to Lizzie.

'I'm just gonna see if I can order any flowers from Mary. It's the wife's birthday next Monday. Ain't many flowers about anywhere, but old Mary seems to get hold of a good supply.'

Lizzie nodded and stood watching the queue of people board the bus and Bill walk over to the shop.

He was, or had been, a very tall man, but his shoulders now stooped and his uniform hung loosely on his lean frame. He should be enjoying his retirement really, Lizzie thought, even his eyesight wasn't all that good. Many a corner he turned with two wheels of the bus hitting the kerb.

Bill came out of the shop and Mary Chapman came with him, pausing only to lock the shop door.

''Allo Lizzie, my love,' Mary said as she heaved her great bulk up on to the platform. 'Christ,' she said, eyeing Lizzie from top to toe. 'This job ain't done you any 'arm 'as it gal. You look marvellous.' And she was right.

Despite the cold weather, Lizzie bloomed with health. Her skin glowed, her fine cheek bones had more flesh covering them and her long fair hair tucked into a lacy black snood shone through like golden corn.

'And rationing ain't made you any thinner, Mary,' Lizzie laughed as she pushed her towards a seat just inside the bus. Lizzie collected her fares and plonked herself down on the long seat next to Mary.

''Ere love, yer don't want a couple of days extra work, do yer?' Mary asked.

'Aw, gor blimey,' cried Lizzie, ''ow many more? I've got two jobs already.'

'Shame,' Mary muttered, 'I could do with someone like you. Knows hows ter keep her mouth shut.'

'I'm not with you,' Lizzie said, 'what's so secretive about your trade?'

'It's the shortages, ain't it? Funerals are like processions now. Sad, but a fact of life. Can't get any decent blooms and as fer the frames fer the wreaths, like bloody gold dust they are.'

'So, what can you do about that?' Lizzie wanted to know.

'Bribe the grave diggers of course,' Mary said. Lizzie looked startled. 'Don't hurt no one, you know. The dead can't see the wreaths, nor smell the flowers. They're only a comfort for the living. Soon as the relatives have gone, the old men pass the floral tributes through me kitchen window and I re-use the frames, even some of the flowers and most of the moss. God won't take umbrage over that, I'm sure.'

The look Mary gave Lizzie defied her to say otherwise. In spite of her misgivings Lizzie had to smile. Mary's sense of self-preservation was quite exceptional. Blame the war, she told herself yet again.

The bitter cold weather continued and the nightly black-outs made trips for pleasure almost impossible. It was weeks since Lizzie had heard from Charlie and she felt depressed. There didn't seem to be any bright spots left in her life.

She was awoken one morning by a piercing scream, a scream that she admitted afterwards she would remember for the rest of her life. She jumped out of bed and ran out to the landing.

Leaning over the banister, she took it all in at a glance and she felt her heart stop. The dreaded yellow telegram lay open on the linoleum. Her mother lay prone on the floor and Aunt Daisy was sitting on the stairs, silently rocking herself back and forth.

She didn't have to give a thought as to whom it was. Lizzie knew. She went bare-footed down the stairs, stepped over her aunt and picked up the flimsy paper. LESLIE COLLINS the words jumped forth. Killed in Sicily. What the bleeding hell was he doing in Sicily! Wasn't Malta bad enough? The lump was so large in her throat that Lizzie almost choked. Her chest felt as if an iron band encircled it, drawing tighter every minute. Her eyes and nose ran, and her ears ached.

Slowly, she went back upstairs, ignoring both her mother and her aunt. She couldn't console either one of them; her own pain was too severe. She loved Leslie so much and she would never see him again.

Then came one of the worst periods of the war. Hitler sent his doodle-bugs to England. Flying bombs without pilots – a mysterious danger droning their way through the sky, flames shooting out from their tails. Londoners raised their weary faces and stared in disbelief. Quite suddenly the engine would cut out, but it would not fall at once. On it would glide for breath-taking seconds before hitting the ground. Everyone held their breath, you could feel the unnatural silence. Lips moved and everyone prayed the same prayer, 'Please God, don't let it fall on us.' It fell elsewhere and people were safe – until the next time.

Aerial bombing had never been like this. The bomp-bomp, thud-thud of British anti-aircraft guns told people that their side was fighting back. Men and women had become defiant, cursed the Germans and got on with their wartime jobs. Now, with these buzz-bombs, they felt defenceless.

It was Sunday lunchtime and all three of them were at home. The sound of a single engine was suddenly immediately overhead. They froze. The heavy droning stopped. 'Down, quick, get down!' Nellie ordered, almost dragging Lizzie beneath the kitchen table. Seconds later, the kitchen door burst open, their last intact window blew in and dust and glass showered down into the passageway.

'Bloody Hitler,' yelled Daisy, forced out of her complacency for once.

They went out into the street. Black smoke and flames shot high above the rooftops of the houses opposite. The doodle-bug had dropped just two streets away. So near and yet, thank God, so far.

Lizzie would be twenty-one years old in August, and Nellie prayed that they would all live to see the day.

Summer came early. The lovely May days were really warm. Lizzie got compassionate leave from her job; she needed a break. *Gone With The Wind* was showing at the Mayfair Cinema and long queues formed to see it. Lizzie paid three and six

each for three reserved seats and took her mother
and her aunt.

Another evening Arthur's mother minded baby
Lucy and he took Polly and Lizzie dancing at the
Streatham Lyceum. Lizzie didn't really enjoy herself; she felt lonely. But returning home with these
happy friends, she spied a 'For Sale' notice posted
up on the front door of a house opposite. All her
determination returned.

Wilton Road was a short cul-de-sac with a dozen
semi-detached houses on the side where Polly now
lived and only six large detached houses on the
opposite side of the road. Colliers Wood was a very
nice surburban district and Lizzie decided that she
could do a lot worse.

The very next morning Lizzie took the tram to
Wimbledon. William Fox & Sons estate agents obviously catered for opulent clients. The only sign of
war was the scrim, glued tightly to the plate-glass
windows and which obscured the comfortable office
from the stares of passers-by. A portly, middle-aged
man turned to greet her as she opened the door. A
smile lit his face, a mass of fuzzy grey hair topped
his head. 'Mr Brownlow,' he said, offering his hand.

Lizzie gave her name and explained that she was
interested in the Wilton Road property.

'Ah!' he exclaimed. 'Come into my inner office,
if you please, Miss Collins.'

Lizzie obeyed reluctantly, staring at him curiously
as she walked slowly after him.

'Be seated, be seated,' he waved his arms towards

an armchair, then he turned his back on her and shuffled several papers from a cabinet. 'Are you in business, Miss Collins?' he unexpectedly asked.

'No,' she answered. Today, she wore an old, but still smart, pin-striped grey suit with a dusty pink tailored blouse. Her long hair hung loose, secured only on the side with two tortoiseshell combs. She wasn't about to tell this stranger that she was a clippie.

'Ah, ah,' he repeated in a low voice. 'Very wise decision,' he went on, 'to buy property at this point in time. Risky, but worth the gamble. Boys will be coming home. Whole streets of houses demolished. Thousands married in haste, nowhere to live.' He thumbed through the piles of leaflets now lying on his desk, his head bent low, his voice only a murmur. He might have been talking to himself. 'Terrible, terrible housing shortage come the end of this war,' he paused, raised his eyes to Lizzie, 'you mark my words.'

He sounded so kind, so reassuring, that Lizzie relaxed. 'Three properties in Wilton Road,' Mr Brownlow said as he held out the details. 'One, an executive sale. Number nineteen, owner in a nursing home, number twelve, family evacuated, decided to stay in Devonshire. Would you like an escort or shall I entrust you with the keys?'

When Lizzie felt she could get a word in edgeways and that Mr Brownlow was listening to her, she assured him she would be able to view the properties quite safely on her own. 'I'll bring the three sets of keys back to this office this afternoon,' she promised.

'How kind, how kind,' he repeated in his low voice as he handed Lizzie the labelled front door keys.

The first house, a few doors away from Polly, was nice and Lizzie was tempted. It was very similar to Polly and Arthur's but, being unoccupied, it looked dusty and wretched. The second one she dismissed straight away; there was too much structural damage.

The third one was on the opposite side of the road. Detached, with a large front garden and a circular drive, this looked like a rich man's house. Lizzie consulted her estate agent's list. Work had been started with the purpose of turning the building into flats, then abandoned.

She used the key and opened the front door. The hall was very long, with black and white ceramic floor tiles. The first room was enormous, with bay windows reaching from floor to ceiling and a huge fireplace with marble surroundings.

At the end of the hall, there was a wood-panelled dining room and, beyond that, a white-tiled kitchen. What she thought was a cupboard turned out to be a modern bathroom. That was wonderful!

The first floor had four rooms and an old-fashioned bathroom, complete with a copper geyser on the wall. The top of the house was a complete surprise. A door at the head of the stairs opened into a self-contained flat, just one large room, a small kitchenette and an alcove that held a toilet and a deep porcelain sink.

From up here, the windows looked down over a neglected garden where several shrubs still fought for survival. It also gave Lizzie a good view of the district and the River Wandle as it snaked its way through grassy banks. What couldn't I do with this place! I could make it pay, Lizzie told herself.

All the way back to Wimbledon, Lizzie was doing her sums. She found the offices of William Fox & Sons closed for the day. She slipped all three keys through the letterbox, glad to have time to ponder on things and make up her mind.

Indoors, Lizzie rushed upstairs and took off her coat. Excited now, she wanted to tell her mother all the news and sound her out over the ideas that were forming in her head.

Nellie was slumped in the chair, staring into space. A quiet 'Hallo' was all the greeting she gave Lizzie. In her lap lay a photograph of Leslie, and she sounded so depressed that Lizzie was alarmed for her.

'I'll tell you what,' she coaxed, 'come and sit nearer the fire while I make us a cup of tea, then I'll brush your hair for you. You always like that, don't you?'

Perched on a foot-stool behind her, Lizzie took out the many hair pins which held her mother's plaited hair in circles on each side of her face.

Then she unbraided it and began to brush her

mother's hair with long, firm strokes. Nellie sighed and closed her eyes and Lizzie's heart ached for her. Now was not the time to discuss buying a house with her mother. She would have to make her own decisions.

June came in wet and windy, a disappointment after the warm month of May. It was three days later when Lizzie, well wrapped up in her bus overcoat and with her hat pulled well down over her ears, braved the biting winds and went over to Wimbledon again. She shook hands with Mr Brownlow, who was obviously pleased to see her and made no reference to the fact that she was wearing the bus uniform.

By the time Lizzie had finished telling Mr Brownlow that if mortgages could be arranged she would like to buy number nineteen Wilton Road in her brother Sydney's name and number twelve in her own name, he was smiling at her with a drowsy, gloriously happy expression. Not much property was being bought. Not with this wretched war going on.

'Leave everything to me, Miss Collins,' Mr Brownlow said. 'First we should talk finances. Number twelve's asking price is £950. I don't think we can get the vendor to come down on that. Nineteen is a different matter.' He shuffled through his papers. 'Ah yes, ah yes,' he was repeating himself again, '£650. Too ambitious. We will make an offer of £500.

'Now, about deposits?' he asked.

Lizzie brought out her notebook and read from it, 'I could pay £250 on number twelve and £120 or nineteen.'

'Good, good,' he mumbled, as he wrote.

'Also,' Lizzie said, 'I would like to pay one year's mortgage on each property in advance.'

This statement did surprise Mr Brownlow, and he raised his eyebrows in question. 'I have quite enough money,' Lizzie assured him, 'and who knows, the war may well be over by then.'

'Indeed. Let us pray that it is, Miss Collins,' he answered, thinking to himself what an astute young lady he was dealing with.

Lizzie went to the same firm of solicitors that had dealt with her grandmother's affairs. They agreed she was perfectly entitled to use the amount the developers of Silverdore had paid over.

Within eight weeks she had signed contracts so that she and her brother Sydney were, in conjunction with the Abbey National Building Society, owners of two houses in Wilton Road, Colliers Wood.

Chapter Twelve

THERE WAS TO be more tragedy for the Collins family before the year of 1944 was out, for Hitler had one last surprise up his sleeve for the suffering Londoners. Deadly rockets, packed with explosives, were launched over the Channel. Because they were supersonic they gave their victims no warning whatsoever – no sound of engines, no rush of air, just the devastating explosions!

Lizzie was in Smith's the drapers in Mitcham Road when one landed on Tooting Bec Common. Luckily, she was only slightly hurt when falling masonry knocked her to the floor.

'What yer doing down there?' two air-raid wardens joked, as they shifted broken sandbags and helped Lizzie over the pile of debris.

'Well, me name wasn't on that one, was it?' she told them as she wiped the dust from her eyes.

But just a week later a rocket hit Balham Station. Aunt Daisy was killed outright.

Lizzie stood in the passage hugging her mother. Both of them were sobbing. 'Oh God!' Nellie cried. 'How much more can we take? I give up. I really do. I just want to die myself.'

Of course she didn't give up, but she raged in her

heart against the cruelty of this war, and her own suffering.

She and Lizzie, like everyone else, lived day by day, month by month, giving each what comfort they could.

The Allied troops had landed in France in June 1944, giving everyone hope that the war would soon be over. But the advance to Paris and beyond was painfully slow, with fierce fighting all the way. Many sons and husbands were lost and many tears were shed. Christmas came and went; it was 1945, and still the war dragged on.

One morning the alarm clock rang loudly and Lizzie, still muzzy with sleep, reached out and only managed to knock the clock to the floor.

'Damn and blast,' she said as she groped around in the darkness. 'Christ, it's only ten minutes past three.'

Still not fully awake she went downstairs and put the kettle on, lighting the gas beneath it. 'Damn,' she said again, as she held the empty tea tin. 'Oh well, if I sign on early enough, I can go into the cafe next door to sort out my ticket box and have a large tea and two slices of dripping toast at the same time.' She had a wash at the scullery sink and struggled into her uniform.

It was the first week in May 1945, still dark at that time in the morning, and still quite nippy, Lizzie decided, as she closed the front door behind her.

Rounding the corner she stood stock still. She was like a rabbit trapped in the headlights of a car.

She just could not move.

Not one, but two trams were standing at the Broadway. Both were ablaze with lights. From stem to stern, every window was unblacked. It could not be true. It had to be a vision.

'Run!' a voice yelled at her to get out of the way of the tram.

'Yeah, come on, run,' other voices chorused.

'The war's over', a deep-sounding response echoed again and again.

The war was over.

Germany had unconditionally surrendered to the western Allies, and the festivities began and continued for days. No one went to bed, street parties were the order of the day. Pianos were pushed out into the roads and were never short of a pianist.

Lizzie persuaded her driver to abandon their regular route and drive the bus to Graveney Road. He sat on an upturned wooden box outside number thirty, a glass of beer in his hand. Their bus, now parked by the kerb, was swarming with kids. They clambered over the wooden seats, they tore up and down the stairs, hung out of the windows and rang the bell non-stop.

And Lizzie did not give a damn.

Bonfires burnt all night; time had no meaning. For the first time in six years, folk felt free to laugh, sing, shout and to cry with relief. Many mourned their lost ones, others thanked God that their menfolk had been spared and would be coming home. For Nellie in particular, the deaths of Leslie and Aunt Daisy had left an unbearable sorrow and no amount of celebration could raise her spirits or comfort her heart.

Patching up the houses began. Boarding was taken down from the window frames and sandbags were removed. Holes in ceilings and walls had to be ignored for the time being. Some returned home, to sleep in their own beds for the first time in years.

But Japan still hadn't surrendered and the awful decision was made that brought about a swift and total end to the war. The first atomic bomb was dropped on Hiroshima on August 6th and, a few days later, a second bomb was dropped over Nagasaki.

'Jesus, Holy Mary,' whispered Nellie as she turned the knob to silence the wireless. 'It's beyond belief what man does to man in the name of war.' She turned ashen-faced to Lizzie, who was sitting silently, staring into the fire, tears running unheeded down her cheeks.

Charlie was coming home.

Lizzie flew about in a fever of anticipation. She had a bath and washed her hair and, wearing her favourite sage green dress, she paced the floor of the front room like a caged lion. She saw him through the window when he was halfway down the road – his cap on the back of his head, his kit-bag perched on one shoulder, his face deeply tanned. She opened the door and ran. The moment she reached him, he dropped his kit-bag and his strong muscular arms went around her.

'Oh, Lizzie, Lizzie,' he murmured.

Regardless of women on the doorsteps, children staring and the milkman in the middle of the road grinning broadly, they stood clinging to each other, lost in a world all of their own on the pavement of war-battered Graveney Road.

Clutching his arm tightly, they eventually went up the road and into the house. Once inside, they literally locked themselves together, their arms about each other, their bodies pressed close. 'Oh, God, I've prayed for this moment,' Charlie whispered.

When at last he released her, Lizzie was trembling violently. Nothing had changed. Charlie still had this extraordinary effect on her. 'I still can't believe it,' she cried as she put out a hand and touched the lean lines of his face and then ran her fingers through the dark hair which still clung in waves to the back of his neck. 'You really are home, Charlie!' she whispered.

Emotions ran away with them; they forgot about everyone except themselves. A discreet cough from Nellie brought them back down to earth.

'Welcome home, Charlie,' Nellie said with a sob in her voice. She was thinking of her eldest son who would never now come through that door.

Charlie walked forward and clasped her in a great bear hug. 'Thanks, Mum,' he said.

They were married five weeks later.

What a rush!

Sadly, Lizzie thought of Aunt Daisy, who undoubtedly would have made her wedding dress. Leslie, too, was uppermost in her mind, for it should have been him who walked her down the aisle.

In the end, it was Sadie Braffman who attained the unattainable – a wedding dress and veil for Lizzie, a cream linen suit for Nellie and a peach-coloured, floor-length dress for Polly who was to be matron of honour. Uncle John, gave her away. St Nicholas's Church was hushed as Lizzie at last became Charlie's wife. The guests were happy and Lizzie prayed that the dear ghosts whom she felt were truly present, were also happy.

Syd was coming home at last and, impossible as it seemed, he was already married! After days of waiting, the couple arrived.

Everyone stared open-mouthed at the slim, rather flashily dressed young lady with peroxide-blonde hair. She wore a bright red suit and a large black picture hat. A brilliant diamanté necklace hung at her throat.

Nellie's disappointment showed on her face as Syd introduced Doris as his wife. She was twenty-four years old, two years older than Syd, very shy and quiet despite her appearance and the fact that she had served five years in the R.A.F.

Lizzie liked Doris instantly. Syd had grown, now six foot two inches tall, but his gappy smile hadn't changed and his blond hair was even lighter. Syd had always been a bit of a devil; more than likely he had chosen Doris's outfit in order to shock. Lizzie understood him so well. Even now she could read him like a book and still she adored him. Doris's front teeth protruded slightly, but because of the frankness of her expression and the sparkle in her eyes, she exuded a bubbling attractiveness that Lizzie warmed to immediately.

Doris obviously liked Lizzie in return, for she said, 'It's nice to meet you; I've heard such a lot about you.'

Lizzie looked across at Syd. 'Don't believe all he tells you,' she said with a grin, 'we can be friends in spite of him.'

And they were.

Chapter Thirteen

AMIDST MANY PROBLEMS, they all moved into Wilton Road and Lizzie carried on with her job on the buses just the same.

Syd and Doris were fairly lucky. Number nineteen had had the carpets (such as they were) left intact, together with several odd items of furniture, so at least they had the basic necessities; and with the dockets and coupons that they were allowed, they set up a comfortable home.

Syd used his demob money to buy an openbacked truck. He was down at the railway sidings each morning before it was light, loading up with hundredweight bags of coal. Touring the back streets, he would sell the coal door to door, sometimes making two or three more trips when the weather was cold.

Polly and Arthur had now bought number seven as sitting tenants, thus securing what had already become a much-loved house with good furniture. Arthur had been promoted and now had a good job in the offices of a brewery firm at Morden.

Things were not so straightforward for Lizzie and Charlie. The rooms at number twelve were vast, the windows enormous. A utility bedroom suite, obtained by docket, looked lost in the bedroom. It was banished to the top flat, while Gran's lovely old pieces of furniture were brought out from Uncle John's shed and thoroughly cleaned. The elaborately carved side table looked well in the hall and two bedside cabinets went one in each of two bedrooms on the first floor. A hand-carved dresser fitted exactly into a corner of the top flat. Lizzie wished she'd saved more.

Beg, borrow, even steal if Charlie had his way, became the order of the day. Second-hand shops, junk yards and markets, everyone foraged for Lizzie. Syd threw thirty bobs' worth of lino off the back of the coal truck one morning. It was a god-send. Charlie cut and shaped it, fitting it into three ground floor rooms.

After a time spent cleaning and decorating number twelve, Charlie took a job on the buses at Merton Garage. He hated it. He hated the hours, the traffic, and most of all the uniform. But he loved the social side of bus life, especially the darts.

A buff-coloured envelope brought another set-back. Inside was a document stating that number twelve Wilton Road had to be registered under the Town and Country Planning Act. A visit to Somerset House was needed.

'No sweat,' said Charlie, 'a day up in town will be great. Go to a show, shall we, Lizzie?' he asked and she readily agreed.

Finding the registrar's department in Somerset House was something of a problem. Everyone in the building seemed hell-bent on rushing some-

where. At last, a kind, elderly gentleman with a thin
face and rimless spectacles explained things. The Act
had only come into being since the war and it only
affected property costing more than seven hundred
pounds.

Stamp duty now had to be paid according to a
scale, which in the opinion of this legal-looking
gentleman was not excessive.

A few moments later, he produced a seal with
which he made an impression over wax on three
sets of documents and indicated where Lizzie should
sign. He looked up and said, 'The duty payable is
ninety-six pounds exactly.' The bottom dropped
out of Lizzie's world.

They didn't go to a show and Lizzie was very
subdued all the way home. Her capital wasn't going
anywhere near as far as she had hoped.

At least they had a double bed, which looked ridiculous standing in the centre of their enormous bedroom. All they had to hang their clothes on were
nails knocked into the walls and Lizzie now felt these
would have to suffice for some time to come.

She had let two bed-sitting rooms on the first
floor. One to Paddy Betts, a tall, red-faced Irishman,
and the other to a city-slicker type who travelled
daily to Whitehall, a Mr Joseph by name.

The top flat had looked so homely and comfortable when finished that Lizzie had been tempted to
move up there herself. Instead, she chose as tenants
Hilda and Wally Saint, both of whom also worked
on the buses out of Merton Garage.

'Oh, well,' Lizzie told herself, 'I will just have to keep our bedroom door locked so that the lodgers don't see we haven't got any furniture.'

Charlie didn't care two hoots either way. 'We have our bed,' he said with a wicked leer, 'what more can any man ask?'

What more indeed? Lizzie often asked herself.

She and Charlie had a relationship that was rewarding, full of warmth and certainly never dull. They had fun together, they argued and shouted at each other, they made love, and Lizzie counted her blessings.

One evening Nellie came in the back door, her face was red and her eyes excited.

'Hallo, Mum,' Lizzie called from the dining room, which only held a folding table and two wooden kitchen chairs, 'bring a cup through with you, I've only just made this pot of tea.'

Charlie stretched out on the hearth rug giving his chair to his mother-in-law. 'Had a win on the dogs, have yer, Mum?' he asked, winking at Nellie.

'No, I haven't,' she answered quickly. 'But I have found you a beautiful wardrobe for two pounds.'

'Two pounds! Crikey that's cheap,' exclaimed Lizzie.

'Well, that's what Mrs Dawson said you can 'ave it for.' Lizzie's hackles rose. The Dawsons again. Still her mother bowed and scraped to them.

'Must be rotten with woodworm if they're letting it go for two quid,' Lizzie said spitefully.

'Never mind her,' Charlie said, acting the peace-maker. He had heard all about the Dawsons and in a way he didn't blame Lizzie. Her mother did work hard for this family, had done for years, and Lizzie resented the fact.

They went to Balham in Syd's truck. Nellie and Lizzie squeezed into the cab with Syd. Charlie rode on the open back.

The Dawsons hadn't changed. They were just as Lizzie remembered them. Mrs Dawson, plump, big, towering over everyone, with hands that were podgy with gold rings on almost every finger. He, dressed in a dark suit, gold watch and chain stretched across his waistcoat, was as pompous as ever.

One glance at the wardrobe and Lizzie bit her tongue and kept quiet. She wanted it, very badly. Charlie paid the two pound notes and Mr Dawson helped Syd to dismantle this huge piece of furniture into three separate parts. Lizzie didn't believe what she was seeing and avoided looking at her mother who was smiling smugly.

Next morning, Lizzie had a rest day. She, Polly, Doris and Hilda Saint sat on the floor of Lizzie's bedroom. They were all seized with fits of the giggles. Each had taken a turn with a tin of Ronuck furniture polish and a yellow duster. The monster occupied the whole of one wall and was shining like a new dollar.

It was never meant for use in a modest home like Lizzie's. Each end section was a separate wardrobe with hanging space and footwear rails. The centre part had a full-length mirrored door, behind which lay glass-fronted drawers. Each drawer, and there were ten, held a slot-in label kept in place by brass fittings. Into the drawer marked 'Socks', Doris very solemnly placed four pairs belonging to Charlie. Polly then made a great ceremony of laying Lizzie's underwear into the space labelled 'Lingerie'. This set them off again, tears of laughter running down their cheeks.

'Well, you must admit,' Polly chortled to the others, 'it is a magnificent piece of furniture. Probably came from Harrods,' she added with a supposedly posh accent.

'One thing's for sure,' Lizzie piped in, 'I'll have ter work all me rest days if I ever hope to fill it.'

Within forty-eight hours Lizzie had added another great object to her room. She had swapped duties with another girl, just for the one day. Now on the 93 route there was a bus stop just outside a newly built parade of shops. A long queue of people moved slowly and Lizzie stepped down from the platform and idly looked at the window displays. A splendid sideboard caught her eye. 'Taken in part exchange', stated the Times Furnishing Company ticket.

Without regard for her passengers, Lizzie was in that shop before she could change her mind. 'How much?' she gasped to the astonished salesman. He must be dim-witted, Lizzie thought to herself, as he stared blankly at her.

She plucked at his sleeve and pointed at the side-board. 'How much?' she repeated.

'Er, five pounds,' he stammered.

Lizzie thrust a ten-shilling note at the now totally bewildered young man and fled, shouting back over her shoulder, 'Keep it for me, please. I'll be back about four.'

Lizzie's temporary driver wasn't too pleased with her, but she didn't care. They were late, the bus was overloaded with passengers and the one behind was half-empty. Lizzie collected fares, hummed to herself and pictured her new sideboard with its great ornate overmantle in her dining-room.

All she had to do now was to persuade Charlie to buy a couple of decent armchairs, or better still, a three-piece suite. Well, tonight would be the best time for that!

Time passed quickly and Lizzie wondered cautiously why she was so lucky. There wasn't a day that she didn't feel totally happy.

Doris and Syd were expecting their first baby. Polly's little Lucy had just started school. They spent evenings in each others' houses, playing cards or just talking.

Syd bought a television set. Well, he would! He would never alter – live for today was his motto, why bother to save, tomorrow could take care of itself. Doris was still a bit of a mystery to them all. Sometimes Lizzie thought she saw a scared expression in those lovely blue eyes.

'If Syd ever gets on ter yer, Doris, you let me know,' Lizzie repeatedly told her.

'No, I'm all right, really I am,' Doris would assure her. 'Syd is real good ter me.' That Doris loved Syd was only too obvious. In fact, what Lizzie feared was true, she was bewitched by him and even sometimes afraid of him.

Hilda and Wally Saint usually joined in their get-togethers and all eight of them would go off to other bus depots to watch two teams play darts. Charlie was the champion of Merton with Wally running a close second. When the game was over the fun began for the women, the home garage would supply food for a buffet, drinks would flow freely and, with any luck, the men could be persuaded to dance with them.

It was a good job that they went by a bus on loan to the darts team; the men were often too legless to walk to a bus stop.

Christmas was fantastic. All four families, friends and relations ate their Christmas dinner at Lizzie's. All, that is, except Doris. She was in hospital after having given birth to a bonny eight-pound boy. Lizzie went to the hospital on Christmas afternoon, armed with a bagful of soft cuddly toys for her new nephew, Raymond, and an expensive lacy nightdress for the sister-in-law that she had come to love so dearly.

The whole party had assembled in Polly's house by the time Lizzie got back and it was there that

Polly's parents and Lizzie's mum dropped their bombshell. They were going to Newquay in Cornwall to run an hotel.

At the end of the war, Connie and Bill had chosen to stay in Plymouth and they had only seen them and little William once since then. Lizzie felt like panicking. Was her whole family to be split up and scattered?

A distant cousin of John Hurley's had, before the war, bought a small hotel in Newquay, but she'd lost her husband in the war, had a bad stroke herself and was selling up. John and Kate had jumped at the opportunity and had talked Nellie into going with them.

'Don't worry, love,' said Nellie kindly, when all explanations had been given. 'I'm not giving up me house. I'm only going to help get the place ready, though I suppose I might stay for the first season.'

A smile crossed Lizzie's face, 'I can't see you, Mum, in a short black dress and frilly apron.'

'Don't be so cheeky. You want to save up and come down there for a holiday. Maybe next September, eh, Lizzie?'

'Yes, maybe,' Lizzie answered, 'but you haven't gone yet.'

Three weeks later, on a bitterly cold, frosty morning, Lizzie stood on the railway platform with Polly and waved until the train was out of sight.

'How d'you think they'll do?' asked Lizzie.

Polly screwed up her face, 'Dunno, bit old aren't they?'

Down the platform came a mobile canteen selling hot drinks and Lizzie immediately thought of her Aunt Daisy; she'd lost her, and now her mum had taken herself off to the back of beyond.

Still in a depressed mood, she suggested to Polly, 'Let's go and have a drink.'

Nearly an hour later they came out of the railway bar, Polly had drunk two gin and tonics and Lizzie had had two whiskys with dry ginger. Both girls were smiling now.

'Good luck to them,' Lizzie muttered.

'Yeah, that's it. If that's what they want, good on them for 'aving a go,' said Polly.

The next few weeks the weather didn't let up. Every day was bitterly cold. Already they had had snow, which hadn't cleared and the gutters were full of dirty brown slush. Nellie wrote each week, giving full details of how they were preparing Bay View Hotel for the coming season. She seemed determined that, come September, Lizzie and Charlie would be taking a holiday in Newquay.

At the end of February, Lizzie stood staring into their bathroom mirror, a satisfied grin spread over her face. A knock came on her kitchen door and she called out, 'Come in.'

'I thought I heard you being sick,' Hilda Saint said.

'I'm all right now,' said Lizzie in a clear, decisive voice, coming out of the bathroom.

'You haven't got the 'flu, have you?' Hilda asked.

Lizzie burst out laughing. 'Nothing could be further from the truth,' she protested. 'I'm on top of the world.'

Hilda stared at her and the truth dawned. 'You're pregnant!' she exclaimed.

'Yes, yes, yes,' cried Lizzie as she did a little jig around the kitchen, 'two months almost to the day'.

'How can you know that?' Hilda asked.

Lizzie smiled knowingly. That was a secret she was only going to share with Charlie.

In bed that night, Lizzie cuddled up to Charlie and reminded him. 'Charlie,' she whispered in the darkness, 'remember when you did a day's work on the 118s and we 'ad a row?'

Charlie had other things on his mind as he ran his hands up her smooth legs. 'We always have a row when we work together,' he said.

'Yeah, I know, but that was different. Oh, leave off, Charlie!' she protested as he tried to silence her by placing a hand over her mouth.

'Oh, all right then.' He gave in and half sat up, resting back on his elbows. 'Get to the point,' he insisted.

Lizzie switched the bedside table-lamp on, nestled close and kissed his rough, whiskery face. 'You need a shave.'

'For Christ's sake, Lizzie!' Charlie exploded.

'All right, all right,' she answered calmly and almost dreamily. She went on, 'We had stopped outside St Leonard's Church and among the people waiting to board the bus were a young couple with a young baby. I stowed their fold-up pram under the stairs for them.'

Charlie sighed and put his arms around Lizzie, pulling her head down on to his hairy chest. He hadn't a clue what she was talking about.

'I stood gazing at that baby, watching as the mother loosened the shawl. Next thing I heard was the cab door slam and seconds later you came around the back of the bus, jumped on to the platform and grabbed me.'

Recollection came back to Charlie. 'Hey,' he roared, 'I told you to stop day-dreaming and ring the bloody bell, and all you went on about was what a lovely baby it was.'

'That's right, go on, what else did yer say?'

'Nothing.'

'Not much you didn't, Charlie! You told the whole damn bus you were quite capable of making your own.'

'Get on,' he said through his wide grin.

'Yes, and that wasn't all,' Lizzie told him, disentangling herself from his grasp. 'You kissed me, and when I told you all the passengers were looking, you said, "Good, let 'em look." Everyone ended up laughing at me.'

'Ah, poor Lizzie,' he mocked, 'but what's made you bring all that up now, for God's sake?'

'Because I am going to leave the job.'

'What! After all this time you're gonna leave the job because I kissed you when passengers were looking?'

'No. Because that night you made me pregnant.'

Charlie sat bolt upright in the bed; he looked absolutely bowled over. Quietly he said, 'Why you sly old thing.'

'Not so much of the old,' she laughed.

'Oh Lizzie, Lizzie, Lizzie,' he murmured and there was deep affection in his voice.

Then suddenly he punched the bedclothes and let out a roar which must have woken up half the street. 'Now,' he said with a wicked gleam in his eye, 'if you've finished talking about the past, can we get back to the present?'

When spring eventually came round again, life seemed to Lizzie to be almost too good to be true. The girls worked hard in their houses during the morning, and then took themselves out for the rest of the day. They went to parks, up on to the Common, even took bus rides to Box Hill, where they lay on the grass, ate sandwiches, drank lemonade and watched Lucy play with Raymond. Weekends they walked to Tooting, bought their fruit and vegetables in the market and haggled with the butcher.

Charlie often said it was a wonder that the girls hadn't worn a triangular-shaped track in Wilton

Road as they went continuously from one house to the other.

Hilda was slightly the outsider, mainly because she still went out to work, but Lizzie knew she was happy enough. She never used make-up, her hair was always sleek and shiny but dead straight, and she adored her Wally. Lizzie thought it was a case of an attraction of opposites. Hilda was big-boned, fair and tended to be a bit overweight, while Wally was slender, dark-haired, dark-skinned, with a pencil slim moustache and eyes that were almost black. They were both good company, especially on the private outings.

These outings had become a regular thing, running every Sunday from each bus garage throughout the fleet to spend the day at the coast. Drivers were mainly volunteers. The cost was four shillings for adults return, and a half a crown for children. Lizzie, Polly and Doris would wash and set each others' hair, paint their fingernails and try on each others' dresses before Sunday came around. Polly was the tallest of the three, still slim, dark and with lovely soft skin that tanned easily. Doris and Lizzie could have easily passed for sisters. Same height, same slim build, same blue eyes and fair hair, though Doris still used peroxide which Lizzie thought was a pity. In all the time Lizzie had known her, she had never heard Doris raise her voice in anger. She seemed so demure and unobtrusive. Kind acts and deeds which she accomplished for elderly neighbours she did without thought of reward or recognition.

It was on one such outing to Bognor that they discovered what a truly lovely voice Doris had. The day had been grand; the girls had hardly left the sands. At lunch time, the men had taken themselves to the pub where they drank a considerable number of pints between them. They came back when the pub closed, sank down into deckchairs, put handkerchiefs over their faces and fell asleep.

The girls didn't mind; they were used to it, they told each other, as they played about at the edge of the sea, their dresses tucked into their knickers.

Everyone sat still and silent on the homeward coach until it was time again for the pubs to open.

'Pull up, driver, nice big coach park at the Wheatsheaf,' shouted Syd, whilst dozens of male voices backed him up.

Soon, Charlie was seated at the piano inside the bar, while Wally, Arthur and Syd belted out the words to the all-time favourites he was playing.

It began low-pitched. Lizzie and Polly turned and looked in amazement. Doris was singing. Gently the words of 'Charmayne' came from her lips; she looked utterly at peace. The whole busy bar became hushed, listening to Doris's soft crooning voice. There was a moment's complete silence as the last notes faded away, then thunderous applause came from everywhere.

Doris blushed and hung her head.

'You're gorgeous,' Lizzie whispered to Raymond,

who was asleep on her lap. She bent and kissed his warm forehead. 'And, young Raymond, there's a helluva lot for you to learn about your mum!'

It was late in August. Lizzie had been feeling rotten for two days when Doris resolutely took her by taxi to the Wilson Hospital.

'Her frame is very small,' the doctors stated, 'we shall transfer her to Hammersmith Hospital.'

Charlie was frantic when he came home and found Lizzie missing. But he was full of pride when, the very next day, she had the baby – a boy of almost eight pounds, with a shock of dark hair and those blue eyes so very much like his own.

Everyone had argued about the baby's name. If it was a boy, Nellie had said, call it Brian. Brian! Never in her life. That was the name of the eldest Dawson boy.

Phillip, Syd wanted. Or Frederick, suggested Polly.

Only hours after he was born, the registrar came around the ward. He peeped at the half-asleep Lizzie, and whispered, 'I won't bother you.'

'Please,' her hand stayed him, 'Robert Leslie Wilson,' she stated firmly, having sought no one's advice, not even Charlie's.

When Lizzie arrived home, they had acquired another addition to the family – an Old English sheepdog puppy. Charlie's conductor had been living in a Nissen hut and, when granted a council house, was told no pets.

'Couldn't let him be put down, could I, love?' asked Charlie.

'No, of course not, he is lovely,' Lizzie quickly assured him. 'What's his name?'

'Bob,' said Charlie.

'Yeah, Bob-Bob,' said Raymond, his big eyes pleading with his auntie to let the dog stay. Stay he did and became everyone's friend.

When the baby was just three weeks old, Polly came across the road waving a telegram from her parents. Doris had tagged in behind and they all laughed in disbelief as Polly read aloud, "Come on holiday now. All eight welcome. Don't forget the children. Love you. Mum and Dad."

They couldn't refuse. They didn't want to.

So it was all arranged. The train fare was very expensive but an overnight coach left Victoria at ten p.m. three evenings each week.

Their tickets cost four pounds return for each adult, two pounds each for Lucy and Raymond and the baby went free. Hilda and Wally Saint were thrilled to be included in the invitation and Arthur Scott assured them that Polly's parents were kind and generous folk and that the season was probably all over and the bedrooms would be empty. Paddy Betts and Joe Frost promised faithfully to take good care of Bob-Bob.

It was barely daylight when the coach driver pulled

into the Newquay terminal, but Nellie, Kate and John Hurley were there waiting.

Utter confusion followed; everyone wanted to hug everyone else, the two little ones were irritable after a long weary journey and wouldn't go to their grandmas, and Baby Robert started to cry.

Arthur took charge. The hotel was only a few yards from the harbour coach park and soon everyone was seated in the basement kitchen, around a huge circular table which had a well-scrubbed top.

Blue and white mugs filled with scalding tea were set in front of each of them. The two toddlers and the baby were already fast asleep and tucked up safely.

Quietly Lizzie took stock. Then she glanced at Polly and they each blinked to take away the tears.

Their parents looked awful! John Hurley had aged ten years in the past ten months; his hair had receded, leaving a shiny bald patch, his eyes looked sunk in their sockets and the amount of weight he had lost was considerable. Kate looked very pale and tired and Nellie was hobbling. She had tripped going up the uncarpeted stairs from the basement to the entrance hall, knocking her shin badly. A lump had formed, which the doctor now said was thrombosis.

Hotel life hadn't proved to be easy.

'Eighteen hours a day, seven days a week,' John Hurley told them quietly. 'We hadn't reckoned on being at the visitors' beck and call every minute, day and night.'

'Never mind,' Kate said, 'season's over and done with now and we'll see you all have a grand holiday. By Christ, we've missed you, ain't we, Nellie?'

'More than you know,' Nellie agreed as she gazed at the group of young friends, which included her son and daughter.

'Now, let's see about breakfast,' ordered Kate as she stood up and prepared to tie an apron around her waist.

'Oh no you don't!' Everyone turned to look at Doris as she spoke. 'We can get the breakfast.' She spoke quietly but with weight behind her words. 'Get your mum and your aunt and uncle upstairs to bed. Then you men can take all the suitcases to the rooms and by that time we'll be ready for you to lay the table.'

The men had been standing open-mouthed. No one had seen Doris in charge before, let alone heard her issue orders.

The gardens at the back of the hotel were beautiful. Lush lawns sloped directly down to Newquay's famous beach.

As a big family they did everything: took boat rides, swam and paddled in the sea, collected shells and picnicked on the golden sand. Everyone looked and felt better as the sun continued to shine down each and every day through that September.

Two days only were left of their fortnight's holiday and all was quiet and peaceful as they sat sipping coffee on the top lawn.

The bell in the reception hall sang, shattering the silence.

'Leave it, Polly,' her father said as she rose to go and answer it. Persistently it rang again, longer this time.

'I don't mind,' Polly said, 'I won't be a minute.'

She wasn't. Almost immediately she came across the grass, her long brown legs showing to advantage beneath her very short shorts. 'Eight people for bed and breakfast,' she called, 'they want four double bedrooms for two nights.'

'Tell them no. We're closed up for the winter,' John Hurley was emphatic in his refusal.

Polly didn't argue. Minutes later she rejoined the group, started to collect the cups and saucers on to a tray and said, 'Move yourselves, the beach is calling.' The matter was forgotten and everyone enjoyed another lovely day.

Except Charlie. It had turned eleven o'clock when they put the cards and the cribbage board away and everyone said a tired but happy good-night.

Lizzie reached over to put the light out when Charlie caught hold of her arm. 'Lizzie, how much does Uncle John charge for bed and breakfast?' he asked.

'Whatever are you on about?' Lizzie stifled a yawn. 'If you're worried about what he's gonna charge us, don't be. Mum has worked for next ter nothing. We won't have to pay him much.'

'No, it's not that. Listen, Lizzie, please. How much do you reckon he charges, have a guess?'

'Well,' Lizzie considered, 'twelve and six a night, maybe fifteen shillings.'

'Yeah, that's about what I thought. So even at twelve and sixpence, eight people for two nights comes to ten pounds.'

'Oh, I get it,' Lizzie cried, 'you're on about those people Uncle John turned away this morning, aren't you?'

'Well, yes I am,' he said thoughtfully. 'I push a bus around the streets of London for six days and all I get is five pounds eight shillings. Don't make sense, does it?'

'Oh forget it and let's get some sleep, Charlie,' she pleaded. 'It's our last day here tomorrow and we want to make the most of it.'

They did go to sleep, but Charlie didn't forget the matter at all.

Chapter Fourteen

BACK HOME IN London, Charlie promptly bought a copy of Daltons Weekly and eagerly scanned the pages which had hotels and guesthouses for sale. He wrote in answer to a few of the advertisements and received prompt replies.

Lizzie listened as Charlie read out the details, showing an interest she did not feel, never dreaming anything definite would come of this pipe-dream.

Two weeks later, a second letter arrived from the proprietor of a guesthouse at Woolacombe Bay in North Devon.

'As you have shown interest in my property, perhaps you would care to view, stay a couple of days,' the letter said. Enclosed were two return railway tickets to Ilfracombe.

'Well, he's keen,' Lizzie cried, as she and Charlie re-read the letter. 'You're not going, are you?'

'Why not?' Charlie asked. 'It's not going to cost us anything and I have got Tuesday and Wednesday rest days next week.'

During lunch, Charlie was very quiet and as Lizzie made a start on the washing-up he called out, 'I won't be long, I'm going to the phonebox.'

As he came back into the kitchen, grinning from

ear to ear, Charlie declared, 'All settled. That Frank Fleming seems a decent bloke.'

Lizzie had to smile; despite her misgivings she could see that Charlie already had a vision of himself as an hotelier.

Oh, what the hell, going to view a place didn't commit them to anything and it would keep Charlie happy. Woolacombe Bay, near Ilfracombe, she muttered to herself as she searched for the previous letter, which contained a brochure. She had never heard of either place.

At six o'clock on Tuesday morning, a taxi came to take them to Paddington. Robert had been left with Doris and Syd. A lot of persuasion had been needed to get Lizzie to agree to leave the baby behind, but in the end she saw the sense of it and it was only for two days.

For the first part of the journey, Lizzie slept and when she woke up the countryside had changed considerably. Through the carriage windows, she watched as the train rattled through tiny villages which had low-built farm houses, tall barns and green fields. Trees and hedges were decked out in all the glorious colours of autumn. She felt much more optimistic.

The train finally came to a halt. There were no tracks left. 'The back of beyond,' Lizzie said to herself, and all her doubts returned. It was raining, fine rain – half-rain and half-mist. Frank Fleming had no difficulty in identifying them for they were the only passengers to come through the barrier. Having shaken hands, he helped Lizzie into the back seat of his car while Charlie took the front seat beside him.

The journey to the hotel took about thirty minutes, during which time Lizzie clutched the seat as the car negotiated hills so steep that she wondered just what kind of a place they had come to. Mrs Fleming waited in the doorway to greet them, but as they climbed the front steps, the wind blew with gale force and the fine rain whipped their faces.

It was not a good beginning.

A hot meal was ready for them in the dining-room and as they ate Lizzie studied their hosts. Mr Fleming was not at all as she had imagined him. He was a good-looking gentleman in every sense. Nicely tanned, with a well-cut suit, a full head of bushy hair, dark but streaked with grey gave him a distinguished look, which was emphasized by thick horn-rimmed glasses. An egg-head type, Lizzie decided, not knowing herself exactly what she meant by that.

Lizzie settled in her mind that Mrs Fleming was about forty years old, tall and elegant. Wavy brown hair framed her oval face and when she smiled her mouth revealed lovely white teeth. Her manner was friendly enough.

They finished eating and went into the adjacent lounge. Mrs Fleming brought coffee for each of them, but made her excuses, saying she had to attend a meeting. Mr Fleming suggested that he and Charlie got down to brass tacks. 'Got a lot to accomplish in this short time,' he said.

Lizzie almost retorted, 'Don't mind me, I'm only here to make the numbers up,' as they began their tour of the guesthouse. There were two rooms they had not seen on the ground floor: one was a double bedroom and the other was the kitchen, which was spacious, clean and with more equipment than Lizzie had imagined.

The basement, a small, cosy sitting-room and just one bedroom, formed the Flemings' private quarters. There were three more floors above ground level, each having large landings and long corridors, four bedrooms and one bathroom on each floor.

All were nicely furnished.

Back downstairs, seated in deep armchairs, drinks were served and a fellow guesthouse owner from nearby joined the group. 'Bill Rush,' Mr Fleming said with a wave of his hand, 'meet Mr and Mrs Wilson.'

Bill Rush was a jovial, outgoing man with a big beer-belly and it was soon obvious, at least to Lizzie, that he was not impartial at this meeting.

Lizzie moved her seat backwards, letting the three men group themselves in a semi-circle. She had decided to be a listener to their conversation rather than a participant. Both Frank Fleming and Bill Rush extolled the virtues of the hotel trade. Besides the high profit on capital outlay, one enjoyed a marvellous way of life. According to them.

Mr Fleming was waging a battle he was determined to win, as he worked on Charlie and ignored Lizzie. He trotted out smooth, plausible reasons why Charlie should lose no time in going ahead with the purchase of this guesthouse.

'Do you mind if I go to bed,' Lizzie interrupted, 'it has been a long day.'

Much later, Lizzie feigned sleep as Charlie crept into the bedroom. She wanted no more discussion tonight. The mood she was in she might say something that she would be sorry for.

After breakfast next morning, they went for a walk. Just Lizzie and Charlie on their own. The beach was breathtakingly beautiful. Sheer golden sand stretched as far as the eye could see, banked by green cliffs and dunes. Hardly a word was spoken as they walked at the sea's edge, each deep in their own thoughts.

Mr and Mrs Fleming were ready to take them into Ilfracombe by the time they got back to the house. 'I've telephoned my bank manager. He will be more than pleased to see you,' Frank Fleming spoke directly to Charlie.

'Bank manager!' Lizzie hissed at Charlie as they went out to the car.

'Leave it out, will you, Lizzie?' he whispered aggressively. 'It's better to sort things out while we're on the spot.'

'What bloody things?' she demanded to know, her temper rising.

There was no time for Charlie to answer; Mr Fleming was holding open the door of the car for her. Perhaps it was just as well; Lizzie was getting a bit tired of being given the cold shoulder and was rapidly reaching the point where she would explode and a blazing row would be inevitable.

Charlie and Frank Fleming went off together; it had been half-heartedly suggested that Lizzie accompany them but she had refused. Mrs Fleming had business of her own to attend to, so Lizzie walked down Market Street to the seafront.

Horrible, was her first impression. Bleak, rugged and desolate. She had never encountered such a place before. Steep, steep hills, huge granite rocks at the base with the angry sea swirling and crashing over them, sending showers of spray high into the air.

'Oh, all I want is to go home,' she mumbled to herself. She missed Polly and Doris, but most of all she felt lost without her baby. This place felt lonely, not a soul was about. No, definitely not for me, she determined; I need folk around me. Give me good old London any time.

They were well on the way home when Charlie came over to where Lizzie was stretched out on the seat.

They had the carriage to themselves, just as they had on the journey down. He lifted her legs and sat down, letting her legs lie across his knees. 'Never seen you so angry, Lizzie, want to talk about it?' he asked.

'What's the point?' she argued. 'They've hooked you good and proper.'

'Oh, don't talk rubbish,' Charlie cried – but that was like a red rag to a bull.

'It's you that's been listening to all that rubbish. Rubbing his hands is Mr Fleming; thinks he's got a right bleedin' daft one in you.'

Charlie's hand flew up, but he stopped short. God, he thought, I almost whacked her one. He sighed deeply and went back and sat across from Lizzie.

'You don't believe it's a good business proposition, then?' he asked quietly. She didn't answer. 'Come on, Lizzie,' he urged, 'get it off yer chest; why are you so dead against the idea?'

Lizzie felt too upset to talk sensibly.

'They're taking you for a ride. I never heard no mention of any work. Do their guests take care of themselves? Who does the cleaning? Who makes the beds? Who prepares and cooks the meals? And, where do yer get the shopping from? I never saw no bloody shops.'

Charlie couldn't help it, he had to laugh.

'And no bloody market either,' Lizzie added for good measure, as she herself began to laugh.

The weeks raced towards Christmas, and although Lizzie was fully aware that Charlie was still negotiating with Frank Fleming she chose to ignore the fact.

An uneasy truce existed between her and Charlie. The parents all stayed down in Newquay but everyone crowded into a telephone box to talk to them on Christmas morning. Doris and Syd hosted the festivities at home and, with the children and an added baby, nothing was left to chance. Chocolate figures adorned the tree and dozens of gaily wrapped presents lay on the floor around its base.

Charlie did make one attempt to bring North Devon and the hotel trade into the conversation, but it was Doris who tactfully and quietly changed the subject. Lizzie had long since come to the conclusion that her sister-in-law was a rare person indeed.

With the coming of January, the pressure from Mr Fleming increased and Lizzie and Charlie rowed openly now. One very bitter argument ended by Charlie shouting, 'Do as yer like, I don't care, but I'm going to Woolacombe if I have to walk there.'

'Well, walk there then, damn you,' muttered Lizzie, but either Charlie never heard or he was past caring what she thought.

Every problem that arose, Frank Fleming found a way around it.

'He's got us an eighty per cent mortgage,' Charlie announced one morning as he read yet another letter. 'And we don't have to worry about the twenty per cent. He's willing to wait for that till we sell this house.'

'I bet he is,' Lizzie said over her shoulder as she left the room.

Lizzie thought she had heard it all until one day when Charlie came home jubilant.

'I've signed the contracts,' he cried. 'Completion day is 15th of February.'

Lizzie felt her heart miss a beat. Until this very moment she had never truly believed that Charlie would do this to her. Not go this far without really sitting down and discussing it with her.

Charlie watched as the tears filled Lizzie's eyes and ran unheeded down her cheeks, and the sight of her affected him so much that he almost cried himself.

'Please, Lizzie,' he began, 'it will be a wonderful life, truly it will. Think about our Robert, growing up down there by the sea, he'll be so healthy.'

'And London would kill him?' Lizzie asked sarcastically.

As usual it was Doris with her gentle, placid ways who became the arbitrator. 'You don't have much choice, do you?' she wisely pointed out to Lizzie. 'Not if you love Charlie and I know that you do. The only alternative is for you to stay here and then, as sure as eggs are eggs, you two will end up getting a divorce. Why don't you give it a try?' she beseeched Lizzie.

To Charlie she spoke outright. 'You've gotten away with murder, you have, Charlie Wilson! Just you remember this was all your idea and watch out for our Lizzie.'

Charlie at least had the good grace to look crestfallen and to keep his mouth shut.

An air of despondency settled over the house as it became obvious that Charlie was to have his way. Everyone made their own arrangements. Hilda and

Wally decided to leave London; a new bus garage was to be opened at Stevenage in Hertfordshire, and to every crew that volunteered, a brand new council house was on offer.

Joe Frost decided to marry a widow lady he had been seeing for the past ten years, and Paddy Betts was going home to his wife Oaife and his two children – he had found out that the streets of London were not paved with gold.

Moving day! Charlie had left with the removal van early in the morning and now it was time for Lizzie to depart. She had deliberately made herself look smart. She dressed in a well-cut suit and a pale blue blouse, her camel swagger coat on top, and her hair was tucked up in a cloche hat that would keep her ears warm.

It was a bright sunny morning and Doris told her that was a good omen. Doris got into the taxi that would take them to the station, while Lizzie gave Polly a final hug.

On the railway platform, the two girls clung to each other, oblivious to the hustle and bustle all around them, the shunting, hissing, steaming trains, the clanging of the wheel-tappers' hammers, the pigeons in their hundreds flying high up into the great glass roof. Taxis, porters, trolleys piled high with mailbags, people of all nationalities, the over-riding smell of soot, dirt and grime – this was the dear old City of London that Lizzie was leaving behind.

Reluctantly, Lizzie took her seat in the carriage, unhooked the lead from the dog and placed it in the bag that held napkins, baby food and sandwiches. Doris kissed the baby one last time and hesitantly held him out for Lizzie to take, then she stretched out her arm and patted Bob-Bob who lay on the floor between the two bench-seats.

'Bye, Bob-Bob,' she whispered and, as if in answer, he twitched his nose and gazed up at her with his soulful brown eyes.

'Stand back, mam,' a porter ordered as he slammed the door of the carriage. To Lizzie the sound had a ring of finality about it.

Hardly out of London, the sunshine disappeared and the weather turned horrible. High winds and sleet. Passing through the countryside, the sleet changed to snow, pure and white, the flakes splashing against the window panes of the fast-moving train. The scene was pretty; hills and fields lay as if beneath a huge white blanket.

Lizzie fed the baby and cuddled him tightly.

There was no one to meet her this time. Lizzie struggled to get everything out of the carriage and on to the platform. The solitary ticket collector offered to fetch the baby's pram from the guard's van. Suddenly a taxi driver appeared and took charge.

At least Charlie had remembered to send a taxi. The removal men had unloaded and gone and Charlie had been busy. The house was warm and the lounge and dining-room were set out, though Lizzie thought that their few bits and pieces looked ridiculous in such large rooms. The basement flat was cosy. The bedroom looked nice and Charlie had even made up the bed and placed Robert's cot close. The sitting-room had rugs on the floor, two armchairs, Gran's carved dresser and their wireless set.

'Welcome home,' Charlie said as he kissed Lizzie.

She didn't answer. A lot of water would flow under the bridge before she regarded this place as home.

They ate a good meal in the basement and Lizzie suggested that, before they settled down for the evening, they should have a walk around upstairs. Charlie seemed reluctant, but Lizzie went ahead.

She felt like screaming, but what good would that do, she asked herself as she slammed yet another bedroom door and ungraciously pushed past Charlie and went back downstairs.

Twelve rooms upstairs, and not a curtain at the windows, not a carpet on the floors and not a stick of furniture to be seen anywhere!

Passing the green baize-covered noticeboard in the hall, Lizzie tore down a handwritten account. Headed Mr and Mrs Wilson, it read: Items not paid for. Stair carpet £75.00, stair rods £10.00, television aerial £10.00, £95.00 to pay.

Now, she did scream.

'We haven't even got a bloody television,' she yelled.

There was worse to come! The kitchen had been

stripped. Only the gas cooker remained. Refrigerator, free-standing cupboards, kitchen utensils, even the china, all had gone!

'Calm down, please, Lizzie,' Charlie implored, as he pushed her down into an armchair and got down on his knees. He held her hands tightly as he explained, 'Frank Fleming is taking me to Bideford tomorrow morning where I will be able to order every single item needed to stock out this guesthouse. He has promised me that no deposit will be necessary. It's the way they do things down here. Everyone makes the total payment at the end of the season.'

Lizzie only gazed silently at him. What she felt at that moment for Charlie was utter contempt. What had he done? That he had been conned was as plain as the nose on his face, but what were they going to do about it? She just did not know.

'Let's go to bed,' she said quietly, and Charlie sighed with relief.

Mr Fleming kept his word and took Charlie to Bideford. Lizzie kept out of his way.

That evening she and Charlie together looked through the order forms. Lizzie gasped as she entered each item into an exercise book. Twelve bedroom suites, ten double beds, six single beds, blankets, sheets, pillows and pillowcases, bedspreads, towels, tablecloths and serviettes.

The total cost appalled her; they were getting deeper and deeper into debt.

She couldn't resist saying to Charlie, 'Let's hope we live long enough to pay it all off.'

Another thought struck her. 'What about chairs and tables for the dining-room?' she cried. 'And utensils for the kitchen, not to mention a bloody fridge!'

'Don't start again,' Charlie begged her. 'Frank said you can get most of those things at the auction sales.'

'Oh, it's Frank now, is it?' she said cynically. 'Well, you go with him and see how you get on.'

'I can't; I'm going home tomorrow.'

'Oh, you bastard,' she screamed, full of frustration, and tears welling in her eyes.

'We agreed, Lizzie,' he appealed, 'I'd stay on the buses at least until Easter. We need the money to live on.'

'Need the money, do we?' she said sarcastically. 'You're a bit late in the day to give that a thought, Charlie Wilson, and what's with this going home bit? You said welcome home when I got here – thought this was home now.'

'Oh, you know what I mean, Lizzie.'

She cut him short. 'Oh yes, I know what you mean only too well, Charlie. You go home, live with my brother and Doris, go to work, play your bloody darts and there's me stuck down here with the baby, no friends, no family, no money and no bleedin' furniture. Well, you want to tread carefully, Mr Bigshot, I might just decide to come home as well!'

Lizzie cried herself to sleep that night but she didn't resist when Charlie drew her into his arms and held her close.

'You needn't come to the station to see me off,' said Charlie. 'It only means more expense, bringing you back again.'

What you're afraid of, Charlie, me darling, Lizzie thought to herself, is that I might just get on the train with you. The taxi moved off and Lizzie closed the heavy front door. She paused a moment; the silence was deafening. She really was all on her own now, just her, the baby and the dog. No Doris and Polly just across the road. No Hilda upstairs. No trips to Tooting Market and a cuppa in the cafe. No dark-haired Lucy demanding a story, no chubby Raymond to throw his little arms around her neck. Slowly, she went to the basement and sat down. She was aware that her head ached and her throat felt so tight she could hardly breathe.

She buried her face in her hands and she began to cry as though her heart would break.

She hadn't felt so lonely before, not in the whole of her life.

Chapter Fifteen

THE BED WAS too large, the reading lamp too low, Lizzie missed Charlie and she hardly slept at all that first week.

The quiet, endless, lonely days stretched into even longer lonely nights.

'What in God's name am I doing here?' Lizzie asked herself a dozen times each day.

The weather did nothing to lift her spirits. It was raining really heavily; torrents of water slashing against the windows. She watched from the lounge windows, the sea showing signs of great turbulence, the high winds droning and whining, not a living soul in sight.

The front garden, which only the previous day had been so pretty, all the shrubs coated with fine snow, was now bare, flattened by the force of the gale.

She shuddered with dismay. There would be no going out today, not even for a walk. Bob-Bob would have to make do with the back garden.

Before leaving London, Lizzie had used the reference section of the local library, searching out which areas of the country had their wake weeks at different periods during the summer. She had placed small advertisements in local papers in such places as Manchester, Blackburn, Bolton, Liverpool, Derby and Birmingham, offering room and full-board for six guineas each person per week with big reductions for children.

One morning, she heard the letterbox click and was up the basement steps in a flash. Loads of letters were lying spread out on the mat.

Without waiting to get dressed, she read each one. For the first time in days her spirits lifted. She couldn't wait to get pen and paper and start to answer these enquiries.

'Dear Mr and Mrs Brown, with pleasure we can offer you a really nice room which looks out over the sea.' That was how she began each letter.

The trouble was, she had to run up and down the stairs, often with the baby in her arms, and always with Bob-Bob at her heels, trying to familiarize herself with the locality and number of each room and visualize whether just a double bed or maybe a double and a single bed for a child would fit into a particular room.

Not easy when every room was bare.

Lizzie was delighted as the deposits started to roll in, and she made a wallchart setting out the weeks from Saturday to Saturday, from Easter until October. As she filled in the definite bookings, it became apparent that she was only fully booked for the four peak weeks. Nothing at all for Easter and very little for May, June or September.

One morning, the post was all answered and Lizzie decided to give herself a break. It was a dry day, cold but bright. With the baby in the pram and the dog bounding along ahead, she took the winding path upwards away from the beach, climbing steadily.

Pushing the pram was no mean feat and Lizzie was thankful that she had worn flat-heeled shoes.

Finally, she reached the top of the cliffs. The view out over the Bristol Channel was glorious. She found a sheltered spot and sat down. Apart from the postman and the lady in the general stores, which served as the post office as well, Lizzie hadn't spoken to a living soul all week.

Not likely to find anyone to natter to up here, she told herself as she listened to the cry of the seagulls and the gentle noise from the sea far below.

It was much later when she set off in the direction of home, reaching the house just in time. As she put her key into the lock of the front door, there was a loud clap of thunder, the light seemed to fade, and an eerie greyness settled over everything, obliterating the cliffs.

'Good job we went out early,' she said to the baby, and to Bob-Bob. 'Do you think we're going to have a storm?' Neither one of them answered her.

At times, the only links she now had with reality were the Saturday night phone calls she received from Charlie. As she listened to him and longed to see him, she wondered why he was working in

London. Coin after coin she would hear drop into the telephone box as he prolonged those precious moments.

The new furniture arrived. Now Lizzie had plenty of jobs to do which would use up her pent-up energy.

She dusted furniture, unpacked bed linen and made up beds. She was a frequent visitor to auction sale rooms, and became quite good at catching the eye of the auctioneer, and soon crockery, cutlery, tables and chairs had all been purchased. Curtains remained a problem. Measurements had been sent to Doris, who purchased material as cheaply as possible from the markets. Charlie gave her the money, but his wages were being stretched to breaking point. He still had the mortgage on number twelve to pay and some weeks he had nothing left to send to Lizzie.

The stream of deposits was now drying up; the main four peak weeks being fully booked.

The day came when Lizzie had no money in the house. There was enough food in the cupboard to keep her going, but she had to have milk for young Robert.

With the baby in the pram, she walked to the clinic. After much hesitation, she swallowed her pride and entered.

The rosy cheeked, plumpish woman seemed nice enough.

'Please,' Lizzie began, 'would you allow me to

have a tin of dried milk and pay you next time I'm passing?'

'Of course we will, mi dear,' the kindly soul said cheerfully as she reached for the large tin. 'Is there anything else you'm be wanting?'

'No, thank you,' Lizzie said gratefully. The cost of the tin was one and tenpence-hapenny and Lizzie was almost in tears as she walked back to the guest-house. 'Jesus only knows how I came to be in this state,' she said to herself. 'One minute I had a big house, rents coming in regularly from three lots of tenants, and Charlie in a good job. Now I ain't even got two bob to me name. Fancy! Having to ask for milk on tick before I could make the baby his bottle!'

Aunt Daisy's old sewing machine came into its own. Evening after evening, when Robert was asleep, Lizzie slaved away on it until she had curtains, of a sort, ready for every room.

Saturday night came again and the telephone rang. 'Hallo, Charlie,' Lizzie said brightly after she picked up the receiver.

'That's where you're wrong, my love, it's me, not Charlie.' Nellie's voice was loud and clear, and Lizzie was so excited.

'Mum, how are you? Oh, it's so lovely to hear your voice. How's Aunt Kate and Uncle John? I'm sorry I haven't got round to answering your letters. Without your letters and those from Doris and Polly I think I would go off my rocker stuck down here.'

'Lizzie, Lizzie, stop it,' Nellie called down the

line, when at last Lizzie had paused to take a breath. 'We're all fine, stop worrying. How is baby Robert?'

'He's been a bit rough all day, wheezy-like, got a croaky cough an' all. What d'yer reckon, Mum, should I call a doctor in?'

'Without delay,' Nellie said and went on, 'I really rang to say I was coming to see you. Could you put up with me for a coupla weeks?'

'Oh, Mum, do you mean it? Really? When?'

'There you go again; like a bull in a china shop you are. It won't be for about ten days, when I've booked my ticket. I'll let you know. I'll be coming by coach.'

'All right, Mum. Make it soon as you can. I love you.'

'I love you too, Lizzie. Watch out fer the baby. Get the doctor to him. Night love. God bless you.' Nellie hung up and Lizzie replaced the receiver and hugged herself.

She hadn't seen her mum since last September and now she was coming to stay.

Lizzie spent the night tramping back and forth across the bedroom floor. Each time she looked into the cot the baby seemed worse, she had tried nursing him but he was so fretful. At last it was daylight and she telephoned the doctor.

'You must be very careful with him, Mrs Wilson,' the young doctor said when he arrived. 'Keep him in one room, constantly warm, no draughts and as much liquid as you can get him to take.'

'Is he going to die?' Lizzie asked with fear apparent in her voice.

'Oh, come now, Mrs Wilson,' the doctor protested. 'Your baby has bronchitis and he does need careful watching, but there is no need for such a pessimistic attitude.' Lizzie shuddered, and the doctor felt remorse. 'You look as if you could do with a rest, Mrs Wilson, have you anyone who will stay with the baby a while?'

'No, no one,' she answered sadly.

'Well, I'll get the prescription for you and you'll see, in a few days' time your baby will be well on the road to recovery.'

Charlie telephoned each night and Lizzie's first reaction was resentment. If she hadn't been stuck down here miles from everyone she knew and loved, in an unfurnished house, Robert never would have caught a cold in the first place.

The days were long and the nights even worse.

She listened to the wireless just to hear somebody's voice and on this particular morning she wasn't paying much attention to what the announcer was saying until the words 'Festival of Britain' made her sit up sharply.

Of course! It was 1951. Immediately all her longing for London returned. How many times had she been the conductor on a number 49 bus travelling from Shepherd's Bush to Crystal Palace! The bus would travel down Kensington High Street, turning right at the Albert Hall and into Gloucester Road, down Onslow Place on into Sydney Street, stopping outside the dear old Chelsea Palace. That had been a real treat that had, being taken by Mum and Aunt Daisy to see music hall at the Palace. On down Oakley Street and into Cheyne Walk. That was the lovely bit, a view of the Thames and, to the left, Albert Bridge. From here the bus turned right and continued on over Battersea Bridge . . . Battersea . . . Battersea Park – that's where it would all happen. For months and months plans had been under way in London ready for this Festival of Britain, and the main base of operations was to be on the South Bank of the Thames, overflowing into Battersea Park.

'Christ!' Lizzie muttered out loud. 'I've leant out from the back of the bus many a time and watched that entrance on the far side of Albert Bridge go up.'

She listened to the voice of the announcer forecasting how many visitors from all over the world were expected to visit Battersea when the Festival was opened by the King and Queen. Londoners in their thousands were certain to flock to the fairgrounds and exhibitions. 'Well here's one Londoner that won't be able to go,' said Lizzie who was now feeling very sorry for herself. It was bad enough being stuck down here in the back of beyond with a sick baby without having to be reminded of all that was going on back home in London.

She got up from her chair and went downstairs to her basement bedroom and tiptoed in to look at Robert. He was sleeping now, although his little

face showed that he was still burning up. Quietly,
she went back up the stairs and into the kitchen.

It wasn't fair, her being here. No family, friends,
or even neighbours. The silence and the loneliness
was driving her mad. What if Robert should get
worse? What if he died? She couldn't wrap him in a
blanket here and run with him through the park to
The Nelson Hospital. She didn't even know where
the nearest hospital was. There were buses, she
knew that. About three a day. Maybe more on a
Friday going to Barnstaple on market day. Market
day! I miss the market every bloody day, she
thought.

Here she didn't have a soul to say good morning
to. For the umpteenth time she asked herself, 'How
did I let it happen?'

It was Charlie who had thought himself the clever
one but look who had ended up being conned rotten;
it was her who has been turfed out of house and
home to cope with this so-called gold-mine, with
him still living in Wilton Road with her friends and
family to see that he wants for nothing. If she stayed
here much longer she'd forget what the sound of
her own voice was like, never mind about other
people's. 'I'll tell yer this, Charlie Wilson,' she said,
'if our marriage survives this, it'll be a bloody
miracle. The way I feel right now I don't know
whether to hit the bottle or cut me throat.'

On the third day, she bathed Robert for the second
time that day, not immersing him in the water,

merely sponging his hot little body and changing his damp night clothes. The doorbell rang just as she was laying the baby back down into his cot.

The doctor had shown compassion, calling in to see Robert each day, but he had already called at nine o'clock that morning and she wondered who her caller could be as she came up into the front hall.

She opened the door and then flung it wide as she stared in amazement. Doris and young Raymond were standing on the doorstep.

'I don't believe it!' Lizzie cried as she swept Raymond up into her arms and nuzzled her face into his hair. Doris flung her arms around Lizzie and they clung together for a long time.

Eventually Doris asked, 'May we come in?'

Lizzie laughed. 'Oh, sorry, come on in.'

'Well, I should hope so after all the miles we've travelled,' Doris said. 'And where is that nephew of mine?' Then, much more sombrely, she asked, 'Is he any better, Lizzie?'

Lizzie still couldn't take it in. She busied herself putting the kettle on, talking all the while, assuring Doris that she felt sure that the critical stage had passed.

'He's not nearly so fretful now. He's sleeping better, but his chest is still tight and that horrible cough seems to rack his little body.'

Lizzie couldn't put her finger on it but something was wrong. Doris seemed drained of energy. Surely the train journey couldn't have been that tiring. No, there was something else, Lizzie was sure of it. She settled Raymond with milk and chocolate biscuits and brought tea for Doris and herself to the table.

'Now,' she said, 'let's have it, Doris. Whatever it is that is wrong with you, you're gonna have to tell me.'

'I know,' Doris said, and she looked so sad that Lizzie felt her heart miss a beat as intuition warned her of trouble.

'Well?' Lizzie whispered.

'It's your mum, Lizzie. She died on Tuesday.'

For a long moment neither of them spoke, then Lizzie stood up and moved to the window.

'Tell me it isn't true,' she pleaded, but she expected no answer and Doris gave none.

'Peacefully. There was no warning. She had a heart attack.'

'I only spoke to her on Saturday. She said she was coming here to stay with me.' Her voice broke suddenly as tears spilled down her face, while Doris watched helplessly.

The funeral was to be in Newquay on the following Monday. Lizzie couldn't take the baby and she wouldn't go without him.

'That's why I'm here, love,' Doris said. 'No one expects you to go. Syd and Charlie are going with Polly and Arthur.'

'Oh,' was all Lizzie managed as an answer.

At two o'clock on Monday, when Nellie Collins was being buried in Newquay, Lizzie sat alone in a church in North Devon. She wasn't at all sure what she was doing there; she couldn't even bring herself to pray.

She did, however, talk to her mother.

'Sorry, Mum, that I am not there. You wouldn't want me to leave Robert would you? I love you, Mum, love you, love you,' she repeated over and over again.

Syd and Charlie arrived late on Monday night. It was not such a happy reunion as it should have been.

The two men did several jobs, such as stretching and laying carpet that Lizzie had acquired as a job lot.

Alone one morning, Syd told Lizzie all the details of the funeral. 'Aunt Kate and Uncle John were really upset,' he told her. 'It was such a shock. Polly and Arthur are staying on with them for a while. They're thinking of selling the hotel and moving back to London.'

'Wish some bugger would buy this place,' Lizzie muttered beneath her breath as Charlie came into the kitchen.

Saturday afternoon, and Lizzie stood forlornly watching the taxi disappear into the distance. They had all gone again, on their way home to London. 'Par for the course,' she said to the dog as she made a bottle for the baby.

Chapter Sixteen

SLEEP EVADED LIZZIE again that night, but rising next morning, looking and feeling like hell, she came to a decision. She was going to pull herself together. Charlie hadn't really forced her to come here. True, he had made it very difficult for her to say no, but all that was in the past and she could hardly back out now.

'So, stop wallowing in self-pity,' she said firmly to herself. 'Who knows, Charlie might just be on to a winner with this place.' If only she could be certain of that, she thought as she came up the stairs and opened the kitchen door.

Bob-Bob came leaping across the room to say good morning, licking her hand with his long pink tongue, his tail wagging furiously. Lizzie was all smiles as she patted him.

'You don't mind living in Devon, do you?' she laughingly asked as she unlocked the back door to let him out. She watched as he bounded off up the garden. 'He's happy enough,' she said aloud, and the thought crossed her mind that perhaps, if she stopped yearning for London, accepted the situation, maybe even started to count her blessings, then life for her would begin to look a lot rosier too.

'Right,' Lizzie decided, having bathed and fed the

baby, 'we'll put you in your pram and push it out into the garden this morning.'

She was wearing slacks, with a pale blue round-necked jumper, but as she looked in the mirror, she wrinkled her nose in disgust. Her hair was a mess. So, she spent a good ten minutes brushing it hard and then she tied it back from her face with a piece of black velvet ribbon. 'Now, how about some make-up?' Her expression was thoughtful as she did her eyes and eyebrows. For too long she had let herself go and she had to admit that she already felt much better for having made the effort. 'Definitely better,' she muttered after having applied lipstick.

Perched halfway up a pair of steps, Lizzie was happily humming to herself as she endeavoured to hang curtains at the lounge windows. She heard a sudden slight movement out in the hall and she almost toppled over, as Frank Fleming appeared in the doorway.

'Good morning, Mrs Wilson,' he said cheerfully as he removed his trilby hat.

'Good morning,' Lizzie replied, not feeling in the least bit pleased to see him. How dare he walk straight into the house without knocking! He must have come down the lane and in through the open back door. Daft old Bob-Bob hadn't even barked.

He came straight to the point. Looking up at Lizzie, for she hadn't bothered to step down, he asked, 'Has the sale of your London house been finalized?'

'Not that I've heard,' Lizzie said.

'Well,' Mr Fleming continued, 'there is the little matter of nine hundred pounds owing to me. Eight hundred to complete the sale of the house and one hundred for goods I left behind.'

Lizzie surveyed him in stony silence.

Mr Fleming's eyes narrowed. 'Time is going on, and I would like the matter settled. Your husband indicated to me that there would be no problem with him finding a purchaser. I, too, have commitments on the hotel that I am buying.'

Not wanting to lose her temper, Lizzie only said, 'I know that.'

'Well,' just the one word Mr Fleming uttered, but his voice had suddenly become much harder.

Lizzie's face went pale and she drew in her breath as she slowly came down the steps.

Now she was at a disadvantage for Mr Fleming was a good deal taller than her. Her temper was rising, but she held it in check as she said, 'You urged my husband to buy this property, you got him a mortgage, you said you'd wait for the balance. I don't recall any time being set for him to pay you the rest of the money.'

Mr Fleming's eyes blazed, 'Dammit, I did everything I could to help your husband. I understand the position you're in, but I have liabilities too. I need that money; I can't afford to wait for it.'

'Bit late now, isn't it? You should have thought about that when you were pushing my Charlie,' she fired back and watched the expression on his face turn to real anger.

Abruptly, Mr Fleming turned to go, then stopped dead in his tracks. 'One week today I'll be back, and let's hope we can sort things out more satisfactorily then than we have today.'

'I'll be here,' Lizzie said stubbornly.

Strangely, Lizzie didn't feel a bit nervous as she watched him storm off down the garden. At least she had stood her ground with Mr Bloody Fleming; she hadn't let him walk all over her.

After dinner that night, Lizzie didn't put Robert down in his cot; she sat nursing him. Bob-Bob settled himself in his usual place at her feet, his head raised to lie against her shins.

She was considering her options.

Suddenly she sat up very straight and Bob-Bob looked at her reproachfully with his doleful eyes, cross at having been disturbed.

Bank managers! That was what they were for, to give advice. She had opened an account at Barclays when the deposits had started to come in and had been given a cheque book. Well, now she was going to make an appointment to see the manager.

Next morning, Lizzie telephoned as soon as the bank was open. At two p.m. sharp she presented herself, together with the baby in the pram.

Graham Blackhurst, attired exactly as she had imagined in a charcoal grey suit, white shirt and striped tie, stood smiling in the doorway of his office.

Lizzie hesitated, her nervousness obvious.

'It's all right, Mrs Wilson, please bring the pram in with you,' he said reassuringly. Seated opposite him, Lizzie unbuttoned the jacket of her navy blue suit and decided that Mr Blackhurst was no more than forty years old, despite the fact that his fair hair was receding.

'Now, Mrs Wilson, how can I be of help to you?' he asked, and his voice was not only soft, but kind as well.

In a barely audible whisper, Lizzie said, 'I would like the bank to lend me nine hundred pounds.'

If Mr Blackhurst had burst out laughing, Lizzie would not have been at all surprised; her request spoken out loud sounded comical even to her. But he didn't laugh, he leant towards her and courteously said, 'Why don't you tell me what you need the money for.'

Lizzie sighed, wondering if she really did have to tell this stranger all the ins and outs as to how she came to be in such dire need.

'Take your time, Mrs Wilson,' he encouraged her.

Slowly, to begin with, Lizzie told the bank manager that she needed the money in order to pay Mr Fleming. Then her hesitation gave way to resolution. No longer were her words faltering; she held nothing back. It was as if she needed to talk. She had bottled things up inside her for so long, only able to speak out loud to herself or to the dog. Now she had the opportunity to unburden herself to another human being, someone who was a good, attentive listener.

She suddenly realized that she had been talking non-stop for a very long time. Not once had Mr Blackhurst interrupted her. Almost in mid-sentence, Lizzie paused and raised her head to meet the eyes of this quiet gentleman. The eyes she now looked into were an unusual shade of grey and Lizzie felt that they were smiling at her.

Very gently, Mr Blackhurst put a question to her, 'Do you have any collateral?'

Lizzie didn't even know the meaning of the word. He sensed her discomfort.

'Additional security?' Still Lizzie made no reply. 'Shares, jewellery or property? Anything of that nature, Mrs Wilson. I am not being inquisitive, I do need to know.'

Lizzie twisted her hands in her lap and bit her tongue, saying angrily beneath her breath, 'If I had all those things, I wouldn't be here asking you for money.'

'Sorry, Mrs Wilson, I didn't hear you.'

'No, nothing,' Lizzie said indignantly. Then, as an afterthought, she added, 'Only my London house.'

Graham Blackhurst straightened himself up in his chair. Already, he had a lot of respect for this young, slim woman who had come into his office, looking so very despondent. He had read her file, only a few pounds in a recently opened current account. It seemed that her resources were stretched to the limit and beyond. Then there was this matter of Mr Fleming. Everyone in the village knew Frank Fleming –

many to their cost. A good businessman, without a doubt, but God help anyone who crossed him.

'Tell me about your London house, Mrs Wilson, is it in both your husband's and your names?' He awaited her reply with interest.

'No, Mr Blackhurst.' Cautiously Lizzie considered the question before she continued. 'I bought number twelve and number nineteen Wilton Road in Colliers Wood during the war, or rather, I paid the deposits and got the rest of the asking price on mortgage.'

More and more, Graham Blackhurst was becoming convinced that this young lady from London had a great deal of common sense. He also suspected that, given half a chance, she could very well become a shrewd businesswoman.

'So, are both properties registered in your name?'

'Oh, no, I bought number nineteen for my brother.'

'And number twelve, is that jointly owned with your husband?' He was fully aware that he had asked this question previously but he wanted to be absolutely clear in his mind on this very important point.

'I wasn't even married then, Mr Blackhurst, my Charlie and I weren't married until the war was over.'

'I see,' he said, and his grey eyes twinkled at her. 'And you've never altered the registration?'

Lizzie was baffled again. Why the hell did he keep on and on about Wilton Road. 'I did have to go to

Somerset House once,' she shot at him. His hopes dropped drastically.

'Do you remember why?'

'Yes, the property had to be registered under the Town and Country Planning Act.' His hopes rose again.

'Did you have any legal papers to sign?' and he emphasized the word YOU.

Lizzie's thoughts went back and, without thinking where she was and to whom she was talking, she burst out, 'Yeah, and I had to pay bloody ninety-six pounds for stamp duty.'

The tension was gone. Graham Blackhurst threw his head back and burst out laughing. Would that all his customers were so straightforward!

Lizzie felt her cheeks flame and her hand flew up to cover her mouth.

She waited a few seconds and then she apologized.

'Not at all, Mrs Wilson,' he said, still grinning broadly, 'not at all.'

The baby, whom they had both apparently forgotten, began to whimper. Lizzie looked at Mr Blackhurst. She was still upset that she had sworn, and now Robert had to start.

He put her at ease straight away, 'Please lift him out of his pram. I only need to get a few details from you and then you can be on your way.'

Lizzie rose, loosened the pram covers, and took the baby up into her arms. Rocking him gently, she soon had him pacified. She liked this bank manager, she liked him very much, but was he going to lend her nine hundred pounds? And if not, why the hell didn't he get it over and done with and say so.

'Now then, Mrs Wilson,' Mr Blackhurst was all at once very businesslike, 'I need a few details from you. Firstly, the name and address of the firm of solicitors who acted for you when you bought number twelve Wilton Road.'

For the next five minutes, he fired questions. Lizzie answered to the best of her ability and he wrote notes on to a pad which lay in front of him.

Finally, he stood up, came around the desk, held the pram still while Lizzie put the baby down again, and then held out his hand.

Lizzie solemnly shook it.

Then Mr Blackhurst did surprise her. He put his arm across her shoulders and looked into her face. 'Now, I don't want you to worry. I am going to make some enquiries on your behalf and I want you to come and see me again on Friday.' He stopped speaking and pondered for a moment. 'If the weather is bad, or for any reason you cannot make the journey, please pick up the telephone. Let me know, and I shall come out to you.'

Jesus! Lizzie thought. Wonders would never cease; she had a bank manager as a friend.

Curiosity was killing Lizzie. She was relieved when Friday came. The bus was late and Lizzie felt flustered as a young fresh-faced boy held open the door of the bank for her.

Graham Blackhurst's greeting was cordial; he

even looked into the pram and asked how the baby was.

Once seated it was down to brass tacks immediately. Professionally, but with a good deal of patience, Mr Blackhurst explained the whole matter.

'It was Mr Wilson who had signed an agreement, undertaking to pay Mr Fleming the balance of twenty per cent of the purchase price of Sea View Guesthouse on the completion of the sale of property known as number twelve Wilton Road, Colliers Wood in Surrey.' Mr Blackhurst had read aloud this information from an official document which lay in front of him.

Now, he raised his head, his eyes met Lizzie's and the smile on his face deepened as he firmly stated, 'Mr Wilson owns no such property.'

What was he saying? Lizzie was no fool, but he would have to be a lot more explicit before she could actually take it in.

'That agreement between your husband and Mr Fleming isn't worth the paper it is written on.' Slowly, Lizzie smiled and Graham Blackhurst smiled with her. She would need a helluva lot of time to clear her thoughts but just at this moment she was cock-a-hoop. She wanted to yelp with joy, grab this bank manager and dance him around his office.

She restrained herself.

It wasn't Charlie she wanted to put one over on. No, never that. It was Mr Frank Fleming.

Graham Blackhurst sat back. Watching Lizzie's face, he saw disbelief turn to glee. He could read her thoughts. He had to chuckle to himself. What he wouldn't give to be a fly on the wall when the next meeting took place between this young woman who had been uprooted from London, and Mr Oh-so-clever Fleming.

'You could go back to London, Mrs Wilson, if you wish to. No one can force you to sell your house.'

'Thank you,' was all Lizzie managed to mutter.

Chapter Seventeen

LIZZIE PUT HER key into the lock, opened the door and let the dog out. 'Come on Bob-Bob, we're going down on the beach,' she declared. The afternoon was still bright since the evenings were drawing out and there were a few people, mainly with their dogs, down on the beach.

She took the zig-zag path down through the dunes and pushed the pram into a secluded recess between the rocks. Turning the baby on to his side, she propped the feeding bottle, half-filled with orange juice, close to his pillow. Baby Robert's chubby, dimpled hands clutched at it eagerly. His eyes began to droop, he blinked a few times, and then he was asleep.

Taking the now empty bottle away, Lizzie tucked the pram covers up around him, then she took off her shoes and stockings placing them into the end of the pram.

'Right, Bob-Bob,' she called out, 'let's go for a run.' The tide was well on the way out and her feet and the dog's paws left clear imprints in the wet sand as they ran. The water was freezing and Lizzie moved swiftly. Up and down at the edge of the sea she ran, kicking water into the air, splashing Bob-

Bob who thought it was a marvellous game in which he heartily joined in.

As she walked towards home, bare footed, for she hadn't brought a towel, Lizzie felt she could easily leap for joy. She had things well and truly in perspective now. But by the time she got home, washed, changed and fed the baby, her feeling of elation had dwindled quite a bit. Whichever choice she made, she knew she would have to bear the consequences.

Did she want to go home to London? All she knew was that she missed Doris pushing open the front door, calling, 'I'm going to the corner shop, Lizzie, is there anything you want?' She missed hearing Lucy's footsteps, as she ran down the side path, coming through the back door panting, 'Auntie Lizzie, Mummy says she's just put the kettle on, are you coming over?' She missed the bus outings, the dart matches and fish 'n' chip suppers in front of Syd's television set. Right now she wished that somebody would tell her what to do.

A sudden thought struck Lizzie – had Charlie known exactly what he was doing all along? Her thoughts flew around in her head. Londoners had a saying, 'Never con a conman'.

Had Charlie done just that? It was inconceivable, or was it?

All along, Lizzie had been thinking that Charlie was a pushover, easy game for Frank Fleming's persuasive tongue. What if she had been wrong?

She tried to see it from Charlie's side. He had

badly wanted a guesthouse and along had come Mr Fleming, doing every mortal thing within his power to get Charlie's signature on the contract.

Just what had it cost Charlie in terms of actual cash. Not one penny! Not even the railway fare to view the house in the first place. Lizzie vowed she wasn't going to think along those lines any further, and she certainly wasn't going to question Charlie.

Should she take the baby and go back to London? No, she told herself, though her decision was very half-hearted.

She thought about Charlie; there had never been anyone else for her from the moment she'd set eyes on him. Just what would it do to Charlie if she packed it all in and walked away? It just didn't bear thinking about.

There was still the mortgage – over three thousand pounds – to be paid. There was the matter of all that new furniture and bedding sitting in the rooms upstairs and not a penny paid on it yet. If she was honest with herself, and she was certainly trying to be, she didn't really have any choice.

Lizzie lowered the gas beneath the boiling kettle and her expression was thoughtful as she spooned tea into the pot. 'Well, Lizzie Wilson,' she said out loud, 'like it or not, I think you're stuck with this guesthouse,' then, as if to boost her morale, she quickly added, 'at least for this season'.

Lizzie looked much the same as she had on his last

visit. She had washed her hair the previous evening and had taken pains with her make-up this morning.

Mr Fleming advanced across the kitchen, hand outstretched, his mouth widening in a broad smile. All animosity apparently forgotten.

'Well, everything sorted out?'

'To the best of my ability,' Lizzie said seriously.

'Good, good. I knew your husband wouldn't let me down.'

'What I have to say hasn't anything to do with Charlie.'

'Carry on then,' Mr Fleming's voice was deceptively quiet.

'I'm afraid you are going to have to wait for the balance of your money.'

His mouth dropped open. With grim determination Lizzie continued, ignoring the fact that if looks could kill she would be dead.

'My husband had no right to sign an agreement stating that when our London house was sold he would pay you the balance.'

Reaching out, Mr Fleming roughly took hold of her arm. Lizzie stiffened instinctively. Her first impulse was to resist forcibly, instead she winced. 'You're hurting me,' she warned. He immediately let go of her arm and stepped backwards.

Leaning forward, Lizzie spoke.

'Our London house belongs to me; to me, Mr Fleming, do you understand? Mr Wilson doesn't own any property, he doesn't have a house to sell.'

Hysteria had made her raise her voice and by the time she had finished she was shouting.

The disbelief on Frank Fleming's face halted Lizzie, but she felt no remorse. 'What the hell are you on about?' he roared.

With a voice that was still shaking, Lizzie answered, 'You understood every word that I said. Now, if you'll excuse me . . .' and she waved a hand in the direction of the back door.

He left and Lizzie heaved a sigh of exhaustion, mingled with relief. She watched him walk the length of the back garden and she couldn't resist a sneer.

Two green-horns, that's what she and Charlie were.

Fancy even considering a twelve-bedroomed guesthouse that was totally devoid of furniture and working equipment, let alone going so far as to buy it. Well, perhaps now Mr Fleming didn't think they were quite as green as he had supposed.

Chapter Eighteen

CHARLIE GAVE UP his job and came to live in Devon two weeks before Easter.

Lizzie was on the station to meet him and spotted his laughing face as he hung out of the carriage window. They hugged each other for a long while and then Charlie lifted Robert from his pram and carried him in his arms.

'Christ, I've missed you,' he told Lizzie.

'Me too,' she agreed.

The house felt more of a home now, with Charlie around.

They only had one booking over Easter, a party of six – four adults and two children, who were due to arrive on Good Friday.

Alan Gregory was tall and thin and his wife, Winnie, was short and a little on the plump side. With them were their two children – a fair-haired girl called Darryl, who was six, and Neil who was four. The two grandmothers, Grandma Gregory and Winnie's mother, Grandma Eaton, completed the party.

No sooner were they inside the house than everyone was on first-name terms. It was more like having friends to stay than having paying guests, and Lizzie liked them all straight away.

Alan had hired a car for the holiday and on Saturday evening after dinner the two grandmothers pressed them to leave the children in their care, so that the two young couples could go out together.

For Lizzie it was a real treat, dressed up and sitting in a country pub, with Charlie sitting close to her side and these new Lancashire friends for company. The weekend was grand.

The following day, Woolacombe looked magnificent in the fine spring sunshine, with its lovely view across the bay and the high green hills stretching down to the vast expanse of golden sands. It was too early for many holidaymakers and the beach was not too crowded. The children threw bread and laughed as the great seagulls swooped low.

On Monday evening everyone was a little downcast, for tomorrow the Gregorys would be leaving. Even baby Robert would miss them, for they had all tended to spoil him.

'When have you got to have the car back?' Charlie asked Alan as he passed him his coffee.

'Oh, not until the end of the week. It wasn't much more money to hire it for the week, rather than just four days,' Alan explained. 'I've still got the rest of the week off from work, so I thought I would take the family on a few day-outings.'

'Why don't you stay here?' Charlie suggested.

'We would love to, but we can't afford it.' Everyone's face dropped.

'Please, be our guests,' Lizzie pleaded.

'Of course,' Charlie echoed. 'It would be our way of repaying you. You've mucked in with the washing-up, helped get picnics ready, taken us out and about in the car, oh, of course, you have to stay.'

'Please, Dad,' Darryl pleaded, and even quiet, shy little Neil added, 'I'd like to stop here.' Everyone laughed and it was decided.

Next morning they all piled on to the bus and went to Ilfracombe. They watched the fishing boats come into the harbour and they bought fish that smelt of the sea for their next day's dinner. It was a wonderful week and when Saturday morning came and the Gregorys finally did have to depart, they promised Lizzie and Charlie that they hadn't seen the last of them.

Several weeks passed before they had any more visitors. Lizzie longed for the season to begin and tried not to worry about their money problems.

During the day, she and Charlie would take the baby for long walks, and each day Charlie would sniff the air appreciatively and say, 'It's so fresh and clean. I love the smell of the sea.'

When summer finally arrived, they were rushed off their feet. Upstairs, doing the bedrooms, Lizzie would look out enviously as the holidaymakers packed the beach and romped in the sea.

Charlie surprised her. Not only was he marvellous at waiting at table, he prepared all the fresh vegetables in the evening, ready for the next day, would bone out a side of bacon, cut up steak and kidney, while she made the pastry for the pies.

In fact, there wasn't one job that he wouldn't tackle.

The height of summer passed all too quickly and then the visitors became far less frequent. Come September and only the odd few bed and breakfast couples came to their door. The situation had to be faced.

Carefully and methodically Lizzie and Charlie went through the accounts together. There was little enough money to pay the bills, let alone to keep them during the long winter months. The local traders, the wholesalers from whom they had bought their meat and dry goods, even the hire purchase on the refrigerator, which had been an essential item, would all have to be paid, declared Charlie as he wrote out the various cheques.

Laundry, rates, gas, electricity and telephone were totted up, and thankfully they agreed there was still enough in the bank to cover these items.

'Now, what about the Bideford Furniture Stores?' Charlie asked, not expecting any answer. 'I'll have to go and see Mr Channon,' he insisted.

'I'll come with you,' Lizzie said, and it was obviously what he had wanted her to say, because he gratefully accepted.

'Lizzie,' Charlie's voice was quiet with apprehension as he paused from packing away the account books.

'Yes?' Lizzie was at the door, about to go downstairs and check on young Robert.

'I'll have to go back to London for the winter,' Charlie blurted the words out. 'I can probably get my job back on the buses.'

Lizzie had been expecting this. She knew it made sense. But in spite of all her resolution the tears came, hot and scalding, running down her cheeks.

'Oh Charlie!' She swayed and he was beside her in two strides. His arms about her, his lips pressed to her hair, he soothed, 'I know, I know, Lizzie. All that hard work, and for what?'

Mr Channon was in his early fifties. A shade shorter than Charlie, he had a mop of hair which was light brown and wavy and his eyes were set wide apart, which gave Lizzie the impression that he was a straightforward kind of man. There would be no pulling wool over his eyes.

Charlie must have had the same impression, for he laid their situation on the line as soon as they were seated in Mr Channon's office.

Silence hung heavily for a few minutes.

'So, you haven't made a fortune during your first season.' Mr Channon's voice was gruff as he continued, 'Too many liabilities. I thought that from the very beginning.'

Lizzie looked at Charlie and her heart ached for him. He was dressed so smartly today in his navy-blue suit, white shirt and paisley tie, now his face was red with embarrassment.

'Can you afford to pay anything now?' the question was shot at Charlie.

He swallowed deeply before answering, 'Only about twenty-five per cent of the total amount.'

Again, the office was quiet and just for a moment Lizzie was gripped by fear. Could they send Charlie to jail for not being able to pay his debts? She couldn't take her eyes off Mr Channon as she waited for him to speak.

'I'm a pretty good judge of character,' Mr Channon said at last. 'Yes, all right, Mr Wilson. I appreciate the fact that you and your wife have come to see me in person. You have been completely honest and that is another factor in your favour. I'll take your cheque for what you can afford and we'll leave the balance in abeyance.'

Despite Mr Channon's generosity, Lizzie couldn't help feeling humiliated as she watched Charlie write the cheque. There and then she made a promise to herself. Once they got out of all this debt she would never owe a penny to anyone, not if she could possibly help it.

A high wind was blowing and the sea was rolling in really rough, bringing with it a heavy rain which lashed against the windows of the house as Lizzie packed socks and underwear into Charlie's case.

'All finished,' she finally said as she straightened up. 'Plenty of time for lunch now before the taxi gets here.'

They sat opposite each other as they ate, each busy

with their own thoughts. Lizzie's blue eyes contemplated her husband thoughtfully. Was it right that they should be separated for weeks on end once again? Right or not, it was a necessary evil, she chided herself. They needed to have money coming in from some source and what other option was there?

'Come with me,' Charlie had urged and she had been sorely tempted. It would be heaven to stay with Doris and Syd, to be part of the family again. Number twelve still hadn't been sold and Lizzie knew that if she went she would never come back to Devon.

Charlie looked at his wife. The weeks of sun and wind had tinged her fair skin to a pale golden tan and brought out the hidden lights in her fair hair. How he hated to leave her, she had never looked more lovely and for the hundredth time he chastized himself. Why on earth had he been so pig-headed? What had made him even think he was capable of running a guesthouse and showing a profit?

The taxi came and Charlie went back to driving a bus around the streets of London while Lizzie faced a long lonely winter.

Chapter Nineteen

JANUARY 1952 HAD been bleak and cold, with snow flurries and bitter gusty winds, but Lizzie still went out whenever the weather allowed, walking miles with the baby in the pram and the dog tagging along by her side. Already it was February and it still hadn't turned much warmer. Lizzie shivered as she walked up the stairs and tugged her dressing-gown more tightly around herself. In the kitchen she filled the kettle and put it on to boil, patted Bob-Bob and let him out of the back door into the garden, then switched on the wireless. The King had died. Oh, how sad! He wasn't all that old.

For the rest of the morning the wireless gave out bulletins and played mournful music which did nothing to lift Lizzie's spirits. Like everyone else in Britain that day, Lizzie's thoughts were all of King George VI. It was a funny old world she said to herself; if his brother hadn't fallen in love with a woman who'd been divorced, an American woman at that, he would never have become the King at all. They said he'd died peacefully in his sleep and she was glad about that. She wondered if there would be a lying-in-state. She had to brush away a tear at that point as she remembered Bill taking her up to

London to see King George V's lying-in-state – all those years ago.

As she thought of the past, she remembered a day during the War when she'd been doing a turn on the 88s. As the driver had turned the bus round by the Tate Gallery he had been stopped by the police from driving down the Embankment. The whole of that area had been badly bombed the night before, and Lizzie had watched from the upstairs windows of the bus as the King and Queen had walked amongst the havoc of the demolished buildings talking to the air-raid wardens and consoling men and women who had lost members of their families in the air raids. From the little she knew of him, he had always seemed a quiet, kindly man.

Well, we won't have a King on the throne now, she thought, because King George only had two daughters. That makes Princess Elizabeth Queen of England. Fancy that! She'd been in the ATS during the war, done her bit for the war effort, so at least she knew how the other half lived.

'Oh well! Life has to go on,' Lizzie said to the dog. 'Seeing as how there's no one else here for me to talk to I have to make do with you. Come on, get yer lead, I'll get Robert ready and we'll go up over the cliffs. A good walk and we might all feel a bit better.'

It was the start of their second year at Sea View Guesthouse and Lizzie threw herself whole-heartedly into the preparations.

Bursting with energy, she worked from early morning until lunchtime. The afternoons she spent writing letters. She wrote to town halls, to Darby and Joan clubs, and to every organizer whose name she could glean from magazines in the local library, offering reduced terms for coach parties either at the beginning of the season or towards the end.

She was delighted by the response she received. But one evening, long after she had settled the baby down, she read through several of the letters again and sighed. Most of the groups that were making provisional enquiries had approximately forty to fifty members. Lizzie hadn't got that many bedrooms to offer. Eventually she went to bed still racking her brain as to what she could do.

She hadn't realized that, to make the long journey worthwhile from northern towns, the coaches would have to be either forty-two seaters or fifty-three.

In the post next morning there was a letter from Alan Gregory and, although she was pleased to hear from him, his news only added to her dilemma.

He had been promoted and was now transport manager for a large coach company in Blackburn. Would she like to send a quotation for four parties, two early- and two late-season, full-board?

'Wouldn't I just,' she said aloud, and Bob-Bob put his head on one side, peering at her, wondering what she was on about.

The doorbell rang and Lizzie picked up the baby and kissed him. 'Come and see the postman,' she said, fully expecting it to be the second delivery, maybe even a registered letter with a deposit on a booking.

Lizzie's face reflected her surprise as she stood in the open doorway holding Robert. The man at the door was Ted Armstrong, the manager of the Round House pub just four doors down the hill.

'Wasn't expecting me, was you, Mrs Wilson,' he said with a grin.

'Well, no,' Lizzie stuttered in bewilderment.

'It's just that the wife and me would like to have a talk to you, maybe put a bit of business your way. Would you like to come along to the pub later on, have a bit of lunch with us?'

'Oh, no, I couldn't,' Lizzie hastily told him, 'I couldn't leave the baby.'

'Of course you couldn't, we didn't mean for you to. Bring him along with you, we're not busy, not this time of the year. Push his pram into the saloon bar or into our sitting-room, whatever, we don't mind. Will you come?'

'Are you sure it will be all right?' Lizzie asked anxiously.

'The missus will be right pleased to see you – about half-twelve then?' He nodded his head and gave Lizzie a reassuring smile, 'Don't worry, love, I'll shut your door; you take the baby in the warm.'

There was an expression of doubt on Lizzie's face as she went back to the kitchen. She knew Ted Armstrong to nod to, even to say good morning, but no more than that.

At Christmas time, she and Charlie had popped into the Round House for a quick drink, but it was the only time, for Charlie had only been down for four days.

Visitors spoke very well about the pub, saying that they always got a good welcome there.

'Wonder what it's all about?' she asked herself.

Two hours later Lizzie sat on the wide window-seat and watched Ethel and Ted Armstrong working behind the bar. She was glad she had changed into her red dress, the long full skirt felt good around her legs, and so did the nylons and high-heeled shoes. It made a change to be dressed nicely.

The interior of the Round House was 'oldy-worldy', nice heavy oak tables and chairs, red velvet curtains and horse-brasses everywhere.

Ted Armstrong was a big-built man with a jovial laugh that was infectious: a typical publican, Lizzie thought, as she watched him squeeze past his wife giving her backside a hearty pat as he went.

Ethel Armstrong looked as if she most certainly did her share of the work. Like her husband, she was well into her fifties, her once auburn hair was streaked with grey, her face red and puffy. She served the drinks while Ted leant against the bar chatting to the customers.

Lizzie sipped her milk stout and wondered what she was doing here.

'I'm here. I'll be with you in a minute,' a female voice cried.

'That's Rosie,' Ethel called to Lizzie. 'She'll take over now; nice friendly girl she is, everyone likes our Rosie.'

Rosie appeared, tall and slim and dressed in a tight-fitting black dress.

'Right then, love, we'll go and eat. Bring your drink with you; it's all right, I've got the pram.' Ethel talked baby-talk to the wide-awake Robert as she led the way through to their private quarters.

The living-room was bright and cosy, the table set for three. Ethel nodded to Lizzie, 'Sit down, you don't mind a cold lunch, do you? I don't cook until the evening.'

'This is fine,' Lizzie answered. Before her was a platter on which lay a pork pie, a wedge of Cheddar cheese, plenty of salad and a baked potato.

As Ted Armstrong took a seat next to her, he blurted out, 'This is daft, I'm Ted and my wife's Ethel. What's your first name, love? Can't keep on calling you Mrs Wilson, can I?'

Lizzie laughed; both Ted and Ethel were regarding her with what could only be friendliness and now she felt very much more at ease. 'Please, call me Lizzie.'

'Right, Lizzie it is. Eat up lass, and then we'll talk.'

When they had finished eating, they moved from the table to sit in comfortable chairs by the window. Ethel lit a cigarette, having first offered one to Lizzie, who had declined, and slowly she blew out the match. 'Wish I could give it up,' she said in an undertone, 'but with this life and all the hours we put in I'd go crazy without my cigarettes.'

Still Lizzie was filled with curiosity, she liked these people very much, was actually thrilled at having been asked to lunch. Company was a rare thing to her these days.

Ted leaned forward and looked directly at Lizzie. 'What we want to ask you, lass, is would you like to rent our bedrooms? We've got nine upstairs.'

A few seconds passed before Lizzie had formed a reply. 'I'm not sure I understand what you mean.' She stared at them both in bewilderment.

'Of course, she's new at this lark, Ted. You go at things like a bull in a china shop,' Ethel rebuked her husband.

'It's quite common for folk to rent extra bed-rooms, Lizzie,' Ethel explained. 'Visitors sleep out and come to the guesthouse for their meals.'

'Oh, I see,' Lizzie said very quietly.

'It's like this; I'm not having Ethel doing meals or even bed and breakfast this year. We've quite enough to do in the pub during the summer.' With a grim smile, Ted Armstrong got up and passed an ashtray to his wife.

'While she's showing visitors up to their bed-rooms, especially on a Saturday night, the blasted part-time staff are giving the drinks away left, right and centre to their damn friends. We don't make a profit, all we do is end up well and truly out of pocket. So, now you've got the picture, Lizzie. Like it or lump it, my Ethel can rent you our rooms or they damn well stay empty!'

Ethel lowered her head, winked at Lizzie and stubbed out her cigarette. 'So now you know,' she said. 'But don't worry, love, his bark is worse than his bite.' Lizzie could hardly believe what she had heard. Maybe, just maybe, it could be the answer to her problem.

Ted smirked at them both, 'I'd best be getting back into the bar, I'll leave you two to sort out the details.' Then he stopped short, turned to Lizzie, and in a fatherly manner he told her, 'You take your time, young Lizzie, think it out well. There's the question of where would you seat these extra guests at meal-times, but there again I know a couple of my customers could sort that one out for you. Just come and see us, as often as you like, whether you say yes or no, don't make no difference. You know us now, so don't be a stranger. You'd be doing my Ethel a favour if you let her spoil that youngster of yours.'

He bent over and gave an affectionate tug to Lizzie's swept-back hair. 'Our two are grown up, both married, both settled in Wales, so no excuses – let's be seeing you, eh?'

'Yes, all right,' Lizzie promised in a voice that was husky with emotion.

The whole afternoon Lizzie just sat. She read through the notes that she had made dozens of times, and still all she felt was disbelief.

For the main ten weeks of the season Ethel Armstrong suggested that Lizzie paid her a set fee of £250 plus three shillings and sixpence per person for each night should she use any of the bedrooms at any time other than during those ten weeks.

Christ! Lizzie did her sums again.

Two pages of an exercise book were covered with figures. Whichever way she looked at it, she couldn't go wrong. There were seven double bedrooms and two singles all lovely and clean, nicely furnished and charmingly decorated. Accommodation for sixteen extra guests.

'They can use the lounge-bar, even drink after time, seeing as how they would be residents,' Ethel had cheerfully told Lizzie.

This arrangement, if it came off, would enable Lizzie to accept full coach parties. She scribbled away furiously; the one booking from Alan, for four weeks, fifty people at four guineas a week, would come to over eight hundred pounds.

She'd have to get some staff. A chambermaid for the Round House at least. It was only four doors away – would guests mind walking that far for their meals? Her head was beginning to ache. This pipe-dream was all very well, but could it become a reality?

That night, Lizzie wrote a long letter to Charlie.

His answer when it came was short and sweet. 'Grab them!'

It was all happening so quickly. Lizzie stood at the

sink, gently squeezing some woollies in the nice hot soapy water. Four workmen were busy in the garden plastering the new extension and in a couple of days' time glass would be in the windows and a large archway was to be knocked through their existing dining-room wall.

Once again, Lizzie had gone cap-in-hand to see Mr Blackhurst. He hadn't hesitated.

'A sound investment,' had been his verdict. 'It could prove to be most profitable, Mrs Wilson, and most certainly will add to the value of your property.' The bank would advance a loan.

As Lizzie thanked him, Graham Blackhurst had pondered on her reasons for staying. He was aware just how disastrous their first season had been in Sea View Guesthouse and his good wishes for the coming season were truly sincere.

The milk boiled over and Lizzie cursed herself for day-dreaming as she mopped up the mess. She made four mugs of coffee, set a plate of her home-made fruit scones and a feeding bottle of warm milk on a tray and walked down the garden path.

'Coffee up!' she called, and the men all grinned and readily stopped what they were doing.

It was the least she could do, Lizzie told herself. Three or four times a day she made hot drinks for the men.

Robert had been as pleased as Punch ever since they had started work. She had to laugh out loud now as he stretched his little hands out for his beaker. Sitting in a mucky wheelbarrow, dressed in dark blue dungarees, a red high-necked jersey and a red woollen hat pulled down over his dark curly hair, he looked the picture of contentment. The bib of his dungarees was smeared with plaster and his face smudged with dirt as he chuckled away to himself. The workmen had been great; even when they had gone off in the van to get supplies, they had taken Robert with them.

He'll miss them when this job is completed, Lizzie said to herself.

Once more, Charlie had left his job and was back in Devon. Everything was ready as they waited for their first coach party to arrive. Unbelievably, Mr Channon had allowed them further credit. Four tables and sixteen chairs, all in a light oak, were set up in the new extension and in the main dining-room there were places laid for a further thirty-eight guests. They were now capable of accommodating fifty-four people in all.

It did not take long for them to get into a steady routine. They had two women who came in every day, plus two extra on Saturdays, all were very reliable and everywhere was kept clean and bright with vases of fresh flowers in the hall and the lounge.

Each meal-time, as the gong sounded, it seemed to Lizzie that people were coming from all directions, down the stairs, from the lounge and through the open front door. She and Charlie would grin at one another, still amazed at their own determination.

Saturdays were a bit hectic ('bloody chaotic' as Charlie put it) as women came from the bedrooms upstairs, arms full of dirty linen, demanding sheets, pillowcases and clean towels. Methodically, Lizzie made out lists and knew exactly what each room needed.

No sooner had the women gone about their tasks than through the front door came the chambermaids from the Round House. Charlie would stop what he was doing and carry the heavy, clean bedlinen down the hill for them.

And then, early in June, Syd got a very good offer for his house, which he accepted. This opened the way for an agreement between Lizzie and Syd which was to solve a great many problems and give Lizzie and Charlie the financial security that they longed for. For Syd and Doris decided to buy number twelve.

It meant that that lovely big old house, where Lizzie had been so happy, would remain in the family and, as Doris assured them, there would always be a bedroom for Lizzie, Charlie and Robert whenever they came 'home'.

When everything was finalized, Charlie went first to Bideford and paid Mr Channon in full.

He came back looking very pleased. 'Mr Channon said to give you his kind regards and to tell you that he hadn't been wrong. He was a good judge of character.'

Lizzie thought of Mr Channon as a compassionate

man. Then, Charlie paid a visit to Mr Fleming. What took place at his new big hotel was never mentioned.

'Did you have a drink while you were there?' Lizzie asked him very cautiously.

'Did I hell,' was all the reply she got.

Later she caught Charlie grinning to himself and she asked, 'What's amusing you?'

'Nothing, really,' he replied; then added, 'eighteen months Frank Fleming waited for his money.'

Lizzie's thoughts flew back; once again she had her doubts as to just who had conned whom. Wisely, she kept her thoughts to herself.

The golden weeks of summer slipped by and soon it was autumn. The early mornings were misty, the days were no longer so warm, and sharp breezes blew in across the sea.

Both Lizzie and Charlie heaved a sigh of relief as they stood on the front steps, waving goodbye to the last coachload of old-aged pensioners.

'I could sleep for a month,' Lizzie declared.

'Nothing to stop you,' Charlie answered.

'Oh, no, and whose gonna see to Robert and cook our meals?'

'Well, tonight no one's doing any cooking.' Charlie tenderly took her into his arms. The quietness was strange and the two of them stood in the entrance hall, locked in a close embrace for several minutes.

'We've made it, Lizzie,' Charlie said, his voice

now quite solemn. 'I shan't have to leave you this winter, and tonight I am taking my wife and my son out to dinner.'

A great tenderness filled Lizzie's heart as she realized that this man of hers was saying 'Thank you'.

Christmas came and Syd hired a minibus.

Lizzie was busy for days getting the rooms ready, taking the blankets out of the wardrobes, making up the beds. Charlie declared he would be the chef and wonderful appetizing smells rose up from the kitchen as he prepared many dishes in advance.

Lizzie could hardly contain herself, she was so looking forward to this holiday.

Syd, Doris and Raymond, Polly, Arthur and young Lucy, Aunt Kate and Uncle John, that would be eight from London.

Her sister Connie and Bill, with William, now wearing his first pair of long trousers, or so Connie had written, were coming from Plymouth. Who wouldn't be excited?

There would be fourteen of them in all over Christmas.

Log fires burnt in the lounge and dining-room and a ten-foot tree taken straight off Exmoor, now glittered with baubles and fairy lights in the hall.

The weather the previous week had been very bad, with gale-force winds and massive waves pounding the shoreline. Lizzie had pretended she didn't care, but when Christmas Eve dawned quiet and peaceful, she said a thank-you prayer.

On Christmas morning they all set off for church, Raymond holding Robert's hand, Lucy chatting away to William. They filled two pews and, as they sank to their knees, Doris reached out her hand to Lizzie and they both smiled – each knowing what the other was thinking.

How wonderful it was to all be together again!

Chapter Twenty

THE NEW YEAR got off to a wonderful start. Scores of letters came daily, many containing postal-orders and cheques. Some were from people from the previous year requesting the same dates, many stating a preference for bedrooms in the Round House. Lizzie made her wallcharts and looked forward to another season.

Forgotten were the days when nothing had gone right, when she had envied guests setting out for a day on the moors whilst she and Charlie had to cook lunch – and dinner again in the evening.

Forgotten were the nights when she had practically crawled downstairs to bed because her legs ached so much. When, just as she had snuggled up to Charlie, the front doorbell would ring at one o'clock in the morning and they would have to climb the stairs again to admit an inconsiderate visitor.

Charlie bought a car. 'Come and see,' he called from the front door, and while Lizzie stopped to dry her hands, Robert beat her up the hall.

Utter astonishment showed on Lizzie's face as she gazed at this immense blue car which stood in the street. Charlie laughed out loud as he swung Robert high in the air before opening the rear door and plonking him down on to the leather seat. Robert chuckled with glee as he bounced up and down and slid from side to side.

'It's a Morris Six,' Charlie told her with pride. 'They only made about fifty of them. Isn't she beautiful?' Lizzie had to agree. The interior was sheer luxury and smelled of real leather, and there were mahogany-faced picnic tables set into the back of each front seat. Oh yes, it was lovely.

Owning a car opened up new horizons for them as a family.

As spring came, they often took a day off from the spring-cleaning and set off with no particular destination in mind.

Exmoor was a favourite, with its wild and beautiful scenery, which Lizzie had read about in *Lorna Doone*, but had never in her wildest dreams imagined that she would see. Charlie played hearty, noisy games with Robert until they would both collapse thirsty and hungry on to the rugs where Lizzie had set out their picnic.

On one such day, Charlie stopped eating and his mouth hung open in amazement. Lizzie, too, stared in wonder and Robert let out a shriek of delight. There, not fifty yards away, stood several red deer. 'Majestic,' Charlie said, 'that's the only word I can think of to describe them.'

Friday became a day to look forward to, because it was market day in Barnstaple.

The produce was all fresh from the farms. There was Devonshire cream, thick as butter and as golden as the sun, plus every vegetable imaginable. Lettuce, cucumbers, radishes, tomatoes and mustard and cress, all had been freshly dug or picked that morning.

Home-made pickles and jams, cakes, sponges which were as light as a feather, home-made treacle toffee which was Lizzie's favourite, all were displayed on snow-white tablecloths and served by rosy, apple-faced women.

Large brown eggs lay on straw in huge china bowls, and plump chickens and fleshy ducks, all plucked ready for the oven.

Out in the street on one side of the road was a continuous line of butchers' shops, hence its name, Butchers' Row. No frozen or foreign meat would be seen here. With the abattoir only a few streets away, everything sold was fresh.

Lizzie never went home empty-handed.

Unlike the London markets, the pubs here stayed open all day. One Friday, while Charlie went off to have a pint, Lizzie did something she had been thinking of doing for a long time.

'Christ almighty, you look like an elf!' Charlie declared when they met up later. She had had her hair cut. Now barely shoulder length, it curled under in a page-boy style.

'It will be easier to manage in the summer,' Lizzie told him.

With the coming of May, the weather became more settled, with nice sunny days and long, light evenings. There still weren't that many visitors about, but Lizzie was hoping that they might pick up some more guests if the fine weather continued.

Hopefully, life for Lizzie and Charlie was not going to be quite so hectic this season and, as their debts were now paid off, Charlie had arranged for two local lads to come in every evening from the beginning of June to do the washing-up of the dinner things. It would make quite a difference – it would enable them to sit down and have their own dinner a lot earlier and enjoy longer evenings together.

But there were still times when Lizzie longed for her London life and her friends and family.

As the month ended and June was upon them Lizzie felt disappointed and angry. She knew she had no right to feel so annoyed but she couldn't help herself, for she would have given anything to have been in London this week. It was 1953 and on the 2nd of June the Queen was to be crowned in Westminster Abbey by the Archbishop of Canterbury.

'Thousands will line the route,' she said to Charlie. 'She's gonna ride in a gold coach. Oh, how I wish I could be there!'

'The newspapers will carry colour supplements every day this week, and you'll be able to read all about it and look at the pictures as well,' he said in that maddeningly tantalizing way of his.

'Get out,' she yelled as she threw a tea-cloth at him, 'we don't even have a television set to watch it on.'

The most galling thing of all to Lizzie was not that she wouldn't see the procession, though that was bad enough, but that she wouldn't be there for the street parties – and you could bet your last farthing that there'd be a party in Wilton Road. Syd, Doris, Polly and Arthur would be out there managing things, you could be sure of that. Christ! I'd better stop thinking about it, she thought to herself. For two pins I'd take Robert and get on that train!

Ah well, nobody gets everything in this life. Though that thought didn't make her feel any better.

One lunchtime, towards the end of the month, the phone rang as Lizzie and Charlie were frying fish and boiling new potatoes and peas.

'It's Ethel, wants a word with you.' Charlie came back down the length of the kitchen and took the bowl of creamy batter from Lizzie's hands.

'Hallo, Ethel.' Lizzie smiled into the receiver.

'Sorry to disturb you, won't keep you a minute. What are you doing this afternoon?'

'Taking Robert down on the beach, same as always. Why? Is something wrong?'

'I don't want to go into it over the phone, but I would like to see you.'

'Well, we've only got twenty-two in for lunch,

rest of them took a packed lunch, so we shouldn't be late finishing.'

Charlie had been listening and had got the gist of what Ethel had been saying. 'I'll take Robert down to the beach,' he volunteered. 'You put the deck-chairs out in the garden; have a cuppa with Ethel.'

'Did you hear that?' Lizzie mouthed her thanks to Charlie.

'Yes, so I'll see you about half-past two,' Ethel was saying, and Lizzie wondered why she couldn't have waited until she popped in to check the rooms, but she had sounded pretty flustered.

Ethel often looked tired to death, and no wonder with the hours she had to keep. Wouldn't have her job for the world, thought Lizzie, three hundred and sixty-five days every year; at least in this trade you get the winter to look forward to, though God knows there are enough jobs to do even then.

Charlie watched Lizzie replace the receiver and then smiled at her. 'Trouble?' he asked.

'I dunno. I hope not.' Yet she couldn't shake off the premonition that there might be.

Ethel looked all in, but when she smiled, her eyes still lit up warm and friendly.

'Sit down, luv,' Lizzie pointed to the two deck-chairs. 'I'll just go in and make the tea, I won't be a minute.'

Ethel's eyes were brimming with tears when Lizzie came back and set the tea tray down on the wicker table.

'Oh, love, don't cry. Nothing can be as bad as all

that. It's the season, gets us all, one way or another, bloody working seven days a week is no pushover.' She held out a cup of tea for Ethel to take. 'Come on, drink that up, a cuppa is everyone's answer when trouble is brewing.'

Ethel struggled not to blink but she couldn't help herself and the tears in her eyes brimmed over.

Lizzie settled herself in her own chair with her own cup of tea. 'A trouble shared is a troubled halved,' she ventured.

Ethel sniffed, 'We've got to go and I'm only sorry for how it's going to affect you and Charlie.'

Lizzie looked puzzled. 'I'm not with you. Where have you got to go to?'

'Anywhere, oh, I don't know. God alone knows, really.'

'Ethel,' Lizzie implored, 'start at the beginning and tell me what's happened.'

Ethel nodded her head. 'You're right Lizzie, there's no way of wrapping it up. My Ted's had an awful row with the brewery. Mind you, I can't really blame him, going to treble the rent. I ask you, treble it! They come down here in the summer, see the bar's packed and they think we're making a bloody fortune. Don't bother to think about the winter, do they? Oh no. Don't want to know about the nights when all we serve is a few pints to the local fishermen.'

Lizzie had an awful feeling that she knew exactly where this conversation was leading, but she did not want to believe it. For the moment she wouldn't let

herself think about it. She held out her hand for
Ethel's cup and poured each of them more tea.

Ethel was miles away, lost in thought. Lizzie
leaned forward and put a hand on her knee. 'So what
are you going to do?'

'What are we going to do? I wish I knew, Lizzie.
I wish I knew.' Ethel stared into space as if she had
almost forgotten where she was.

'Ted will sort something out, I'm sure he will,'
Lizzie's voice was full of compassion.

'That's just the trouble. My Ted blew his top,
told them what they could do with their so-and-so
pub.' Ethel's face was blood-red now, as she con-
demned the brewery. 'Took him at his word they
did. He couldn't keep his big mouth shut, could he?
Oh no, played right into their hands. Just what they
wanted. Get us out, new tenants in, agree a new
lease and charge what they like. One month is all
we've got. That's all we are entitled to. One month
either way, it's in our lease, can't get away from
that.'

The truth was out now and Lizzie had to face the
reality. Ethel's voice droned on. 'My Ted says he is
finished working for the brewery. Gonna see if he
can find a small place to buy, somewhere in Wales
probably; be nice to be near the children.'

She was rambling on, half to herself, saying anything that came into her head. Suddenly she seemed
to pull herself together and her eyes were alert again.

'Sorry to worry you, Lizzie, but I thought it best
to tell you myself. Mind you, nothing is definite

yet, no dates set. When Ted calms down, perhaps Charlie will come and have a chat with him; let's hope they can work something out for all our sakes.'

'I don't believe it!' Charlie sat forward in his chair and stared at Lizzie. She had waited until they had finished eating to tell him. 'Bloody hell! You realize what a mess this will leave us in.'

Lizzie took a book down from the shelf and rifled through the pages. She had known Charlie would go mad and who could blame him, it was a dicey situation to be in. There were the peak weeks of the season yet to come and they had accepted bookings on all nine of the bedrooms in the Round House. What if they couldn't fulfil that contract? If Ethel and Ted Armstrong went, who's to say that the new tenants would want to let out their bedrooms. They might have a family of their own and need some of the rooms for themselves. They may even want to take in visitors.

Dear God, the repercussions didn't bear thinking about.

Lizzie found the page she was looking for and pointed a finger to one of the paragraphs as she handed the book over to Charlie. Tension mounted in Lizzie as she watched him reading. 'Damn it, Lizzie, have you read this?' She nodded her head.

'So, if we can't keep our side of the bargain, guests are legally entitled to go to another guesthouse or even an hotel and claim the difference in cost from us!' Charlie's face was red with anger. 'Right bloody mess, ain't it?'

Lizzie wanted to calm him, she was just as worried as he was, but a screaming match wasn't going to help anyone. They were both tired, much better to leave things to quieten down and then sit down and talk about it.

She placed a bowl of fruit on the table. 'You haven't had any sweet yet,' she said eagerly; 'the grapes are nice and juicy, real sweet, or would you like some ice-cream?'

Charlie burst out laughing. 'If you don't take the cake, Lizzie, I'm damned if I know who does. You're talking in deadly earnest about us not having had any pudding, when all the time we're up to our ears in trouble. If it weren't so serious, you know, it would be downright funny.'

Even Lizzie grinned. 'Would it help if I burst into tears? Nothing's for certain yet, we may be jumping the gun.'

'And if we're not?' he asked.

'Well, we could wait until we know for certain before we blow our brains out, we don't have to meet trouble head on, do we?'

Charlie stood up and came to stand in front of her. 'You really do take the biscuit.' He was laughing now, fit to bust, his dark head thrown back, his mouth wide open showing his perfect white teeth. 'You're bloody marvellous,' he said as she stood laughing with him. 'Bloody marvellous!'

★

The following week was filled with anxiety, and though neither Charlie nor Lizzie broached the subject, each knew that it was uppermost in the other's mind.

'I've got the bloody jitters,' Lizzie muttered to herself as she picked up the broken pieces of a cup she had just dropped.

Ted had phoned and asked Charlie to pop down about eight o'clock. It was ten minutes past ten now – he had been gone over two hours.

One minute Lizzie had sunk into the depths of despair, and the next she'd been telling herself that Charlie wouldn't have stayed so long if the worst had happened.

She was baffled and worried, but just when she felt she would have to pick up the phone, she heard Charlie coming down the basement steps. The tilt of his head and the laughter in his bright blue eyes made Lizzie sigh with relief.

'Everything's all right, love. Put the kettle on; we've got a reprieve. The Armstrongs are going, but not until September, somewhere around the tenth.'

Almost all of their free time was now spent discussing their future. Charlie's ideas were well thought out and Lizzie listened attentively to all that he had to say.

'With just twelve letting bedrooms, we would be back to square one and our income would be greatly diminished,' he pointed out. 'But I don't care what happens, even if we sell up and go back to London, we are never again going to rent rooms from other people. It's far too precarious. God, we were lucky. I still break out in a sweat every time I think about what could have happened.'

It was a lovely afternoon, the sun shone down, the sky was cloudless and the beach was packed with holidaymakers.

'Let's go for a swim,' Charlie suggested.

'You know I can't swim,' Lizzie's voice was sullen, 'besides, I'm too tired and I look a right mess.'

'Poor old thing,' he teased, as he pushed towels and a beach ball into the bag. 'Come on, I'm not taking no for an answer, we'll pick Robert up on the way; he's only playing in the lane.'

Half an hour later and Lizzie felt a new woman. They had clambered over the dunes to a fairly deserted part of the beach, changed into their swimming costumes and romped in the warm sea. Now Lizzie lay back, resting on her elbows, and watched her son and his father as they swam quite a way from the shore.

Charlie was a fantastic swimmer and he had insisted on Robert being taught. 'I swear that kid could swim before he could walk,' she said to Bob-Bob as he came across the sand. 'Oh you horror,' she yelled as he vigorously shook himself and then lay down next to her, taking up more than half of the blanket she had spread out. 'Have they gone and left you too?' she said to him as she rubbed his wet sandy fur with his own doggy-towel. 'Well, they've both got webbed feet, you see, that's the difference between them and us.'

'I heard that,' Charlie sounded happy as he pushed the dog out of the way and lay down, all wet from the sea, beside Lizzie.

'I know what we're going to do,' he said grinning like a Cheshire cat, 'we're going to buy a big hotel.'

'Oh, no,' was Lizzie's first reaction, 'not again, not go through all that palaver all over again!'

Chapter Twenty-One

SEPTEMBER CAME, THE Armstrongs departed for Wales, new tenants with three children took over the Round House, and young Robert went to school.

Lizzie dubbed the school 'arsenic and old lace'. Not that she didn't like it, quite the reverse. It was called Adelaide College and it was owned and managed by two middle-aged sisters, both of whom were spinsters, with the help of just six dedicated staff.

The building itself was like a Southern plantation house straight out of a film. Wide wooden verandas, painted white, ran the length of the frontage; large, comfortable rocking-chairs placed at intervals gave one a view of the wonderful grounds. The whole place seemed unaffected by time.

There were only eight pupils to each class; it was an intimate friendly school and Robert loved it from day one.

It was Lizzie who shed a tear as she walked away and left him clutching Miss Warrell-Bowring's hand.

'He's only three years old,' she had reminded the stately lady with the black velvet ribbon encircling her throat.

'All the better, Mrs Wilson, and his classmates

will be of the same age,' she spoke flawlessly as she showed Lizzie to the door.

Just four weeks of coach parties and their third season in Sea View Guesthouse was over.

'Our final one an' all,' Charlie declared as he scanned estate agents' lists.

'Oh, for Christ's sake, let's have a rest before you start dragging me off to view hotels,' Lizzie pleaded.

They had a good rest. They stored all blankets away in mothballs, disinfected all toilets and bathrooms, cleaned the gas cooker, washed out the fridge and threw out all bits and pieces of perishable food. They bagged up piles of linen for the laundry and went back to bed every lunchtime and only got up again when it was time to fetch Robert from school.

Before they knew where they were it was October and Robert had a week's holiday from school for half-term.

Lizzie didn't ask Charlie, she told him. 'I'm going home.' She had all of her arguments ready in case he tried to stop her, but in the end she didn't need any of them. With a straight face Charlie said that he was going to suggest that they did just that. Lizzie wasn't quite sure that she believed him. But this time her face had shown such determination that he had known she really would have up-sticks and gone on her own if he had tried to stand in her way. Far better to go together and travel by car.

'Doris, Doris, Doris,' Lizzie called as they ran towards each other, arms spread wide ready to hug. It was Polly's turn next, as Lizzie broke free from Doris to put her arms around the girl who had been her friend for as long as she could remember. Lucy and Raymond were also claiming her attention and, as she bent and cuddled them both, Raymond whispered to her, 'Auntie Lizzie am I still your superman?' They were all still in a group, on the pavement outside number twelve, chattering away and laughing, when Syd came back out from the house.

'We've taken in all the gear, are you silly cows going to stand there all night?' he called out in a loud voice.

'Ssh, Syd, mind the neighbours,' Doris said in that little girl's voice of hers.

'Sod the neighbours. Charlie, Arthur and me want something to eat if you lot don't, so get in 'ere an' see about getting a meal; just because my daft sister's come 'ome it don't mean we've all got to starve.'

The three girls looked at each other and burst out laughing.

Doris had hold of Robert's hand, Polly had Raymond and Lizzie had Lucy up in her arms as they all went inside what had been Lizzie's first house.

'God, it's great to be home,' she said as her brother gave her a great bear-hug.'

It was after nine o'clock on the Saturday morning when Lizzie came down the wide staircase, through the tiled hall and into the living-room. They'd sat up half the night jabbering away, and when she'd got out of bed this morning she had stood for a long while gazing out of the big bay window at Wilton Road.

My, she'd done right to buy the two houses during the war, especially this one. It really was a beautiful house, so well built. It was all thanks to Gran though; without her legacy none of them would be so well off today.

I must ask Doris about the people that bought hers and Syd's house; being right opposite she must know all about them, Lizzie promised herself as she finally turned away from the window.

'You timed that right,' Doris called from the kitchen as Lizzie sat down. 'The kettle's just coming up ter boil.'

'Where is everyone? It's so quiet, what 'ave yer done with the boys?'

'They've only bin gone about ten minutes. Syd an' Charlie's taken them out; they didn't say where they were going an' I didn't ask.' Doris gave Lizzie one of her slow, mischievous grins before asking, 'Yer don't mind do yer? Got the whole morning ter ourselves.'

Lizzie laughed. 'Still scheming in yer own quiet way?'

'Got to ain't I? Don't do ter let Syd know what I'm doing half the time nor yet what I'm thinking come to that.'

Lizzie shook her head in disbelief as she drank her

tea and watched Doris cook bacon and eggs for each of them. Doris, so quiet, almost timid at times. I never thought she'd last, she thought to herself, not with my Syd and his ducking and diving I never. She's a proper little dark horse, but she seems to be holding her own all right.

They had finished eating their breakfast and the pair of them lapsed into silence, comfortable and happy to have each other's company, each absorbed with their own thoughts. The clock on the mantelshelf ticked loudly, a cheerful fire glowed in the grate and Lizzie remembered when she had sat here in this same room and nursed and breast-fed her baby. Automatically she asked herself the question for which she had no answer. Why did I ever leave London? How did I come to be living in Devon? Working seven days a week when the sun was shining and not seeing a soul through the long winter months.

The door opened and Polly's voice broke the silence. 'So how are we this morning, an' what are we doing?'

'Has Arthur gone with the boys?' asked Doris. 'Yes, thank God. Lucy wasn't going to be left behind either.'

'We're all going ter get our hair done,' declared Doris.

'Oh, no,' Lizzie groaned. 'You don't want me ter bleach yer roots, do you?' she asked, remembering the times she had done them and what a messy job it was.

'No. I told yer we're all getting our hair done, fer free, at 'alf past eleven.' Seeing the glance that passed between Polly and Lizzie, Doris said, 'Do you remember Vi Dolby? Used ter do women's hair in 'er front room. Well, she bought a sa—lon.' They laughed at Doris's exaggerated use of the word salon. 'Right next door ter Colliers Wood tube station, but it ain't done any good and she wants ter sell it. I met her yesterday and she told me she'd got people coming ter view the place. She hopes they'll buy it. She wants ter make out that the place is always busy an' she said she'd do me hair for nothing if I'd come down there this morning, an' I told her I'd do better than that, I'd bring you two as well.'

'Are you serious?' Lizzie asked in amazement. 'Poor woman going to do all our hairs and not make a penny out of us?'

'We won't be the only ones; she's gonna fill the shop. Got two assistants coming in ter work there as well. It'll be a good laugh and the prospective buyers will think it is a good business, an' Vi will do all right out of it, so yer see it's us what is doing Vi the favour.'

Both Polly and Lizzie fell about laughing. The logic of Doris wanted some beating!

'We've got a good hour yet, so while Lizzie an' I make our faces up you make a fresh pot of tea Polly.'

'Yes, marm,' said Polly giving Doris a mock salute as she went into the kitchen.

They were sitting around the table drinking their

tea when Lizzie remembered she wanted to know about the folk who had bought Syd's house.

'Go on, tell her,' Polly urged Doris with a wide grin on her face.

'Don't laugh then or I won't.' They both agreed and did their best to keep a straight face.

'For a start there's Mr and Mrs Watkins an' they've got a son Tom, an' a daughter Mary. They let two rooms upstairs to an old lady on her own, her name's Thelma, or at least I think it is, though I got told off for calling her that. She said I didn't 'ave to be all lardy-dah with her. She calls herself Felma. Funny old girl, really nice but a bit queer, ain't got much. I took her over a cardigan and a warm dress, she put them on straight away, on top of what she was wearing.'

'Tell Lizzie about Felma's gas meter,' Polly insisted.

Doris shot a look of embarrassment at Polly, before turning to Lizzie and declaring very self-consciously, 'It isn't much. I started putting her money in the meter for her, that's all. Her hands are bad, crippled up with arthritis, and she couldn't get the coins in the slot.'

'That's not the end of it,' Polly took up the story. 'Felma was giving Doris a shilling an' moaning that the gas only lasted a couple of days; said Doris wasn't putting the shillings in right; so what does dozy Doris do now?'

Lizzie had no need to be told. 'She puts two or three of her own two-bob pieces in the meter.'

'You got it,' Polly said.

'Well it don't 'urt me, a couple of bob now an' again, does it?' Doris asked Lizzie with a pleading note in her voice.

'No, 'course it don't,' Lizzie assured her, at the same time thinking what a saint this sister-in-law of hers was turning out to be.

'You were going to tell me about the family themselves,' Lizzie reminded her, and once again Doris looked across at Polly and was obviously embarrassed.

'Don't tell me you're helping them out as well?' Lizzie couldn't help smiling as she spoke.

'I'll tell yer this story,' Polly volunteered. Doris half closed her eyes and gave Lizzie a saucy grin as Polly began.

'The father an' the mother 'ave a fruit stall outside Tooting Baths. Sell good stuff they do, always a queue ain't there, Doris?'

Doris was busy adding more boiling water to the pot so that they could all have another cup of tea, but she looked up and nodded her head in agreement.

Polly took up the tale again and Lizzie wondered when the pair of them were going to get to the point.

'The son an' the daughter work the streets, you know, pushing a barrow; well that Tom does the streets but in the fine weather his sister Mary has been selling from her barrow up on the Common.' Polly paused and giggled at her own thoughts and Doris nearly choked on her tea. 'Syd an' Doris,

Arthur an' me, we'd all been up to Streatham Lacarno for the evening. Well, as we came out it started to rain an' by the time we got to the bus stop it was coming down in torrents. As yer know the bus comes down by St Leonard's Church and runs right along side of the Common. There we were, minding our own business, when at one of the stops on the Common who should get on the bus but this Mary, looked like a drowned rat she did, water was dripping from her 'air and she was soaked ter the skin. Came an' sat on the seat right opposite to Doris an' me an' what do yer think our Doris said to that Mary?' Lizzie shook her head, speechless for once. 'She looked at Mary an' said, "You poor thing, you're soaked, get caught in the downpour did yer and run for it? What yer done with your fruit barrow? Left it under the trees?" I thought my Arthur was going to explode an' as for your Syd, you never heard anyone blow their nose so hard in all yer life. I didn't know where to put me face. I tell yer, Lizzie, we were all damn glad ter get off that bus an' I ain't bin able ter look that Mary in the face since then.'

'I'm not with you,' Lizzie said with a baffled look on her face.

'Oh, not you as well!' Polly screamed, while Doris almost fell off her chair because she was laughing so much.

'You silly cow, Lizzie, ain't yer fell in yet? That Mary's on the game. She weren't up on the Common that time of night selling no fruit!' Then the living-room was ringing with the boisterous laughter of all three of them as they clutched at each other for support.

When they'd wiped the tears from their eyes and settled down again, Doris, never one to mind others having a laugh at her expense, said, 'Here Lizzie I've just got time to tell yer about me taking a lodger, an' then we'll 'ave ter get going if we're gonna 'ave our hair done.'

'I don't know if I can take any more,' Lizzie gasped as she gave her eyes another wipe.

'Oh, you've got ter hear this,' Polly stated as she, too, struggled to stop laughing.

'Well,' (it seemed to Lizzie that all of Doris's stories began with 'Well') 'I thought I might try letting the top flat, like you did ter Wally an' Hilda. We weren't short of money but you know your brother, a millionaire this week, treats the world and his wife ter drinks in the pub, come the next week and he's selling anything he can lay his hands on. Not that me an' Raymond ever go short, far from it, but I thought a bob or two put away for a rainy day wouldn't come amiss. So I wrote out a postcard an' put it in the window of the corner shop. Same day I had a man come ter the door. He was lovely looking; tall and handsome . . .'

'Get on with the story,' Polly begged. 'We'll never get our free hair-do at the rate you're going.'

'He said he was a doctor at the Grove Hospital, went mad about how nice the flat was an' said fifty shillings rent was very fair. I let him move in the next morning. Syd said at the time that I was mad. Anyway, at the end of the first week I went up to clean his rooms an' to change his bed. Young Lucy was with me. No sooner had we got in the room than Lucy asked where the clock had gone to from off the mantelshelf. Then I stripped the eiderdown and the bedspread from off the bed an' I couldn't believe me eyes. My two big thick white blankets were missing an' a blooming old overcoat was lying on top of the sheet. I'll cut the story short. Syd nearly throttled the bloke. Made him turn his pockets out; he hadn't got any money but he had got two pawn-tickets. Syd put his toe up his arse an' kicked him out there an' then. It turned out I'd taken two weeks rent off him in advance, five pounds, an' it cost Syd a fiver ter get our stuff back out from the pawn-shop. I won't tell yer what your brother's threatened ter do ter me if I even think about taking any more lodgers.'

'Oh, my sides are killing me, I shall ache for a week,' Lizzie moaned as the tears of laughter were once more blinding her.

'You 'aven't heard the best bit yet.' Polly was ready with her two pennyworth.

'We were coming back from Tooting, Doris an' me, at the beginning of that week, the bloke had only been in the house for a couple of days. When we passed him, he said good morning ter us polite as yer like, but underneath his arm he had this dirty great big parcel; he even shifted it from one arm to the other as we watched him. What we didn't know at the time was that it was Doris's blankets and clock that the cheeky sod had got wrapped up in there.'

'Pack it in the pair of yer,' Lizzie pleaded with them as she held her arm to her side, which really was giving her gip and her laughter was in danger of becoming hysterical.

'Come on, then,' Doris said, 'get yer coats on an' I'll take yer ter get this free hair-do, and don't forget if the woman asks yer, we 'ave a job ter get booked up in this salon 'cos Vi is always so busy.'

All the way to Colliers Wood Lizzie was chuckling to herself. I knew I was missing a lot by living down in Devon, but not this much; it's worse than a Brian Rix farce.

Lizzie's hair had grown during the summer and was now just beyond shoulder-length. She had had it set on very large rollers, brushed out and clipped back with a wide orange hair-slide which Vi had sold her for one and tuppence. Polly still wore her dark hair fairly short, with a fringe and the ends curling upwards. Doris's hairstyle was the most elaborate; bleached almost white, back-combed until the front was piled high and sprayed with this new-fangled lacquer which Vi told her would keep the hair in place even in the rain, it felt as stiff as a board when Lizzie touched it. All three of them gave the two assistants a couple of bob each as a tip, called cheerio to Vi and walked about twenty yards up the road. There they fell against the wall and none of them could move for the next couple of minutes because they were laughing so much.

'I've never seen anything like it in me life,' gasped Polly.

'I told yer Vi was going ter do anything she could to sell that shop, didn't I?' Doris said as she fumbled in her bag for a handkerchief.

'Yes, you did right enough, but ter go to those lengths!' complained Lizzie as she tried hard to control her giggling. 'I don't know how those two girls kept a straight face. There was one of them kept opening the door to make the bell ring, then saying in a loud voice, "No sorry can't do anything for you today, we're fully booked." An' the other poor cow kept answering the phone that never stopped ringing, saying that they couldn't fit the customer in for at least a fortnight. The woman out in the back room with Vi must 'ave thought the place was a bloody gold-mine!'

Lizzie's description of events set them all off again and their uproarious laughing caused two old biddies who were passing to stop and stare at them. 'Painted molls,' one sniffed to her friend. 'Yeah, drunk this time in the day, should be bleedin' well ashamed of 'emselves,' said the other.

'Painted molls!' exclaimed Polly and this time they really were helpless with laughter.

It took some time for them to compose themselves and to start walking towards home.

'What will we give them to eat now?' asked Doris.

'I've got all the dinner ready for ternight but they'll want something now.'

'How about pie an' mash?' suggested Polly.

'No, can't be bothered ter walk all the way to Tooting now. 'Ere, Lizzie, d'yer, still like faggots an' pease-pudding?'

'Cor, yes, can't remember when I last 'ad them though.'

'Good, 'cos there's a cooked-meat shop opened up at the top of Marlborough Road, we can get some there.'

'What we going ter carry 'em home in?' Polly wanted to know. 'We ain't got a dish with us.'

'I'll buy one at the oil shop. I can do with a new one fer me rice puddings.'

The three of them trooped into the dark, smelly, oil shop and started sorting out the pile of baking tins and pie-dishes that were stacked on the floor.

'They must 'ave been here since the year dot,' Lizzie muttered under her breath as she spat on her handkerchief and rubbed at her fingers.

Doris walked towards the shopkeeper, a biggish man with a round red face, not a hair on his head and a beer-belly that overlapped the top of his trousers. 'Friar Tuck of Tooting,' Polly said in a stage whisper to Lizzie.

'Excuse me,' Doris said in a quiet voice, putting on her little-girl act once again, 'you wouldn't 'appen ter 'ave a kettle boiling out the back would you?'

'As a matter of fact I do, miss,' the bald-headed

man answered her, not in the least put out by Doris's question.

'If I buy one of those enamel pie-dishes, the big eightpenny ones, would you scald it out fer me 'cos we want ter take some faggots and pease-pudding 'ome with us; an' if we get them in paper bags we can't get no gravy, an' we all think the gravy is the best part, don't you?'

'Yes, I most certainly do. Without a load of gravy a faggot just don't taste the same. I'll scald a dish out an' dry it fer yer with pleasure, miss.'

Lizzie couldn't stay and listen to any more; she had to get out of the shop before she started to laugh again. Doris wasn't taking the mickey; she was deadly serious and the shopkeeper was treating her with the utmost respect. Only Doris could act like that and get away with it.

They walked three abreast down the street with their faggots and pease-pudding, Doris carried her pie-dish well out in front of her, very careful not to spill any of the rich thick gravy. As soon as one of them stopped chuckling another one started. 'What a morning,' Lizzie said to herself as she opened the gate and stood back to let Doris go in first.

With their midday meal over, Syd spread the pages of the *Sporting Life* out over the table and, with pencil and betting-slips at the ready, he said to Charlie, 'Come an' see what yer fancy fer the three o'clock. There's racing on the telly all the afternoon.'

Without saying a word, Doris got up from her chair and went to the dresser. From the drawer she took out a tin box that had a picture on the lid of the Changing of the Guard at Buckingham Palace. She spread the contents of the tin all over one end of the table – bottles of different coloured nail varnish, cotton wool, wooden tooth-picks, nail scissors, nail files, and a large bottle of nail-varnish remover.

'Oh blimey! We're not gonna 'ave ter put up with that bloody stink all the afternoon are we?' roared Syd as he got to his feet. With a swipe of his hand he swept the various bottles into a heap. From his pocket he pulled a roll of notes and, with a flash of anger, he pulled a fiver from the roll and threw it towards Doris. 'Here,' he yelled, 'take the kids round the park or something; buy yourselves all the ice-creams an' sweets you can eat but stay out of our way till the racing's finished.'

Doris still didn't say anything as she got the boys' coats out of the cupboard, but as she passed Lizzie a hint of a smile was playing round her lips and she dropped her left eye-lid and winked.

They had a marvellous afternoon, and when they got back Syd was in a really good mood so it was obvious that he had beaten the bookies for once. Polly and Arthur brought Lucy over to number twelve about half-past seven, and Mrs Thompson's daughter from the corner shop came at a quarter to eight to stay with the children while the grown-ups all trooped along to the Horse and Groom.

The pub had a piano and a pianist was always

hired for Saturday nights. As the evening wore on, and the drinks had taken effect, the pub became very lively with all the customers joining in singing the ever-popular old songs. This was Lizzie's idea of a good night out.

All too soon, though, it was time to go back to Devon. But there was one thing that Lizzie vowed and declared to Charlie as he packed their cases away in the boot of his car. 'I don't care what yer do or say; it's not gonna be three years this time before I come home again.'

Chapter Twenty-Two

THE WEATHER HAD stayed pretty good. There was not much warmth in the sunshine now, and the dark nights were cold, but for October it wasn't at all bad. At least there was no sign of rain.

They had had breakfast with Doris and Syd on the Monday morning and set off from Wilton Road just after ten o'clock. Charlie had made good time, stopping only once in Taunton for them to have some lunch and go to the toilet. He had pulled into their own garage just as the village church clock was striking four. By the time Lizzie had unpacked the cases, put the dirty washing in the sink to soak, cooked the dinner and seen Robert to bed she was whacked. Slouched down now in an armchair in front of the fire, which Charlie had lit in the lounge, she was half-asleep, her mind miles away, when suddenly she was brought up with a jerk as Charlie said, 'I think we'll keep Robert off from school for another week.'

'What the hell for?' she muttered as she struggled to sit up and gather her wits about her.

'Because I want this thing settled one way or the other,' he snapped back.

'Well, there's no need ter be so crabby; just say what's on yer mind an' we'll talk about it.'

Charlie had been in a funny mood from the moment they had arrived back and now Lizzie decided that her best bet would be to tread warily. She knew he had discussed the matter with Syd and she understood why he would like the sale of this guesthouse to go through. If the local agent was to be believed, there wouldn't be any problem finding a purchaser, but what was the point if they had nowhere to go?

Yet to stay on here now would be ridiculous. Without the extra rooms at the pub, there wasn't enough income to give them a good living, unless they had another string to their bow. Lizzie knew exactly what she would like to do – sell up and go back to London. But at this point it wouldn't be fair, she told herself, even to suggest it to Charlie. What would he do for a job? He'd been really good all the time they'd been staying with Syd and Doris. Lizzie chided herself; Charlie deserved a chance to see if he could find an hotel that would be for sale at a price that they could afford.

'I'd like to take a look at Bournemouth,' Charlie's statement broke into her thoughts again. 'What d'yer think? We could take Robert, set out early in the morning, stay a few days in an hotel an' check out the estate agents. By all accounts, Bournemouth has become one of the most popular pleasure resorts in the country.'

Lizzie just stopped herself in time from making an ugly grimace; Bournemouth! Still, if that's what he wanted to do she'd do well to go along with him.

'All right,' she agreed in a happy tone of voice which was far from what she was really feeling. 'Why not? A few days being waited on in someone else's hotel will be a nice change.'

They were in Bournemouth by lunchtime and Charlie booked them into the Royal Exeter Hotel. The large bedroom they were assigned had one double bed and one single bed and looked right out over the sea. By the time Lizzie had freshened up she was feeling much more relaxed, determined to enjoy this unexpected holiday. After they had had lunch, Charlie declared that he was going to visit some of the local estate agents and if possible obtain details of any hotels that might be for sale in the vicinity. Lizzie breathed a sigh of relief when, instead of asking her to accompany him, Charlie suggested that she took Robert on the pier.

Later that night, when Robert was in bed and fast asleep, Charlie persuaded Lizzie to come downstairs into the lounge-bar and have a drink. Settled comfortably at a table near the window, their drinks in front of them, Charlie began to read through the particulars of properties that he had managed to collect.

'Interested in buying an hotel, are you?' A tall, middle-aged man in a well-cut suit held out his hand. 'Martin Fenwick,' he said and, with a grin, added, 'joint owner of this place with the bank.'

Charlie laughed as he got to his feet and shook the fellow's hand. 'Charlie Wilson, and this is my wife. She won't mind you calling her Lizzie, everyone does.'

Martin Fenwick shook hands with Lizzie. 'How do you like Bournemouth? Bit quiet here at this time of the year.' Without giving Lizzie time to reply he went on, 'You're staying a few days, aren't you? You must meet my wife and my two sons. Stephen is just four, the other one, John, has turned six.'

He was a likeable man, Lizzie decided as she went upstairs, leaving Charlie to have one for the road. He hadn't put on any airs and graces, even though he owned this large hotel. Quite the opposite, he had made her feel very welcome and he might turn out to be very useful to Charlie. At that thought Lizzie smiled to herself; she certainly didn't want Charlie getting himself involved in any more complicated deals. The buying of Sea View Guesthouse had proved to be enough of a headache for one lifetime.

Sunday was a lovely autumn day, not in the least bit cold. There was bright sunshine and the few clouds that there were in the sky were the white fluffy kind like cotton wool.

Lizzie felt a great deal more relaxed as they walked along the seafront in the direction of the hotel they were about to view.

It was Mr Fenwick who, having made several phone calls on their behalf, had finally arranged this appointment.

'Seems a bit odd viewing on a Sunday,' Lizzie had ventured.

'Not at all, quietest day of the week,' he had assured her, 'and, by the way, no need to drag your son along with you. Leave him with us; he'll be happy enough with my two.'

When Robert had been shown the electric train set, he had made no fuss about being left.

Charlie wore a new overcoat, which wasn't really necessary on a day like this, but it made him appear even more broad in the shoulder. His beige cavalry twill trousers were sharply creased and his feet were shod in the very finest brown brogue shoes, for if there was one thing Charlie was particular about it was footwear. Only leather would do, nothing imitation.

Lizzie looked up into his face as they came to a halt outside the hotel. You wouldn't think he had just finished a season; his face glowed with health and his hair was still thick and glossy.

Lizzie herself had lost over a stone in weight since last Easter, and although the brown skirt she wore fitted well, the jacket hung a little loosely.

As if reading her thoughts Charlie said, 'Come on, my Skinny Lizzie, let's go in.' Lizzie was taken aback. No one had called her that for years!

The outside of the building hadn't impressed either of them. Dingy, they thought. The brick-work was dirty and colourless. The entrance hall wasn't much better, gloomy and shabby with arm-chairs that were frayed and faded. No one came, in spite of the fact that they had rung the bell twice. Sounds of music and laughter were coming from below, and they trod the wide staircase that led downwards. A game of bingo was being played in a colossal basement lounge that was crowded with elderly folk.

It was mainly the ribald remarks of the gentleman seated on the raised platform calling the numbers that accounted for the amusement of the players. 'Bit near the knuckle!' Charlie said beneath his breath as the caller's jokes became more and more indelicate.

They wandered off to one side of the hall and found themselves in what could only be described as a casino. Every conceivable type of gambling was there, plus machines which dispensed hot and cold drinks, bars of chocolate, packets of sweets and nuts, even packets of aspirin.

Lizzie thought of the endless hours that she and Charlie had spent in the evenings making pots of tea or coffee and boiling milk for Ovaltine or Horlicks.

They retraced their steps and each of them was embarrassed as a pot-bellied man with a high-coloured complexion stared angrily at them.

'Are you Mr Petrock?' Charlie asked in a composed voice.

'Yes, you must be Mr and Mrs Wilson; didn't expect you this early.' He ignored Charlie's outstretched hand, and merely said, 'I'm the warden.'

'Warden?' Lizzie spoke without thinking.

'Yes,' he replied, giving no further information.

'We'll start with the bedrooms.' He stalked off, leaving Charlie and Lizzie to follow.

'I don't like him,' Lizzie thought, 'miserable old beggar.'

The corridors were forbidding, very narrow, with no windows and badly lit. The decor and colour scheme consisted mainly of fawn paint. At first, Lizzie couldn't grasp the layout at all, as Mr Petrock opened door after door without saying a word.

Suddenly Charlie clutched at Lizzie's arm and held her back for a moment. His voice a harsh whisper, he said, 'I've just fell in. I've got it now. Apart from the main building, this place is a series of terraced houses with connecting doorways.'

There wasn't time for Lizzie to answer. Mr Petrock flung wide yet another door and stood back, though why he is bothering himself, I don't know, Lizzie thought, every room is exactly the same.

Each contained the maximum number of beds it was possible to squeeze in, and the vacant floor space was hardly enough to enable the occupants to walk around the beds. No chairs, no wardrobes, just a hanging space on the back of the door, covered by a dingy curtain.

The rooms were barren even of necessities, let alone any items of comfort. Door handles were broken, dripping taps over wash-basins needed new washers, carpets were frayed, rucked up in some places, light bulbs were burnt out, leaving sections of the corridors in complete darkness.

'Do you have a maintenance man on the staff?' Charlie asked.

'This is not The Ritz,' was Mr Petrock's ill-tempered reply.

Lizzie was about to say that they had seen enough when she saw that the room she had just entered was occupied. 'I'm so sorry,' she murmured, as she backed away towards the door. She suddenly felt frightened, although she could not have said what of. All she knew was that something was very wrong.

She turned, seeking Charlie, who, seeing the fear showing in her eyes, hastily pushed Mr Petrock to one side. Lizzie had to stifle the scream that rose up in her throat as her glance fell upon a seagull. The huge, fat, grey and white bird was perched on the window sill, not outside but *inside* the room.

As she watched, it took off in flight around the room, its great wings beating and thrashing in frustration. It appeared incredibly menacing at such close quarters, as it swooped low, squawking and shrieking, heading straight for Lizzie.

She screamed and covered her face with her arms, but Charlie shoved her aside. With long strides he was across the room to where an elderly man lay wedged between two beds. Kneeling, Charlie raised the man's head by placing his arm under his neck. Softly he murmured over and over again, 'It's all right, old chap, it's all right; you're safe now.' But the man was in such a state of agitation, rocking himself frantically from side to side, that he finally collapsed heavily against Charlie.

Quickly enough, Mr Petrock caught the gull and put it out through the window. 'Rough high-tide last night. Must have got in through the window and couldn't find its way out,' he complained – though there was a slight hint of an apology in the tone of his voice.

'Get some brandy, man, don't just stand there,' Charlie was fast losing his temper. Mr Petrock didn't bother to reply, he just went.

Judging from the shocking state of the room, the gull had been imprisoned for some length of time. Its droppings had soiled everything – the counter-panes on the bed and the carpet were liberally spattered, even the curtains were covered.

Charlie wouldn't leave until the man was obviously a lot calmer, and as Lizzie waited in the dingy hallway she asked herself what would have happened if they hadn't gone into that particular room.

The estate agent's list had detailed that this hotel was not an orthodox hotel in the accepted sense, rather a balance between a holiday home and a rest home for elderly people. The owners had contracts with various city councils and civic homes to take old-age pensioners, some on a long-term plan, others for shorter periods of approximately a month.

What had attracted Charlie was the hint that all-the-year-round trade was possible, rather than just a seasonal period.

That was all very well, but elderly people needed constant surveillance. If you took on the responsibility, you should damn well carry it through, Lizzie thought angrily. Like Charlie, she had been appalled at the conditions in which these old folk were roaming about. The whole place was fraught with danger.

'I've made you some tea,' Mr Petrock called from the top of the stairs.

'Have you now,' Lizzie said in a mocking voice, just as Charlie emerged from the bedroom.

'Leave it out, Lizzie,' he ordered. 'Christ, I can do with a cup of tea, the stronger the better, then we'll get out of here.'

A few minutes later they were seated in a private sitting-room. No penny pinching here. There were deep armchairs with plump cushions, thick pile carpet on the floor and full-length velvet curtains hung at the windows. They drank their tea in silence, then, reading each other's thoughts, Charlie and Lizzie stood up.

'Just one question, Mr Petrock,' Charlie said, 'where are the owners of this hotel, is it their day off?'

Mr Petrock was in a cold sweat, the incident upstairs had frightened him. The old man might have died. His hands dropped limply to his sides and he moistened his thick lips before he answered, 'No. They're abroad on holiday.'

'So, you're in sole charge?'

'In a manner of speaking.'

'Oh no, there's no two ways about it. Either you are in charge or someone else is,' Charlie's manner was furious by now. 'For God's sake, man, aren't you at all worried about what happened?'

Mr Petrock looked about him vaguely, then, turning to Lizzie, he murmured, 'I'll show you out through the kitchen, save you going upstairs again.'

The kitchen was the last straw! Both Lizzie and Charlie were horrified. Lizzie couldn't move, she just stood and gawped. Everything was so disorganized, and the smell was dreadful!

The flagstone floor was thick with grease. A complete wall of shelves held vast numbers of cups, saucers, plates and dishes, and even a quick glance showed that the china was far from clean.

Two beautiful, expensive commercial cookers made Lizzie feel sick just to look at them. They were not just messy or mucky, they were plain filthy – absolutely soiled with grease. Unwashed saucepans cluttered the top of each stove.

Neither of them could wait to get out into the fresh air.

Having related the whole experience to Mr Fenwick they sat together quietly, deep in thought until Martin Fenwick made a profound observation. 'You know, Mr Wilson, someone will come along and buy that hotel. They'll have a lucrative business for a few years, then they'll sell it and end up just as rich as the present owners no doubt are.'

Under his breath, Charlie muttered, 'Well, it

won't be us.' Aloud he said, 'I don't understand how they get away with it. Aren't there regular checks on establishments that take elderly folk on a permanent basis? Surely, the local authorities should be involved.'

'I shall certainly raise the matter at the next meeting of the local hoteliers' association,' Mr Fenwick said and Charlie knew that his concern was genuine.

Chapter Twenty-Three

CHARLIE HAD TAKEN Robert to school and Lizzie was not yet dressed when the telephone rang.

'Phillips and Ashfield here, Mrs Wilson,' a smooth voice stated as soon as Lizzie picked up the receiver. 'We have a property on our books which may interest you, would you like me to mail you the details?'

'Well, we shall be coming down to the village later on. We'll call in and pick them up.'

'Thank you, Mrs Wilson, goodbye for now.'

Lizzie and Charlie were in Mr Phillips' office by ten-thirty.

'My, you're keen,' John Phillips said as he shook hands with Charlie. 'I've never had the pleasure of meeting you before, Mrs Wilson, though I have downed the odd pint with your husband before now.' Actually, he was quite surprised – Mrs Wilson wasn't at all what he had expected: small-boned, slim, sleek fair hair, a woollen two-piece with shoes, gloves and handbag which all toned in extremely well.

She was no Devon dumpling.

'How does the Manor House Hotel at Milton grab you, Charlie?'

Lizzie watched closely as Charlie scanned the typed sheets of paper. First name terms, these two. Well, well.

This John Phillips was big, and handsome with it, and to be fair, he was the type who would be popular with men as well as women. He turned now and smiled broadly at Lizzie. Yes, he could be a useful friend, she thought approvingly.

That evening, Charlie looked through the motoring guidebooks.

'Yes, here it is,' he pointed out to Lizzie enthusiastically. 'Manor House Hotel, well established, popular with tourists and near a famous beauty spot.'

They were on their way before ten o'clock the next morning. The countryside, though not at its best, still looked fresh and good. The hills were green, the cattle in the fields looked well fed and contented, and the agricultural land was tilled ready for the winter frosts.

Even from the outskirts of the village, the hotel was visible. Perched on a hilltop site, it was very prominent. Clearly sign-posted, Charlie soon drew the car to a halt. Ahead lay a surprisingly lengthy driveway.

Lizzie held her breath for a long time before letting it out in a loud gasp. Formal gardens with low hedges lay each side, and groups of trees and flowering shrubs were still vivid with colour.

They sat in silence as Charlie drove up to the hotel.

Four wide marble steps led up to a huge oak door.

'What do you think of it?' Charlie asked.

'Beautiful,' Lizzie said, 'but we could never afford anything like this.'

The big door opened before they had got out of the car and a slim young woman in a flowered dress walked down the steps to meet them. Lizzie thought her to be about thirty-five. She had a country look about her, rosy cheeks and her cotton dress was stained with earth as if she had been working in the garden.

She came towards them eagerly. 'I'm Phyllis Martin, my parents are expecting you. I'm their youngest daughter. Come in, you're staying for lunch, aren't you?'

Lizzie was amazed at such a welcome.

Mr and Mrs Jeffries were waiting in the entrance hall. Both Charlie and Lizzie soon surmised that Jeffries was not the original surname of this nice couple.

Charlie found holding a conversation with Mr Jeffries heavy going. His birthplace had been Poland and, although he had lived in England for a good many years, his English was not that good. Approaching seventy, he was pleasantly fat, but he had a further handicap, a gammy leg. When seated, it stuck out straight in front of him and, even with the aid of a stick, he couldn't walk without difficulty.

Mrs Jeffries was a homely type of woman; an older version of her daughter, uncomplicated and easy to be with. She ushered them through into a very large kitchen, sympathizing about their long journey, exclaiming over the rawness of the day despite protests from Lizzie that it wasn't at all cold outside. Moving quickly, she drew chairs near to a roaring fire. 'Take your coats off, come along, make yourselves comfortable. Phyllis is just making the coffee. Do you know this area?'

Charlie and Lizzie smiled at each other, Mrs Jeffries didn't seem to expect any answers.

Phyllis came through from what looked like a smaller kitchen, pushing a loaded trolley. The cups and saucers were attractive, white patterned with bold blue stripes, almost matching the gingham curtains which hung at the kitchen windows. The aroma of the coffee was good as Phyllis poured and handed the cups around. Mrs Jeffries handed out matching plates, insisting that everyone must eat a scone, piping hot and served with thick yellow clotted cream and strawberry jam.

While they were eating, Mr Jeffries told them that he had another older daughter. 'Karie . . .' the old man actually stopped smiling as he spoke her name. He took a deep breath and continued, 'Karie, she is on holiday in Jersey with her husband,' and Lizzie felt sure that his expression indicated his relief.

'If you're all set, shall we start the inspection? Are you coming with us, David?'

'Yes, yes, my dear, I'll tag along behind you all. Slowly it might be, but I'll make it.'

Mr Jeffries smiled apologetically at Lizzie and Charlie, then nodded gently to his wife and daughter. 'Go ahead, go along,' he shooed them.

The main staircase swept up to a semi-circular gallery which led to the bedrooms.

On this floor, the rooms were large, light and airy, not at all like the usual hotel bedroom. Lizzie's first thought was that they were typical of a country manor house, then she laughed at herself. How would she know? She'd never seen the inside of any manor house. Each room had an enormous, high, double bed, massive sized furniture and deep, comfortable armchairs which were drawn invitingly into the bow-shaped window recess so that any resident could view the grounds through the windows while relaxing.

The hotel had twenty-five bedrooms and, as they proceeded, Charlie and Lizzie exchanged glances. They were able to read each other's thoughts.

To each of them, it was obvious that Mr and Mrs Jeffries not only had a deep affection for each other, but also treasured their hotel and were proud of what they had achieved. Lizzie even felt a little guilty; the whole place had such a warm atmosphere, much more like a home than an hotel. She felt that she and Charlie were intruding and even began to ask herself why this dear couple had decided to sell up when, without a doubt, they loved this place.

On the second floor, the rooms were not so spacious but were equally charming. A lot of thought had been given to the furnishing of the bedrooms, although Lizzie got the feeling that most of the furniture had been installed there since the place was built many years ago.

It was the little final touches which added to the attractiveness of this floor. The windows were much smaller, yet the curtains were exactly right; each set was made to be in keeping with the surroundings. Rich, heavy, fully lined fabrics had been hung at the windows of the rooms on the floor below, with bedspreads and chair coverings all co-ordinated, but here the accessories were totally different in style and manner. Bright floral, cotton chintz had been the main choice. In parts, the carpets were old, even showing signs of being threadbare, but bright soft rugs had been scattered to compensate for this.

At the far end of this top landing were three rooms set apart up a further short flight of stairs, each so in keeping with the character of the house that Lizzie exclaimed, 'Oh, aren't they marvellous!'

'Not when it comes to working them, they're not,' was Phyllis's quick retort. 'They're very popular with the foreign tourists though.' Everyone laughed. Americans would term them 'quaint'. There was no running water here, only hefty marble-topped wash-stands on top of which stood ornate china jugs and bowls, each elaborately decorated with gilt.

At the base of the staircase, a panel of wood was

fixed to the wall from which hung two rows of brass bells, each suspended loosely by means of a hook-shaped spring. Above each bell, a plaque bore a number which presumably corresponded with a bedroom.

Lizzie's imagination ran riot. Supposing several rang at once, noisy, jangling, ear-splitting sounds – and how many staff would you need to keep running up and down the stairs in answer to their summons?

'It's all right, my dear,' Mr Jeffries chuckled, 'they don't work. The bell push-buttons are still in each bedroom, but they are all disconnected. I fear the days when such service was given are long gone.'

Lizzie and Phyllis exchanged conspiratorial glances.

'Thank God for that,' was their silent answer.

Charlie declared the dining-room to be his favourite.

All the tables were made of oak, and the high-backed chairs had upholstered seats. There was no carpet but the parquet flooring was so highly polished that one could have used it as a mirror.

'We cheat; we use an electric floor polisher,' Mrs Jeffries said proudly.

Next came the lounge. Lizzie unintentionally let out a shriek of amazement. Stepping further into the room, she felt that she had gone back in time – a high, moulded ceiling, an enormous white marble fireplace, bright wood panelling on the walls and a view of the sea in the distance from the windows.

Armchairs and settees were arranged into groups, even a chaise-longue, all covered in uncut moquette of a deep, rich red colour. The floor-length curtains were velvet with a deep valance which was decorated with heavy silk tassels. Small side tables and reading lamps had been placed at strategic points around the room.

By now, Mr Jeffries was visibly tired and limping badly.

'Do you mind if we ask to be excused? Phyllis will finish showing you around; lunch will be ready soon. David come, rest your leg; leave the youngsters to it.' Mrs Jefferies ushered her husband gently out of the room.

'You'd better come and see my quarters,' Phyllis frowned as she spoke.

'You've been marvellous, Phyllis,' Charlie patted her shoulder, 'we don't want to bother you if you'd rather not.'

'No, it's all right, really it is.'

Two minutes later, Lizzie understood the reason for Phyllis's reluctance.

Coming out into a courtyard, Phyllis led them down a ramp and opened a heavy door which was set into the brickwork, revealing a flight of steps leading downwards.

As they hesitated, two bonny little girls, aged about seven and eight, came running up the steps.

'Mummy, you've been a long time, may we go

over to Grandma's now?' the taller of the two pleaded.

'Just a minute. Say hallo to Mr and Mrs Wilson, and then we are all going to have lunch with Grandma.'

'Hallo,' they chorused, now happily hopping back down the steps. Lizzie chuckled as she watched them; they both looked so pretty, shining and spotless in identical blue dresses and hand-knitted white cardigans. Even Charlie was struck by their open smiling faces.

Phyllis's home was a basement apartment; nothing would disguise that fact. Clean and comfortable, but Lizzie concluded that not much daylight ever penetrated down here.

Soon they were back up in the yard, the two little girls, now running and skipping ahead of them. 'We've got plenty of garage space,' Phyllis said, pointing to what could have been a stable block in years past.

'Are these more sleeping quarters?' Charlie asked, stopping and raising his eyes to what appeared to be a recently built apartment over and above the whole block.

'No, that's where my sister Karie and her husband Ray live. It was built for them three years ago.' Then she added, with abruptness, 'They don't have any children.'

With a sigh, Phyllis led the way up the outside staircase. 'I don't have a key, you'll have to peer through the windows.'

It was very modern in appearance, with wide, clear windows, but this one-storey apartment was totally out of keeping with the main building. Noses pressed to the glass, hands cupped around their eyes, they could see that white was the predominant colour – the walls, the furniture, even the carpets were all white.

Lizzie thought it gave a clinical effect, you could tell at a glance no children lived in there. They almost tip-toed back down the iron stairway, acting as if they had been trespassing.

Charlie hung back and, taking hold of Lizzie's arm, he nodded towards Phyllis's back and murmured, 'A sight different to where she has to live.'

Lizzie was still curious and, as she entered the main door held open for her by Phyllis, she asked, 'Where do your mother and father sleep?'

'In one of the main bedrooms during the winter months, but they use a bed-settee in the preparation room when we're busy in the summer.'

At their age! Lizzie almost answered back, for there was something terribly unfair about this set-up.

Charlie quietly asked, 'Why do your parents want to sell this lovely place?'

Phyllis shuddered and, for a moment, Lizzie thought she was about to cry; instead, she changed direction, moving back towards the dining-room.

'Sit down, it's better if we talk in here; I don't want my dad to get upset.'

Slowly, almost reluctantly, she told them, 'When

my father reached the age of sixty-five, which was almost five years ago, in order to be eligible to draw his old-age pension he officially resigned from the business. Legally he made Mum, Karie and me a three-way partnership. We each, from then on, owned one-third of the hotel and all its assets. The trouble started from that very moment, and it was all Karie's fault.' Phyllis sat forward in her chair; her dark eyes were blazing.

'We came close to getting a divorce, my Ron and me. Sorry, Ron is my husband. He's a skilled engineer with a good job in Exeter. That's almost seventy miles and he does the journey every night and morning. Mind you, I freely admit, Ron does his fair share of moaning; he doesn't like living where we do, calls it an underground rat-hole.'

Who could blame him? Lizzie thought. An apt description in her opinion.

Charlie smiled and shook his head. 'I doubt you're any different to any other family, everyone has their squabbles.'

'Um, well,' Phyllis sighed, 'he doesn't like me to be working when he gets home, says the girls are left too long on their own.'

'What about staff?' Charlie stuck his neck out and asked, 'Couldn't you take on more?'

'There's no bus service that comes up here. Besides, the year before last Karie sacked two girls on the spot – caught them putting tinned stuff into their bags on the way out. She should have turned a blind eye, but no, that's not Karie's way. The people down in the village are a tight-knit community, they only heard those girls' side of the story. Anyway, they have never trusted us. Foreigners we are to them in every sense of the word; you'd think we'd all just got off the boat from Poland only yesterday. My mother and father have been in this country for forty-two years.' Her last sentence was said with bitterness in her voice.

Pulling herself together, Phyllis stood up, 'We'd better go and find Mum and Dad.'

Mrs Jeffries had food ready in the lounge and, in answer to Lizzie's protests, she insisted, 'It is only a light lunch to hold you over until you get home.'

They were each given a tray on their laps in order to eat the crisp cheese salad and hot rolls with butter. Rosie and Linda, Phyllis's two little girls, threw themselves down on to the floor and their grandma lovingly placed a tray in front of each of them. It seemed to Lizzie like a cosy family party.

Later, Phyllis left the room and returned with a glass of milk for each of her daughters and a cup of tea for everyone else.

Soon, Charlie stood up. 'We mustn't intrude any longer,' he said, but Mr Jeffries waved him back into his seat and leaned forward himself.

He was agitated, a fact that did not improve his speech. Mrs Jeffries did her best to calm him down, while Phyllis asked, 'Father wants to know, are you interested in buying our hotel?'

'Yes, we are,' Charlie said without any hesitation. 'Naturally, there's a lot to sort out. We have to sell our own place and we'll need a loan from the bank. Depends a lot on the bank, really.'

Mr Jeffries, calmer now, spoke slowly. 'If additional finance is a problem, I myself would be prepared to give a second mortgage.'

'Well!' the one word burst from Charlie's mouth. 'I don't know what to say,' he stammered, 'only, thank you.'

As Charlie drove away, Lizzie felt that their day had been spent in a completely different world. She sat day-dreaming, picturing herself cooking in that pleasant kitchen and reading in the long winter evenings, snug and warm in that wonderful lounge.

Turning his eyes away from the road for a moment, Charlie looked hard at Lizzie and considered his words carefully. 'Don't build your hopes too high,' he said, 'there's something wrong with the set-up there.'

'Oh Charlie, don't put the dampers on it. It was a lovely day, wasn't it?'

'Yes, it was,' he readily agreed, 'and nicer people you couldn't wish to meet. I'm just saying . . .'

What he was just saying Lizzie would never know, and she had the good sense not to ask, yet for one awful moment she had doubts. She shook her head hard; she wasn't going to let anything interfere with her dream of living at the Manor House Hotel.

That same evening, Charlie was on the phone to John Phillips for quite a long time. 'He feels sure he's got a cash buyer for this place,' Charlie said, smiling as he sat down, and that was all that was said on the matter that evening.

The following morning, Phyllis Martin rang. 'Would it be asking too much for you to come back again tomorrow?' her voice sounded strained.

'We'd love to,' Lizzie assured her, then her inquisitiveness got the better of her. 'What's happened, are your parents all right?'

Phyllis ignored the latter part of the question. 'Karie's home,' she said, and Lizzie heard her make a cynical sound. 'Father said it's best if we all meet. Mother said lunch would be ready at one o'clock, so we'll see you then, Mrs Wilson,' and the phone line went dead.

'Bit quick, isn't it?' was Charlie's only comment.

He was ready first next morning, wearing a suit, collar and tie, looking every inch a businessman. He scowled as he looked at his watch. Lizzie came through the door, her thin silk dress rustled as she walked.

'Do you think I shall be warm enough in this dress?' she asked and she smiled at him with eyes filled with excitement.

'How the hell should I know? You're taking a big coat, aren't you?'

'Yes,' she said, 'I'm ready.'

'About time, too,' he retorted, still scowling a little.

Lizzie came near and kissed him on the cheek. 'Something worrying you?' she asked.

'I don't know,' he moved quickly towards the door. 'I'll feel a lot better when I find out why the Jeffries have invited us back so soon. At least I hope I shall.'

'Why? Do you think they've changed their minds?'

'Just let's stop supposing things and get going, shall we?' Charlie said abruptly as he opened the door of the car.

When they arrived, it was Phyllis who came down the steps to greet them.

'Come inside first. Mother said we'll have a drink together.' Seeing their puzzled expressions, she quickly explained, 'We're having lunch at Karie's.'

The sherry was good, and the Jeffries seemed exceedingly pleased to see them both again. Phyllis's husband Ron was there, an ordinary, everyday type of fellow, rugged in appearance as if he spent a great deal of his time out of doors. Charlie and Ron Martin hit it off from the moment they shook hands.

Lizzie wasn't prepared for meeting Karie. She gaped almost open-mouthed until Charlie nudged her.

Inches taller than either her sister or her mother, Karie had a fantastic figure. The cream silk dress she was wearing didn't just fit well, it looked as if it had been moulded around her. Most lovely of all was her thick, shiny, auburn hair. Most probably the colour comes out of a bottle, Lizzie thought enviously. Everything about Karie was immaculate, her sheer stockings, elegant court shoes, even her long red fingernails. She was most certainly different to any other member of this family and Lizzie felt sure that this was no accident. One could tell that Karie strove hard to be different. Her husband introduced himself first to Charlie and then to Lizzie.

'Ray Daniels, pleased to meet you,' he spoke quietly.

He was a tall young man in silver-grey trousers and a well-cut black velvet jacket. His eyes were brilliantly blue and shiny, and his smile was warm and friendly. In fact, his whole air was open and boyish, even if his dress was a bit showy.

The lunch was excellent, down to the last detail, but what surprised both Lizzie and Charlie the most was that a dark-haired and dark-skinned young lady in uniform waited on them as they all sat around a glass-topped dining-table.

The mood while they were eating was very different to that of their previous meeting. There were long silences, especially between courses.

Finally, when the last dishes had been removed by the maid, Karie said brightly, 'Shall we have our coffee in the lounge?'

Mrs Jeffries's eyes never left her husband's face as they sat drinking their cups of coffee. The atmosphere felt decidedly strange and Lizzie was beginning to feel uncomfortable. As she repeatedly said to Charlie afterwards, 'I'll never know in God's name what sparked that lot off.'

Until that moment the whole family had been tolerant of each other, then suddenly it was as if a bubble had been burst. Everyone began to talk at once and in seconds the place was in an uproar.

Karie dominated the scene. Staring directly at Charlie, she left him in no doubt as to the frame of mind she was in. 'You are here under false pretences. I don't know why my father contacted an estate agent.'

'Now, dear,' Mrs Jeffries said, seeing her daughter's temper getting out of hand, 'there's no need to be rude to our guests.'

'Well, it can't go on. I won't stand for it. All he thinks about is selling the hotel. An hotel in which he has no legal part.'

'Oh, how can you be so cruel,' Mrs Jeffries uttered a groan while Mr Jeffries took out his handkerchief and wiped the sweat from his face and hands.

Lizzie had never felt so uncomfortable in all her life.

Charlie looked hot under the collar, and, but for the fact that he had just eaten a meal at Karie's table plus the kindness of the old couple, he would have stormed out there and then.

The argument continued in earnest now.

Ron Martin taunted Ray Daniels with the fact that he had no job. 'You live off your wife you do,' he spat out, his face only inches away from his brother-in-law's.

Karie turned on Phyllis. 'You only want money. Sell, sell, sell, is all I hear from you, just so that you can get your hands on a third of the money.'

'Christ! You're the right one to talk about money. You spend it quicker than we can make it. Yes, and I do mean *we*. Mum and Dad and me, we're the general dogs-bodies around her. It's us that does every job imaginable while you swan around playing the lady.'

Mrs Jeffries, her complexion quite flushed by then, placed herself between her two daughters.

And only just in time, thought Lizzie, she'd seen women row, even fight, in London, and this little do was fast getting out of hand.

'Do as your father wants,' Mrs Jeffries pleaded. 'If we sell this place, you can each buy a nice house, and your father and I can have a nice little bungalow; why not be reasonable?'

'It's nothing to do with our father; how many more times do I have to tell you?' Karie shouted.

Mr Jeffries, struggling to stand on his feet, implored his eldest daughter, 'All I ask is that you sign the contract.'

'No. I've told you and I mean it, no.' With a defiant look in Charlie's direction, Karie turned her back and walked out of the room.

Lizzie found that her thoughts were all mixed up. No way did she condone Karie's attitude towards her parents nor yet tolerate the fact that she was ashamed of them, for it was obvious that she was. In spite of all that, Lizzie found a part of herself admiring Karie. Who could blame her for being so stubborn? The business here provided her with a lifestyle she enjoyed, she was well set-up in a home of her own choosing, and she wasn't about to give it all up without a struggle.

She was utterly selfish, of course she was, but Lizzie couldn't help wondering how she might have reacted, given the same set of circumstances. Twice she asked herself the same question and still she honestly didn't know the answer.

To be fair, Ray Daniels did try to ease the situation. He went into the kitchen and made fresh coffee, offering brandy with it as he handed it round. The silence in the room hung heavy and both Lizzie and Charlie were relieved when at last they could say their goodbyes and make their escape.

It was a relief to be out in the fresh air.

Mr Jeffries had been visibly upset and had tried to apologize to Charlie. The women had kissed each other goodbye and all three of them had been close to tears. The journey home promised to be a solemn one indeed. For they now realized that owning the Manor House Hotel had been nothing more than a pipe-dream.

Chapter Twenty-Four

IT WAS GETTING towards the end of October now, and neither Lizzie nor Charlie had much enthusiasm left in them to go searching for another property. And yet the prospect of only having twelve bedrooms to let for the next season was not very encouraging.

John Phillips had twice shown the same couple around the guesthouse, a Mr and Mrs Sadler from Birmingham. They had both expressed an interest in the property. Lizzie had liked them well enough and on each occasion she had cut sandwiches and made coffee for them, but when it came to answering Mrs Sadler's questions as to the running of the guesthouse, Lizzie couldn't be bothered, and even Charlie refused to discuss business details with Mr Sadler.

'What's the point?' Lizzie overheard Charlie saying to John Phillips. 'We can't sell this place until we find an hotel for ourselves, and if we don't do that before Christmas, we might as well forget it.'

That's true, Lizzie agreed with Charlie. Once Christmas was over, there was never much time to spare. The mail had to be the number one priority. Every morning, letters had to be answered and replies back in the post by noon whenever possible.

After all, one could get the place looking like Buckingham Palace, but without any subsequent bookings, you'd be wasting your time.

Lizzie felt sorry for the Sadlers, they wanted an answer; their future was in the balance just as much as Charlie's and hers.

Two weeks slipped by during which nothing of importance took place and Lizzie was quite glad when Friday came round again and they could have their day out in Barnstaple. Having finished the weekly shopping, Charlie asked, 'Where would you like to have lunch?'

'Anywhere that suits you, I'm easy,' Lizzie replied.

'Right, let's make it the Imperial.'

They had almost finished eating when Mr and Mrs Farrant stopped by their table. Mr Farrant was a local solicitor with his own firm in a nearby village. On two occasions, Charlie had taken Lizzie to his office, once when needing advice, and a second time when Mr Farrant had taken care of the legalities when Lizzie's mother had died. Lizzie had also formed a friendship with Margaret Farrant while doing voluntary work for the WVS.

'When are you moving?' Mr Farrant asked.

Charlie's face must have had a blank look, because Mr Farrant immediately said, 'Didn't John Phillips put you in touch with the Jeffries out at Milton, the Manor House? I understood you were going ahead with that.'

Charlie laughed, 'I only wish we were. It all fell through.'

'Oh, I'm sorry to hear that. Well, finish your meal and come through to the bar, I may have some interesting news for you.'

Fifteen minutes later the two couples were settled with their drinks, on a window-seat in the lounge. After the usual small-talk, Mr Farrant said, 'Well, now to business.'

Taking a card from his wallet, he wrote a few words on the back of it, and then, passing it to Charlie, he spoke quietly.

'Take that to Freddie Clarke and he will arrange for you to view an hotel. It's a bit hush-hush, not yet officially on the market, but ideal for you two, I should think. Anyway, Freddie will fill you in on the details.'

Today, Charlie thought, it is not *what* you know but *who* you know that makes the difference.

Freddie Clarke was a well-known local character. His main occupation was as estate agent but by no means was it his only method of earning a living. He had earned the reputation of being a Mr Fix-It.

Not much was said over the telephone when Charlie rang him, except that he would be in to see them that same evening.

It was a little after seven o'clock when he arrived and the first thing Charlie did was offer him a drink, which he readily accepted. When they were all settled comfortably in the lounge, the two men with whisky and soda, Lizzie with whisky and dry ginger, Freddie opened his case and took out some papers and, nodding grimly, he said, 'These are the only details I have got. This hotel will be going up for sale but with certain drawbacks.'

'Oh, no, here we go again,' Lizzie said beneath her breath.

'Why all the mystery?' Charlie questioned.

'Because the owners don't want to sell,' said the up-to-now serious Freddie Clarke, then he leant forward, picked up his glass and drained it quickly.

'Mind if I smoke my pipe?' he asked, and Lizzie was surprised at just how old this man looked as she waited while he filled the bowl of his briar with tobacco and Charlie refilled his glass. Without his trilby hat, which he always wore when he was out, she could see that he was almost bald and he appeared tired and sluggish. He once more turned his attention to the papers which lay in front of him.

'It's not an unfamiliar story,' Freddie began, 'especially in this trade. Four proprietors, two couples, own one hotel, living in each others' pockets seven days a week, and you end up with friction. Plus the fact this lot has no business sense. Spent more than they earned. It has reached the stage where they have no option. The bank is about to foreclose.'

'Oh, no!' Lizzie muttered to herself. 'Does every family fall out if they work together in an hotel?'

'We can't do anything over the weekend, I'll make an appointment for you for Monday, shall I?'

Charlie agreed and they all got to their feet and shook hands.

'Remember now, just look over the property, don't discuss any business while you're there. It's a Mr and Mrs Fletcher and a Mr and Mrs Kirkland you'll be seeing. Good-night, Mrs Wilson, sorry to hurry off, but I've had a helluva day. Good luck.' He placed his hat on his head, shrugged himself into his raincoat and went with Charlie to the front door.

On Monday morning, if the weather was anything to go by, it was not a good omen.

'As filthy a morning as I ever remember,' Charlie said as he came in from having taken Robert to school; he shook his raincoat before hanging it up and Bob-Bob gave a low growl.

'Who's upset you, old boy?' He patted Bob-Bob on the head.

'You just shook all the rain off your coat on to him,' Lizzie said.

'Has he been out yet?'

'No, not yet,' Lizzie answered.

'Well, it's about time he did. Come on, Bob-Bob.'

Lizzie watched as Charlie opened the back door. The rain was simply lashing down and the high winds blew at gale force.

Bob-Bob took one look, turned tail and went back to lie on his bed in the corner. Charlie stood, and hesitated.

'Leave him be,' Lizzie laughed, 'he'll go out when he's good and ready.'

'Yeah, he's got more sense than we give him credit for,' and Charlie laughed with her as Bob-Bob barked at them both.

They started off on their journey, but with less enthusiasm than before.

Highland Heights was the name of the hotel, situated close to a small harbour just the other side of Ilfracombe, which meant that they hadn't too far to travel.

After about forty minutes they found the place and they looked at each other as they took stock of their bearings. Winding down the window, Charlie exclaimed, 'Look, it's only built about nine foot from the sea!'

The sound of the sea was deafening as great waves rolled in to crash on to the rocks far below.

'Cor blimey,' Lizzie cried, reverting back to her cockney dialect. 'Ain't it rugged here? Look at those cliffs, they look like masses of great boulders.'

Straining her neck, she saw that the building was at least five storeys high. 'The texture and colour of the outside makes it look as if it's built of granite,' Charlie observed. 'Really intimidating on a day like this!'

They both ran from the car to the side entrance, where a man signalled for them to come in.

'Do take those wet coats off,' said a woman standing inside.

They introduced themselves, which wasn't necessary as obviously they had been expected. In turn, the gentleman said, 'We are Mr and Mrs Kirkland. Come through to the kitchen, I have the kettle boiling.'

By now, Lizzie was feeling cold and Charlie reached for her hand as he said, 'a hot cuppa wouldn't come amiss, will it, love.'

Their footsteps echoed with a hollow ring as they crossed a large tiled hall and went into what seemed to be a small kitchen. Mr Kirkland made the tea and set the pot down on to a tray that was already laid out with cups and saucers. Then he excused himself, saying, 'I'll be back shortly.'

His wife had disappeared already. Gratefully, they drank their tea and Lizzie poured a second cup for each of them. Still, no one came. Restlessly, they began to wander.

There were three kitchens, each one leading through from the other. It was amazing the amount of equipment there was, mainly of stainless steel, each item scrupulously clean. Catering-sized saucepans and steamers, machines for peeling potatoes, a washing-up machine, three trade-sized washing machines; 'Perhaps they don't send the linen out to a laundry,' Lizzie whispered. There were two double-bowled sinks, each with double drainers, an electric slicing machine which Charlie switched on and, as it burred into life, quickly switched off again.

There were two commercial cookers, each with six burners and a vast oven, beside which stood a massive cast-iron grill. 'This lot must have cost a fortune,' Charlie said in a hushed tone. 'It's certainly a very professional working area. You could cook for an army with this lot.'

Mr Kirkland reappeared. 'If you're ready, I'll take you up to meet Mr and Mrs Fletcher.'

Going up a narrow flight of carpeted stairs, they found themselves in the main entrance hall, one wall of which was taken up by the reception desk and glass-fronted office. They both now realized that the side door through which they had first entered led only to the kitchens. The hotel was built on steeply sloping ground so that the kitchens, though on basement level at the front of the building, had large windows at the back overlooking the sea.

They were ushered into a small, but comfortably furnished sitting-room where Mrs Kirkland was sitting in an armchair close to a bright log fire. Again Mr Kirkland said, 'I'll be back shortly,' as he closed the door behind Lizzie and Charlie.

Without being asked, they both sat down and in silence Lizzie looked at Mrs Kirkland. She seemed a fragile, timid lady and Lizzie noticed that her thin, fair hair was streaked with white which added to her general appearance of delicacy. Lizzie thought that the poor woman must have been very ill. By comparison, her husband had appeared an active, vigorous man, bursting with good health.

A log moved in the fire, sending sparks up the chimney and at the same moment the door opened;

Mr Kirkland was back and with him were Mr and Mrs Fletcher.

'How d'you do?' said the short man with bloated features. He spoke gruffly as he took Charlie's out-stretched hand and merely nodded in Lizzie's direction.

Funny how opposites attract, Lizzie thought, as she said good morning to Mrs Fletcher. She was a striking-looking woman; her shiny brown hair was brushed into a French pleat at the back, leaving a few curls on the top of her head, but it was the deep suntan, set off by the white jumper she was wearing, that gave the greatest effect.

After the polite greetings were over, Mr Kirkland said, 'I'll show you around.'

The back of the hotel faced the sea. The layout had been so well designed that in the majority of the bedrooms, which were spaced out on three floors, one could lie in bed and watch the sea.

There were twenty-seven bedrooms, not lavishly furnished but adequate. All had wash-basins and hot and cold running water. Landings were spacious. On each floor there were two bathrooms and three separate toilets.

The staircase was grand. 'A work of art,' Charlie remarked as he walked down the wide treads and Lizzie ran her hand over the dark grained wood of the banister rail, noticing how elegantly it curved at each floor.

The public lounge was on the first floor. A plaque over the doorway stated, 'To stay here is to be on board a luxury liner'. Hardly inside the room and Charlie and Lizzie knew that was no exaggeration. An uninterrupted view of the Bristol Channel stretched before them. The size of the room threw Lizzie off balance for a moment.

There were five sets of windows!

Curtain material alone must have cost a fortune, she thought. The windows were gigantic, reaching from the floor almost to the exceptionally high ceiling.

The many deep armchairs all matched, having floral, chintz loose covers, but the dominating feature had to be that view of the sea directly outside.

Lizzie and Charlie held hands as they looked out of one of the bay windows and they were speechless. The huge panes were being lashed by the rain, and the turbulent sea beyond rolled in and crashed on to the huge jagged rocks, sending mighty plumes of foaming spray high into the air.

Reluctantly, Charlie and Lizzie turned away. Reaching the ground floor once more, Lizzie this time noticed port-holes set into the walls of the entrance hall and a board above the reception desk which read, 'The Captain's Cabin'.

On into the dining-room, almost an exact replica in size and shape of the lounge. Here, the nautical look had been maintained. A large anchor entwined with ropes was fixed to an end wall with more port-holes in evidence around the room. Here also, the grey angry sea, with huge waves topped with what looked like galloping white horses, swept over the rocks immediately beyond the windows.

Mr Kirkland had hardly spoken a word while they had been doing the rounds. He had merely opened doors and stood back.

Returning to the sitting-room, Mr and Mrs Kirkland said a cordial goodbye to Lizzie and Charlie and left them alone with the Fletchers. There was a curious hesitation to all of Mr Fletcher's movements. Eventually he asked, 'Would you like to look over this lot?' and he pointed to a table which was placed beneath the window.

'Incredible!' Charlie said without thinking. The whole table was covered with stationery: menu cards, account forms, booking forms, memo pads, wage slips, writing paper that looked almost regal it was so heavily embossed. There were small envelopes and large envelopes all of which were overprinted on the outside in royal blue with the name and location of the hotel. Not just a few of each, but boxes and boxes of them.

Again, Charlie spoke aloud, 'God! The printing bill for this lot must have been colossal.'

Behind them Mrs Fletcher coughed and her husband said indignantly, 'The brochures are in those boxes on the floor by your feet.'

The brochures were coloured. Views of the interior and exterior of the hotel were on every page. The write-up had been done by experts. The coloured plates and blocks were also there and this time, as he examined them, Charlie kept his thoughts to himself, for this also must have been a very expensive operation.

Mr Fletcher was pouring himself a stiff drink as his wife led them back downstairs and struggled against the wind to open the side door for them.

'Well, that was over quick enough,' Charlie said as they reached the safety of the car.

Lizzie gave him a sudden quick smile, 'We do get around, don't we? At least we're seeing how the other half live.'

Then, to her astonishment and delight, Charlie leaned across his seat, put his arms around her and very tenderly kissed her. He held her close for a long moment and when he did release her, he said with all seriousness, 'We're going to have that hotel, Lizzie.'

Chapter Twenty-Five

DURING THE DAYS that followed, Charlie walked about the house singing to himself and occasionally grinned from ear to ear.

He had numerous telephone conversations with Freddie Clarke and twice Lizzie got the impression that he was speaking to Mr Farrant. Lizzie had attempted to ask questions, but all she got from Charlie was an instruction to be patient.

Then, one Friday morning, as Lizzie took care with her make-up and hair while deciding what to wear (for she was never quite sure where Charlie would end up taking her for lunch) she heard the telephone ring yet again.

A few minutes later and Charlie almost bounded into their bedroom wearing an open-necked, short-sleeved shirt and still looking very tanned.

'Mr Farrant is sorry for the short notice, but he wants us to be at his office two-thirty this afternoon.'

'What for?' Lizzie asked, squinting into the mirror as she softly pencilled-in her eyebrows.

'How the hell do I know? I'm going to get changed.'

'You don't have to be so irritable,' she muttered and then thought to herself, of course he knows what it's all about, it has to be concerning Highland Heights.

Beyond that she would not let herself think, but if they got a bank loan . . . If – Oh stop it, she told herself angrily, don't build your hopes up again.

Mr Farrant's office was one of several sited above the bank, all were occupied by professional men.

A clerk looked up from his work. 'Mr and Mrs Wilson?' he enquired, then led them through from the outer office and opened a door on which gold lettering spelt out 'Farrant, Day and Dalston'.

Mr Farrant himself welcomed them, giving Lizzie a charming smile which immediately put her at her ease.

Two other men were sitting comfortably in chairs placed behind the huge desk. 'Mr Harding you already know,' Mr Farrant said, as indeed they both did, for he had acted as their accountant for the past two years, preparing Sea View's books for the Inland Revenue, 'and this is Mr Sims. He is here to take notes. We are only waiting now for Mr Parker.'

Only recently, Graham Blackhurst had been promoted, moved on to a much larger branch of the bank, and this had made Lizzie sad. He had been a good friend to both her and Charlie, always available for a chat, ever ready with good, sound advice. She wondered what this new man, Mr Parker, would be like.

She didn't have long to wonder.

A sharp tap at the door and he entered, earnestly

shaking hands with Charlie first and then Lizzie, before taking a seat. He was very tall. The tallest of all the men present. At least six foot three inches, he looked every inch a successful bank manager, if a trifle flashily dressed.

An informal meeting began, though Lizzie was conscious of the fact that both she and Charlie were being scrutinized. Weighed up and judged, she thought to herself.

Mr Harding read out facts and figures on their progress since taking over Sea View Guesthouse. Mr Parker had a bulky file in front of him, which he flicked through, pausing now and again to scribble columns of figures on to a pad.

Mr Farrant caught Lizzie's eye, and again he smiled at her, this time in an encouraging way. She thought, not for the first time, how handsome he was.

Mr Parker took off his heavy-rimmed glasses and looked directly at Charlie. 'I understand that, in principle, the bank has agreed to grant you a loan. Well, on your past record and on the recommendations of Mr Blackhurst, you can go ahead now with your purchase of Highland Heights. That is, if you are willing to comply with certain conditions.'

His pause then was so long that Lizzie felt everyone in the room could hear her heart thumping and she saw that tiny beads of perspiration had formed on Charlie's forehead.

'The main condition being that a company be formed, thus allowing the bank to take a debenture on the hotel.' Maybe Mr Parker sensed Lizzie's confusion. He explained more fully. 'A debenture would acknowledge the debt to the bank, repayable with guaranteed interest.'

Mr Farrant and Mr Parker, now with heads close together, had a quiet exchange of words.

'All right? Are you happy about everything?' Mr Farrant, with pleasure showing on his own face, directed this to Charlie.

Apparently, Charlie was more than happy, for he leaned forward and gravely shook hands, first with the new bank manager and then with Roger Farrant.

'Providing all the searches and paperwork can be got through, all loose ends tied up, shall we suggest January 11th for completion date?'

Charlie's mood could only be described as exuberant as he drove to Adelaide College to pick up their son, while all Lizzie felt was utter bewilderment.

Forces behind the scenes must have been working on their behalf, she told herself, but why did they warrant such help? They were going to buy Highland Heights. Even a completion date had been set and yet they had only had a brief look over the hotel.

They had had no real meeting with the owners. Sadly, Lizzie reflected that if the bank was foreclosing because it was owed money that must effectively make the bank the owner.

What misery and anguish those two couples must be going through, the very thought of them having to leave that lovely place made her feel wretched. I hope to God it never happens to us, she mused.

Minutes later, a smile spread over Lizzie's face as she watched Robert raise his cap to Miss Warrell-Bowring and set off at a trot down the drive.

The run-up to Christmas was spent in cleaning rooms, washing blankets and generally making the place look nice. Charlie did all the repairs that were necessary, including replacing tap washers. They were selling Sea View Guesthouse to Mr and Mrs Sadler, fully furnished as a going concern, goodwill included. Lizzie was more than pleased that she had already taken quite a few bookings for the next season and had quite a tidy sum of money taken as deposits to turn over to the young couple.

The Christmas period was spent very quietly, just Lizzie, Charlie and young Robert alone in the guesthouse.

There were several reasons for this, the main one being that they were short of money. The cash left over from the previous season had been used to place a deposit on their new hotel. The guesthouse deal was not to be completed until 10th of January and even then the profit from the sale would have to go towards the purchase of Highland Heights.

Once again they were getting into very deep waters. Lizzie had worried herself sick when all these negotiations had begun, but now she kept telling herself that Charlie knew exactly what he was doing and that this time he wasn't on his own. He seemed to have professional men not only acting for him but decidedly on his side.

She hoped with all her heart that her assumptions would prove to be right. God help them if they didn't!

Lizzie kept telling herself that she was enjoying Christmas and she was to a certain degree. When she thought back over the years of the war, with their austerity and danger, she realized just how lucky she and her family were – a roaring log fire, plenty of good food to eat and presents and toys spread out beneath a glittering tree. But it was the sight of the Christmas cards standing on the furniture and strung around the walls that brought on the wistful thoughts.

Doris and Syd wouldn't have ordered their turkey from the butcher. They would have waited till it was dark on Christmas Eve before they'd have gone down to Tooting Market and along the Mitcham Road in search of their bargains. She could imagine Syd and Arthur, with a few pints of beer inside them, playing Father Christmas, filling Lucy's and Raymond's stockings, letting the kids put a carrot out for the reindeer, which Syd would probably have a good old gnaw at to show that the reindeer appreciated their kindness.

Boxing day made Lizzie really homesick. The Horse and Groom always put on a party for the kiddies during the afternoon. What wouldn't she give to be there. Whistles, drums, cymbals, trumpets, anything that made a noise would be used; hats, funny masks, streamers and indoor fireworks – the place would be like bedlam!

The men would be making utter fools of themselves, crawling about on all fours. It was the one day of the year when that pub was geared to nothing more than ensuring that every child in the neighbourhood had a good time and received at least one Christmas present. Jack and Dolly Hawkins were publicans of the old type and their customers loved them.

Lizzie didn't voice her thoughts aloud, but she vowed silently to herself that never again would she willingly spend a Christmas away from dear old London – unless, that is, her family came to Devon again for the holiday. For Christmas was a time to be with one's family and to have those that loved you and whom you loved around you.

The Sadlers came and stayed with them as their guests from the 6th of January.

Having their company eased the strain of the last few days. At last, it was the 11th, and Lizzie, Charlie and Robert had breakfast with Mr and Mrs Sadler at seven-thirty in what, legally, was now the Sadler's house.

In the basement bedroom, Lizzie viewed herself in the familiar mirror for the last time. Was she dressed suitably? She had spent ages pressing the grey suit and white blouse she was now wearing. Oh well, she sighed, too bad if she wasn't.

All her other clothes were packed, and already the cases were in the boot of the car. Charlie stood in the doorway, looking spruce and smart. Robert clutched tight at Bob-Bob's lead. Margaret Farrant had offered to have both Robert and the dog for the day, since two of her boys were Robert's school chums.

They kissed the Sadlers goodbye; everyone called out their good wishes. Charlie started the engine and then, with a final wave, moved off.

Assembled in the chambers were five men, Roger Farrant, Gordon Parker, Mr Harding, Mr Sims and one rather young-looking clerk, and now, Charlie made six.

This meeting was vastly different from the previous one, nothing informal about these proceedings. A small table had been positioned against a far wall at which Mr Sims and the young clerk now sat, one on each side. Mr Parker and Mr Farrant sat in their usual position behind the vast leather-topped desk.

Mr Harding sat next to Charlie, facing them, with Lizzie on his right. He agreed to be the company accountant. Mr Farrant used a very authoritative tone of voice to say, 'Charles James Wilson and Elizabeth Louise Wilson as sole directors. Elizabeth as company secretary, Charles to be treasurer. The company to be known henceforth as Highland Heights Hotel Ltd.'

At this point, Mr Harding bent forward and, from

a case which lay at his feet, he took what to Lizzie looked like a heavy press.

'The company seal,' he said, and very formally got up and placed it on the desk. Returning to his seat, he again reached into his case and took out a cheque book which was at least twice the size of an ordinary one. On each cheque, the name of the company was embossed, together with both sets of initials and the surname Wilson. Mr Harding passed the book over to Mr Parker, who immediately began to write out cheques, stating aloud each amount and giving a clarification of the purpose for which it was needed, pushing each one towards Charlie for his signature.

The amounts seemed enormous to Lizzie. She felt queasy. It was all much too complicated. She screwed her eyes up tight and bent her head forward. The next thing that she was aware of was Mr Farrant standing near, a shadow of a smile on his lips.

'All right, Mrs Wilson? I've opened the window, we'll take a break, have some coffee.'

When a young lady, dressed in a severe dark outfit, came into the office bearing a tray on which were several cups and saucers plus a large coffee pot, Lizzie's only thought was, thank God I haven't got to stand up and pour it out, for she felt that her legs would buckle beneath her.

While they were drinking their coffee and Charlie was deep in conversation with Mr Harding, Roger Farrant did his best to put Lizzie at her ease. 'It's not every day one becomes a company director.' His lovely grey eyes sparkled as he teased her.

The cups were cleared away and it was back to business. Try as she might, Lizzie couldn't keep her hands from trembling as first Charlie was asked to sign several legal documents and then herself. During the whole of this time, Mr Sims and his clerk had been busily writing and entering figures into a ledger.

Mr Sims looked up, coughed discreetly and drew the attention of Mr Farrant who left his seat and joined him at the table. The two men had a quiet conversation during which a lot of head nodding and hand gestures took place, resulting in Roger Farrant returning to his desk and turning towards Mr Parker.

'Gordon, how about granting Mr and Mrs Wilson an extra five hundred pounds on their loan? They are on a very tight budget and an extra five hundred would see them in with a lot more ease. In fact, from their point of view, it is almost a necessity.'

It seemed to Lizzie that whole minutes elapsed before the silence was broken. She glanced furtively at Mr Parker; his face was stony, his lips set in a firm line. Lizzie wished she was anywhere but in that room.

Finally, shaking his head, Gordon Parker said, 'No. From bus personnel to company directors in three years is not bad going. As from today, they are on their own.'

Lizzie felt the colour drain from her face. Quickly

she turned to look at Charlie; she was choked. She wanted to put her arms around him, there and then, to tell him to ignore that bank manager. What did he know about them? He'd only just come to the village. Her anger was now getting the better of her. If Mr Parker said just one more word, I'll tell him to shut up, she vowed.

Poor Charlie, he looked so embarrassed; his cheeks were red and his hands clutched together so tightly that the knuckles showed white through the skin. Even Roger Farrant seemed speechless; you could have heard a pin drop, the silence was so great. No answer, not a comment from anyone was made in reply to Mr Parker's judgement.

Finally, it was all over. Everyone in the room, including Mr Parker, shook hands with Charlie and Lizzie and congratulations were offered.

'The keys to the hotel are in the outer office,' Roger Farrant said, insisting that he escort them to the car park.

Although he did not show it, Mr Farrant felt responsible for Lizzie and Charlie. It was he who had set them on this road. From what he had heard, Mr Wilson was a conscientious man, a hard worker, and as to Mrs Wilson, well, Graham Blackhurst had had great admiration for what he had described as a gutsy woman.

He hoped they hadn't gone too deeply into debt.

When they reached the car, Mr Farrant turned to Charlie, saying, 'I'd like you both to listen to what

I have to say. I am convinced that you two, working together, will make a success of Highland Heights. You'll be all right, you're going in at the right time, deposits should be coming in.'

He stopped speaking, looked at them both as if considering something, then, slowly, he continued, 'The forming of the company and preparing of the documents, plus the registration fee has been calculated in your accounts at five hundred and five pounds. That amount is what is owed to my firm. What I am trying to say is that we won't be sending you our statement for at least one year. That will give you a little more time to get on your feet.'

Charlie held out his hand and in silence the two men shook hands.

Lizzie was stunned – such generosity! She swallowed deeply before she was able to say, 'Thank you, Mr Farrant.'

She couldn't get over it. Roger Farrant was everything a woman likes in a man, naturally sophisticated, with a nice sense of humour, but it had always been his jaunty, almost flirtatious manner that had made Lizzie like him. Not a bit stuffy like the usual run-of-the-mill solicitors. Now she was overwhelmed.

Not only was his offer very generous, it was also a face-saving gesture towards Charlie.

It was eleven-thirty when Charlie drove up to Highland Heights. He unlocked the side door, and they smiled at each other, held hands and went in.

Relief! All the waiting, the tension and anxieties were over. They were in their own hotel.

They spent the rest of the morning exploring, in and out of bedrooms, gazing over the banisters from what seemed a great height, staring out of the windows of the lounge, still utterly amazed at the sea that was so close. They lingered in the dining-room watching the seagulls swoop and listening to them screeching. Finally, they went to the kitchens downstairs.

'What's through there, Charlie?' Lizzie called as she watched him disappear.

'My God!' she heard him exclaim.

'It looks like a ballroom. Never been used for years, I shouldn't think.'

'There's three more small bedrooms down here,' Lizzie cried, 'I think they must be staff rooms. Come on, let's put the kettle on. You did put that box with the tea in it in the car, didn't you?'

There was no need for Charlie to go to the car and fetch the box. On one side of the cooker there was a caddy filled with tea, a bowl of sugar, two pints of fresh milk, and further back was a crusty new loaf, a half-pound packet of butter and a wedge of Cheddar cheese.

A hand-written note lay on the cabinet. 'Good luck', was all it said, but it had been signed by M. and T. Fletcher, and H. and D. Kirkland.

'Isn't that kind?' Lizzie murmured.

'Certainly makes a nice beginning,' Charlie answered.

*

The telephone rang, and from then on it never seemed to stop all afternoon. Good wishes from all sides; a florist's van arrived with two bouquets, one from Syd and Doris and one from Arthur and Polly, the postman brought 'Welcome to your new home' cards from Connie and Bill and Aunt Kate and Uncle John.

By the evening they had two adjoining bedrooms on the first floor made up, plus the private sitting-room, now bright with vases of flowers, and their own china ornaments and photographs set out. Though they were thoroughly exhausted, they were both very pleased with the results.

During the rest of the week, apart from taking Robert to school and meeting him, they only went out once. Charlie remarked, 'You'd better come out for a walk, get some fresh air into your lungs.'

It was a very raw, cold morning and, though the sun was shining, there was a keen January wind blowing in from the sea. The surrounding hills were extremely steep and the coves very rugged. Bob-Bob was in his element as he bounded on ahead. Having walked as far as the harbour, they were both glad to turn back. Nevertheless, Lizzie admitted that she felt better for having been out in the open air and their faces were glowing by the time they got back indoors.

At the weekend, the question of insurance arose. Up until now, Charlie had only obtained temporary coverage. Now a more clearly defined policy had to be considered, on this the bank was most insistent.

'Ten o'clock Monday morning, they are all meeting here,' Charlie said as he replaced the telephone receiver.

Promptly on time, Mr Hutchinson, an inspector from the insurance company, arrived. Mr Parker and a colleague from the bank were late.

'Better open the main entrance doors before the bank officials arrive,' Mr Hutchinson whispered to Lizzie. She ignored his advice.

Mr Parker and the official from Head Office came in through the side door. He introduced himself as Mr Thompson, and Lizzie took to him straight away. 'How does it feel to own one's own company?' he asked Lizzie in a friendly, almost jovial kind of way.

'First, we have to assess the building and the contents,' Mr Hutchinson said and Charlie led the way.

Mr Parker hung back. 'I would have appreciated it if you had opened up the main entrance for Mr Thompson,' he said, and his manner was aggressive.

'Why? The side door is good enough for us,' Lizzie answered, and her tone of voice was insolent.

'Careful!' he spat the word out sharply, but before he could say more Lizzie stopped him. Tall as he was, she wasn't about to be intimidated by him, not this time.

'Mr Parker, you have made my husband and myself company directors and this hotel is now the registered office of that company, but it is also our home.' Without pausing for breath, because her courage might have failed her, Lizzie pressed on. 'Please, don't think we're not grateful for all the help and advice the bank has given us, but as I understand it, we shall be paying a large amount of money in interest on the loan and, as you so aptly pointed out the other day, from here on we are on our own. We don't have to kow-tow to anyone.'

To Lizzie's utter astonishment, Mr Parker threw his head back and laughed, a vigorous, strong sound which had Lizzie staring at him open-mouthed.

He took a step towards her and, placing a hand across her shoulders, he said, 'You'll do. You'll make it, Mrs Wilson, without a doubt you'll make it.'

As he turned away to join the other men, Lizzie could still hear him chuckling to himself as he walked down the corridor. Thankfully, she sank down on to a chair. She had made her first impression as a company director.

Talk about being thrown in at the deep end!

Life in an hotel, especially one where the trade was seasonal, was vastly different to living and working in a guesthouse.

They needed staff. Waiters, chambermaids, kitchen boys to prepare the vegetables, work the dishwashers and clean the ovens, girls for the still-room to make endless pots of tea and coffee and wash the silverware, Saturday boys to carry luggage and show guests where the garages were.

They decided not to employ a chef. Charlie boned his own sides of bacon, roasted numerous legs of pork and lamb and huge, succulent pieces of beef. He spent hours preparing chickens, turkeys and cutting up pounds of steak and kidney for pies. Ham cooked on the bone was his speciality. Lizzie made all the pastry, she also made the soups, gravy and sauces and prepared large quantities of fresh fish and side salads.

The sweet trolley, cheese trays, plus the hors d'oeuvres were tasks that they shared. They prided themselves that they could make sixty cold decorative sweets in individual sundae glasses in just fifteen minutes.

All did not go smoothly. Not all the time.

Staff failed to turn up. Guests arrived late, sometimes past midnight. Laundries failed to return the linen on time. The poultry man's van was not the most reliable of vehicles and Lizzie would hold her breath some mornings as she cracked eggs into an oval pan that cooked ten at a time and prayed that some guests would prefer kippers or smoked haddock, because their stock of eggs was running low.

It was no exaggeration when Charlie spoke of an eighteen-hour day, seven days a week. Six in the morning until midnight at least.

From two p.m. until four p.m. was their free time. Maybe! Except on Saturdays, when folk were leaving and arriving all day long. Not Thursdays either because guests' accounts were made up then. Lizzie would write while Charlie would call out names, room numbers and whatever extras, such as early morning tea, had to be added to the bill.

On Fridays Charlie would sit at the reception desk while visitors paid their accounts. The money had to be sorted, staff wages made up and then Charlie would dash into town to bank the remaining money, while Lizzie counted the clean laundry, hoping it had all been returned safely.

There was a bright side. Charlie applied for and was granted a licence. Women dressed in their pretty summer dresses, men in flannels and open-necked shirts would sit, making friends, chatting and laughing in the bar at the end of warm, sunny days.

All were exceedingly sociable to Lizzie, whenever she decided to join Charlie for a drink. Everyone complimented her on how well the hotel was run, insisting that she look at the photographs they had taken and would not take no for an answer when requesting Lizzie and Charlie pose for a photograph together.

We shall have enough snaps to fill a dozen albums by the time we retire from here,' was the thought that struck Lizzie.

The first week in July 1954 turned out to be a week that Lizzie would remember for a very long time. The hotel guests were mostly from London, which was unusual, since the majority of bookings, Lizzie had found, came from northerners, and during the wakes weeks every guest in the hotel would be from Lancashire or Yorkshire.

The newspapers had been full of the fact that America had sent two of her special sons to England. One was Billy Graham, a Southern Baptist minister, who had, in May, held a mass meeting in Wembley Stadium. The papers had reported that thousands of people had attended and that hundreds had surged forward pleading to be converted.

The other American to cross the Atlantic was an entirely different kettle of fish. Bill Haley and his Comets were to introduce a new rock beat to country music, an exciting combination which immediately achieved immense popularity. Their first recording, 'Shake, Rattle and Roll' sold thousands of records up and down the whole country.

It was on a warm sunny night in June, that Charlie played this record and, although space in the bar was limited, a couple in their early thirties got to their feet and started to dance to the music. Lizzie had just walked into the bar with a plate of sandwiches and she stood stock-still staring in amazement. 'You couldn't call it dancing,' she remarked to Charlie, as she set the plate down behind the counter. It was all arms and legs as the fellow swung his partner from side to side, twirling her like a top to the beat of the music, finishing by sliding her through his wide-apart legs.

As the record came to an end a spontaneous burst of applause came from almost every guest in the bar.

Whenever Lizzie was to tell this story in the future she always emphasized that not everyone approved. A dear old couple, well turned seventy, rose to their feet and the man, speaking in a very loud voice, said, 'Barbaric! Like a pair of savages. You'd do better to listen to Billy Graham and turn to the Lord.' You could have heard a pin drop as the old folk, quietly and with dignity, made their way through the tables and left the bar. Lizzie hadn't dared to look at Charlie as she beat a hasty retreat muttering as she went, 'Oh well. It takes all sorts to make a world.'

Chapter Twenty-Six

EARLY IN THE new year of 1955, the weather-men on the wireless had forecast that the country was in for a bad winter. That had been putting it mildly! January wasn't even halfway through yet and already the weather was absolutely terrible.

During the last seventy-two hours it had never stopped snowing. Heavy falls meant that most villages in north Devon were already cut off. There was ice everywhere and the roads were treacherous. Lizzie moaned to Charlie that despite all the extra woollens she was wearing she just couldn't seem to keep warm.

'Yer don't wonder at it do yer,' said Charlie, lowering the scarf that he had wrapped round his neck and face so that he could be heard. 'The bloody temperature dropped well below freezing last night and it hasn't risen at all this morning yet. Not likely to either, by the look of that sky.'

The week wore on and they felt like prisoners in the hotel as the weather worsened. The hotel gardens jutted out to the sea, and were reached only by climbing several stone steps. To Lizzie it was madness even to think about climbing up there. Nevertheless that was exactly what Robert and his father insisted on doing every morning. Lizzie watched anxiously from the dining-room windows as the two of them, muffled to the eyeballs, did the precarious climb. Robert had both hands free and was able to clutch at the rocks for support. Charlie had only one free hand, because in the other he carried a shopping-bag filled with soaked bread, dried fruit and dishes of fat. It was the only way that they could think of to keep at least some of the birds alive.

It wasn't too bad for Charlie, his feet were much bigger and he had strong sturdy boots. All Robert had on his feet, other than two pairs of thick socks, was a pair of wellingtons. More than once Lizzie's heart came up into her mouth as she watched Charlie put out his free hand to steady Robert.

Face flushed and excited, Robert would come bursting in again through the back door calling, 'Mum, Mum, you ought to see them all, they were waiting for us to feed them.' But it was a sad little boy who came back a few days later. There had been no let up in the great freeze, in fact the winds had whipped up the snow into drifts, making matters very much worse. Charlie had picked up five dead birds, all frozen stiff.

By the end of the week Charlie declared he had had enough of being indoors. 'Come on, muffle up well an' we'll go for a walk. See how far we get. We can always turn back if the going gets too tough.'

It was slow going as they turned towards the hills, their feet leaving deep imprints in the snow. Already the dog was racing ahead of them. 'He seems to like it even if we don't,' Lizzie said, her voice muffled by her thick scarf.

On the way back, the noise from the sea was deafening, the wind was almost up to gale force and as they no longer had the wind at their backs it was a job for them to get along. Charlie stopped and, much to Robert's delight, swung him up on to his shoulders. As they got near to the hotel Lizzie exclaimed, 'What a welcome sight.' Before they had left, Charlie had switched on every light in the porches and around the building.

Their private sitting-room on the ground floor was cosy and warm, but going up to their bedrooms on the first floor where the wind howled and rattled the huge bay windows was another matter. The kitchens being downstairs didn't help either. The entrance hall became known to them all as No Man's Land.

One night, as Lizzie came up from downstairs carrying a loaded tray, she plonked the tray down, shivered and hugged herself, then held out her hands to the blazing fire.

'I wish we had a smaller cooker,' she said half to herself, 'it takes ages for one of those huge ovens to heat up, and those great big burners are ridiculous when I only need to heat a small saucepan of milk.'

'You're always wishing for something,' Charlie murmured, not really paying any attention to what Lizzie had been saying.

Busy putting the hot pies on to three plates, Lizzie

suddenly exclaimed, 'OK, clever clogs. I've forgotten the teapot. I've only brought the hot-water jug. You cross No Man's Land, go down the stairs and through to the second kitchen and fetch it for me.'

Rather sheepishly, Charlie got to his feet, but had to laugh as Lizzie added, 'If you run quick enough, you won't freeze.'

They were grouped round the fire tucking into their meat pies and jacket potatoes, which Lizzie had split open and lavishly spread with butter, when Charlie asked, 'How about a separate house, or even a bungalow?'

'What?'

'We could live in it in the winter. Be less expensive than to heat this hotel. You and Robert could even live in it during the summer. I could sleep in this room on a divan, and we could then let our two bedrooms.

Lizzie put her hand behind her back, drew out a small cushion and chucked it at Charlie's head. It missed. Robert and his father both chuckled. 'You never could bowl, Mum,' Robert said.

'What's the matter?' Charlie wanted to know. 'Don't you like the idea? I thought you'd be all for it.'

'Oh, I like it all right,' she leant forward and nudged Charlie with her elbow, 'it's you. You've got our bedrooms let to guests before we've even moved out. Besides, talking about another house and buying one is an entirely different matter, and by the way, if, and I said if, this comes about, do you think I might have a choice?'

'Lizzie, my darling,' Charlie bowed his head in mock adoration, 'the choice shall be entirely yours.'

The weather gradually improved and, armed once again with details from estate agents, they were out and about looking at small properties. Nothing suited.

Charlie's arguments were, one, they had to live close enough to the hotel to keep an eye on the place and, two, from Christmas onwards, they would have to pick the mail up every morning. It was essential that all enquiries were answered on the same day, otherwise they would start to lose bookings.

The agents had given details of every property on their books, but Lizzie hadn't seen one that she wanted as a home.

Charlie grew bad tempered. 'You're too critical,' he flung at her.

'Waste of time to look further,' Lizzie decided. The subject wasn't mentioned again for at least a week.

They were sitting in the car outside the gates of Adelaide College waiting for Robert, when Charlie came out with another suggestion. 'How about having a place built?'

'How? Where? How much would it cost?' the questions poured from Lizzie.

'Hold your horses, for Christ's sake, I dunno any

of those answers yet, do I? It was only a thought I had.'

But early next morning, Charlie was off. Curiosity was killing Lizzie as she made the beds and washed her hair to pass away the time.

It was three o'clock in the afternoon before Charlie drove his car up the drive and behind it came the conspicuous car of Freddie Clarke – Mr Fix-It had come to call.

To see Freddie was a tonic, bright and breezy, with his trilby tilted jauntily to the back of his head. The way in which he greeted Lizzie, arm around her shoulders, kiss on both cheeks, made her feel that all was well with his world.

'I've bought a field of Christmas trees,' Charlie blurted out.

Now what? Lizzie had visions of Charlie going to London in December and selling Christmas trees on street corners. Before she could tell him that this time he had gone too far, that he ought to be certified as mentally insane, Freddie calmed her down.

'It's a plot of land. Residential building permits have already been granted. I've got three adjoining plots to sell. I never gave it a thought before. Be just right for you, Lizzie, I promise you'll love it.'

'Where it is?' Lizzie got a question in at last.

'About two miles out on the old road. Get your coat, we've just got time to show you the plot before it gets dark.'

They all piled into Freddie's car.

The surroundings where the plots were situated was truly lovely.

'Makes a change from being right on the sea's edge,' Lizzie said as she stood on the sloping hillside and sniffed deeply at the smell of the pine trees and noticed that there was still a good view of the sea, shimmering away in the distance.

She understood why Charlie hadn't let the grass grow under his feet.

Locally there was only one builder, whose name was Ron Geering, and he was honest enough to admit to Charlie that the job of building a house was too big for him to handle. He admitted he would very much like to be considered for sub-contracted work on the project, but as to being the main builder, definitely no.

Meanwhile, he was prepared to give as much help as he could and Charlie gratefully accepted the benefit of his advice. Discussions began.

'Talk a lot,' he advised, 'before approaching an architect. They charge a helluva lot of money for their time. What type of dwelling do you prefer – house or bungalow? What type of heating – electric or gas?'

No sooner had they settled one thing, than Ron Geering would suggest another point to bear in mind . . . it went on and on. Reluctantly, Lizzie agreed she didn't have the technical knowledge needed for her to join in these discussions. Even Charlie began to wonder whether this time he had bitten off more than he could chew.

Ron advised them to leave it a while. 'The ground won't lose any value,' he assured them. 'You both want to give a great deal of thought to all the matters that I've raised. Don't make any decision in a hurry.'

Charlie thanked him and promised to keep him informed of whatever conclusion they came to.

Lizzie felt defeated.

About ten days had passed during which Charlie had twice driven Lizzie out to visit their plot. Sold notices were now on the two adjoining lots.

It was a quarter-past eleven at night when the shrill ringing of the telephone made Lizzie jump; she had her book in one hand and a hot drink in the other and was on her way up to bed. She left Charlie speaking into the receiver.

'Who was on the phone?' Lizzie raised herself up on one elbow as she spoke.

'Freddie Clarke. He's bringing a chap called Michael Gale to see us in the morning.'

'Who's Michael Gale?'

'I can't rightly say, Freddie said he's known him for years.'

Promptly, at ten o'clock next morning, Freddie was in the hotel introducing Mr Gale, who was a tall, athletic-looking man in his early forties, with blond, almost white hair.

Lizzie made coffee and soon everyone was on friendly terms. Mr Gale certainly had a way with women. While he was speaking to Charlie and Freddie he had Lizzie feeling that she was included, that nothing would be decided without her knowledge or participation. Lizzie liked that.

Having established the fact that Charlie had bought a plot of land and that, yes, it was his intention to have a private dwelling of some kind built there, Mike, as Charlie was by now calling him, stated that he was a member of the Federation of Master Builders.

'How would you feel about a package deal, involving all three owners of those plots?' he tentatively asked.

Charlie looked dubious.

'Have you approached any firms?'

'Only a local builder,' Charlie told him.

'Right,' the self-assured Michael Gale began. 'On such a project as this, insurance is absolutely vital. You must make sure that you don't sign any contract which makes you legally liable for accidents to contractors or workmen. Don't make yourself liable for theft or damage to materials and equipment whilst on your site. Some insurance companies will arrange special temporary cover for building materials and machinery, but would probably charge very heavily for materials that were being left out in the open on your site . . .'

Charlie sighed heavily and Lizzie suggested more coffee.

Freddie Clarke winked at her as she took away his cup to refill it.

'You must also insist on setting a completion date . . .'

Mike Gale was off again with his dire warnings as he spooned sugar into his cup from the bowl that Lizzie held. 'Equipment doesn't always arrive on time. At various stages during the building, inspectors have to attend. Inspectors lead very busy lives, probably have a long way to travel each time to your site, Charlie. You'd have to make appointments to fit in with their schedules, not yours. My firm could save you all those headaches . . .'

Lizzie could see that Charlie was almost ready to surrender. She found her courage and spoke up. 'When you say a package deal, exactly what do you mean? Do we end up with what you want us to have? Have the other two owners agreed yet? Or haven't you spoken to them?'

'Whoa, whoa, you're going too fast for me, Mrs Wilson, let's take your questions one at a time. Package deal first. You allow us to tender for a prototype external house or bungalow, to be decided at a later date. All three properties to all extents and purposes would be very similar, though not exactly the same from the outside. All your personal preferences and ideas could and would be incorporated inside. It could work out very much cheaper, save all three plot owners a great deal of money. Secondly . . .' and on, and on.

At last Charlie was able to chip in. 'You still haven't said whether the other two owners have agreed.'

Very reluctantly, Michael Gale said, 'No, they have not. They are still considering the matter.'

Then he played his ace card.

'Come to Bristol. The other two couples have agreed to that. An architect and several members of my firm will be there. We'll show you plans, a film and several colour slides to help you make a final decision as to the type of building you would all choose and decide on. Nothing definite, you don't have to sign anything, just come as our guests. Nice hotel . . .'

'OK, Mike,' Charlie said as they shook hands, 'we'll come to Bristol. Make a nice change for Lizzie if nothing else. Beyond that, I'm promising nothing.'

Turning to Freddie, he grinned, 'Probably cost me a bloody fortune, if I let Lizzie loose in Bristol.'

Freddie hung back and his face became quite serious. 'I didn't pull Michael out of any old hat, you know, Charlie. He *is* trustworthy. His firm is bona fide, honestly.'

'I know,' Charlie told him, equally serious, 'it's just that I need time to think and talk things over with Lizzie.'

When the two men had left, Charlie turned to Lizzie, saying, 'We'll go to the bank in the morning, together. I'll ask Mr Harding to meet us there.'

The meeting at the bank didn't take long. Mr Harding produced copies of the company's returns. Mr Parker approved the idea of a private house as a sound investment and put forward the suggestion that the purchase should be a private one. Outside the company.

'Repayments on the loan can be made from your own income,' Gordon Parker smiled at Lizzie, 'just in case.'

He laughed now, and Lizzie turned to Charlie, 'Just in case of what?'

'Just in case the company should flounder,' Charlie told her. 'No creditors would be able to claim on our home.'

'Oh,' was all she said, but inwardly, Lizzie liked the sound of that.

'Make a detour, Charlie, please, let's go and look at the site again,' Lizzie pleaded as they drove home from the bank.

Charlie just nodded, and before long they were there. They held hands like a couple of teenagers and climbed right to the top of the hill. Out of breath and trying to breathe deeply, Lizzie stood still while Charlie wandered off on his own.

The view was fantastic. The winter sunshine was streaming through the green trees and suddenly she felt a surge of excitement. This spot was going to be their home. Not the company's property. Not to be used in any way for business purposes, every room would be theirs. All of it would be theirs.

All this surrounding natural beauty, it was breathtaking. She wished she could wave a magic wand, have the house built now. She hoped that if and when building did start, as few trees as possible would be disturbed.

From that vantage-point, so high up, she could

see right across the Channel and, way below, the surf was still booming on to the rocks. Here, please God, they would eventually have stability, an environment of normality, a home where their son could bring his friends.

Charlie made Lizzie jump as he came up behind her and nuzzled his face into her neck. 'You were day-dreaming, miles away, do you know we've been up here for over an hour?'

By lunchtime, a week later, Charlie and Lizzie were in Bristol. Robert was safely away on a school trip, and Mr Gale had arranged everything perfectly.

The Hydro was a nice hotel. Charlie registered at the reception desk, and booked them in for a stay of at least four nights.

They freshened up and then went downstairs into the bar. Michael Gale bought a drink for each of them and introductions were made.

The other two purchasers were a Mr and Mrs Courtney and a Mr and Mrs Marshall. Not local people, in fact, one couple had travelled from Birmingham.

After a very nice informal lunch, during which everyone seemed friendly and at ease, they moved off into a large room which was obviously used for business meetings, and here everyone gathered around a circular table as drawings and plans were laid out. There was talk amongst the men of ground-floor plans, upper-floor plans, south elevation, north elevation. Lizzie heaved a sigh and withdrew to the back a little and so did Mrs Marshall.

'Do you understand the drawings?' Mrs Marshall asked in a quiet voice. Lizzie shook her head and whispered, 'No, I don't.'

'If you will all take a seat now,' Michael Gale gestured to where chairs had been set out in a row, 'we will show photographs of suitable dwellings designed with your situation in mind. If any of you spot anything with which you feel you would be happy, both in size and type, please stop me and I'll be happy to discuss such a property at length and in much greater detail.'

Blinds were drawn down over the windows, the projector started to make a purring sound and the first colour slide appeared on the screen.

The second slide came up, much the same as the first, a dull, long, low type of bungalow.

It was when the third slide came up that Lizzie let out an exclamation of surprise without stopping to think. It wasn't that the house being shown was large or even very impressive. It was different.

'This is a split-level bungalow,' Mr Roberts, the architect, was saying. Lizzie glanced quickly at the other two ladies; both smiled and were very clearly impressed.

Now, having everyone's full attention, Mr Roberts showed more slides of this bungalow from various angles, the interior, lower floor, entrance hall, bedrooms, shower room, bathroom and separate toilet.

'Why bedrooms downstairs?' Mrs Courtney asked.

Mr Roberts grinned, 'I'm coming to that.'

Technical drawings came up on the screen. 'Split-level means that by building the second half high up on and into the hill, one will gain all the benefits of the views. The upper-ground floor, as it is known, would house the kitchen, dining-room and lounge. The lounge would be thirty-five foot long, one wall of which would be mainly glass.'

Suddenly, another slide appeared and even the men gasped. It showed the exterior of the lounge. The glass doors in the photograph were opened on to a huge veranda fenced in by ranch-style white slats and the solid floor was two-toned concrete slabs.

The decision was unanimous, at least amongst the ladies it was. Was all of this real? Lizzie asked herself.

She was bursting with excitement. Had they found the ideal bungalow? Would it eventually be built? Would it look exactly like those colour slides or would it all turn out to be an unachievable dream?

She wanted to laugh, yet she also felt like weeping.

She wanted to throw her arms around Charlie, hug him, kiss him, share all this excitement, but there were too many people around. He must have been having similar feelings, as he tucked his arm through Lizzie's and squeezed so hard it hurt.

That was a very intimate moment.

No one else in the room mattered, just each other.

Chapter Twenty-Seven

THE SECOND SEASON hadn't proved too difficult, the weather had been good most weeks, which must play a great part in any holiday. The guests could get out and about and there were less moans to contend with.

However, with the coming of their third season in Highland Heights, Lizzie felt she was a lot wiser and certainly not so starry-eyed about the job.

They were well into July 1956 when Charlie put the fear of God into her. The pair of them were in the court-yard, which was outside the main kitchen, slumped in deckchairs, having a quiet hour before lighting up all the ovens and getting the evening dinner on the go. Suddenly Charlie lowered the newspaper he was reading, leant forward and touched her knee. 'Do you realize Lizzie, it's quite possible I might get called up?'

Lizzie's heart missed a beat. 'You shouldn't joke about a thing like that,' she quickly rebuked him.

'Who's joking?' he retorted. 'I know you don't get much time to read the papers but even you must be aware of all the trouble there is with Egypt over the Suez Canal.'

Lizzie didn't answer. Of course she had heard rumours, but she took the attitude that she had quite enough of her own problems to contend with without trying to solve matters that were going wrong on the other side of the world.

Charlie continued to read his paper, now and again making a comment out loud. 'Sir Anthony Eden's not very popular with the Americans. Both Eden and France want to send troops in. There's talk of it going to the United Nations.'

'Well, wasn't that why the United Nations was formed? To act as peacemaker?' she asked.

Charlie only mumbled something about her having her head buried in the sand.

Lizzie got up, folded her chair and leant it against the wall. 'Let's 'ope to God that all these men in power see a bit of sense for once,' she flung back over her shoulder at Charlie; 'surely one war in anyone's lifetime is more than enough. Come ter that there's many a person still alive that is still suffering from the First World War.'

The days and weeks of August and September seemed to drag. Life became monotonous, the same old routine day after day, sweltering in the hot kitchens while the guests lay on the beach or swam in the sea, the scorching sun shining down on them.

By the time the season was over once again Lizzie was thoroughly disillusioned. Despite all the promises that she'd made to herself, she had not been back to London since 1953. Doris phoned regularly and she herself would often telephone Doris or Polly. But these conversations only made her feel worse.

Her thoughts would be back in London and it didn't take much for her to conjure up pictures in her mind of what her friends and relations were up to.

This particular Friday seemed endless to Lizzie as she wandered about the hotel. She found herself doing the same job over and over and the silence was becoming eerie; her footsteps sounded loudly each time she crossed the tiled entrance hall and she prayed that the telephone might ring. It could be anyone on the other end, she didn't care who it was as long as it was someone to talk to.

Charlie had gone to Cardiff for the weekend, to see a football match. It was a long-standing arrangement, an outing for the local darts club that Charlie played for. The men had caught The Cardiff Queen at eight o'clock that morning, the last paddle-steamer to leave Ilfracombe harbour this season. Lizzie didn't begrudge Charlie his weekend with his mates but it had coincided with the weekend that Robert was away, staying with a school friend named Stephen Banks, whose father and mother owned holiday flats and a caravan park out at Heale, a very picturesque village on the way to Combe Martin.

Lizzie had found it hard to make friends down here in Devon; she fell between two stools. The largest of the hotels in the vicinity were company owned and run by managers put in for the season only. During the winter months such hotels would be closed up. No one there to get friendly with. She liked some of the women who worked for her and

Charlie, especially the real Devonians and she had tried hard to get one or two of them to go into Barnstaple with her for a day's outing or even into one of the local pubs for a drink. She'd had no luck. They regarded Lizzie as a foreigner from London, their boss and not someone with whom they could socialize.

As the short October day drew to a close and the daylight began to fade, Lizzie could hear the wind howling and the waves crashing on to the rocks. It would probably be a very high-tide tonight and she was thankful that Charlie wasn't making the return crossing until Sunday.

What could she possibly do with herself during the long evening that stretched ahead? 'I know what I would do if it weren't fer you,' she said crossly as she opened the door at the foot of the stairs and let Bob-Bob bound up to the sitting-room. 'I'd be on that first train up ter London. What the 'ell 'ave I got ter keep me 'ere.'

With that thought came the action. None of them had to stay here. Not for another long dreary winter. 'Jesus Christ!' she exclaimed and the sound of her own voice seemed to mock her. People were fond of saying that seasonal hoteliers only worked six months of the year. Well, she now knew for a fact that you did a year's work in that six months. Then what did you get? Maybe October, November and December off, but you had to be here every day from the beginning of January to answer the mail each day and to do all the running repairs that were necessary.

Lizzie dialled the number of her brother's house, but when the phone rang and rang with no one there to answer it Lizzie could have cried with temper. It seemed that everyone else in the world had somewhere to go and more than likely someone they could go with.

It was only after the third attempt that Doris finally answered the phone.

'I can't stay in this bloody place a minute longer. Charlie's took 'imself off to Cardiff, Robert's staying the weekend with his school friend, an I'm stuck in this blasted hotel on me own with no one to talk to but the bloody dog.'

Doris listened to Lizzie's outburst and now in her own placid way she calmly said, 'Why don't yer come up? We've got stew for dinner.'

That was exactly what Lizzie needed. The logic of Doris. She threw back her head and laughed so hard she almost dropped the phone. Stew for dinner!

'Doris, much as I would love a plateful of your stew I don't own an airplane. What I want you ter do for me is ter go to the estate agent's at Wimbledon first thing in the morning, see if they've got a furnished house to rent for three months, tell them it's for me, maybe someone there might remember me.'

'Who's the house for?' Doris's sing-song voice

came down the line and Lizzie was sure she was taking the mick.

'You know damned well it's fer me and Charlie. If we don't get away from 'ere, at least for a while, I shall end up killing him.'

'Anyway, why d'yer want a house, you can all stay 'ere.'

'Doris, if I were near you at this moment I would strangle you!'

Lizzie heard Doris's soft tinkle of a laugh and she relaxed.

'Seriously Doris, it would be better if we rent a house, that way we won't get under one anothers' feet and Charlie won't be able to moan so much if he's in a place of our own.'

Suddenly Doris's voice sounded very serious as she said, 'OK, Lizzie, I'll be round at Wimbledon nine o'clock in the morning. I'll phone you as soon as I've found you something, and Lizzie . . .' Doris hesitated.

'Yes, love?' Lizzie queried.

'Take it easy tonight. Have a drink and go to bed early. I'll ring you before ten in the morning. Night Lizzie. God bless.'

'Good-night Doris. God bless you.'

Lizzie felt a whole lot happier as she replaced the receiver, though she was a little apprehensive when she thought about how she would tell Charlie of her decision.

'Sod him,' she said aloud in an attempt at bravado, 'if he don't want ter come 'ome he can bloody well stay down 'ere in Devon an' see how he likes talking to himself.'

Lizzie spent an awful night, tossing and turning, punching her pillow and moving from side to side in the big double bed. When she did finally fall into a light sleep it was almost day-break and it wasn't long before the noise of the sea and the screech of the gulls had her awake again. She gave it up as a bad job, got out of bed, pulled her dressing-gown tightly around her and made the cold trek down to the kitchens.

'Talk about madness,' she mumbled to herself as she waited for the kettle to come to the boil, 'all in all there must be more than thirty rooms in this hotel an' there's me rolling around the damn place like a bloody pea in a colander.'

It was twenty minutes past ten when the phone rang and Lizzie snatched it up with a sigh of relief.

'I've found you somewhere, Lizzie, only five minutes' walk from us.' Doris sounded excited as she poured her news down the line. 'No houses I'm afraid, but I've put a deposit on a maisonette. Do you remember the big 'ouse on the corner of Longley Road, we used to call it the two-faced 'ouse cos it 'ad windows side and front.'

'But that place is enormous,' protested Lizzie.

'Wait, just let me tell yer, it's bin turned into flats an' they're all being let furnished. Only the bottom one is still vacant and the old boy at the estate agent's said they'd only take a six-month let, nothing less. Well, I told 'im all about you. He said he remembered yer, but I don't know if he did. Anyway, I said you only wanted somewhere ter stay while you were looking for another house ter buy, 'cos you were coming back ter live in London and you 'oped he'd be able ter find you something nice.'

'And?' Lizzie asked but she knew what was coming and there was laughter in her voice.

'You got the garden flat, as the old boy called it, for three months as from a week terday. Next Monday yer can move in, that's if Charlie don't kill yer first.'

'Oh Doris, trust you!'

They talked for another few minutes till Doris said, ''Ere this is early morning rate an' if I don't soon put this phone down Syd will kill ME when he gets the bill.'

Charlie's reaction surprised Lizzie. He put up no resistance to the idea, not even any argument. She had fully expected that they would have a right old barney, and had been prepared to tell him exactly what he could do if he didn't want to go with her to London. Instead, he had smiled in such a way that would normally have aggravated her, and from then on had been thoroughly cooperative, going so far as to offer to go to Adelaide College and make it right for Robert to be absent until the new year.

It was the end house in a row of terraced houses with a bay window in the front which looked out at the houses opposite, and another bay window at the side of the house which looked out on to the High Street. Situated on the opposite corner was a small shop which seemed to sell every imaginable thing.

The furniture in all the rooms was adequate, but nothing at all to get excited about. Mostly it was 'utility' – furniture that had been available during the war, and then only on dockets issued to newly-weds or people who had been bombed out.

The first thing they set about doing was finding a local school that would take Robert. They were lucky. The headmistress of Colliers Wood Junior School was most understanding and said they would be happy to offer a place to Robert for as long as his parents deemed it necessary.

Their first week in London was progressing nicely. Syd had started his own business, hiring out cars for weddings and such like and had taken a lease on premises in Totterdown Street at the back of Tooting Market. It was Thursday morning, Charlie had gone off with Syd, and Doris and Lizzie had just arrived back at Doris's house from taking Raymond and Robert to school. Raymond was in the junior section, while Robert had settled into the infant department.

'We'll wash up these breakfast things, 'ave a cuppa an' then go down Tooting, shall we?' Doris asked as she put the bung in the sink and poured a kettle of boiling water over the dirty plates.

'Yeah,' Lizzie said, picking up a tea-cloth ready to dry up. 'We can give Polly a knock as we go.'

Doris laughed, 'Polly'll be over 'ere before we're ready ter go. We always go down Tooting on Thursdays.'

At a quarter to eleven the three of them were just going out of the front door when the phone rang. 'I've a good mind ter let it ring,' Doris moaned. 'It's more than likely only Syd wanting me ter do something or other.' The ringing persisted as Doris closed the door, and then something made her change her mind. Putting her key into the lock, she opened the door and ran down the hall. Two minutes later she was back and the colour had drained from her face.

'It's Robert! He's missing! They've rung the bell after playtime an' no one can find 'im.'

'Oh my God!' Lizzie's heart was already beating like a drum inside her chest as she threw down her shopping bag and purse and ran back inside the house. 'I'm gonna phone the police,' she called back to Doris.

'Lizzie! Lizzie! He's 'ere.' Polly was out at the front gate and was pointing a finger up the street.

Lizzie spun round on her heels and was up and out in the road in a few strides, then she stopped, staring in disbelief. Her young son was a few feet away from her, looking very bedraggled, his cap was on crooked, his plimsoles, tied together, were strung round his neck and he was dragging his satchel along the pavement. 'I'm never going to go to school ever again,' he declared as Lizzie swept him up in her arms.

'How did you get home? How did you manage to cross the main road? How did you know to come ter Auntie Doris's house?'

'Lizzie leave him be for now,' Polly put out a restraining hand on to Lizzie's shoulder. 'Come on, let's get him back inside the 'ouse. Doris has gone ter phone the school ter tell them that he is all right.'

'All the boys keep calling me a Devon dumpling,' was the only explanation that they could get from Robert.

They phoned Syd and within twenty minutes Charlie was home. Having found that his son was safe and sound Charlie laughed, which was a great relief to Lizzie. She had fully expected to get the blame.

At one-thirty Charlie took Robert back to the school and once again the headmistress was most kind, promising that she would sort the matter out. Both Lizzie and Charlie were outside the school gates at a quarter to four when Robert came running towards them with three other bigger boys in tow. 'Dad, Dad,' he yelled, 'will you take Jimmy, Sam and Freddie home in our car because they're my friends now, Miss Thompson said they're to look after me.'

From then on Charlie gave all three boys a ride home every afternoon, because, as he said, 'What choice have I got. I've got to look after my son's minders!'

The third weekend that they were 'home' Syd got

tickets for the six of them to go to Chelsea Palace on the Saturday evening. He couldn't have picked a worse night.

They got off the tram outside The Weatsheaf at Trinity Road and walked to the bus stop. It was almost impossible to see a hand in front of your face because the damp thin fog, which had swirled round during most of the day, had now become much denser. How glad they were when they at last saw the headlights of the bus penetrating the blackness. The journey took longer than usual but they were grateful to the driver of the bus when it pulled up safely outside the theatre.

'Don't fink we'll be going much ferver, it's turning out ter be a right pea-souper,' the driver called down to his conductor who had come off the bus and was standing on the pavement looking up at his mate in his cab.

'Did yer 'ear that?' Polly called to the men who had walked on in front of them. 'If the buses stop running 'ow the 'ell are we gonna get 'ome?'

Arthur, usually the one with the least to say, turned his head and called, 'You can start walking now if yer like. Yer silly cow, we've only just got 'ere an' you're worrying about 'ow we're gonna get 'ome. Fer Christ's sake, let's git ourselves inside an' maybe we'll 'ave time to 'ave a drink before the show starts.'

''Ark at 'im getting out of his pram,' Polly said in a whisper to Lizzie, and they were all laughing as they went inside the warm foyer and made for the bar.

The applause was thunderous as Winifred Atwell seated herself at her Honky-Tonk Piano. 'Ma, she's making eyes at me', 'Bye, Bye, Blackbird', 'California here I come', 'Who were you with last night?', 'Fall in an' follow me', all these great songs were belted out as the audience sang at the tops of their voices and the rafters of the old Chelsea Palace rang as they hadn't done for many a long day. The audience was loath to let her go and for an encore she played a quiet tune, 'Who's sorry now?', which was sung by men and women alike with a great deal of feeling.

When they came out Syd suggested that they walk over Battersea Bridge. A wind had got up and the fog had lifted a little, but as they crossed the bridge the dampness from the river Thames below seemed to Lizzie to spread right over her and she was glad when Syd broke into a run flagging a taxi down.

'I'm on me way 'ome mate, I live at Wimbledon an' I ain't about ter make a detour fer nobody ternight.'

'That's all right. Can yer drop us anywhere between Tooting Broadway and Colliers Wood?' asked Syd, adding ruefully, 'But there's six of us.'

'Must be your lucky night,' the old cabbie said as he put his arm backwards and unlocked the door of his cab. 'Me son's just drawn in behind me, he'll take a coupla yer.'

On the short walk to the house Lizzie huddled up

close to Charlie; the wind might be a good thing, getting rid of that acrid smell of fog, but it was bitterly cold. There was one thing, though, that they were both agreed on; it had been a smashing night out.

Doris and Lizzie were making their way home from the shops, their coat collars turned up against the cold. 'Doris, Doris!' a voice called out as they reached the front gate. ''Ang on a minute, I've got somefink I wanna show yer.'

'Oh hell! Aggie Baggie!' Doris told Lizzie as she put the key in the lock. Half turning she said to the scruffy-looking woman who was by now right on their heels, 'I suppose you'd better come in.'

Lizzie started to take the shopping from the bags while Doris took a poker to the fire. Lifting the banked-down coal, letting a draught through, she soon had bright flames darting up the chimney. Getting up from her knees, Doris spoke to the woman, 'Aggie make it quick, I gotta get the dinner and yer know what my Syd's like.'

Aggie sniffed and, lifting the large patchwork bag from her arm, she emptied the contents on to the table. Lizzie's eyes lit up. There were four or five skirts, real quality, expensively tailored skirts.

'I like the grey one,' Lizzie murmured as she picked it up and fingered the cloth.

As if on cue, the door opened and Syd came into the room. He took everything in at a glance. Thumping his fist down on to the table he shouted at his sister, 'Lizzie, you must be out of yer bleedin' mind, they're Braffman's skirts.' Taking a step towards Aggie, he spoke with menace in his voice, 'You bin up ter yer tricks again? You nicked them, an' all right it ain't nothing ter do with me what you get up to, but I've told yer before keep out of my 'ouse and don't try flogging yer stuff ter my family, 'cos if we get the coppers round 'ere so 'elp me God I'll see you pay for it. As fer you, Lizzie, you might 'ave known she was a tea-leaf. An' you, Doris, what the bloody 'ell did yer let 'er in 'ere for?'

Lizzie put the skirt down on the table and, as she looked up, she saw Charlie was leaning back against the door; she hadn't heard him come in.

Syd wasn't finished by a long chalk. He grabbed the bag from Aggie and shoved the skirts inside it. Charlie moved and Syd shoved Aggie through the door and up the hallway. When he came back he spoke, taking in both Doris and Lizzie, 'If either of you 'ad worn one of those skirts down the market, Wally Braffman would 'ave recognized it an' he'd 'ave the coppers on ter yer as soon as yer put yer foot in the place. Yer pair of silly cows! Ain't yer learnt? Yer never make a mess on yer own door-step.'

The pair of them decided it was safest to keep their mouths shut as they bustled about making a pot of tea and setting the cups out.

'Shall we not bother to cook tonight?' Doris suddenly said as they all sat near to the fire drinking their tea. 'We gotta go over the road ter get the boys from Polly's and we could pop up the road an' get fish 'n' chips fer us all. You might as well stay 'ere for yer dinner, eh Lizzie?'

Lizzie looked across at Charlie and he nodded his agreement.

'It's lovely fish up there, cheap an' all,' Doris said; 'anything yer like as long as yer don't mind waiting while old 'Arry cooks it. Even get a Dover sole if yer fancy it.'

Charlie brought his head up with a jerk, looked at Syd and asked, 'Is she joking?'

'No. 'Arry's brother works at Billingsgate Market; he keeps his brother well supplied with fish that's how come he can do it so reasonable.'

'Gawd blimey! Every bugger up 'ere seems ter be on the fiddle!' Charlie muttered and then, looking at Doris, he spoke in a voice that was very quiet, 'Mind you I could really go a nice thick Dover sole.'

It had become a regular thing for the six of them to go out together on Saturday evenings and the word had got around that the King's Head in Merton was putting on a live show at weekends.

'Come on, we'll give it a go,' said Syd, as he pushed open the swing door and held it back for the girls to go in first.

They had a job to find a free table and were about to walk back and stand against the wall when a thick-set fellow, who was obviously acting as a bouncer, called out, 'Syd, 'ere Syd, over 'ere.' He then spoke to a couple who were sitting alone at a

round table and they immediately got to their feet
and moved over to join another group where there
were two free seats.

'Thanks Mike,' Syd said. 'Ain't much good
though, mate, there's six of us.'

''Old yer 'orses, will yer, Syd? Let the girls park
their backsides an' I'll git yer another table from out
the back an' we'll push 'em together.'

When they were all settled, the men with pints in
front of them and the girls with shorts, Doris leant
across the table and touched Syd's arm. 'Why did
that bloke do that fer us? Do yer know 'im?'

''Course I bloody know 'im, yer daft cow! 'Ow
else would he 'ave known me name. I'm doing 'is
daughter's wedding next Saturday; booked all three
of me cars he 'as. Nice little earner that'll be.'

Part of the show was this new craze for mime.
The master of ceremonies stepped to the front of the
stage and, with the mike close to his mouth, bawled,
'Ladies an' gentlemen, I give you, JOHNNY RAY.'

Behind the curtains a record was placed on the
record-player. A slim, blond young man in his early
thirties, flashily dressed in a checked suit and wearing a spotted bow-tie, crossed the stage and took the
mike. The music blared out.

The young man's impersonation of Johnny Ray
was fantastic; he imitated every action of the well-
known singer as he mimed – 'Let your hair down
'n' go on 'n' CR – Y – Y'.

The applause was deafening and as the customers
stamped their feet and yelled 'More', Arthur

remarked, 'He wouldn't 'ave done 'alf so well if he 'adn't 'ave been 'alf cut.'

'Yeah!' Syd agreed. 'A right piss artist!'

Lizzie fell about laughing. Saturday nights in Devon were nothing like this!

Lizzie loved the trips they made to Tooting Market. There were still some of the old traders left who remembered her from when she had worked there during the war. No matter how many times she went there, they would still call out to her, 'Watcher, Lizzie, 'ow are yer, me old darling?'

There was old Annie, still running her salad stall, lively as ever. She had gazed in wonder at Lizzie when Lizzie had first gone to say hallo to her.

'Cor blimey, you've put some meat on yer bones,' she had cried as she flung her arms around Lizzie. 'I remember you as a skinny bloody urchin; I used ter fink that was why yer mum sent you on the errands, 'cos every bugger felt sorry fer yer, fought yer needed a damn good meal so they always gave yer a good whack fer yer money. Yer mum was a good'n', God rest 'er soul; she was an' all. There's many a one still around 'ere what yer mum helped out of 'n 'ole.'

That had brought a lump to Lizzie's throat and made her smile at the same time as she remembered how, in this very market, she had given her mum rations which they hadn't been entitled too.

And what a fuss there'd been over that!

*

One morning Lizzie was feeling particularly happy. Christmas was only weeks away and, although she was suffering from sheer exhaustion because Doris and Polly had dragged her round so many shops looking for presents to buy for the men and the children, she was really looking forward to the holiday. 'At last!' Lizzie breathed a sigh of relief as they reached the cafe in the centre of the market and they dumped their shopping-bags down and lowered themselves onto chairs.

'Must admit I'm dying for a cuppa,' Polly said as she got straight back up on her feet again. 'I'll go an' get us three large teas while yer make up yer minds what yer want to eat.'

It was about twenty minutes later, as the girls were tucking into hot meat pies and a second steaming mug of tea, when a gruff voice boomed at them, 'Ah! Just the three luvverly girls I was 'oping ter see this morning!'

'Watch out!' Doris said in a stage-whisper. 'When Fred 'Arris pays anyone a compliment it only means one thing. He's after something.'

'Yer right, Dorris me ol' luv,' he said as he took a chair from another table, swung it round and placed it back to front next to Polly. Then he straddled his legs across the seat and rested his arms over the back and faced them all.

'Next Saturday week, ten days before Christmas, we're giving a party in the Central 'All fer the widows, widowers and pensioners. Could do wiv yer 'elp all day if yer ain't got nuffin' better ter do.'

The three looked at each other and all nodded but it was Polly who said, 'We don't mind, glad ter 'elp, but we can't make it all day; what would we do with our kids?'

'That's just it.' There was a beaming smile now on the face of Fred Harris as he licked a stub of pencil and wrote the girls' names down on a long grubby sheet of paper. 'We've told all the 'elpers ter bring their kids along wiv them. Brighten up the place they will an' the old folk'll enjoy watching the antics some of the little sods get up to.'

'Why do yer need us all day? Isn't it just a tea that you're giving them?' questioned Lizzie.

'No it ain't!' declared Fred. 'It's gonna be a proper Christmas dinner wiv all the trimmings. Hemming-way's the bakers are gonna cook the turkeys fer us an' boil the puddings an' all. There's still the soup ter get on early in the morning, all the veg ter do, the tables ter be laid and before yer can do that we 'ave to set up the trestles an' see ter them blasted folding chairs. The bloody china will probably need a good wash, we'll need gallons of custard – there's about an 'undred coming. An then there's the car-rier-bags ter fill 'cos every one of 'em is going 'ome wiv a load of goodies, all given free by the stall-'olders of this market.'

The tears of mirth were by now running down their faces as Doris tried to stop laughing and pleaded, 'OK, OK.'

*

The talk now was of nothing else. Arthur, Charlie and Syd were all for giving their services. Syd offered his cars to transport any of the old folk who would have difficulty in getting to and from Central Hall, Charlie put his own car at the organizers' disposal and also said he would come to the hall with the girls early in the morning and help with any of the more heavy type of jobs.

When the day arrived, Charlie made two trips before nine o'clock in the morning, taking first the girls down to the hall, where they were pleasantly surprised to see about twenty other women already there, about the same number of children and six men, mostly retired costers. On the second trip, Charlie brought Lucy, Raymond and Robert with him, and everyone, kids and grown-ups alike, got stuck in.

It was a long, hard day for all the helpers; many more would have gladly been there to give a hand but being so near to Christmas, trade was brisk in the market and they had to be on their stalls. Placards had been displayed for days stating that the market would be closing at six o'clock that night but would make up for it by remaining open every other night until nine o'clock right up to the holiday. Every man and woman who owned a stall would be coming straight round to the hall as soon after six as possible to help with the entertaining of the old folk.

The hall looked marvellous, hung with chains and

bunches of balloons, and holly and mistletoe adorned with tinsel hung in bunches from the walls.

At last dinner was over! Nobody quite knew how they had coped. It had fallen to Charlie to carve the large turkeys and to plate up the meat, while the women strained pots and pots of vegetables into dishes and did their best to keep everything piping hot while the guests had their oxtail soup.

Roars of approval had gone up as the male helpers carried in ten big, round puddings, all ablaze from a liberal soaking of brandy.

It was now seven o'clock and the women all breathed a sigh of relief as they stacked away the washed china and put the saucepans back in the cupboards. The men would take over completely now and they could have a well-earned drink, sit back and watch the fun.

Even the kerb-side barrow boys, who had their pitches outside the rear entrance to the market, had turned up to do their bit. While the band was being set up, two of these young lads came on to the stage with accordions strapped around their chests. They started the ball rolling by playing 'Maybe it's because I'm a Londoner' and there wasn't a silent voice in the hall. As the last notes died away someone shouted, 'It's old Lil's birthday.'

Instantly the men ran, forming a line in front of the raised stage, and with a nod from Fred Harris the music started to play and the men sang at the top of their voices: 'It's 'er blooming birthday, so wake up all the town, Oh, knees up, knees up, knees up, knees up, knees up, Muvver Brown'.

Suddenly all the chairs were vacant. Everyone was on their feet. Kids were in the middle as the old women lifted their skirts and bounced up and down to the music, urged on by the men who were clapping like mad. Not to be out-done, the band took over and within minutes the crowd was shouting 'Oi!' and stabbing the air with their raised thumbs as they sang and danced 'The Lambeth Walk'.

'Take a breather,' Fred told them as he announced that Maureen, who had the flower pitch, would now sing to them. You could have heard a pin drop in that vast hall as she sang 'I'll take you home again Kathleen, to where your heart will feel no pain'.

This was quickly followed by one of the young lads who gave them his version of 'I wanna girl, just like the girl that married dear old Dad'. Lizzie felt a great surge of tenderness fill her heart as she watched Charlie raise a white-haired lady to her feet and stand there, holding her hand. Oblivious of everyone, he sang, in a voice that tugged at every mother's heart, 'To that old-fashioned mother of mine' and as he finished he raised the lady's hand to his lips and gently planted a kiss on her fingers. It became too much for Lizzie, she burst into tears which only made Doris and Polly burst out laughing.

'Come on Syd!' Fred Harris called across the room as he watched Syd toss his head back and drain his pint glass. 'Yer turn ter give us a song.'

'This one's fer the kids,' Syd said into the mike, then, after wiping the back of his hand across his lips, he took a deep breath and began, 'There'll be pennies from heaven fer you an' me'. As he sang the words he tossed handfuls of pennies up into the air and of course the kids were running everywhere, dashing here and there, scrambling to see who could pick up the most. Minutes later, Robert held his hand out and said, 'I got seven, Uncle Syd.' 'I got twelve,' Raymond proudly told them.

'I only got three,' Lucy sadly announced. Doris bent her head and whispered into Raymond's ear. After a moment's hesitation he held out four pennies to Lucy and said, 'You have these, Lucy, then we've all got nearly the same.'

The lights were now turned down low; lanterns were lit, the band quietly played all the old Christmas carols and, as the old folk sang, imitation snow fell gently down on them from the rafters. It was a perfect end to the day.

It took a long while to help the old folks on with their coats and to organize which car or coach was taking them home. As they filed past the table behind which all the women helpers were lined up, each person was given a carrier-bag which contained a gift from every stall-holder in Tooting Market. There was everything from fruit, nuts, oranges and dates, right down to a packet of cocoa, a quarter of tea and packets of dried peas and haricot beans. A bar of chocolate hadn't been forgotten nor had bags of boiled sweets. There was even a two-bob voucher for each of them to change at the butchers.

'Won't buy 'em a turkey but it will buy the sausage-meat for the stuffing,' Fred Harris had joked as the women had spent more than an hour packing those bags.

'Gawd bless yer,' was said over an over again as the folk accepted their gift and many leant across the table to give a hug and a kiss to the women who had helped to give them all such a happy day.

When Doris turned to Lizzie there were tears in her eyes. 'Did yer see the look on those old folk's faces as they peered into those carrier-bags?'

'Yeah,' said Lizzie.

For Lizzie, Christmas was a time of sheer enjoyment and high hopes. She wasn't lonely, she was surrounded by her family, friends and neighbours and to her that meant more than anything.

On Boxing Day they took the children to the pantomime, and the biggest thrill for the three sets of parents was to watch the expressions on their children's faces as they cheered the good fairy and booed and hissed the wicked uncle. Muffled up against the cold wind in brightly coloured woollen scarves and gloves, the kiddies faces shone with excitement as they waited at Wimbledon Broadway for the train that would take them home.

Next morning when Lizzie came out into the kitchen she couldn't find Charlie or Robert. She hadn't slept that late, it was only ten minutes to nine;

surely they hadn't gone up to the Common this time of the morning. But even before the kettle had come to the boil she heard the front door being opened and, poking her head out into the hallway, she saw Charlie coming in.

'Where's Robert?' she shot at him as he stood wiping his feet on the doormat. 'He's all right. Give us a chance ter get inside the door an I'll tell yer.'

When Charlie had taken his overcoat off and hung it on a peg in the hall, Lizzie was ready for him. 'Well where is he?' she demanded.

'I've told yer, he's all right. He's round at Syd and Doris's; I've asked them to 'ave him fer a while 'cos I want ter take you out somewhere.'

'Oh yeah? Well, you had me worried,' Lizzie grumbled. 'Why didn't yer wake me?'

'You were sleeping so peacefully. Anyway it's all settled now and I thought we might 'ave a run out ter Epsom, 'ave a bit of lunch out, 'cos I want the two of us ter 'ave a good talk.'

'On our own!' Lizzie laughed. 'What 'ave you got ter say ter me that is so important that you're going to wine an' dine me?'

'Who said anything about wine?' Charlie cut in loudly, putting his arm around her shoulder. 'Look, Lizzie, it's almost time for us ter go back ter Devon an' I don't want us two ter end up 'aving a screaming match. Far better if we clear off this morning, away from everyone, an' discuss our problems sensibly. Then it should be easy fer us ter work things out.'

'Easy!' Lizzie said sarcastically.

*

By the time Charlie had got the car out and they were on their way, they had both calmed down. The weather wasn't at all promising; it was bitterly cold and the dark grey clouds that filled the sky looked full of snow.

When they had left Sutton behind and were approaching Banstead Downs, the scenery was much more interesting. Although most of the trees had shed their leaves and just the long bare branches reached up to the sky, there were still several shrubs wrapped in glory, their foliage shining with rich dark colours made all the more beautiful against the stark background of winter.

At a quarter to one, Charlie drove the car into the forecourt of a hotel at Tattenham Corner. Lizzie excused herself to go to the toilet while Charlie went to the reception desk to request a table for two for lunch. Having combed her hair and refreshed her lipstick, Lizzie came out of the ladies' room to see Charlie standing waiting for her at the entrance to the bar. 'About twenty minutes before they'll 'ave a free table,' he told her, as he put his hand under her elbow and propelled her towards the bar. 'Might as well 'ave a drink while we're waiting.'

Lizzie walked to the other side of the room and stood staring out of the immense plate-glass windows. Even on a dull day like today the view was stunning. Epsom Race Course! Where great horse races such as the Derby and the Oaks were run.

'What yer standing up for?' Charlie's question

broke in on her thoughts. She smiled at him and he smiled back as they both chose a seat near the window. Charlie had finished his pint and Lizzie was just draining the last of her schooner of Bristol Cream when a waiter came to tell Charlie that their table was ready.

The dining-room was elegant, the food superb and they lingered so long over their meal that it was turned half-past two by the time they went into the lounge and found two empty chairs near the enormous fire-place in which a bright log fire was burning.

It was impossible to raise one's voice in such surroundings and in that respect Charlie had the advantage as he put his points to Lizzie.

'Spending three months in London is all very well,' he said softly, 'but coming back to live for good – is that what you really want, Lizzie?'

Lizzie made no answer as she picked up her cup and saucer and sipped her coffee. It seemed that Charlie expected none, for he went straight on talking in low tones. 'Have you given a thought ter Robert's schooling? There's his future to take into consideration. At the moment he's 'aving all the advantages you or I never 'ad.' Charlie paused and picked up his cup of coffee and the silence hung heavy between them for some while.

When, finally, Charlie spoke again he sounded even more serious, if that was possible. 'The prospects of me finding a job in London that will enable me ter provide you and Robert with all the things you've both become used to are pretty slim, wouldn't yer say? I 'aven't got a trade to fall back on.'

'Oh, Charlie,' Lizzie sighed. Her heart ached for him! And at that moment she felt she had been thoroughly selfish.

Again, the silence was long and Lizzie refilled their cups from the silver coffee-pot.

'By the way, it's about time you learned to drive.'

'What?' Lizzie had raised her voice and Charlie laughed at the expression on her face.

'It makes sense yer know. Why don't we give Devon a few more years, at least until Robert is older, see him off to college. As hoteliers we're not doing so bad are we? And if we get you driving you won't feel so isolated; you'll be able ter get out an' about a bit more. Even pop up ter yer brother's on yer own now an' again.' The last statement Charlie had said with a saucy grin on his face.

'Oh, I see! A sprat ter catch a mackerel, is it?' Lizzie asked and there was no smile on her face. 'Don't tempt me too much,' she said beneath her breath. To be honest she did see the benefits of all his arguments. To stay in Devon, at least for the time being, was certainly the wisest choice. Reluctantly, she admitted to herself she didn't have any alternative. They had put up with all the hardships and the rough times of being up to their ears in debt. Charlie was right, damn him, when wasn't he? They would have to be mad to walk away just when all their problems were being ironed out and they were becoming successful.

'All right,' she said grudgingly, 'but it's still the back of beyond and the seasons are bloody 'ard work.'

'Lizzie, if they cut your head off you'd still 'ave the last word!'

Chapter Twenty-Eight

Now it was time to start thinking seriously about yet another season.

Easter wasn't too far away and the hotel was fully booked for that long weekend. Charlie's time was taken up with repairs and decorating; he reckoned to paint and re-paper between six and eight bedrooms each winter. Lizzie's mornings were spent entirely in the office answering on average forty letters at a time.

Many were from previous guests with cheques enclosed to reserve a particular bedroom for their holiday. These, Lizzie would set aside. They could be answered and receipts sent later in the day; they were definite bookings. Any new mail, either enquiries from the Town Guide or recommendations, she answered straight away and had them back in the post by midday.

They had come to know only too well that hotel life was a highly competitive business. Only by working on the enquiries received, giving each one full personal attention, were they going to achieve the maximum amount of bookings.

To Lizzie, it now seemed a very long time since they had been to Bristol. All the legal formalities had been taken care of, but still she was barely able to contain her impatience.

Week followed week, and nothing seemed to be happening.

'You just have to be patient,' Charlie told her time and time again. 'They can't dig the footings while the ground is still freezing.'

Patience was not Lizzie's strong point.

When the thaw finally did set in and Michael Gale telephoned to say that work could now begin in earnest, Lizzie was up there on the site to see the machinery close in to start on the footings.

With the improvement on the roads, Lizzie was able to take her driving test. The whole village must have known she had passed! Driving back from Barnstaple in the green Austin 1100 that Charlie had bought for her and which Robert had immediately nick-named 'Brussel Sprout', the examiner's words were still loud in her head.

'Congratulations. I wish you many happy years of safe motoring.'

Approaching the hotel, she put her finger on the horn and kept it there until she reached the main entrance.

'Cocky, aren't we!' Charlie said, grinning from ear to ear.

With the season, came the usual problems. One morning, while doing her rounds, Lizzie heard the Hoover going but couldn't see where.

She opened a bedroom door. There, sitting on the bed, reading a magazine, was the young chamber-maid who had only recently come to work at High-land Heights. The Hoover was plugged in and switched on, but stood there quite stationary.

'What are you doing?' Lizzie asked firmly.

No answer.

Lizzie looked around the room. Under the wash-basin there was sand, the dressing-table was dusty and the towels needed to be changed.

The girl got to her feet and turned on Lizzie, prac-tically screaming, 'The trouble with you is you think this hotel is a ruddy palace!'

Lizzie held her temper in check, but her big blue eyes flashed. In low-pitched, precise tones, she said, 'If it is, then I'm the queen that reigns here and your services are no longer required.'

The older, more conscientious chambermaids, who had worked for Lizzie since she had first taken over, were huddled together on the landing; they hadn't missed a word.

Lizzie heard what they said as she swept by. 'Missus must be in a good mood. Wonder she didn't grab that one by the scruff of the neck.'

Lizzie had to laugh to herself. They didn't know just how near she had come to doing just that.

In what free time they did get, Charlie usually opted to go for a swim, mainly in the sea, using the swim-ming baths in Ilfracombe only as a last resort if the weather was too foul.

Lizzie would drive out to the site. She was a bit disappointed in the early stages, the area of the footings looked so small.

'Not to worry, mi-dear,' the workmen told her, 'that be everyone's first impression.'

To get up there over the weekends was an impossibility. So, four or even five days might pass without Lizzie being able to pay a visit. Then the progress would be noticeable.

The framework developed at an amazing rate and the buildings began to develop character. At each stage, they were consulted by both Michael Gale and Mr Roberts, who wanted to know their preference for the interior work and design, even down to the smallest detail, such as door design for the garage.

Charlie and Lizzie thought it was great to be actively involved in the building of their house and each trip that Lizzie made out to the site could be guaranteed to bring her back to work in a very happy frame of mind.

Miraculously, by mid-August the house was completed.

Strangely, Lizzie lost the urge to visit it so often. The season was at its peak. Days for them both still had to start very early in the morning and finish very late at night, so, not surprisingly, their energy began to flag and they were often very tired by the end of the day.

But at last another season was over; it was the

second week in October and they were standing in the grounds seeing the last coach party of guests off on their homeward journey.

During the next few days, with the help of all the staff, the hotel was shut down. Bedrooms were closed up, silver cleaned and packed away, all kitchen equipment scalded and thoroughly cleaned and dust sheets thrown over furniture in the first-floor lounge. The place took on an air of despondency.

Charlie paid off the staff, adding a bonus for each of them and everyone was well satisfied.

The next few days were grim. Charlie wisely said, 'Don't rush things, breathe out. No one is so resilient that they can spring back to a normal way of life after working seven days a week since last Easter.'

So they were lazy, sleeping a lot, eating when they felt hungry, not watching the clock at all. Ten days later, with batteries recharged, they were both raring to go.

'Furniture for the house or a holiday?' Charlie queried.

'What d'you think?' Lizzie asked, giving him a smug look.

That evening they talked and talked, made lists and wrote out suggestions as to what they would like to buy for their new home, and the next morning they set off for Bideford to see Mr Channon. This time they didn't need credit, they would pay cash for whatever they purchased.

The memory had never dimmed for either Charlie or Lizzie. Mr Channon had not only treated them fairly, he had been an absolute brick. When all the odds had seemed stacked against the pair of them ever making a go of Sea View Guesthouse, he had shown faith and understanding. Neither of them would have dreamt of going to any other furniture store.

Lizzie had a whale of a time. She quickly chose a bedroom suite and a smaller, slightly more masculine suite for Robert's room. Upstairs in the showrooms, she bounced on beds and divans. Brass headboards? Wooden headboards? She couldn't make up her mind. In the end, she settled on newly imported continental ones, woodgrained to match the suites. One was nine feet wide with bedside tables attached and individual reading lights. Robert's was similar, but half the size.

The dining-room suite was also a relatively easy choice. Charlie liked good wood and traditional styles. Lizzie, in her imagination, was already seeing the oval table with its claw feet, set up and laid. Candles lit, a bowl of flowers set in the centre, she couldn't wait for them to eat their first dinner in their own dining-room.

There was still the question of what to put in that gigantic lounge. They sat on comfortable sofas and easychairs; nothing seemed right. Even with the addition of occasional tables and various lamps the room needed more than an ordinary three-piece suite.

'How about these?' Mr Channon asked, producing three glossy brochures.

This furniture was unique. Expensive for sure, but even Charlie exclaimed that he'd never seen anything like it before.

'It is going on show in London from next week. I've got swatches of colour and fabrics I can show you,' Mr Channon said.

Charlie made a snap decision. 'No, we'll go to London. I'd like to see the actual furniture, wouldn't you, Lizzie?'

'Not half I wouldn't,' she answered, thinking at the same time, a weekend in London, great!

Friday afternoon, with the car well packed, they were outside Adelaide College to meet Robert. Charlie broke their journey in Taunton where they all had a meal in a steak house. Soon they were on their way again and Robert was asleep. Lizzie, lulled by the steady motion of Charlie's driving, also began to doze.

Doris and Syd had the front door open before the car had stopped. Raymond practically dragged Robert out, and there were hugs and kisses for everyone.

At nine o'clock next morning, Charlie and Lizzie set off for the West End. Although it was Saturday, traffic seemed horrific and Charlie had great difficulty in finding somewhere to park.

The three gentlemen in the showrooms, most would say, looked the perfect image of success. To

Lizzie, they looked like tailors' dummies with their pin-striped trousers, cut-away dark grey jackets and starched white shirts.

One man stepped forward and introduced himself, 'Mr Westland, how may I help you?' He shook hands, but his fingers hardly touched Lizzie's. Yet, as he showed them around these expensive showrooms, Lizzie found herself liking this Mr Westland. He wasn't the cold fish she had first taken him for and neither was he stupid. He knew his job; he was intelligent and interesting to listen to.

See! She chided herself, you shouldn't be so quick to form an impression.

The furniture was upholstered in leather. Leather so soft and supple it felt like velvet. The design just as exciting as the brochure had promised. They chose an enormous settee, five-seater open-ended. It had a wide armrest at one end, the other end curved and rounded off to a half circular shape. Also a traditional three-seater settee together with two large, well-cushioned, deep armchairs.

Mr Westland was a little persuasive when it came to pouffes. 'One cannot imagine you would ignore them,' his rather grand voice beseeched as he ran his hand through his mop of blond curls. 'These are the *pièce de résistance*.'

They ordered two. Each three foot square; the top cushion, when removed, revealed a well-polished grained wood table top. 'Great for playing cards on,' Charlie commented.

'You'd have to sit on the floor to do so,' Lizzie retorted.

Import licences and delivery dates were discussed. The actual retailer would be Mr Channon of Bideford. Charlie asked several questions all of which Mr Westland answered with ease. Lizzie, in the end, felt that neither fire nor flood would ruffle that young gentleman's composure.

Saturday afternoon, Syd and Charlie took the two boys to watch Chelsea play an at-home football match, while Doris and Lizzie set off for Croydon and the shops.

At seven-thirty, a taxi came. They were off to the Selkirk Pub for a drink, taking the boys with them. 'Do they still have a children's room?' Lizzie asked Syd.

''Course they do.' Brother and sister grinned at each other, recalling the old days when they themselves had been kids.

Pushing through the swing doors at barely eight o'clock, the place was jam-packed. The band struck up; 'For he's a jolly good fellow' was sung with gusto. Everyone rushed towards Lizzie and Charlie. It was a party in their honour!

All their friends, and what few relatives that were left, were gathered there. Half the street where Lizzie had been born had turned out. Neighbours Lizzie only half remembered. She had forgotten what a cockney welcome could be like.

Lizzie was choked; fancy wanting to cry on such a happy occasion. What an evening! Drink flowed like water. The band never seemed to stop playing and Lizzie told herself over and over again how lucky she was.

On Sunday evening, Polly and Arthur had the two boys while Doris, Syd, Charlie and Lizzie went to Kensington. Flanagan's Restaurant had sawdust on the floor, and a menu chalked on an old blackboard. A pianist sitting at an upright piano belted out all the old songs non-stop.

Lizzie ordered skate and chips.

Charlie was astounded. 'You've never come all the way from Devon to the Royal Borough to eat fish 'n' chips?' he cried.

'It's not fish 'n' chips, it's skate 'n' chips,' Lizzie hurled back, smacking her lips in anticipation.

From Flanagan's, they took a taxi to the Victoria Palace. Tonight's performance was in aid of Jewish Benevolent funds. All the stars were giving their services free. For Lizzie, it was Ann Shelton who stole the show as she sang 'My Yiddisher Mamma' and there wasn't a dry eye in the house.

Monday came and it was back to north Devon.

'That was some weekend!' Charlie said as he shook hands with Syd.

'Yeah, wasn't it?' Doris whispered to Lizzie, as once more they hugged and said, 'See you soon.'

It took nearly a month for the carpets to be delivered and laid. Furniture arrived and was set out in appropriate rooms. A local lady had made the curtains, and Charlie put up curtain tracks and poles and saw to the hanging of them.

Lizzie became a constant visitor to the nearest garden centre. Vans drew up delivering shrubs, small trees, earthenware urns, tubs of all shapes and sizes, colourful hanging baskets, and bag upon bag of peat and John Innes' mixtures.

'Might as well bury money in the earth, the amount you spend,' Charlie grumbled, but Lizzie only smiled sweetly.

The actual day dawned; they were moving their personal belongings from the hotel into their own home.

By evening, the bungalow was filled with familiar, well-loved things and had really begun to feel like home.

Robert's bedroom looked lovely, with his belongings already scattered about and his books all set out on the shelves. The bathroom was a dream, everything co-ordinated, beautiful soft towels – none here with Highland Heights printed in red running through the middle.

Upstairs, the dining-room was to the right, perfect in every detail. Beyond was the kitchen, the only room in the whole house that did not give a view of the sea. It was, however, a cheerful, bright kitchen with large windows looking out over the steep sloping garden where several Christmas trees and other shrubs had been left intact and which Lizzie now thought of as their rural area.

The lounge was open and spacious, the end wall, apart from two foot on either side, was entirely glass, the centre being an enormous set of sliding doors which led on to the upper terrace. Running the whole width of the house, the terrace was so big that Lizzie remarked, 'You could hold a dance out there.'

The concrete paved slabs forming the base were alternately green and white and with the white ranch-style railings all around it looked splendid.

Charlie and Lizzie were very pleased.

Chapter Twenty-Nine

THE NEW YEAR of 1958 was only a few weeks old and every morning Lizzie's first job was to sort and answer the mail.

'Has the postman been yet?' Lizzie called up the stairs to Charlie.

'I haven't heard him but I'm just gonna pick the paper up, I'll bring the mail down if he has.'

Two minutes later Lizzie heard Charlie shout, 'Oh no!' The tone of his voice was so distressed that Lizzie ran to the foot of the basement stairs. 'Charlie,' she called loudly, 'are you all right?'

'Yes, Yes, I'm coming down. I won't be a minute.'

Lizzie was halfway up the stairs before she could see him walking very slowly across the entrance hall with the newspaper opened wide and his head bent low as he read. Lizzie hurried to see the headlines. There had been an air crash in West Germany. The whole of the Manchester United football team had been on board.

They sat facing each other at the kitchen table and listened to the news being relayed over the wireless net-work. The crash had happened because the plane had failed to clear a fence on take-off; the weather was foul and the rescue workers were being hampered by driving snow. Charlie looked thoroughly dejected, eight members of the team were among the twenty-one dead. Lizzie got up and went to the gas-stove. 'I'll make us a coffee,' she said as she filled a saucepan with milk and put it on to heat.

'Poor old Matt Busby,' Charlie said half to himself. 'He's a damn good manager, he's become so popular that the team has been nick-named the "Busby Babes". Eight of the boys dead! It's not fair!'

All day Charlie couldn't get it out of his mind and Lizzie let him rattle on about football because it seemed to make him feel better to talk about it. On the six o'clock evening news they heard that Matt Busby had been seriously injured in the crash. 'It's not bloody fair,' was all that Charlie could mutter.

Life went on and Lizzie concentrated on getting as many bookings as possible for what would be their fifth season in Highland Heights Hotel. With the coming of the very busy weeks of July and August the weather was as good as it had been bad at the beginning of the year, which was fine for the visitors but not so good for the hotel workers. A veritable heatwave had the beaches and the surrounding little coves packed with holidaymakers. The hotel kitchens became unbearable as the scorching sun beat down relentlessly.

Lizzie sighed with relief one Monday evening about nine o'clock when Charlie switched off both ovens and the hot plate.

'I think I'll come home with you, love, for an

hour or so, there's plenty of staff on duty.' Charlie sounded really done in.

They walked in silence to the garage. Lizzie backed her car out first, then Charlie did the same, taking to the road first while Lizzie drove home behind him.

Dawn had hardly come and Lizzie was up again, after a hot, restless night.

On the upper terrace they kept a set of wrought-iron garden furniture, four chairs, table with centre umbrella and two sun-beds. She carried out the green and white striped mattresses, returning indoors to fetch the matching seat-cushions for the chairs.

A breakfast of toast, marmalade and orange juice, eaten out on the veranda, and Lizzie felt much better.

The sky was a clear blue; the heat was still there and it seemed certain to be another hot day. In the silence all she could hear was the gentle whirring of a lawnmower and even that seemed miles away.

It was almost ten o'clock and Lizzie stood by the railings looking down the hill and beyond to the sea. She saw Doctor Whittaker's car coming along the lower road; there was no mistaking it – a dark green MG sports car, roof down. He slowed, tooted his horn and waved. Lizzie raised her cupped hand to her mouth and mimed, drink. He tooted his horn again and gave a thumbs-up sign.

Lizzie had first met Jeffrey Whittaker while

delivering meals on wheels with the WVS. He wasn't their family doctor, he belonged to a panel of three doctors.

The WVS covered a wide area, including many outlying villages. The volunteer women often saved the doctors a journey by delivering a package or even reporting to them how the elderly folk were getting along.

Although quite young in comparison to the other doctors, Jeffrey Whittaker was conscientious about his work. Unmarried, scrupulously clean yet never formally dressed, he mainly wore slacks with sporty-type shirts and, when necessary, a zip-up jacket. He would come bounding into the building where the WVS ladies cooked and packed the dinners, and so invigorating was his attitude that Lizzie always half expected him to call out, 'Anyone for tennis?'

Everyone was on first-name terms with this young doctor. But only being able to do voluntary work during the winter months, it was weeks since Lizzie had had a chance to talk to him.

She heard his car park below, in front of their garage. He used the outside staircase which brought him directly up on to the terrace without going into the house.

'Gee! This is absolutely marvellous, Lizzie,' he exclaimed as he threw himself down on to one of the sun-beds.

'Yeah, fantastic,' Lizzie called back as she went inside to make the coffee.

He must have noticed the weariness in her voice

because, as she came out and put the tray with the coffee cups and saucers on to the table, he gently asked, 'Everything not right with your world?'

'Oh, don't mind me, Jeff, I didn't sleep that well last night, that's all.'

He sat up straight and proceeded to pour out the coffee. 'Milk and sugar? Help yourself,' he stated as he handed a cup to Lizzie.

She had to laugh. Talk about making yourself at home. He certainly was an easy person to be with.

She glanced at her wristwatch, 'What are you doing out so early, Jeff? No surgery this morning?'

'I've been out to Combe Martin. The church camping site. You know the big hut come hall; the scouts use it and the girl guides. Well, they've got a party of young boys staying in there this week. Managing well really, mattresses on the floors. Hotels, guesthouses, cafes all mucking in, helping to give the little lads a free holiday.'

He stopped talking, took out his handkerchief and wiped his forehead. 'It's hot again, isn't it? I can't remember it being as hot as this. When this weather does break we'll have such a storm.'

'Jeff,' Lizzie grasped his arm, 'go on, tell me more about those boys.'

'Well, they probably come from your part of the world or near enough. East End of London, some home, not Doctor Barnardo's, but similar, can't recall the name. You'd have laughed, Lizzie, climbing about the rocks wearing thick, knee-length socks, heavy laced-up shoes, most likely they've never seen the sea before.'

Lizzie winced, 'Thick socks on a day like this? Who's in charge of them?'

'Four men.'

'I might have guessed that.'

'Now hold on, Lizzie, I doubt even you could have got those youngsters to part with their clothing. You should have heard them; they were in their element but still highly suspicious of change or anyone that wanted to do things for them.'

Lizzie's mind took her back in time. Charlie had spent his childhood in an orphanage. When she had first met him, he had been starved of love, yearning for a home to call his own. Look what they had now. She thought of the advantages her son had and then she got cross with herself. Seeing the anger appear on Lizzie's face, Doctor Whittaker wondered whether he had gone too far.

'Have I upset you, Lizzie?'

'Hell, no. There's me wallowing in self-pity all night, worried sick because Charlie was so tired, and there's those unfortunate kids out there glad of a free holiday.'

Jeffrey Whittaker smiled to himself, he had achieved what he wanted to; it had helped to snap Mrs Wilson out of what could have been a nasty spell of depression, had it gone on too long.

Aloud he said, 'You mustn't blame yourself, Lizzie. You and Charlie are both hard workers. You put the maximum effort into every job you tackle.

Now you're both strung up like overwound clock-springs. It'll be September come next Monday, season will soon be over. Book yourselves a holiday; best tonic in the world having something to look forward to.'

Later, when Jeffrey Whittaker left, he tooted the horn of his car and Lizzie stood leaning over the balcony until he was out of sight.

What a kind, caring person he is, she said to herself as she went indoors and picked up the telephone.

'Please, Charlie,' Lizzie pleaded, 'I'll come down to the hotel when we get back. Help get the dinners through. I don't need the evening off.'

'All right. I'll organize it,' his reply came quiet and firm over the line, 'be at the foot of the hill; I'll make it by a quarter to two.'

She had told Charlie everything that Jeffrey Whittaker had told her and really he hadn't hesitated for a second.

The couple of hours that she and Charlie spent out at Combe Martin would remain vivid to Lizzie for a very long time. Charlie had met the organizer of the party, established the name of the children's home and offered a week's holiday to a party of children for the following year at Highland Heights. He had also been to the local haberdashery shop.

'You're too late,' a beaming shop assistant told him. 'Local people have already bought up our entire stock of swimming trunks for the boys. My guvernor has gone to Barnstaple to get some more.'

Lizzie had to smother her sobs as she watched Charlie romp with a couple of five year olds and her heart almost burst with love as she watched him quietly hand some notes over to one of the men in charge.

'See they have a few ice-creams and what nots,' he said in a voice that was barely audible.

Chapter Thirty

'COMING WITH ME tonight?' Charlie asked enthusiastically.

Lizzie was doubtful. Darts matches in Devon were sombre affairs compared with those in London. No food provided, no dancing afterwards, in fact, few wives bothered to accompany their husbands.

On the other hand, this match was being held at The Foxhunter's Inn, a rather lovely road house well out in the country. Young Robert was going to play water polo, they could pick him up on the way back.

'Yes, all right,' she agreed, having weighed up all the pros and cons.

Just as she thought, she was the only woman.

'You don't want to stay in this public bar,' Charlie whispered rather sheepishly. 'Go through to the lounge, I'll bring you a drink.'

She had finished her drink and was sitting, idly looking through the evening paper, when she heard a loud cheer go up in the public bar.

'Is that the first leg over?' Lizzie asked as Charlie came through the archway carrying a fresh drink for her. With him was the captain of the team Charlie played for, Harry Baldwin, well known to Lizzie because it was he who delivered fresh fruit, salad stuff and vegetables to their hotel during the season.

'Harry's been telling me there's to be an auction at Rillage View,' Charlie said as he placed the glass and a fresh bottle of dry ginger down on to the brass-topped table.

'Coming up soon it be, Mrs Wilson. Several properties, contents an' all. Make a nice day out it will. Shall us be seeing 'ee there?'

'More than likely,' Lizzie smiled as she answered. She liked Harry, no side with him. A good-natured, down-to-earth sort of bloke.

Rillage View was a local landmark, a very old type of hotel standing high up on what was known as Harbour View Terrace. Difficult to gain access to, the road being narrow and steeply winding, but once there, as its address implied, you had a commanding view of the harbour.

On the morning of the sale they laughed at each other, both had opted to wear what they described as their country outfits. Charlie had on cavalry twill trousers, a suede-fronted jerkin and a Harris tweed sports coat.

'You look every inch a squire,' Lizzie scoffed at him.

'You'd pass at a horse show,' he retaliated.

'Thanks a bunch,' Lizzie said as she half turned to check herself in the hall mirror. She wasn't too happy with the low-heeled shoes she was wearing, but she liked the heather-coloured woven costume.

The pale lavender cashmere jumper with its high neck toned in extremely well, 'At least I think it does,' she muttered, determined not to let Charlie put her off.

'Well,' Charlie made a mocking bow, 'Rillage View, here we come.'

Within minutes of their arrival Lizzie had lost Charlie. She wandered off into the hall and up the staircase. Every item of furniture she passed was marked with a lot number. Looking in through the doorway of each room, Lizzie found it all unbelievable. Everything looked as if it had come out of the Ark.

Having got to the top floor and been really nosey, peeking in all the corners and opening cupboard doors, Lizzie began making her way downstairs. She had to be very careful since the staircase was not only very narrow, it twisted and turned quite sharply at every landing. She reached the first floor and was frightened for a moment; not only was the landing crowded with people, but, looking over the banister rail, she saw that the staircase was also jam-packed.

The auction had started. Lots were being sold from exactly where the various items were situated. Presumably the ground-floor contents had all been disposed of and the auctioneer was moving upstairs to start on the sale of bedroom furniture.

It was like a stampede. Lizzie panicked. There was no way she could possibly get through that crowd. She felt herself being half pushed, half carried into a bedroom. Packed like a sardine, she couldn't move. The auctioneer climbed up on to a wide window sill and the sale carried on. Small objects were held high in the air by men in brown overalls, while large items were pointed to with the aid of a long cane. The auctioneer's gavel fell with monotonous regularity as each article went to the highest bidder.

Lizzie looked around; the room was very large. One double bed, two single beds, each having old-fashioned brass rails at the head and foot. Large cumbersome furniture. A marble-topped wash-stand complete with an ornamental china jug and bowl. God help the chambermaids who had to work in this hotel, Lizzie thought to herself.

Suddenly, Lizzie felt a tug at the hem of her skirt. Moving her feet and knees as much as was possible, she looked down. Charlie's face was peering up at her.

'What the hell are you doing?' she uttered almost under her breath.

He was on his haunches almost underneath the double bed. 'Bid, bid!' he ordered in an undertone.

'What?'

'Don't ask questions, just bid for this carpet,' he hissed.

She glanced at her programme. The carpet was lot number 315. Now she paid attention. 'Lot three one three, a unique pair of vases . . . ' the auctioneer's voice droned on.

Only two lots to go.

'Three one five, ladies and gentlemen, the carpet

on three one three which you are standing.' There was a general shuffling of feet as folk attempted to look down.

'Who will start me off with a fiver?'

Lizzie was too nervous to do anything; three bids had been taken, her skirt was being yanked at again.

She didn't bother to look down, just raised her programme high in the air. Two counterbids were made, each time Lizzie waved her programme.

'Going, going, gone,' the gavel fell. 'Name?'

'Mrs Wilson,' Lizzie said in a voice that didn't sound a bit like her own.

Lot number 315 was hers, whether she wanted it or not.

The crowds moved on and Lizzie made her escape – down the winding stairs and out into the fresh air. Within ten minutes, Charlie had joined her.

'Dirty old carpet,' she shot at him straight away, 'what in the world do we want it for?'

'That's a *real* carpet. One hundred per cent pure wool Wilton. Cost a fortune to buy one that size today. All it needs is cleaning, you'll see. Got ourselves a great bargain there.'

Lizzie gave up. No use arguing about it now, was there!

'Come on, we'll have lunch. Nothing I'm interested in now, not until this afternoon.'

The brightness in Charlie's eyes and the colour in his cheeks as he grinned at her told Lizzie that he was more than pleased with his purchase.

Charlie drove the car down to what was the only

public house on the harbour. Lizzie sat outside on the quayside while Charlie went into the pub. The fishing boats were in, unloading basketfuls of shining herrings and pots which held struggling crabs and lobsters. Huge gulls were screeching overhead, swooping in low for scraps, and yet the whole harbour had a peaceful air.

They had crusty bread, local cheese and big pickled onions to eat, washed down by cool, sparkling lager, and were back at Rillage View by a quarter to two.

The afternoon's sale was to be conducted in the original dining-room. A makeshift platform had been set up at one end, with rows of chairs placed in front, most of which were already taken. Charlie led Lizzie to where there was a single empty seat on the end of a row by the middle aisle.

'What about you?' she asked.

'I'll be all right,' Charlie answered, 'I'm just going to have a word with the auctioneers.'

There were more than a dozen men clustered in front of the platform. Charlie was soon in their midst, having quite an animated conversation with two of them.

'Wonder what he is up to now?' Lizzie asked herself.

To one side of the room, two men were seated at a table with lots of legal-looking papers spread out in front of them. One man was quite old, the other, barely thirty, was writing with his head bent low, intent upon what he was doing.

'Solicitor and his clerk,' the woman sitting next to Lizzie obligingly said, nodding her head in the direction of the two men.

What are they here for? Lizzie wanted to ask, but merely murmured, 'Thank you.'

Groups of men were standing around the sides of the room, some talking so loudly that Lizzie thought they were having an argument.

Suddenly, the auctioneer rapped loudly with his gavel, and all the men made a general movement to the back of the hall. Lizzie couldn't see where Charlie had got to.

Now there was complete silence in the large room.

'Before the commencement of this sale, I must impress upon you all the legality of these proceedings.' The gentleman conducting this part of the sale was totally different from the previous auctioneer.

His voice was that of a well-educated gentleman, although to look at him, he seemed a typical north Devon farmer. A real open-air type of man, his tweed jacket had leather patches at the elbows, his shirt was open at the neck and he wasn't wearing a tie.

'The highest bidder to whom each property will be sold must be prepared to sign contracts this afternoon and pay to the vendor a deposit of ten per cent of the selling price which will be irretrievable.'

He paused, consulted his programme and went on, 'Mr Button, the gentleman on my right, is acting for each and all of the vendors. We have five properties to be disposed of this afternoon, so if you are all clear in your minds as to the legal points, we will make a start.'

There was a shuffling of feet, a clearing of throats, and the auction began.

'Lot number one. Agricultural land known as Dene's End.'

Lizzie lost interest. She looked around the room. All the furniture had been pushed aside leaving the floor space free. It was all heavy-framed dark wood pieces now bearing 'Sold' labels.

There was an extremely large glass-fronted book-case filled with books which were so dusty they looked as if they hadn't been taken down from the shelves for years, never mind opened and read.

The auctioneer startled Lizzie, his voice got louder, his movements more rapid. 'T'be done, t'be done, t'be done. Sold to Mr Hutchinson,' his gavel fell loud and final.

'Look at your programmes, ladies and gentlemen, lot number two, Hampton Cross Farm.'

Only two serious bidders, same procedure, it was all over.

'Lot number three, known as Ivy Cottage, Larks Lane, and number one, Leigh Lane.' Murmurings came from the audience.

'That's perfectly correct,' the auctioneer said. 'This cottage does in actual fact have two postal addresses. Dilapidated, needs renovating, will take low bid to start.'

Very quiet now, no takers. Lizzie was reading her

programme. The two addresses had intrigued her.
She heard the auctioneer plead for someone to start
the bidding, but it was slow and she wasn't taking
much notice.

'The bidding is against you, Mr Wilson.'

Wilson, did he say Wilson? There was no mistaking this time as she heard the auctioneer say, 'Thank
you, Mr Wilson.'

Lizzie jerked her head round so quickly her neck
snapped and it hurt. She still couldn't see Charlie.
She twisted the other way, still no sign of him. Too
many men crushed together at the back of the room.

The gavel fell again with a firm, loud bang.

'Sold to Mr Wilson of Highland Heights.'

Lizzie sat through the rest of the sale in a daze.
Charlie had done some daft things in his time, but
this beat the lot. Lovely new split-level bungalow
built especially for them and he goes and buys a run-
down ramshackle old cottage.

The sale was finished and refreshments were
being offered. Lizzie pushed her way through and
made for the car. She couldn't really analyze her
feelings.

She saw Charlie coming and wrenched open the
car door. Even before he reached her, she yelled,
'You've just bought a cottage!'

'I know.'

'I know you know. What I want to know is what
you are intending to do with it?'

People were looking. She knew she was being
stupid.

'Don't be so emotional,' Charlie rebuked her.

Well! That was like showing a red rag to a bull. 'We haven't even seen the place. Come to that, I don't even know where it is, don't suppose you do either. It's got to be derelict, nobody else wanted it. Did you have it surveyed? No, 'course you didn't. You're the great man, Charlie Wilson.'

'Calm down,' Charlie said very quietly, 'trust me. I'll tell you all about it later. Come back inside and countersign the contract.'

'What?' Lizzie was off again. '*You* bought the bloody cottage; *you* sign the bloody contract.'

'God give me patience!' In exasperation, Charlie grabbed her arm and his words to her now were hissed through teeth that were almost clenched. 'This property has been bought by the company. It is an investment. I should have discussed it with you, but I didn't. I'm sorry. None the more for that, it's done. The company has purchased it, and that means you, Lizzie, as well as me. Joint company directors. You and me. Now, will you please sign the contract?'

Lizzie jerked her arm away from his hold; he had said sorry, probably for the first time in his life. Still, that didn't alter things much. He was still an impulsive know-all.

'You haven't left me much option,' Lizzie said, still showing ill-feeling as she walked away.

They each signed the contract, Lizzie wrote out a

cheque for the ten per cent deposit and Charlie signed it.

'You've made a good buy today,' Mr Button said as he took hold of Lizzie's hand. 'I've known Ivy Cottage since I was a lad. Sadly neglected, very sad, but its structure is sound.' Wistfully he turned away to shake Charlie's hand.

'Wise decision, young man, so near to your own hotel. It would have been a mistake to let it go to others.' For the first time, Charlie smiled.

'Thanks, Mr Button, thanks for your help.'

Lizzie watched and waited while Charlie took his leave of several men. 'What now?' she asked as they walked to the car.

It was a foolish question, she knew. Mr Button's comments had aroused her curiosity but her pride would not let her question Charlie outright.

He didn't answer her, but as he held the car door open for her, he said, 'I'm sorry, Lizzie.'

Two apologies in one afternoon, she smiled briefly. 'I am too.'

Before starting up the engine, Charlie placed his hand on Lizzie's knee. She dropped her head a little and clenched her hands together in her lap. She was fed up. Charlie was headstrong and her own temperament wasn't all it should be. That was the whole damn trouble, they clashed.

'Lizzie, look at me.'

She raised her eyes and Charlie chuckled, 'Perhaps you would like to see this cottage?'

They had almost reached the hotel when Lizzie exclaimed, 'I thought you were going to show me this cottage.'

'I am. We'll leave the car in the hotel drive.'

Lizzie was even more confused now.

When the car stopped, Charlie was out and off down the hill like an excited ten year old, his dark hair fluffed up high by the breeze as he ran.

'Come on, run!' he yelled back over his shoulder, and Lizzie found herself doing just that.

She stood there panting, her chest still heaving as she gasped for breath.

Minutes passed and still she could hardly believe it.

Finally, she turned to Charlie, amazement uppermost in her voice. 'I must have passed Leigh Lane hundreds of times. I had no idea that there was a cottage here.'

'Well, you know now,' Charlie said, grinning broadly, 'and what's more, it belongs to us.'

Lizzie stepped back and scrutinized the cottage. It looked as if it hadn't been occupied for years. The windows had odd pieces of wood nailed together covering them. Even the roof was covered with what looked like boards and a waterproof sheet.

Suddenly, she couldn't help herself, she burst out laughing. It was hilarious, it had to be a joke; she laughed so much she had a stitch in her side. Her laughter was infectious.

'You can scoff,' Charlie said as he, too, let out a great belly laugh, 'this place will make us a fortune.'

For once in her life Lizzie kept her mouth shut and listened with deep interest to what Charlie was saying as he sat opposite her at the dinner-table.

'I knew I could buy it for next to nothing and, as Mr Button said, I would have been mad to let it go to somebody else. Staff quarters!'

The sharp and sudden explanation had Lizzie wanting to bombard him with a dozen questions, but no, she still kept silent. Charlie waited for her outburst and grinned when none was forthcoming.

He continued, 'We're losing money in the hotel. Since we've had our bungalow built our private rooms hardly get used. Then there are the three rooms downstairs taken up by staff living in. That's why it is money well spent, that cottage will pay for itself over and over again.'

I must be thick as two planks, Lizzie thought to herself. She couldn't keep quiet any longer.

'So you do that cottage up. Probably cost us a bomb just to make it habitable. Then, you use it as sleeping quarters for the staff? Have I got things right so far?'

'Yes,' Charlie confirmed.

Lizzie smiled at him brightly, then, with a sigh, asked, 'How will the cottage ever make money if we are only going to use it to sleep staff in?' Lizzie put down her knife and fork. 'You are deliberately trying to rile me, Charlie, you know I haven't got the foggiest what you're on about. You just keep throwing out scraps of information, and you sit there watching me get more and more confused.'

'OK, OK,' Charlie threw his hands up in mock surrender. 'Pour me a cup of coffee and I promise I will explain everything, down to the last detail. The huge ground floor dining-room could easily be divided into five bedrooms. All would have sea views and, being on the ground floor, they would be easy to let during the summer and absolutely invaluable for the coach parties of old folk. Do you agree?'

'Yes, of course I do,' Lizzie said but she couldn't keep a hint of sarcasm from her voice as she asked, 'then, just what do we use as a dining-room?'

Charlie thrust out his chest as he delivered his masterpiece. 'All the lower ground-floor rooms beyond the kitchens we turn into a complete new dining-room.'

Excitement now showing on his face, Charlie got up and came round the table, drew Lizzie to her feet and hugged her.

Speechless, absolutely stunned, that's how Lizzie felt. The very idea staggered her. Finally, she did manage to mutter, 'Charlie, you're forever conniving some new scheme.'

Now Charlie held her closer, eagerly as if he would never let her go. 'It will all work out fine, you'll see,' he assured her, and as Lizzie broke free from his arms, she believed him. His eyes were brilliant, he was smiling his loving smile, his whole mood was frank, even boyish, and he was certainly very pleased with himself.

Next morning, Lizzie was awake early. She got out of bed quietly and went upstairs.

The kitchen clock said five minutes to five. She made a pot of tea, drank several cups and was bathed and dressed by the time Charlie came upstairs.

'Seldom seen you ready to go so early in the day,' was Charlie's greeting as he kissed her cheek. 'Can't you wait to get cracking?'

Breakfast was all ready and as they sat eating Charlie seemed so calm and self-assured that Lizzie kept trying to smother her giggles.

They say nothing ventured, nothing gained, but boy, this was some venture even for Charlie!

The kitchen was bright and cheery, the windows were open and, although the breeze was fresh, there was a bite in the air – a sure sign winter was coming again.

Lizzie thought of the hard winter they had experienced the year that they had had this split-level bungalow built, and silently she prayed that this new venture they were about to embark on would turn out just as successfully.

Glancing at his watch, Charlie said, 'Come on, get your coats on, time to go.'

At the first stop they dropped Robert off at school, and at the second stop, the offices of Roger Farrant their now long-term solicitor and friend.

'Success breeds success, eh Mrs Wilson?' Mr Farrant said warmly as he shook hands with them both and offered his congratulations. Lizzie's smile deepened, she liked coming to this office. She sniffed the smell of good leather upholstery as she sat down on a high-backed chair and listened to what the men were saying.

'Mr Harding will present the company accounts to the bank, no problem there,' Roger Farrant confirmed.

Lizzie's thoughts again went back over the past. The bank had been marvellous, helping them at every turn. Without their help, they could never have achieved so much. In the early years, though, it hadn't exactly been easy or without anxiety trying to borrow money. Yet now, it seemed, Charlie had only to ask and further loans would be granted.

Roger Farrant was right, success must breed success.

As always, Lizzie felt the urge to kiss Mr Farrant as they said goodbye.

He still had that flirtatious manner about him as he held her hand longer than was necessary and said in that soft drawl, 'We'll meet again soon.'

Charlie swung the bunch of very odd-looking keys.

'What will it be, coffee or a drink to celebrate?'

'Celebrate what? Our personal disaster?' Lizzie asked, but she smiled as she spoke.

'Pessimist,' Charlie taunted.

They settled for a quick cup of coffee in a nearby restaurant. Lizzie wanted to get to Ivy Cottage as quickly as possible. She fervently hoped it would look better in broad daylight, but her hopes were not fulfilled. If anything, it looked worse!

There was a short rise of steps leading to the front door. Charlie went up these and tried several keys from the bunch, all to no avail. One large key he was able to turn, but even with his shoulder to the door it wouldn't budge.

Looking down over the steps, they saw what they thought was a basement, but which had been detailed in their programme of sale as the ground floor with an address of Ivy Cottage, Larks Lane.

'This door must be bolted from the inside,' Charlie said. 'Now all we have to do is find Larks Lane.'

They walked further down the hill, turned a sharp corner and eventually discovered Larks Lane. Neither of them had been aware of its existence before.

Originally, the pathway must have been coarse cobbles. Now it was covered with a thick growth of moss. The surface was wet and slimy and Lizzie was afraid of slipping. Quite clearly, they heard the sound of water gurgling and bubbling. On one side of the lane, overgrown bushes were forming a fence, even a barrier, and into these Charlie thrust his arm, making a parting. He had discovered a brook. Rushing along, crystal clear, the water flashed and sparkled.

'Oh, it's lovely to watch,' Lizzie declared as Charlie let go of the branches and they fell together again.

It was quite a walk further on before they reached the cottage. Lizzie stood and looked silently at this old dwelling.

'Gran,' she whispered to herself, and then she had to moisten her lips with her tongue. She couldn't have explained her feelings at that moment, not for all the tea in China! It was nothing like Gran's immaculate cottage in Silverdore, and yet it brought memories flooding back. It had the same air of tranquility. Lizzie began to feel optimistic.

It had a front garden, albeit in an extremely overgrown state. They had virtually to fight their way through masses of green foliage and numerous tangled shrubs and bushes.

The front door was almost completely concealed by foliage and Charlie had to clear many branches away before he was able, this time, to turn the key and open the door.

It appeared that this door opened directly into the kitchen. Cobwebs were everywhere.

'It's so gloomy and dusty; put the light on,' Lizzie called to Charlie.

'There isn't electricity in the house, nor gas,' came his answer. 'No water either.'

Dear God! Lizzie didn't believe him.

Taking candles and a box of matches out of his coat pocket, he laughed as he said, 'See? I've come prepared.'

Lizzie was at a loss for words.

Charlie lit several candles. It didn't make much improvement. The guttering sounds from them seemed weird and they sent shadows flickering around the walls. But soon their eyes became accustomed to the gloom.

All the walls appeared to have been painted but

had become so dirty that whatever paint had been used was now an indistinguishable grey.

There was a fair-sized kitchen with an old-fashioned, coal cooking range, on which still stood a large soot-blackened kettle.

Above the range, a high overmantel took up one wall and each side of the range was flanked by two deep cupboards.

'Have them out and you could have two lovely inglenook seats,' Charlie said.

Lizzie wrinkled her nose in disgust and didn't bother to answer.

The centre of the kitchen was taken up by a table. It was a mystery to Lizzie how it had ever got to be in that room. Certainly not through that low, narrow doorway. It must have been there forever. It was thick with dust but she could see that over the years it had been well scrubbed.

Under the small window, which they couldn't see out of because the panes were so dirty, was an old brown china sink, badly cracked and very chipped. Two built-in cupboards underneath the sink didn't look much better.

From the kitchen, a stone-floored corridor led to the only other room on this level, a preparation room of sorts which housed two enormous walk-in larders.

A short flight of steps led up to the ground floor. Charlie's assumption had been right; the front door was bolted and barred from the inside. There were two rooms on this floor, both dirty and bare.

Another short flight of stairs and they came to two bedrooms. These rooms seemed brighter with windows front and back.

'It's because they are on a higher level,' Charlie said, 'they get more daylight.'

One thing Lizzie did like about these two rooms was that each had a small outside balcony, skirted by a wrought-iron trellis, well in keeping with what she was by now thinking of as their rustic cottage.

Coming out into the garden again, having finished their tour of inspection, the daylight was so bright after the gloom inside that, for a few moments, Lizzie had to shield her eyes. Charlie was busy pulling brambles and other prickly hedge plants away from an old garden shed.

Lizzie picked her way cautiously through weeds and stinging nettles to join him as he cleared the door to the shed and, with a tug, opened it.

Inside was a lavatory pan. Spread across the top were wooden planks forming a seat, in the middle of which was a circular hole. They looked at each other and fell about laughing.

A few feet away stood another creeper-covered shed. Charlie hesitated a second before lifting the rusty latch.

Surprise, surprise. It was a wash-house. It had a sink and one tap, which Lizzie couldn't turn but Charlie did. It spluttered into life spitting out filthy rust-coloured water.

'Marvellous,' Lizzie said, 'I had visions of having to draw water up from an underground well.'

'You might have to yet,' Charlie said with a grin. There was a large copper and across the far wall, wooden slats were fitted, like rungs of a ladder.

'Marvellous,' Lizzie said again. 'We could do the hotel washing in here. Hang it all up there to dry and air.'

Charlie swiftly came to where she was standing and grabbed her. 'Any more bright ideas like that and I'll put you in that copper and put the lid on.'

Lizzie tried to wriggle away from his grasp but he held on to her tightly. 'Two kisses before I let you go,' he said.

'I knew you were mad,' she retorted.

It didn't matter one jot that Charlie's suit was covered in dust, that his hair looked as if birds had nested in it and that one of Lizzie's stockings now had a long ladder in it. They had each other and that was enough.

Chapter Thirty-One

WORK COMMENCED ON the cottage first. This would
enable the furniture from the staff rooms to be transferred, leaving the entire area clear for the dining-
room.

Top two priorities were the roof and electricity.
The roofers did a grand job. Two days and they
were finished.

It turned out that the roof was structurally quite
sound. The steeper upper part needed no attention;
the lower part had several slates which had worked
loose and quite a few that needed replacing.

The gas company declined to run a supply to such
a remote area unless Charlie agreed to bear the
whole of the cost. He came to the conclusion it
would be far cheaper to rely solely on electricity.

The electricians were very efficient. Lizzie constantly took them hot drinks and certainly didn't
envy those men their job. Just taking up all those
old floorboards seemed hazardous and dangerous to
her. When they had finished the job, Charlie said he
was well pleased, although Lizzie thought that the
new white power-points looked out of place on the
ancient skirting boards.

Next came the plumber – just one local man who
had previously done work for Charlie.

As well as running a water supply into the cottage, installing an inside toilet, and turning one of the walk-in larders into a shower cubicle, he also replaced the old cracked sink with a gleaming stainless-steel unit above which the electricians positioned an electric water heater.

Now the job of cleaning the whole place right through could begin.

Three of their regular chambermaids said they were only too willing to help, even though Lizzie stressed how dirty the work would be. So at nine o'clock on a Monday morning, the three of them set off from the hotel with Lizzie.

'A right bunch you look,' Charlie joked and he had to duck to avoid being hit by a brush which Lizzie threw at him.

He was right though, they did look peculiar! All four women had their hair tied up in turbans, and they all wore old slacks. Armed with buckets, scrubbing brushes, numerous cloths and old rags, they made their way down the hill. It was an unanimous decision for each of them to tackle a separate room rather than the four of them working together in a restricted area.

By midday, all the windows of the cottage were flung wide open and the women had worked really hard. Charlie came and was warmly welcomed, for he had brought with him ham and cheese rolls and two large flasks of coffee.

They ate, sitting on upturned boxes in the garden. The weather was kind – a good drying day with a stiff wind and pale sunshine. They didn't feel cold, for the overgrown hedges gave great protection from the wind, and they all agreed that it had been a satisfying day.

'It being so dirty, us is bound to see an improvement,' said Mary with her down-to-earth Devonshire logic.

Over the next few days, they stumbled upon some interesting discoveries.

They came to learn just how good most of the woodwork was beneath the layers of old paint. By continuous use of sugarsoap and Brillo pads, they ended up with lovely surfaces which Charlie decided to varnish, thereby showing the natural grain of the wood.

In the kitchen, they decided to leave the coal fire cooking range intact. Not that there was ever any likelihood of its being used, but it did make a good focal feature.

Lizzie had great difficulty in finding a shop which sold old-fashioned black-lead, finally tracking one down in Barnstaple. After the use of much energy and elbow grease on her part, she declared the end result well worth the effort.

By the end of the second week, the whole place looked different. With the windows open to the morning breeze, the panes now sparkling and clear, the whole place smelt fresh and nice. No more dirt or cobwebs.

Cupboards had been scrubbed out and lined with

fresh paper. Cups and saucers, plates, a milk jug, together with a matching sugarbowl and teapot had been brought over from the hotel.

On the draining board beneath one of the new powerpoints stood an electric kettle. Little things such as these would make their seasonal staff more independent.

Here, during their time off, they would be able to unwind and relax in pleasant surroundings.

Downstairs, there was now a gleaming kitchen, one shining chrome shower unit with sparkling white tiles on the wall and one modern toilet. As they walked through, viewing all that had been accomplished, Charlie leaned forward and pressed the flush lever of the toilet – it was almost a ceremonial act!

Of the other rooms they had made one on the ground floor into a sitting-room, while all the others were now twin-bedded rooms.

The windows were so small that Lizzie had been able to make all the curtains herself. She had chosen cotton material in bright colours. And at last the furniture had been transferred over from the hotel and installed into Ivy Cottage. It was ready for occupation!

Chapter Thirty-Two

TO CONVERT THE existing hotel dining-room into five extra bedrooms presented no problems. Mr Roberts, the same architect who had done such a superb job on the bungalow, agreed to draw up and submit the plans to the council, but where on earth could they store all the furniture?

Only one solution. It had to go into various bedrooms up on the first floor. Tradesmen and friends all offered their help. Numerous trips were made up and down the elegant staircase. Soon, all bedrooms were packed with tables, chairs, china and glassware. Cutlery and silverware were packed away in boxes. The overspill of trolleys and two sideboards had to be left on the landing and covered with dustsheets which gave the place a dismal, abandoned look.

Just shut your eyes to the muddle, Lizzie repeatedly told herself, hoping that the end would justify the means.

When drawing his plans, Mr Roberts had been able to utilize all the existing windows, including the two large bays which almost jutted out to sea. They would eventually have three additional double bedrooms and two single bedrooms on what would now be an entirely new corridor.

It was surprising, indeed, how quickly these rooms took shape, and very luxurious they were, too, with coloured hand wash basins, backed by tiled vanity units which housed strip-lighting and shaving points. Because of their size, they were able to make the end of each bedroom into a lounge-type area, thus creating bed-sitting rooms rather than just functional bedrooms. And there were bathrooms and toilets where the old still room had once been.

The construction of the new dining-room on the lower-ground floor, was entirely different. It was a much more arduous and lengthy job.

The workmen had erected sheets of hardboard which sealed off the area and at least partially diminished the amount of dust and dirt which must inevitably rise when the walls were demolished and the floors dug up – for every single interior wall at the rear of the hotel had to come down.

Charlie was totally involved in the project, while Lizzie did her best to keep out of the way. When work was nearing completion, Charlie coaxed her to take a look. She was amazed at how spacious the new dining-room was. The windows, with their immense panes of glass, were truly colossal. In future, when the guests were seated, they would no longer have to look down on the sea, they would henceforth be almost at the same level as the waves.

As much cleaning as possible having been done, the carpet layers arrived. Rolls and rolls of dark red

Wilton, patterned with gold scrolls, had to be laid.
The finished effect was rich, bold and regal.

Everyone pitched in to help carry the chairs and
tables down the stairs. Every person who was working that day seemed caught up in the excitement of
having a dining-room in a completely new setting.

Early spring had arrived once more, and in a few
days from now, their first coach party of the season
would be arriving.

Lizzie decided to take a tour of the hotel by herself, beginning on the very top floor. Every bedroom was well co-ordinated; bedspreads and
cushions matched the curtains; even wastepaper bins
Lizzie had covered with remnants of material.

Reaching the first floor, she opened the glass
doors of the lounge; they were bright and clear, no
finger marks. She stood a while on the threshold.
The whole room looked fantastic. The sun was shining through the huge bay windows, a bit weak perhaps, but bringing a promise of summer days to
come.

Outside, the sea was calm and way over in the
harbour a few gaily painted boats were already bob-
bing about at their moorings.

Everywhere smelt fresh and clean and the green
foliage plants banked up in front of the fireplace
looked bright and healthy.

Back then to the ground floor. The reception desk
was ready for business, with plenty of writing paper

in the pad, pens at the ready in their holders, a vase of fresh spring flowers standing on a ledge.

The new bedrooms still gave Lizzie great pleasure as she checked them once again.

On now to the kitchens, all three were clean and bright, all was shining. The boys had done a good job here.

Last of all she went into the new dining-room. Standing there surveying this magnificent room, Lizzie found it hard to believe that Charlie had brought everything to such a successful end. Had they really accomplished so much that winter? The tablecloths were snowy white, serviettes were folded neatly and everywhere silver was glistening, glasses were sparkling, all in all a picture of elegance.

The following morning Lizzie decided on a visit to Ivy Cottage. Living-in staff would be moving in the next day.

She walked slowly down the hill, approaching the cottage from Larks Lane, which she thought was by far the most attractive entrance. The front garden was neat and tidy by now. It would be a good place to take a deckchair, relax in the sun, read a book or have a snooze.

Going from room to room, the beds had already been made up; Lizzie decided that everything was fine. It felt like a quaint old-fashioned cottage. As she locked the door and walked back down the cobbled path, she looked back at the shining windows and she felt proud of a job well done.

So, they were all set for yet another season.

On her walk back to the hotel, Lizzie began to deliberate in her mind about all the past events. They had achieved so much – their beautiful hotel, a staff cottage and their own lovely bungalow out in the country – it was all a far cry from what they had started out with when leaving London to purchase that first guesthouse.

How lonely she had been in the beginning. God alone knew how much she had missed London. But would she go back now, given the chance?

She wasn't quite sure. She thought back to the years of the war, the humdrum existence, the air raids and the rationing. What of her friends, and Doris and Syd? They still lived there.

She thought of the crowds, so much traffic, travelling perhaps on the stuffy Underground trains. Having to go to the same job day after day. And then she thought of her life here, never far away from the sea.

Lizzie knew better than most that life offers no guarantees, but as far as she could tell Charlie's, hers and their son's future was secure so long as they continued to run an hotel. It was a good living, they had everything they could wish for, and more, but material things weren't everything. People mattered too! At least they did to Lizzie.

She considered, taking everything into account, that she had done very well over the years. She had coped with being dumped in an unfurnished guesthouse in a strange village where she hadn't known a soul, with a young baby to look after, a mountain of debts and a business, which she had known nothing at all about, to get off the ground. If you looked at it that way it had been like taking a small London sparrow, bringing it to north Devon and setting it down amongst the seagulls. And clipping its wings so there was no way it could fly back, she mused with a wry smile on her lips.

If she lived to be a hundred she would never forget the loneliness of those first few months.

Dear daft Charlie! Never happy unless he was thinking up some scheme or other. Well he wasn't the only one who could be a bit foxy. She would let this season get well under way, pick the right moment, and then put her proposition to him, she solemnly vowed. If he could acquire all these properties in north Devon, what was to stop her buying a place in London? Lizzie grinned to herself at the thought, but why not? She was a director of this company, she earned half the money.

Not a big place, she mused wistfully, a flat would do. Just so that she would always have somewhere to go to, even if it were only for weekends and holidays. Charlie loved London just as much as she did, but it was actually getting him there that was so difficult. Perhaps if they had their own place he wouldn't always be so reluctant. A sudden thought came to Lizzie and she stopped in her tracks and laughed out loud. The bugger would more than likely want to let it when they weren't using it themselves.

'Ready?' Charlie's voice called to her, bringing her back from her day-dreaming. 'I've done enough fer today,' he said as she drew level with him.

Lizzie nodded and looked up into his eyes with love and affection, then, reaching up, she softly kissed his cheek.

'What brought that on?' he asked as he put his arm around her waist.

'I just felt you deserved it,' she answered. She was thinking of that day, long ago, when she had first glanced across the hall at the sevenpenny dance and found Charlie, a blue-eyed, wavy-haired young corporal. There had never been anyone else for her. Just him.